**AN ISOLATED ESTATE IN GERMANY**
where Eddie Livingston first met the
youthful Count Alexander, and plunged
into a family drama of shimmering
elegance and secret shame.

**THE OPULENT SALONS OF VIENNA**
where the young Englishman became the
official lover of Princess Marie Therese,
and joined an exclusive circle that turned
from a paradise into a hell.

**THE ANCIENT CITY OF PRAGUE**
where Nazi jackboots echoed on the
cobblestones and an explosion of violence
was planned that could savagely rip the
Old World apart.

All were part of a game of power and
passion where all appearances were
calculated to deceive and betray, and only
the peril was undeniably real. . . .

**MASQUERADE**

# Big Bestsellers from SIGNET

# Masquerade

## CECILIA STERNBERG

A SIGNET BOOK
NEW AMERICAN LIBRARY
TIMES MIRROR

## PUBLISHER'S NOTE

This novel is a work of fiction. Names, characters, places, and incidents are either the product of the author's imagination or are used fictitiously, and any resemblance to actual persons, living or dead, events, or locales is entirely coincidental.

NAL BOOKS ARE AVAILABLE AT QUANTITY DISCOUNTS WHEN USED TO PROMOTE PRODUCTS OR SERVICES. FOR INFORMATION PLEASE WRITE TO PREMIUM MARKETING DIVISION, THE NEW AMERICAN LIBRARY, INC., 1633 BROADWAY, NEW YORK, NEW YORK 10019.

This is an authorized reprint of a hardcover edition published by Rawson, Wade Publishers, Inc.

SIGNET TRADEMARK REG. U.S. PAT. OFF. AND FOREIGN COUNTRIES REGISTERED TRADEMARK—MARCA REGISTRADA HECHO EN CHICAGO, U.S.A.

SIGNET, SIGNET CLASSICS, MENTOR, PLUME, MERIDIAN and NAL BOOKS are published by The New American Library, Inc., 1633 Broadway, New York, New York 10019

First Signet Printing, February, 1981

1 2 3 4 5 6 7 8 9

PRINTED IN THE UNITED STATES OF AMERICA

For Alexandra

# PART ONE

PART ONE

# Chapter One

After nine years in the Diplomatic Service, followed by the years of the Second World War, I have finally returned with my wife to Gloucestershire and to the house in which I was born. My mother still lives in it.

Though called the Old Parsonage, it no longer belongs to the Church. It is a spacious, architecturally perfect Queen Anne house standing in walled gardens on the banks of the Thames. My father had bought it when he was Professor of History at Oxford. It had been sold by the Church for very little because it had proved too large and its upkeep too expensive for the modest needs and means of twentieth-century parsons.

Neither of my parents seemed to have considered at the time that they, too, would have the same problem and that a large house, built in the late seventeenth century, would be in constant need of costly repairs and demand living standards they could not afford. After my father's death my mother was to find it even more difficult to manage and to pay for my education at the same time.

Now, thanks to an unexpected inheritance, the house has a new roof, the tall Georgian windows that give so much light and air to the house have been repaired and painted, the stonework restored and its exterior is as elegantly perfect as it was when it was built. Inside it has remained unchanged, most of the rooms still have their original panelling and fireplaces and a certain amount of rather fine eighteenth-century furniture, that had come from Ireland with my mother.

I have been married now for the last seven years and my son has what used to be my room. The battered old desk is littered with much the same assortment of miscellaneous objects as it was when I was a boy. Except that among it all stands the most beautiful and valuable object I have ever owned.

It had travelled with me wherever I was posted since I had

3

been presented with it nearly thirty years ago at Schwarzen-see. Rome, Copenhagen, Vienna, then Prague, transforming every room I lived in with its splendour. It is a heavy gold box studded with emeralds and diamonds. Engraved on it is the double-headed eagle of Russia, the Imperial Crown and the initials of Catherine the Great. Its gold still glows untarnished, the precious stones still glitter, so do the emblems of supreme power; nevertheless I can now contemplate it at last without guilt or shame. My mother calls it Pandora's Box. This is its story and much of my own.

In 1929 I had taken my degree in modern languages at Oxford. After that I had hoped to go to the Foreign Office and eventually to join the Diplomatic Service, which I later did. I had even then given up all ambition to become an artist. Though I drew moderately well and could produce pleasing watercolour sketches, I had had to accept that I would never be anything more than a gifted amateur.

It was in early summer. My mother had rather hoped to close the house for some months, in order to economize and to visit relations in Ireland whom she had not seen for many years. She expected me to accompany her. The idea did not appeal to me, knowing I would have no leisure to work on my thesis there, nor to improve my proficiency in languages. Though I was fluent in French, having spent two vacations with a family at Tours, I was not so certain about my German and I did not know that country at all. Why not go there for a couple of months, I had thought. But where to? The Rhineland, with its medieval castles and terraced vineyards? Eighteenth-century Dresden? Heidelberg, Göttingen or Jena? All attractive small university towns, equally tempting. Unfortunately, I had no German friends who could have advised me or whom I might have gone to stay with, which might have lessened the expense of travel.

Then, looking through *The Times* personal column, I found the following: "Wanted, English postgraduate to tutor fifteen-year-old German boy this summer in exchange for board and lodging in historic house in Holstein. Applicant must speak German and French and have good knowledge of history and literature."

Sounds all right, I had thought. I read on. "Applicant must be a gentleman and have a pleasing appearance." This seemed a rather surprising request. Though I felt reasonably sure about being able to satisfy the first condition, I was most uncertain about the second.

I remember I had gone to the mirror and looked at myself closely: rough brown hair, liable to curl untidily. Well, perhaps I could have it close-cropped in the German manner. Eyes, greenish hazel, a most undistinguished colour, a nose that would have been straight had a cricket ball not left a permanent bump on its ridge, a mouth neither as firm nor as masculine as I would have wished and a chin with an ugly dent. I noted nothing pleasing about my face. Still, up to now no one had looked at it with distaste either. I straightened my shoulders, thrust out my chest and pulled in my stomach. At least nothing much wrong with my physique, I had thought.

I had resumed reading the rest of the advertisement: "Apply by handwritten letter to Rev. David Hollington, The Vicarage, Little Paston, Nr Burford."

Why, that wasn't more than a half-hour's drive from our house, I had realized with amazement. I went to my mother and handed her the paper.

"It's rather what I had been hoping to find, except—well, you'll see. Read it!"

She did and laughed. " 'Pleasing appearance' indeed," she looked me over fondly. "You'll do," she said. "But I must say it's an odd request."

"The address given couldn't be more respectable," I pointed out. "Surprising you don't know this man Hollington since he lives so near us."

"Why should I? I'm bored enough with our own vicar and his tiresome fussy wife. I carefully avoid meeting others of the same kind."

"Perhaps he isn't married."

"Nonsense, they always are. Not one of them has the decency to stay celibate as a good priest should."

My mother has remained a Roman Catholic in spite of having fallen from grace. She hasn't gone to mass for years, instead even occasionally attends the Anglican service in our village church. My father is buried in its yew-dark cemetery and she is fearful she might not be permitted to join him later if she doesn't give some semblance of participating in the rites of the Church of England.

"Well, I suppose you had better write," she said, "and state your qualifications. At least it will be interesting to find out what connection there can be between a vicarage and a German family in search of a good-looking tutor."

I felt myself blush. My mother has a biting sense of humour at times. Besides, though she lived the quiet, dignified life of most respectable widowed gentlewomen of her kind, she is rather unpredictable, impatient of the mediocre and ordinary and fascinated by anything strange or bizarre. In her fifties then, she was still attractive as well as rather intelligent. She spent most of her time not in gardening, taking dogs for walks, gossiping with neighbors and going in for local charities, as did most country-living ladies of her age, but in trying to complete my father's last unfinished book on the Tsars of Russia,

Though she had worked on the book with dedicated persistence, and had even tried to learn Russian, I doubted she would ever finish it or really wanted to. She would have missed the research involved and the correspondence with various scholars interested in the same subject. Besides, I sometimes thought she found in it the sort of satisfaction as people do in crossword puzzles or in playing solitaire or in detective stories—solving problems.

I sent off my letter and received a prompt answer. I was expected for tea at the vicarage on a Saturday.

I borrowed my mother's car and went. Though I had asked her to come with me, she had quite rightly refused. There are occasions when too much unconcealed maternal pride and affection are not advantageous if one hopes to make a mature impression.

I found an unexpectedly large house, built of Cotswold stone, still partially Tudor with Victorian additions adjoining a small, square-steepled village church. It stood in a well-tended garden. Since it was June there were roses everywhere, climbers, ramblers and shrubs, colourful and very fragrant.

There were almost as many in the house in vases and even patterning the chintz curtains and the sofa and chairs in the drawing-room, which contained a few pieces of quality furniture, polished through centuries I felt, and family portraits better than one would have expected to find. The high-arched Tudor fireplace with its heaped-up ashes was a reminder of warmth frequently rekindled.

A pleasant room and house, revealing modest wealth, unpretentious good taste and solid respectability. A typically English house—and what connection it could possibly have with a historic one in Germany was puzzling to say the least.

It was to take quite a while until this was explained. An

elderly couple received me. There was no doubt as to Mr Hollington's calling, though he was not wearing a dog collar. A handsome old man with a sonorous voice and a complexion that would have revealed, if he had not, that he still hunted. He greeted me with rather ponderous benevolence, ascertained that I was not only a relation of Professor George Livingstone whom he had known at Oxford, but his son. After that only the very briefest of interrogation followed. Then, apologizing at having to prepare his sermon for the morrow, he left me with his wife.

Once fair, her hair had dulled into grey and her complexion reminded me of dried rose petals. She poured tea with the grace and precision of long practice but seemed rather at a loss for words. Evidently she was shy and only after the second cup could she bring herself to apologize for the peculiar text of the advertisement, explaining that her daughter's mother-in-law, the old Countess, had insisted on it.

After that she talked freely.

"I have never met the old lady," she said, "but from all I can gather she is rather eccentric. Nor do I know Schwarzensee, my daughter and my grandson's home in Germany. It is fourteen years now since I last saw Elaine or Alexander." She sighed.

"Your son-in-law is German?"

"He was. He is dead. Killed in the war like so many of our boys."

I said I was sorry, as one so casually does.

"Yes, tragic. We were fond of him. At first, of course, we did not like the idea of Elaine marrying a foreigner and going to live so far away. She didn't lack admirers. She had plenty to choose from at Oxford but, romantic as young girls are, she thought marrying a Count and living in a castle more exciting. Besides, he was really very nice, spoke quite good English, and had charming manners. A splendid horseman too. He hunted with the Duke of Beaufort's. He remained with us for over a year and Alexander was born in this house—Do have a scone while they are hot—"

I ate my third,

"You see, I managed to persuade Paul that Elaine was not very strong," she gave me a small conspiratorial smile, "and that she needed a mother's care throughout the time of her pregnancy. And even though he wanted his child to be born in Germany he let me have my way. I did so want my grandchild to be English. Will you have some more tea?

"Then when Alexander was three months old," she resumed, "they left for Germany, with a good nanny of my choosing, of course. A year later war came. I had no news from my daughter for years, then only once through the Red Cross, a message that my son-in-law had been killed in action. How I longed to go to Elaine to comfort her but that was impossible. I could not even write to her then. After it was all over, of course, I wrote immediately, urging Elaine to come home with Alexander. There seemed no reason for them to remain in Germany after Paul's death and I felt the boy should be educated here."

"Most understandable."

"Well, Elaine didn't seem to think so. She wrote back saying that though she longed to return, she could not for the present leave Schwarzensee, nor could Alexander."

"Black lake," I translated.

"Oh, is it? I'm afraid I don't know German very well. In any case it is the name of the estate. However, the reason Elaine gave for not returning was that her mother-in-law, Countess Plevke, would not let Alexander go. It seems that after Paul's death she became somewhat deranged. It was the second tragedy in her life. She lost her husband, true it is half a century ago now, but the circumstances were rather dreadful. He was found drowned in the lake. Now all she has left is Alexander, whom she adores. Elaine thinks it might kill her if she took him away.

"And there are other reasons. Elaine felt she should remain loyal to the country for which her husband died. As you know, after the war things went very badly in Germany: revolution, inflation, poverty and hunger. She felt to escape it all would be like leaving a sinking ship—all quite comprehensible at the time—but by now I don't understand why she can't make up her mind to even visit us. So many years have passed."

Mrs Hollington raised her faded blue eyes. There were tears in them.

"And you never thought of going there?"

"Of course I did, again and again. Even if it is difficult to leave my husband—he does need my help in the parish, you know—I would have gone if Elaine had wanted me to. But she does not. One excuse after the other. That the house is not modernized, that there is no plumbing or electric light, that I would be too uncomfortable—as if I cared—that they don't even have a maid and that her mother-in-law dislikes guests. I hope this won't put you off," she added hastily. "After all, it will only be for the summer months and you would be doing us the greatest of favours. That Elaine should feel that she wants someone English to tutor Alexander fills me with so much hope. It seems her first move in the right direction—and perhaps you would write and let us know if there is anything wrong. I can't help feeling that Elaine is trying to conceal something from me and that it concerns Alexander."

"His health, perhaps. Is he very backward in his studies?"

"Oh no. Elaine says he is a brilliant scholar and she has never mentioned his being ill. He looks such a healthy, normal boy too and what a bonny baby he was." She took some photographs out of a folder and handed me one after the other.

"This is Elaine with him just after he was born." A pretty young woman was bending over an infant, contemplating it with that pensive brooding expression painters give the Madonna. The child looked to me much like any other baby, though perhaps fatter.

"And this one she sent soon after the war. Of course I had to write to her that she really must have his hair cut," Mrs Hollington added. "He looks like a girl with those corkscrew curls and that lace collar. Still, isn't he sweet?" Indeed he was.

"And here, aged nine." More fancy dress, I thought with distaste. The boy was clothed in a sort of tightly-buttoned old-fashioned uniform and was holding a gun. "It's the traditional shooting dress they wear there," Mrs. Hollington explained.

I looked at the face more closely. The hair had been cut and sleeked down and clung to the small head like a helmet. Large eyes, set very wide apart, a finely chiselled nose and a smiling mouth, somehow more endearing since it showed a missing tooth.

"And these are the last photographs Elaine sent."

There were two. A slim youth, clad only in shorts, leaning against a tree trunk in an attitude of almost conscious grace. The other, in profile, outlined against what looked like an expanse of water. He seemed to be contemplating something in its depths.

Narcissus, I thought. "Good-looking," I said.

"Yes, isn't he. And very intelligent too, so Elaine writes."

"And he doesn't go to any school?"

"No. His mother teaches him English, his grandmother

French and German. However eccentric the old lady may be, she is a well-educated woman. Also there have been tutors, though they never seem to have stayed. You see, going to school is not compulsory in Germany yet as long as the necessary exams are passed. Alexander has had no difficulty at all in doing this. He is so clever."

I was starting to feel somewhat uneasy at having to tutor such a prodigy of intelligence and beauty.

Perhaps Mrs. Hollington noticed.

"Yet he is still such a child," she said. "He writes me the most amusing and affectionate letters."

She handed me a page of copybook paper. It took me some time to decipher what was on it. Not only were many words misspelt, but the German gothic script was difficult to read. However, the writing itself with its elaborate flourishes was as beautifully and carefully penned as that on a medieval manuscript.

"Dear Granny," I read. "Thank you for the poems by Rupert Brooke. I like some very much. The one about the fishes and the one about the benison of hot water and furs to touch. It's very cold here in the winters and we have neither. How kind of you to send me the Meccano set I so much wanted. There are, so it says on the instructions, several more kits, which would help me build something larger. Please send also some more strawberry jam and ginger biscuits and chocolates. The Tsarevna ate all the last. She is very greedy."

"The Tsarevna is his dog, I suppose?"

"No, no," Mrs Hollington laughed. "It's his grandmother. They call her that. It is because of the Russian connection, I imagine."

"Why Russian?" I asked, surprised.

"Oh, didn't I tell you? I thought I had. The Empress Catherine the Great of Russia presented the estate of Schwarzensee to one of Countess Plevke's ancestors and the house was built and furnished by a French architect according to her plans."

"How extraordinary," I said, thinking how much this would interest my mother.

"It's a beautiful old house, I am told, even if very old-fashioned. Nothing has been changed in it since the eighteenth century. Not only does Countess Plevke not allow any modernization, but even if she did, Elaine says they couldn't afford it. The estate brings in very little and they are not at all well off. We send what we can spare, of course, but it is not much."

Considering the remarkable economic recovery Germany had made in the last years, in spite of its defeat in the war, I rather wondered at this but perhaps Schleswig-Holstein had not been included in its reviving prosperity.

"Oh, you will go! Won't you?" she pleaded, and I was startled by the sudden emotion in her voice.

"Of course I will, if you think I'd be the right kind of person for the job," I reassured her.

She wiped her eyes, blew her nose in a small, lace-edged pocket handkerchief and rewarded me with a very sweet smile.

"Forgive me," she said, "but I do so worry about Elaine and the boy."

She then asked me when I could leave. I said in two weeks' time and she wrote down how best I could travel to Schwarzensee, saying she would advise her daughter when to expect me. "And please, please write," were her last words before we parted.

■

"And how were the Hollingtons?" my mother had asked on my return.

"Much as you expected," I had to confess, "though she was rather nice. It is her daughter, Elaine, who was married to a German who wants a tutor for her son."

"Elaine," my mother exclaimed with extreme distaste. "What a revoltingly romantic name—Elaine the fair—Elaine the . . ."

"An elderly widow, mother. Certainly no Lily Maid of Astolath."

"All the worse I would think, still languishing for Sir Lancelot. You'd better beware—tell me more."

I did and soon she was fully informed as to what I could remember of my conversation with Mrs Hollington. As I knew it would, the Russian connection intrigued her most.

"And you say this Schloss belonged to Catherine the Second? But when can she have possibly lived in it? She was fifteen when she left Germany to be married to the Tsar and as far as is known never returned to her country."

"I don't think they said she ever lived in Schwarzensee, only that it was a gift of hers to a Count Plevke."

"Plevke?" my mother repeated, wrinkling her brow. "Never heard of him."

"Probably one of her many lovers."

"Impossible, I know them all. Besides, she became very patriotic. Except for one Pole, they were Russians."

"Patriotic, even in bed?"

My mother gave me one of her stern looks. "Obviously you know nothing about her. Though of an affectionate nature, most of those she favoured were a matter of political expediency. She needed the help of loyal men to govern Russia. People are so mistaken about her—even history seems more interested in her love affairs than in her remarkable achievements. She was the most enlightened woman of her time. She brought Western culture to Russia. She corresponded and exchanged ideas with all the great minds of the eighteenth century."

"And had her husband murdered."

"It has never been definitely proven that she did, though he was mad, cruel and impotent."

"But didn't she have a son?"

"Of course—Paul. Though he was murdered too. Now what did you say that Count's name was?"

"Plevke," I repeated.

"Of course, it's just possible," my mother pondered, "that he came to Russia with Peter, who was Duke of Holstein before he became Tsar, as a member of his guards regiment, and proved himself more loyal to Catherine than to her husband, since she rewarded him so generously. Well, you will have to find out all about that since I take it you have decided to go to Holstein. It may be of some historical importance and it would certainly help with your father's book if we could reveal some, up to now, unknown facts."

So interested did my mother remain in the discoveries I might make at Schwarzensee, that she had parted from me without the usual warnings and regrets.

# Chapter Two

Having crossed the Channel, I had travelled by train to Kiel, a small town in Schleswig-Holstein notable only for its Canal that unites the Baltic with the North Sea. It was raining when I came out of the railway station, the same gentle, warm summer drizzle I knew so well from home. I had been advised by a telegram that I would be met.

There were only a few cars waiting but all of them empty, their owners presumably seeing someone off or shopping in the town. There was, however, one old-fashioned high-wheeled carriage, a species of hooded Victoria, from which a youth jumped.

Alexander, I thought. But as he drew nearer I saw he was much older than the boy could possibly be and his face, though quite comely, only vaguely resembled the one I had seen in the photographs.

*"Der Herr Engländer?"* he enquired.

I nodded.

"Fritz," he said, shook my hand, then took my luggage. The two suitcases were mainly full of books and I was rather ashamed at their weight, but he swung them into the carriage with ease and then helped me in, covering them and my legs carefully with a black, shiny waterproof sheet. The rest of me was sheltered from the rain by the hood.

He covered his straw-coloured hair with a cap, jumped on to the front seat, took the reins and we were off. The two big roans, heavy-limbed like carthorses, trotted briskly at first, encouraged by a fierce cracking of the whip, though I saw to my relief that it never touched their fat rumps. Once out of the grey streets of Kiel they fell into a more leisurely pace.

"How far is it to Schwarzensee?" I asked in German.

He turned round. *"Der Herr spricht Deutsch?"* He grinned amiably. *"Zwei Stunden."*

Not his kind of German, I thought, since he pronounced both *"Spricht"* and *"Stunden"* as one would in English, without the "Sch" sound I had been taught to use when an "S" is followed by a consonant. However, I was soon to grow accustomed to this oddity in the Holstein dialect though it did not do my German pronunciation much good.

The landscape through which we were passing reminded me of parts of southern England: rolling country, very green, hedges enclosing fields in which cattle and horses grazed. But there was more water—we passed innumerable lakes, large and small, and there seemed more woodland than we had been able to preserve at home. The villages were all built of red brick, so were their tall steepled churches. I had not enough knowledge of north-German architecture to recognize what was old or new. Occasionally there were picturesque thatched farmhouses with high-eaved barns on which storks nested. Now and then Fritz would turn to point out a "Schloss". Not castles, but pleasant-looking manor houses, surrounded by parks. A gentle land, I thought, unspectacular as to scenery, untroubled by extremes of climate, as peaceful as its inhabitants would probably prove to be. Not that I had seen many of these. It was still raining hard and few people were about, but I had noticed that the village women were dressed very much alike in blue flowered cotton and that both men and women had white-blond hair and pale sunless complexions.

I had slept very little in the train and the rhythmic tapping of the horses' hooves, the swaying of the high-wheeled carriage and the good homely smell of horse and leather. must have lulled me into sleep.

When I woke we were passing through an avenue of gigantic limes, their stems like pillars upholding the arched roof of a cathedral, the interlaced branches and foliage above forming gothic patterns against the grey sky.

"Schwarzensee," Fritz said.

But no house was as yet visible. We left the avenue, pulling into a narrow drive which led through a forest of oak, beech and coniferous trees, which I thought must have once been a park before it had reverted to nature and formed this dense jungle. The undergrowth of saplings, ferns, ivy and brambles was so thick one could not see more than a few yards into that wilderness. The forest had even encroached on to the drive, so narrowing it that Fritz had to bow his head to escape overhanging branches and shrubs that brushed against the horses and beat against the carriage hood. The air was very close and there was a foetid smell of damp, rotting vegetation and mud.

Then suddenly something so amazing, that I thought I hadn't woken from sleep at all but was dreaming.

We had stopped in front of a gate. It was at least fifteen feet high and as wide, forged of magnificently ornate, partially gilded ironwork, decorated with the double eagle of Russia, its Imperial Crown and the initials "CR" interlaced. Through its intricate scroll-work a group of pink buildings was faintly visible.

Fritz jumped down, inserted a key into a large padlock and the gate swung open, then he resumed his seat and we drove into a paved courtyard to halt in front of what looked to me very like Versailles in miniature: sentry boxes first, then small lodges to right and left, stables, then two wings flanking a central building. The steep roofs all with mansard windows, the architecture entirely French, except that the house was built of brick which had faded into a pale rose colour.

I thought I had never seen anything more enchanting than this perfectly proportioned toy palace: a royal court, lacking nothing, even if it was all diminutive as to size. And the unexpected suddenness of coming upon it after the dark wilderness of forest through which we had passed like some dream fantasy. There was no sign of life in the courtyard. One can never completely banish fairy tales read to one as a child from one's mind. *La belle au bois dormante (Sleeping Beauty)?*

Then a man dressed much like Fritz in a semi-uniform of dark green opened the front door. He introduced himself as Ivan. He too was well-built and obviously muscular, carrying my suitcases as if they were weightless, but his features were marred by an ugly scar that only a sword could have inflicted. A thick red welt distorted them and had left his mouth oddly twisted.

He took me into a hall that rose right through the house. A staircase with an elaborately carved banister curved upward from one galleried landing to the other.

There was scarcely any furniture, except for two tall and ornate mirrored console tables and a bench of lesser importance. There were no coats, sticks, umbrellas or boots or tennis racquets such as litter most English halls and no dog barked a welcome.

Ivan led me through one of the tall panelled doors into a corridor which was narrowed by a quantity of horns of deer and stags' antlers, all still attached to their bleached skulls and hung on the walls. The dark empty eye-sockets seemed to stare reproachfully. I had a sudden feeling of oppression and of fear at so much evidence of death.

It was with relief that I contemplated the pretty room into which I was finally taken. It had pale green panelling, a window that looked out on to the courtyard and a French window opposite that led on to what must once have been a formal garden. Unclipped box hedges still outlined squares and triangles that were now flowerless, a mass of weeds. An overgrown path led to a small Greek temple, part of its roof gone, and in the further distance there was a dark gleam of water. The Black Lake, I thought.

I turned to inspect my room. The narrow bed was recessed into the panelled wall and covered with frayed silk. On an eighteenth-century writing table, part of its ormolu decoration missing, stood a large vase of roses arranged with care and taste. Elaine, I wondered?

Perhaps she shared her mother's love for these flowers. Nevertheless I felt some concern that no member of the family had as yet deigned to welcome me. But then what did I know of German aristocratic customs? Perhaps tutors were ranked as servants. Both Fritz and Ivan had shaken hands with me, as if they thought me their equal.

"*Das Badezimmer?*" I asked. I was in great need of it after the long journey.

"*Das Bad?*" Ivan pulled out a round tin tub from under the bed.

"*Und die Toilette?*"

"*Hier.*" He opened a door into a sort of cupboard in which there was a wooden seat with a hole in it and a bucket underneath.

"I will fetch hot water from the kitchen," he then said, "for the bath." And was gone before I could ask him not to bother, having noticed an old-fashioned wash-hand stand with jug and basin in a corner of the room.

I walked out into the garden, there was no one about, and relieved my most urgent need behind the Greek temple.

On my return I found Ivan pouring water into the tub. He then measured the temperature by inserting his hand. "Too hot," he said, "but it will be right by the time *der Herr* has undressed." Evidently he was waiting for me to do so because he did not leave. I thanked him and indicated the door.

He looked at me without comprehension, his twisted mouth either expressing derision or concern.

"But *der Herr* cannot do it alone." He pointed to another large jug. "I must pour the water over when he is soaped. I always do that for Her Highness, the Tsarevna, and Alexander, though the English lady prefers to bathe herself."

"So do I," I said.

Finally he shrugged and left me.

By the time I got into the bath, the small amount of water was tepid. I poured the rest in and had a partial wash, since whenever I moved I splashed the floor.

I put on a clean shirt and decided the time had come to find some member of this odd family who were bathed by their manservants. I went into the hall to find one of the doors open on to a delightful-looking drawing-room, the walls yellow silk and the furniture black Chinese laquer.

A woman rose from a sofa, laying aside some needlework. She was indeed fair and much younger than I had expected her to be. I remembered my mother's warnings, though there was certainly nothing in the stiff formality of Elaine's greeting to merit them.

How had my journey been? Was my room comfortable? Did I know Germany at all? My answers as conventionally polite didn't seem to interest her much. Not a warm welcome, I felt. Perhaps I had failed in pleasing appearance. She had beautiful large blue eyes, if rather vacant as to expression, and a mouth that would have been pretty, except for its discontented droop.

"What a wonderful old house. When it emerged so miraculously from that dark forest I thought I was dreaming."

"So did I when I first came here."

"Your parents send their love."

"Oh, how are they?" By her tone of voice she might not have cared at all.

"Both very well,"—but remembering her mother's pathetic pleas—"rather worried about you and the boy."

"There is no reason for that," she said coldly.

"They do very much want you to come home."

"And perhaps I will. After all, we are not prisoners here." I was startled by the sudden note of defiance in her otherwise so listless and apathetic intonation.

Then, as if regaining her composure, "No doubt you would like me to show you the parts of the house that are of historical interest."

"How kind," I said.

She led me into a library that adjoined the drawing-room. It was a small room but so high-ceilinged that a gallery on to which a step-ladder led divided it horizontally. Its walls were lined with books, most of them in gold-tooled bindings. I noted nearly all of them were French or German, though there was Milton and Chaucer, several volumes of Shakespeare and a whole shelf of Tauchnitz novels.

"I keep the more modern English books my mother sends in my room. Some are really not suitable for a child."

"Such as?" I asked curiously.

"Oh, Aldous Huxley and D. H. Lawrence—rather too frank—I only allow Alexander to read classics."

"Surely many of them are just as explicit? Probably he knows Shakespeare and the Bible?" I couldn't help saying.

"Of course, but surely that is different?" She looked genuinely puzzled. Was this pretty woman rather stupid, I wondered?

"And does Alexander read a lot?"

"Oh, avidly—everything he can find, in three languages," she said, a genuine smile momentarily transforming her face. But then the listless apathetic look returned. "There is so little else to occupy him here, except for shooting and fishing. He has no companions of his own age. He has never been allowed to play with the village children."

"But why not?"

"The Tsarevna does not permit it. She does not think it suitable because of his rank."

"The Tsarevna?" I asked. "Does everyone call your mother-in-law that?"

"Why, yes—it is a sort of whim of hers that we indulge. She is a very old lady now and somewhat peculiar. She identifies herself more and more with the history of this house. She lives very much in the past. Come, you must still see the ballroom." Only reluctantly did I part from the library and a closer inspection of its books.

"Would I be allowed to work here?" I asked before we left it.

"Oh, they expect you to teach Alexander here and perhaps if you can spare the time you could put the books into some sort of order. No one has for centuries."

"I can't imagine a pleasanter occupation," I said gratefully. Visions of finding precious first editions passed through my mind. A brief glance had sufficed to assure me that the works of Voltaire and Rousseau were of the earliest date.

But Elaine didn't seem to want me to linger. She opened another door and led the way into a room not only remarkable for its size (it must have occupied one entire wing of the house) but for its elaborate white and gold stucco ornamentation. At its far end was a large picture compelling attention, a sort of focal point, all the rest leading up to it. Elaborately set in a richly carved gold surround, it was a painting of what I took to be the portrait of a young man. He wore a cocked hat and a sort of uniform trimmed with silver, a wide blue sash crossed his chest. He was brandishing a sword and riding on an immense white stallion.

"The Tsarevna," Elaine said. "Catherine the Great."

Only then, looking more closely, did I discern any femininity in the painted features: dark, sparkling eyes under arched, very black brows, a pale regular oval countenance, pleasing except for a rather heavy chin and an expression of fierce determination. A long tress of soft brown hair had escaped from under the cocked hat, loosened, presumably, by the speed of the galloping horse.

"It was when she became Empress, dressed in the uniform of her loyal guards regiment and, riding at their head, forced her husband to abdicate," Elaine explained as we returned to the drawing-room.

A very large man, both tall and broad, was standing by the window looking out to where, beyond a group of weeping willows, a portion of the lake was visible. He was dressed much as were Ivan and Fritz, in a green uniform, though his was much better cut. That he was not a servant became evident as he turned to greet me with an air of affable authority. An old man, his close-cropped hair was white but he moved with youthful ease and his rather coarse-featured face shone with robust good health. The grip of his big hand as he shook mine convinced me painfully of undiminished strength. I winced, which I think he noticed because his eyes twinkled with amusement.

"I am Beck," he said. "Welcome. It will be good for our dear Elaine to have the company of a compatriot."

I was rather surprised that he spoke of her with such familiarity in her presence. She had taken up her needlework once more and did not raise her eyes. He then dropped into a chair that creaked ominously under his weight, stretched out his booted legs comfortably, reached for a bottle that was on a table at his side and filled three glasses, handing one to Elaine and then to me. *"Prost,"* he said, emptying his. It was strong Schnapps, I noticed, as I downed mine and was not surprised that Elaine did not touch hers.

"Have you met Alexander?" he asked me.

"Not yet."

"No doubt he will make his appearance when and how it suits him. What the boy needs is stricter discipline. The ladies spoil him." Elaine remained silent, but it seemed to me that she pulled harder at her thread than was necessary."

"Well, I will not interrupt any longer," he said, rising. "You will no doubt have a lot to discuss." He looked from her to me and back with almost paternal benevolence and left the room.

Only then did Elaine look up.

"Does Mr Beck live here?" I asked.

"No. He lives in one of the lodges. Why?"

"Only that he seems very much at home."

"Well in a way it is his home. He was born on the estate. He was a stable boy when my father-in-law was still alive and after his death befriended my husband as much as his inferior position permitted. He taught him to ride and shoot and though there was such a difference in age and class, they became friends. With the Tsarevna's approval, Paul gave him the rank of Oberförster—head forester. When the war came and Paul joined his regiment, Beck went with him as his batman. How it was managed I don't know, but his being with Paul all through the first year of the war was a great reassurance to myself and my mother-in-law, knowing how devoted he was to my husband. When Paul was mortally wounded, Beck carried him out of the trenches, risking his own life in trying to save his. But it was too late. When they reached the field hospital Paul was dead. He is buried in Flanders. Beck was decorated with the Iron Cross for his courage, became an officer and only returned to us when the war had ended.

"By then the estate was terribly run-down, we had very little money. The Tsarevna, ill-advisedly I suppose, had mortgaged it. Beck took over managing Schwarzensee. If not an educated man, he is shrewd and capable and the Tsarevna trusts him absolutely—and even made him Alexander's guardian—and I, well, I have every reason to be grateful to him for what he did for Paul and is now doing for Alexander, who will inherit this place if it so suits the Tsarevna. You see, it is hers to dispose of as she wishes. Paul would have legally inherited it after her death, but she need not leave it to Alexander. Perhaps now you will understand why I cannot take him to England, since she threatens to disinherit him if I do."

She got up, carefully folding her embroidery. "I have to see about dinner. The Tsarevna has insisted on coming down to welcome you. We will have to dress for the occasion."

I returned to my room rather puzzled at what I had heard. Feeling that Elaine had at last somewhat lessened in impersonal reserve and showed me some confidence, I wondered nevertheless how she had been able to speak so calmly of her husband's death, even if it had happened many years ago. And her excuse for not being able to leave Schwarzensee, though comprehensible from a materialistic point of view, did not sound genuine somehow. Whatever sort of woman she was, I did not think a matter of inheritance would be of paramount importance to her. Besides, her parents were obviously quite well off and would no doubt welcome supporting her and the boy if she came home.

She had, when she had shown me the rooms, manifested no great enthusiasm for the uniqueness of Schloss Schwarzensee, so it could not be attachment to the house that held her.

Was it fear of some sort, I wondered? Was she afraid of Beck, perhaps? Much as she had praised him, she had certainly not encouraged his friendly familiarity. In fact I remembered she had not spoken to him or even looked at him while he was in the drawing-room.

# Chapter Three

When I returned to my room I looked out of the window. It was still pouring. I sat down at the desk and started a letter to my mother. My back was turned to the glass door that led into the garden. I had closed it because of the rain. Suddenly I had the unpleasant feeling one gets when one is being watched. I turned. A face was pressed against the wet pane, flattened, featureless except for enormous eyes, a toad-like mask.

For seemingly interminable minutes it remained there observing me. I have a certain amount of courage when angry. Whatever the creature was, it had no right to be there staring at me. I opened the window.

A rain-drenched laughing youth stepped into the room.

"For goodness' sake lend me a towel," he said. "I'm soaked." I handed him one. He rubbed his hair vigorously until it stood out like a golden halo around his head. His appearance was even more startling than the gargoyle features I had seen before.

I had not known that the human face and form, if not translated into art by a great painter or sculptor, could be so beautiful. Mere mortal flesh, bones and hair, I reassured myself, trying to dispel the awe and yet joy one feels in recognizing perfection.

The boy tore off his wet shirt, draped himself in the bath towel and adopting an attitude confronted me with a remark all too familiar: "Doctor Livingstone, I presume?"

I was, however, too surprised that he knew it to resent the trite joke that my name encouraged.

"Of course, it's I who should be Livingstone and you Stanley," he added, "since it's you who have come to rescue me from the natives." He threw himself on to my bed and drew the cover over him. "God, I'm cold," he said. He spoke English with a faint French accent.

"Why did you stare at me through the window?" I asked.

"Because I wanted to see what you looked like before I came in. I've had the most monstrous tutors up to now. Thanks to the eels I got rid of all of them."

"Eels?"

"Yes, as thick as my arm." He stretched out his. "I fish them out of the mud in the lake. The teachers didn't like them in their beds—nor would you I imagine—still I hope we will be friends. They were all so ugly, the tutors I mean. I don't like ugliness—do you?"

"I don't think I notice it very much in people as long as they are interesting," I said, rather pompously I knew. "The very intelligent are rarely beautiful."

"Oh, really?" His large, luminous blue eyes were thickly lashed by crescents of gold. "What are you going to teach me, I wonder?"

"To spell in English, for one thing. Your grandmother gave me one of your letters to read."

"Oh that." He buried his head in my pillow and shook with laughter. "I wanted her to feel I was still a child, since I had some favours to ask her. I haven't any difficulties in spelling in any language. But I like to please people, to seem what they want me to be—don't you? It makes life so much easier—even here, as you will soon find out."

"And what will I be expected to do?"

"Oh, to humour the Tsarevna and indulge her in her fantasies. You've met my mother, I suppose? Did you find her attractive?"

"She seems a very charming person," I said, conventionally. I was not really convinced that she was.

"Well, they expect you to fall for her. That's why they wanted you to be good-looking. It's one of their little plots."

"And who are they?" I asked, startled at such frank revelations. No wonder, if this was true and the fair Elaine knew of it, that she had welcomed me without warmth. I was shocked, too, at the sophistication with which this fifteen-year-old expressed himself.

"Oh, Beck and the Tsarevna, even the servants—they all want to separate me from her. But I'm just as clever when it comes to intrigue. Besides, I'm heir to Schwarzensee and they know it. Meanwhile I play many parts—a different one with each of them of course—even with Mummy."

"Such as?"

"Oh, quite the English gentleman, you know, stiff upper lip, brave and chivalrous," he mimed, composing his features into a semblance of sternness. "With Beck I become the German officer he wants to turn me into." He jumped from the bed and clad only in shorts marched across the room, his arms pressed stiffly against his sides, then standing at attention and saluting me. "The servants like me to play and joke with them, so I do. They are fools rather. Poor Ivan. He was quite good-looking before I slashed him. Oh, not intentionally," he laughed, probably having noted the expression on my face. "We were fencing and my sword slipped."

"And with your grandmother—what part do you play?"

"Oh, that's easy—just kiss and cuddle. She's very much in love with me, you know—but then so is Beck. Damn, what time is it?"

"Half past seven," I said, looking at my watch.

"I've got to get her dressed and laced into her corset—Fritz is so clumsy at it."

"Doesn't she have a maid?"

"No. She won't have any women in the house. She says they gossip. Even our cook, who is a doddering old idiot, is a man—or was one once."

Draping my towel round himself like a toga he gave me a radiant smile, then padded out of the room on bare feet, leaving wet marks all over the floor and me to the confusion of my thoughts.

I put on my dinner jacket and on sudden impulse picked a budding rose from the vase and put it in my buttonhole. Something I certainly had never done before, yet its sweet and familiar fragrance seemed a sort of reassurance that I had not, as yet, strayed too far from home.

I found my way through the darkening passage and hall into the drawing-room. There, though there was still some daylight outside, the damask curtains had been drawn, a cheerful fire was burning and candles in silver stands shed a gentle and flattering light on Elaine's fair hair and face. She wore a long blue silk dress and her slender arms were bare. She was alone in the room.

I felt awkward and shy in her presence, all the more because I realized that she was much prettier than I had thought at first and that she resembled Alexander.

"I have met your son," I said, "and we had a long talk."

"Oh?" She looked at me questioningly and rather fearfully, I thought.

"He seems very intelligent and imaginative," I added.

"Imaginative?" she repeated. "Too much so sometimes.

You must not believe everything he says. It is not that he tells deliberate lies but he invents things and ends up by thinking they are real. I suppose many lonely children do."

"Most understandable," I said, trying to conceal my relief. So probably nothing he had told me was true.

There was a sound of heavy steps descending the stairs and of a deep, booming laugh.

"The Tsarevna," Elaine announced. Leaning on Beck's arm she made her spectacular entry. Not tall and very fat, draped in a robe of pink satin, her ample, partially-exposed bosom covered with glittering gems, more of them pinned into the elaborately arranged brown curls of what could only be a wig. Her face was a painted mask, powder and rouge having been applied with careless abandon to features in which only the eyes, sharp and lively, had kept their youthfulness. Yet somehow, in spite of her extraordinary appearance, she did not look ridiculous. She moved with a sort of regal grace as a proud and beautiful woman might have done and when she stretched out her plump much-beringed hand to me it seemed quite natural to bend and kiss it.

That she was a person accustomed to command homage and attention was evident. Beck carefully settled her on the sofa and Elaine adjusted her draperies.

"*Ach,*" she exclaimed, her voice as loud and rich as her laughter, as she tried to straighten her bulk. "*Quelle peine de vivre comme moi maintenant—entre ventre et derrière.*"

It was a remark of such witty eighteenth-century frankness that I smiled appreciatively, which she noticed. "*Venez ici.*" She patted the small space left beside her. I sat down. She looked me over, her black eyes gleaming.

"*Tiens,*" she said for all to hear. "*Il n'est past mal. Il a même l'air d'un gentilhomme.*"

Then with a strong German accent in English, "I like the English and you resemble Harris. Not that all his reports were accurate."

"Harris?" I repeated, without comprehension.

"Later Duke of Malmesbury," she said.

"I am afraid I never met him."

"It doesn't matter but I will show you his picture some day. Just like you. I will call you Harris—*Ah voilà, Alexander!*" she exclaimed. "*Comme il est beau!*"

There was no doubt about that as he stood in the doorway, displaying his costume: cocked hat, sword and all, it was identical with that on the portrait in the ballroom. Only the horse was missing.

"Ah, youth, youth," she sighed. "To think I was once slim enough to wear that uniform."

She broke into German. "Do you remember the saddle, Beck?" She shook with sudden laughter and so did the jewels on her breast.

"Of course, Tsarevna, since it was I that altered it for you." But though Beck smiled it was only with his lips. It seemed to me as if his eyes expressed some sort of warning.

If so, it went unheeded. "I was a good horsewoman," she said, turning to me, "but I liked to ride like a man which was not considered proper in those days, so I had this saddle made with a pommel I could remove the moment I was unobserved."

Fritz came into the room dressed as a footman in an ancient-looking livery and wearing white cotton gloves.

"*Es ist angerichtet,*" he said.

The Tsarevna heaved herself from the sofa with Beck's help and supported by his arm led the way into the dining-room. I had not seen it before. It was darkly panelled, hung with portraits only dimly visible in the candlelight that illuminated the long table covered with a white cloth. There was a centre-piece of small and large urns joined to each other by fretted balustrades like in a diminutive formal garden, the vases filled with roses, the porcelain green and gold.

I sat between the Tsarevna and Elaine. Alexander was acting as host facing his grandmother.

"Your work, I'm sure," I said politely to Elaine, indicating the table decorations. "You must be as fond of roses as I know your mother is."

She flushed, I hoped with pleasure. "Indeed I am, though we hardly had such valuable vases in which to display them."

"Priceless!" The Tsarevna exclaimed. "Sèvres. The whole service comes from the Hermitage—plates and dishes."

"And most of them cracked and glued by now," Alexander said.

"It is only used for special occasions, of course," Elaine explained.

"Such as tonight in your honour, Mr Harris," the Tsarevna boomed.

Fritz served a red soup with dollops of cream on top in green and gold plates.

"See the Imperial Eagle," the Tsarevna pointed, almost obscuring it as she stirred the purple mess and spooned it into her mouth avidly. "My favourite Borsch! You do spoil me, Elaine. She is the best daughter-in-law in the world," she said, turning to me, "always orders what I like. If only she herself ate more."

Elaine had indeed not touched the soup.

"Do you like your women thin or plump? Plump as a partridge as they used to say in Russia, where they prefer them fat." And she laughed her deep-throated laugh. Ivan, also in livery, was pouring wine with a shaking hand. I saw he was grinning quite unashamedly.

"You must have travelled a lot, Countess," I said, feeling it might sound presumptuous of me to call her "Tsarevna".

"Only in mind, Mr Harris. I have never been able to leave my realm, as you surely know."

Chunks of something covered with a thick oily black skin were being served.

"Smoked eel," Beck who had been silent up to now explained. "Out of our lake. In fact, everything you will eat comes from the estate."

"We have become quite self-sufficient by now, haven't we, Beck? Thanks to our joint rule." He bowed politely.

"And my shooting and fishing," Alexander called across the table.

"But of course, *mon amour*," the Tsarevna said, looking at him fondly.

Then adroitly she dissected the white flesh from the leathery skin and forked it into her painted mouth. *"Comme c'est bon,"* she said. Nor did she seem averse to the excellent saddle of venison that followed and downed glass after glass of what even I could recognize as potent vintage wine with equal gusto. I cannot remember all she said, except that she dominated the conversation totally and that the more she drank the more confused what she said became. It was almost a monologue—questions and answers given by herself. Except for Alexander none of us dared venture to interrupt. But he, obviously familiar with the wanderings of her mind, encouraged her to continue—if from affection or in a spirit of mischief, I could not tell.

That she could not differentiate at all between the more recent past or earlier epochs was soon only too obvious when she started confusing the French Revolution with what had happened after the war in Germany.

"It was when the Navy mutinied in Kiel," Elaine tried to explain to me.

"A bad time," said Beck. "The Kaiser driven into exile. Officers like me stripped of their insignia and insulted—the Russian Imperial Family murdered by the Bolsheviks."

"*Ach*, but we were a match for the Sans Culottes—for the rabble—when they came here," the Tsarevna exclaimed. "We barred the big gates, the servants manned the sentry boxes, all of us—even Elaine—armed with guns ready to shoot stood at the windows. In the end it was not necessary," she added with regret.

"All they wanted was food," Elaine said. "Not that we had much to spare."

"But, of course, much of the Revolution was my friend, Monsieur Voltaire's fault," the Tsarevna declared, "and other writers with equally advanced views. I always knew what it would lead to once the masses learnt to read. Though I was all for progress and enlightenment, I never went too far with my reforms. In any case, Voltaire had a nasty character, disloyal, unpatriotic and a scrounger. Why he even went and lived with that awful Bismarck who stole Holstein, stayed in his palace in Potsdam."

"You mean Frederick the Great," Alexander called, but the Tsarevna took no notice.

"Now Diderot," she said, "he really was a good friend, even came here to work on his encyclopaedia."

"Here to Schwarzensee?" I asked, feeling by then totally confused.

She frowned at my interruption. "Here or there. Then or now—it is all the same, Mr Harris. Don't the philosophers say that time and place are just figments of our imaginations?"

Suddenly she clutched at her throat, gasping as if she could not breathe. Both Elaine and Beck were at her side instantly, helping her up out of her chair and guiding her out of the room.

Alexander, who had not even risen, poured himself some more wine. "Don't worry," he said. "It's only indigestion. She eats and drinks too much. She has these fits quite often. She will be all right tomorrow."

"I hope it wasn't something I said that upset her?" I asked anxiously.

"No, I don't think so—except that she doesn't like to be recalled to reality. Yet except for occasionally thinking that she is Catherine the Great, she is quite sane, even if she mixes up the different centuries—but that's just old age, I think."

"Catherine the Great?" What a fool I had been not to realize it before.

"Do you believe in reincarnation?" Alexander then asked, fixing his large luminous eyes on me.

"Not really," I replied.

"Perhaps I do. Still, it may be caused by all the history she reads and the letters that Catherine wrote to my ancestor that she studies."

"But how interesting," I exclaimed. "Do you mean there are some? Have they ever been published?"

"No. She keeps them under lock and key and won't even let me read them. But I've seen them spread out on her bed—piles of them—quite often when she is sorting them—and of course there are certain real similarities between her life and that of the Empress. She too was married off by her parents when she was fifteen, to a man she didn't love and, by all I hear of my grandfather, no one did, and he too was murdered like Catherine's husband."

"Your grandfather was murdered? I thought it was an accident and that he was found, drowned, in the lake."

"Well, so he was. But by the time they fished his body out of the mud they only recognized him by his clothes. The eels, you know."

I shuddered, grateful I had not even tasted the black slice on my plate.

Walking astonishingly softly and lightly for so big a man, Beck approached without my having heard him do so. Alexander's ears were sharper.

"What were you talking about?" Beck asked with his usual warm and friendly smile.

"Surely you must have heard," Alexander said. Even when he sneered, as he did then, his face lost none of its beauty. "We were talking about my grandfather's death."

"What a grim subject with which to entertain your guest," Beck said mildly, sitting down beside me. Then, noticing Alexander's flushed face and the empty bottle in front of him, "It's long past your bedtime, my dear boy, and no doubt Mr Livingstone will want to start lessons with you tomorrow."

"I'm not a child any more to be ordered around." Beck's eyes held his for a moment then Alexander lowered his golden-lashed lids. "Oh, no doubt you want to discuss me," he pouted. "Good night." He rose from his chair with diffi-culty and walked unsteadily out of the room.

"Doesn't he drink rather too much for his age?" I asked.

Beck made a helpless gesture. "If so, it's the Tsarevna's fault. She wants him to learn to keep his head even if drunk."

"Fortunately not on Vodka."

"*Ach so,*" he said, giving me a sharp glance. "You have understood the old lady's preoccupation with the past."

He went to the sideboard and carefully uncorked another bottle of wine and brought it to the table.

"What was Alexander telling you about his grandfather?" he then asked, stretching comfortably in his chair.

I repeated what the boy had said.

"I must warn you that Alexander is liable to invent things, though in this sad case I fear he has hit on the truth. I have tried to keep it from him, but even our loyal servants gossip and I can't entirely hinder him from associating with the gamekeepers and farm-hands.

"I scarcely knew Count Plevke," Beck then said, contem-plating the wine in his glass. "I was not much older than Alexander is now when it happened. Once or twice he would come to the stables where I then worked. But I noticed that he was hard to his horses, that the grooms were angry when they had to bring them back all in a lather and that they had welts where he had thrashed them.

"It's said that he mercilessly whipped his dogs too and ac-cording to all accounts he was a cruel, vicious drunkard. He recruited young men from the villages around here, training them as a sort of private regiment and forcing them to obey his orders at gunpoint. This was not popular. We Holsteiners are not to be disciplined by force and it may well be that one of his recruits hated him and that he was murdered.

"However, nothing was ever proved and for the Tsarevna and Alexander's sake I hope it never will."

"Did she mourn him?" I asked.

"I don't know," Beck said. "In my inferior position then, how could I? And now she never speaks of him. Only after her son, Paul, was born and as he grew up was I able to be-come of service to her. She came to trust me with him abso-lutely. We were almost like father and son."

"Was he like Alexander?"

"No, he was neither as intelligent nor as handsome as the boy, but more reliable. A good man, a brave soldier and a loyal friend. It was he who gave me the rank of manager of the estate, with the Tsarevna's agreement, of course. What a tragedy, his death! I tried to save him." I saw there were tears in Beck's eyes.

"I know," I said with sympathy.

"Elaine told you? *Ach*, that poor young woman, wasting away here. If only she would return to England where she belongs and start a new life.

"Perhaps you might persuade her to do so," he said.

"It might be better for Alexander too if she did," I replied, "and he went to school there. After all he is English by birth."

Beck's genial expression changed. "There is no question of that," he exclaimed, almost angrily. "That the boy was born in England was a mere accident; all his roots are here. Schwarzensee will one day be his. All my efforts at clearing the estate of debts, in making it productive once more—it has all been for him. He will not leave Germany as long as I'm alive." His thick fingers pressed the slim stem of his wine glass with such force that it broke.

"Besides, it would kill the Tsarevna if he left," he said, more calmly, licking a drop of blood from his finger and mopping up the spilt wine with his napkin.

He got up. "Well, tomorrow is another day. I still have work to do and you must need sleep after your long journey." Politely he escorted me into the hall, then bade me good night and let himself out of the front door, unlocking it and relocking it from outside.

# Chapter Four

So deep, dark and dreamless had my sleep been, due, I suppose, to exhaustion, that I woke with a happy sense of restored energy. I looked at my watch. It was only six o'clock. My windows were uncurtained. It had stopped raining and what promised to be a sunny day painted the panes with a faint glow of pink.

I heard the sound of a car, which surprised me. Surely no such modern vehicle belonged to Schwarzensee? I went to the window that overlooked the courtyard to see Beck drive away in a long, low, open, expensive-looking black Mercedes.

I washed and brushed my teeth at the wash-hand stand. No use trying to shave without hot water, I knew. Anyway I had done so the night before. It could wait. I dressed hastily; there were some things that could not. I didn't like to use the bucket in the cupboard, nor the thought of Ivan having to dispose of its contents later. I preferred to make my own arrangements and walked out through the window to reach my retreat in the shrubbery behind the ruined temple. After that I thought I might as well explore the grounds. I walked as far as the lake's rush-fringed edge. Ducks rose, squawking, from its dark surface. The mud-black water was translucent only where rays of the rising sun lanced through the dense shade of trees. A kingfisher, blue, scarlet and gold, flashed past, so close that except for its speed I could have caught it in my hand. Water lilies, large, white and smaller yellow ones, reclining on beds of leaves, were unfolding their petals as if waking from sleep. It was a large, if narrow, lake encircled by forest. I could only just see its far end.

On trying to find my way back to the house, I knew I had lost it. Though I could see its high roofs, I must have taken the wrong turning back and, having reached an unfamiliar part of the garden, suddenly encountered Elaine on her knees. weeding a rose-bed.

She jumped up, startled, drawing what was no more than a

scant cotton dressing-gown around her. Flushed with embarrassment or exertion she looked quite lovely, I thought. Her fair hair tied into two thick plaits gave her the appearance of a school-girl.

"I didn't expect anyone to be around so early," she stammered, tightening the belt around her narrow waist. "You see, we can't afford a gardener so I do the best I can in the early hours."

"Let me help," I said. "Though I'm no expert, I do know the difference between garden plants and docks and dandelions and I would be glad of the exercise."

"Well," she said, "I'm grateful for any help I can get these days. It seems such a shame to let what once was a beautiful garden go to waste."

She took a knife from a basket beside her and handed it to me. "I find it easier to get at the roots with this than with a trowel."

We worked in silence, side by side, stooping or kneeling. A pleasant sensation of being at one with nature came to me as I touched and smelt the moist earth and the fresh green weeds. Birds twittered in the trees and the rising sun was warm on my back. Soon I felt very much at peace with no thought except for what I was doing. Of Elaine's presence beside me I was soon almost unconscious.

Then a cuckoo started to call. "We must count the years of our life," she said, standing up and smiling. "Listen."

Again and again the bird called, thirty or forty times or more. Finally I lost count.

"A ripe old age for us," I said and we both laughed. Somehow I felt that I had been accepted as a friend, which was certainly all I then wanted to be to the fair Elaine.

After that, both of us squatting down once more to our tasks, we talked quite naturally of home, of Oxford where she had spent a year, and of mutual acquaintances. But as if in secret agreement neither of us spoke of Schwarzensee and its inhabitants. Not even Alexander was mentioned.

Suddenly there he was looking down at us. His bare feet had made no sound on the grass.

"I went to your room and didn't find you," he said to me in a reproachful tone of voice. "I looked for you everywhere. I certainly didn't expect to find you here, grubbing around with Mummy."

"You haven't even said good morning, darling," his mother reproved him gently.

He flung his arms around her neck and kissed her full on the mouth, then, still holding her possessively, he turned to look at me over one shoulder as if to make sure I had noticed and understood.

I certainly had.

Elaine disengaged herself, laughing and blushing. "Take Mr Livingstone to breakfast, darling, he's been a great help but I'm sure he must be hungry."

The boy did not move except for kicking the turf with his bare toes, which were as perfectly formed as the rest of him.

"I got lost and couldn't find my way back to the house. I was lucky to meet your mother." It was meant as an apology.

"Show Mr Livingstone the way back," Elaine said.

Alexander obeyed but remained sullenly silent as we regained the path that led to the house.

"Come in while I clean up," I suggested.

He hesitated for a moment, then followed me through the French window.

"Herr Beck driving away woke me so early," I said. "What a luxurious car."

"Yes, paid for by us, while we have to use the old carriage or walk."

"But doesn't he take you for drives?"

"Oh occasionally, but not to Kiel or Hamburg when he goes there to put his money in the bank."

I had cleaned my hands of earth and turned from the wash-stand to see Alexander leaning over my desk, reading the letter to my mother that I had left unfinished.

"Look here," I said, "one doesn't do that."

"Why? Do you have anything to hide? Who is this 'dearest' of yours, anyway, a girl?"

I took the letter from him. "It's none of your business," I said.

"I thought we would be friends and have no secrets from each other."

I relented. "If you really want to know, it's my mother."

I was rewarded with an amused smile. "I can't go on calling you Mr Livingstone," he then said. "Why, you aren't much older than me. At least, I don't feel you are. What's your name?"

"Edward, though my friends call me Eddie."

"That's nicer, not so stiff—tell me, have you known many girls, Eddie?"

"Oh, lots."

"I mean known like the Bible says—'And he went in unto her and she conceived.' "

I was at a loss for an answer. He did not seem to mind.

"Shall I tell you a secret?" he asked. "Of course you must swear never to reveal it to anyone. Do you promise?"

I hesitated. Obviously something to do with sex. Still, what harm could there be in the fantasies of a fifteen-year-old boy. Perhaps he needed help to sort things out. He could hardly go to his mother with his problems, I thought, remembering my own at that age.

"I promise," I said solemnly, trying not to smile.

"I have a girl in the village."

"Good for you," I said, relieved that he was confessing to nothing worse than a romantic attachment.

"She has conceived—that is, she's pregnant," he added, with evident pride.

Both Beck and his mother had warned me that he did not always tell the truth and assured that this was just a display of bravado, in order to convince me of his masculinity, I said lightly: "You will want to marry her, no doubt, when you are old enough to do so?"

"A peasant? Certainly not! I'll pay her off somehow when I inherit Schwarzensee. Give her some pigs or a cow so she can find a good husband. It's quite usual here, you know."

"Poor girl," I said; though I believed her imaginary, I didn't like the callous way he spoke.

"Not at all. The peasants around here prefer to marry a woman who has a child. It proves she is fruitful. And they don't mind if it's fathered by the Schlossherr at all—in fact, they are rather proud if it is. So I've really done the girl a favour.

"You have promised," he added, scanning my face rather anxiously. "It would upset Mummy terribly if she knew. As for Beck—I think he'd kill me."

"I always keep my word."

"Come on then, let's have breakfast," he said, linking his arm in mine, "and afterwards we can start lessons."

On the sideboard in the dining-room there were a variety of smoked sausages, ham and eggs, black bread, fresh golden-yellow butter and home-made jam and, to my surprise—porridge. Fritz brought coffee, then loaded a tray with all we had left over.

"It's for the Tsarevna," Alexander said. "I'll have to go up to her now to amuse her while she breakfasts. I do that every morning before Beck comes to discuss affairs of state with her."

"I do hope she feels better," I said.

"Oh, she recovers quickly from her fits. She will want to know what impression she made on you."

"I thought her a most remarkable character."

"That's not enough. She likes flattery. I will have to say that you were overwhelmed by her charm and intelligence and how much you admired her looks and her jewels. She wore them especially for you. Usually she keeps them locked in a chest in her room."

"Russian eighteenth-century, according to the settings. I thought them magnificent, especially the emeralds. They must be very valuable."

"So indeed they were. Now they are fakes," Alexander said, pouring milk on to his porridge. "Beck sold the real ones in Hamburg. He told her that they had to be revalued for insurance and back they came looking as good as before. He knew a man who copies antique jewels for the theatre."

"Do you mean to suggest that he stole the real ones?"

"Well, not exactly, I suppose, though I often wonder how much went into his pocket. It was when he had returned from the war. I was still a child, of course, but he managed to persuade Mummy that the jewels must be sold if we were to survive. There was this mortgage, you see, on which the Tsarevna had quite simply not even paid the interest. He told Mummy the bank would foreclose and that Schwarzensee would have to be sold, if some means to at least partially pay off what was owing couldn't be found. Mummy, knowing that it would kill the Tsarevna if she had to leave Schwarzensee and that she was responsible for my inheritance too, gave Beck her permission to sell the jewels."

"It can't have been a very easy decision for someone like your mother to make."

"Yes, she is still bothered by it."

"And the Tsarevna never found out?"

"No, except that she occasionally bites her pearls to see if they taste right. She is quite happy with the rest of the jewels—and anyway, she still has her precious golden box. No one could fake that. It's too perfect. A gift of Catherine the Great to my ancestor. She keeps it in her bed under her pillows. Perhaps one day I can persuade her to show it to you. It's very beautiful."

"I would be rather more interested in the letters," I said.

"My mother studies Russian history and they might be important. Are they written in French or German?"

"German, I think. But they must contain horrible secrets, since she won't let anyone read them. Look, I've got to go; she may have another attack if I don't. I'll meet you in the library in half an hour."

I remained at the table for a while, pouring myself a third cup of strong coffee and smoking a cigarette, trying to sort out my impressions of the boy that I was to teach. Was his appearance of almost angelic, child-like innocence a mere cover? What went on underneath that perfect face? Occasionally, as he spoke, I had the fleeting impression of a mind much more mature than his age warranted, shrewder and more calculating, only to be dispelled a moment later by his so obviously childish fantasies.

Well, no doubt the next hours would tell me more about him. I went to the library and while I waited I examined some of the books, handling the finely-bound volumes, frail with age, with reverent care. Some had the Russian coat of arms on their covers and must once, I thought, have formed part of Catherine's library. And there were big folios of prints, reproductions of famous paintings and copies of architectural drawings. The time passed so quickly, due to my interest in the books, that when I looked at my watch Alexander was an hour late. Finally he did appear.

"She kept me so long," he excused himself. "She wants to see you this afternoon. She hopes you can do some translating for her from the English."

"Nevertheless, I will expect you to be more punctual in the future, Alexander," I said severely. "And why haven't you brought your lesson books?"

"But they are all here," he said, with wide-eyed astonishment. "What more do you want? Geography, astronomy, alchemy, theology, mythology, philosophy, botany, history, mathematics, novels, memoirs and plays and poetry."

"But they are all by eighteenth-century authors, or earlier writers."

"Well, does that matter?—" I wondered if it did—"Besides, there are quite a few modern ones that my father bought." He showed me a shelf which I had not noticed before. On it were the Russian classics in a German translation, the works of Dickens and Sir Walter Scott in English.

"I've read nearly everything that's here."

"And understood it all?"

"Well, not everything, of course," he admitted modestly. "I find philosophy rather difficult—and mathematics." So indeed did I.

"And how is your Latin?"

"Pretty good. At least that's what the school inspector who examined me said. It was certainly better than his."

I had noticed Virgil's *Aeneid* on a shelf. I took it down and gave it to him.

"Read me some," I demanded.

"Oh, I don't have to read," and he recited at least three pages faultlessly without opening the book.

"And have you had any religious instruction?" I asked, when I had got over my surprise.

"Oh yes, from Mummy 'Gentle Jesus' and 'Our Father' every night and Bible reading and hymns. But now, since I've been confirmed by the local pastor, she thinks I'm old enough to pray for myself."

"And do you?"

"Occasionally, when I want something very much. After all, that's what He is there for, to grant our requests."

"And what do you like reading most?"

"Plays," he said, without the slightest hesitation.

"Such as?"

"*Faust,* for instance."

"*Werd ich zum Augenblicke sagen. Verbleibe doch Du bist so schoen,*" I quoted, pleased with myself for having remembered.

"*Dann darfst Du mich in Ketten schlagen dann will ich gern zugründe gehn.*" He completed the sentence with which Faust sells his soul to the Devil with a smile of triumph. "I know most of it by heart, but I'm surprised you do."

"I've studied German literature," I said, hoping he would not expect more samples of my knowledge. "And what other plays do you like?"

"Oh, Schiller and Kleist and Racine and Corneille and Molière, of course, and most of all Shakespeare. I know the whole of *Hamlet* by heart too."

I was glad to be on more familiar ground. "So do most English schoolboys," I said, "but prove it."

To my amazement he did, speaking not only Hamlet's lines but taking all the other parts perfectly with changing voice and gesture.

"You should become an actor," I said lightly, trying to

conceal how impressed and, yes, moved I was by his faultless performance.

His reaction to my words was totally unexpected. He hid his face in his hands and started to sob like a child.

"Oh come on," I said after a while, but he continued to cry, tears seeping through his fingers, his golden head bent.

"What is it?" I finally asked, putting my hand on his shoulder and shaking him gently. "Pull yourself together, old boy."

He raised his wet face to mine. "Stiff upper lip expected once more, I suppose. Sorry to have made such a fool of myself, as Mummy would want me to say—Oh, no one understands," he wailed.

"You could at least let me try," I said.

At that he seemed to regain some self-control. "You see," he said, almost calmly, "I want to become an actor more than anything in the world. I know it's the only thing I can do well. Even the Tsarevna enjoys it when I play for her. And I can learn any part in a few hours."

"And why shouldn't you become an actor?"

"Because they will never let me. I daren't even tell them. To them it's the lowest of professions. Actors are people one cannot associate with."

"I'm rather surprised your mother should think so," I said, "since in England we respect our good actors. In fact, many are socially most acceptable and even become knights."

"Oh, Eddie, you do understand. You don't think it's a shocking, degrading ungentlemanly thing to be?"

"No, I certainly don't."

He threw his arms around me and hugged me. "Oh, Eddie darling, will you help me?" he pleaded.

I disengaged myself gently.

"I care nothing for Schwarzensee or its history really. If I make believe I do it's just to please them. Help me to become an actor!"

Was it just a childish whim, I wondered? Yet of his having talent he had left me in no doubt. Or that, for the moment at least, he cared intensely about realizing his ambition.

"If you studied hard," I said tentatively, "you could probably get into Oxford in a couple of years and join the OUDS—the dramatic society there—that is if you don't prefer a German university."

"I don't. I'm English, am I not? Being born there."

"I suppose you are."

"But what's the use," he sighed. "Beck and the Tsarevna

will never let me go and even if they did there would be no money."

"I'm sure your grandparents would help. Besides, you might try for a scholarship."

"Do you think I could?"

"Alexander, how can I know if we don't start work."

For the next two hours, using books I took from the shelves almost at random, I tested him on various subjects. That the boy had quite phenomenal gifts of memory soon became evident. I was not so sure, however, if there was any profounder understanding of what he had learnt with such ease; when I asked him to explain the meaning of one or the other literary works of importance he became evasive.

"Why should I put into my own stupid words what is much better said by the writer? As long as I can remember and repeat them, what more do you want?"

"Your own thoughts on a variety of subjects," I said firmly. "I will have to ask you to write them down in the form of compositions as homework."

"I will do anything you want, as long as you help me become an actor." His smile was irresistible.

"Then let's work towards it—together."

Beck was not at lunch that day, neither did the Tsarevna appear.

"How did the lessons go?" was Elaine's first question.

"Splendidly," Alexander said.

She looked at me for confirmation.

"It seems there is not much I can teach him that he doesn't already know."

"I hope you didn't show off too much," she said to Alexander, but looking at him fondly.

"Mummy, that's not fair—Eddie thinks I'd have a chance of getting a scholarship to Oxford if we went to England."

"He would need a year or two in a good school before that though."

"A scholarship," she repeated. I saw she was impressed.

"I'm writing to your mother today. May I mention the subject? She would be so pleased, I know, if she felt there was any hope of you both coming home at last."

"I thought I had fully explained to you, Mr Livingstone," Elaine said firmly, "why I can't even consider it. At least not at present."

Was that a slight concession? Alexander seemed to think so.

"Mummy, when? I'll be sixteen next year."

"Oh, I don't know, even if the Tsarevna might, Beck would never allow it."

"Alexander would come back for the holidays. It's not as if he was leaving Schwarzensee for ever."

"If I threatened Beck with certain revelations," the boy calmly suggested, "he might let us go."

"Alexander!" his mother warned, looking startled. "I don't know what you think you mean. Nor do I want to and I doubt Mr Livingstone will be interested in your fantasies. Herr Beck is a good and decent man and does his best for you and Schwarzensee."

"I hate Schwarzensee!" Alexander jumped up from the table and rushed out of the room.

Elaine sighed. "He's so wilful and temperamental and overimaginative."

"Most artists are."

"What do you mean?" she asked, evidently surprised. "He can't draw or paint nor is he really musical. I know he is intelligent, but except for acting he has no artistic gifts."

"And isn't acting one?"

"Most children like getting dressed up and mimicking people and acting out the stories they read. Even I did at his age. It's just a passing phase."

Obviously the boy had not dared confess his ambition to his mother.

"And you really think he could make Oxford?"

"I'm almost certain. Considering he is more or less self-taught, except for your and the Tsarevna's help, of course," I added hastily, "he seems more advanced on most subjects than any boy of his age I've met and his capacity to memorize is close to genius. Also, as you said before, he has considerable histrionic gifts."

"But what is the use of them since he can't possible become an actor?"

"To speak well and dramatically is useful in many professions," I suggested. "In politics, in diplomacy and in the pulpit. Who knows, he may want to go in for theology at Oxford and follow in your father's footsteps."

The last seemed to please her as much as I hoped it would.

"My father's sermons were famous. People came from afar to hear him preach. Possibly Alexander has inherited the gift."

"It may well be," I said, though the Church was hardly the

future I foresaw for him. "Look here," I then said, "may I be quite frank?"

"Of course," but she gave me an anxious look.

"Though this is a very beautiful place, is it right to force a talented and intelligent boy to practically vegetate without companions of his own age in this—well, rather stagnant atmosphere of decay and ancestor worship?"

"No, of course not," she exclaimed.

"I can help him a little," I added, "by opening up avenues of modern thought, but I cannot offer him the stimulus of competitive study among those of his own age which every boy developing into manhood needs."

"You are quite right," Elaine admitted with a deep sigh, accepting my rather pompous speech, "but what can I do? If you only knew how helpless I am." Her large blue eyes filled with tears. Eyes so like Alexander's but, whereas his dazzled and tantalized, hers merely expressed sad resignation.

On a sudden impulse, prompted more by pity than by any other emotion, I stretched out my hand and took hers in mine. She didn't withdraw and I was touched when I felt the pathetic response of her clinging fingers.

"Elaine," I said. It was the first time I had ventured to call her that, but I was carried away by a wave of compassion. "You need just as much help as Alexander. Your youth is as wasted here as his gifts. You cannot go on living in this gloomy isolation with no company but an insane old woman and Mr Beck—a man with whom you have nothing in common except the memory of your husband. Trust me and let me be your friend! Let me help you."

She gently withdrew her hand but not her eyes and I was startled by the sudden light in them. They shone like Alexander's and she looked lovely. Fear that I was becoming more involved than I wanted to and remembering with secret amusement my mother's warning not to play Sir Lancelot, I nevertheless felt I could not back out of my chivalrous offer to the fair Elaine.

"Thank you," she said softly. "I do trust you. I know I have been foolish but for so many years I have been out of touch with reality."

"Then come home," I urged. "We might even travel back together."

"Without Alexander?" This was certainly not what I wanted.

"You have more right to decide what's best for your own

child than they," I said. "If you are firm and stand up to
them, they will have to let him go." Certain that firmness was
about the last thing one could expect from her, I added,
"Leave it all to me. The Tsarevna has asked to see me this
afternoon and I will do my best to persuade her."

"If you knew how grateful I feel."

We both got up from the table. The hope and trust her
face expressed moved me to take her hand once more. Did
she sway towards me or was it I who drew her into my arms?
Even now I don't know and I believe all I then felt for her
was pity.

At that moment, perhaps fortunately for me, Fritz entered
the room. Probably he wanted to clear the table, believing because of our silence that we had left.

He saw, of course, and though he retreated hastily I did
not like the expression of sly amusement I had seen on his
face.

Elaine, too, must have noticed it.

"He will tell them," she said. She had gone quite pale and
her lips trembled as she spoke.

"And so what?" I exclaimed with sudden irritation. "That I
gave you a friendly hug, such as I would give Alexander or
any man, woman or child that I liked and felt sorry for?"

Was it relief or some other emotion that brought the
colour back to her cheeks so suddenly?

"Of course," she said, raising her head proudly. "I only
hope they will understand as well as I do."

# Chapter Five

I completed the letter to my mother which I had started that morning, describing in some detail my journey, arrival and the events of the last two days.

Of Alexander I merely said that he was clever and scholastically quite advanced for his age and that Elaine, in spite of having spent so many years in Germany, was still very English and very much the daughter of the Reverend Hollington.

I described Beck, the reason for his having become Alexander's guardian and his position as almost a member of the family.

But mainly I told her about the Schloss itself, its architectural beauty, its unique library with books that must have once belonged to Catherine the Great, about her portrait in the ballroom and her letters which I hoped the Tsarevna would allow me to read. I also mentioned the sinister black lake in which Alexander's grandfather's body had been found.

Then, having assured her I was well, the food good and plentiful and that I was enjoying my stay, I sent her my fondest love.

■

At four Ivan came to fetch me and led me up the wide stairs into a part of the house I did not know as yet.

"Does Alexander live up here?" I asked.

"Yes, and the English lady." Did I only imagine that he grinned knowingly because of his twisted mouth?

He knocked loudly against a door, and was answered by a faint *"Entrez"* from within.

I entered a room that, though large, was dominated by an enormous bed. From a kind of crown suspended from the high ceiling, decorated with dusty ostrich feathers, flowed crimson velvet curtains, frayed and stained but embroidered

with tarnished gold and looped and tied back with tasselled
gold cords.

In this bed sat the Tsarevna, supported by a quantity of
rather grimy lace-edged pillows. She was not wearing the wig
of the night before but a sort of frilly bonnet tied with co-
quettish blue bows. It framed a face that was, unpainted, a
healthy pink and looked with its fat round cheeks and double
chin more like that of a giant baby than that of an old
woman.

She was—what I think one would term—lightly clad in a
type of lace negligée that revealed more than it covered, leaving her opulent breasts partially bare. On her stomach rested
a tray. On it were folders, reams of paper and books. On the
floor all around her bed too, books were stacked one on top
of the other, the high piles also seemingly used as tables and
covered with a most varied assortment of objects: plates of
biscuits and cakes, articles of clothing, wine bottles and
glasses, tubes and jars and boxes presumably containing cosmetics. There was an overpowering smell of incense-like
scent. The room was very hot. In spite of its being a warm
summer afternoon, the windows were closed and a big fire
was burning in the fireplace. A silver-framed icon hung on
the wall, an oil lamp lit beneath it.

"Well, Mr Harris, or should it be Sir James?" she asked
with a chuckle, stretching out her pudgy, dimpled hand to be
kissed.

The sleeve of her gown fell back revealing a round, fat,
unwrinkled arm.

"Sit down."

I looked for a chair. There were several standing pushed
against the wall.

"That is much too far away," she said. "Sit down on my
bed. It's always been big enough for two. There is something
I want to show you."

I hesitated.

"*Mais venez donc!* I won't eat you. How shy you English
are—not however with your compatriots. You and Elaine
have become good friends already, I hear."

So she had been told of that brief embrace. I probably
blushed.

"Don't think I blame you, Harris," she said amiably, her
dark lively eyes searching mine. "*C'est tout à fait naturelle.
Quand on est jeune—et même après.*

*"Mettez-vous là,"* she ordered. I obeyed, if reluctantly, perching on the edge of the gold-embroidered bed-cover.

Our conversation continued from then on in a mixture of French, English and German, though I give what I can remember of it in English.

She took a book from the tray before her, briefly searched through it and handed it to me. The open page showed the reproduction of a picture signed "Reynolds". "Sir James Harris" was written underneath.

"Do you see the resemblance?"

The man portrayed had elaborately curled and powdered hair and was obviously older than I and more heavily built, but I had to grant that feature for feature our faces were extraordinarily alike.

"He came as English Ambassador to the Court of St Petersburg when Catherine was no more young. He was only thirty-two then. I have heard you also hope to become a diplomat. Who knows, you may one day have the same post, though in a very different Russia. Hers was the most splendid court in the world and she the most remarkable of women—The Semiramis of the North, they called her."

She closed her eyes and leant back on her pillows as if exhausted. But the moment I moved, her eyes opened and looked at me as alertly as before.

"Are you tired?" I asked.

"No—I was just remembering those days." For a moment she looked away from me. "Harris was a gossip and an intriguer," she then said, "but a clever diplomat. The Empress liked him but then she was always fond of the English. Not that she wasn't just as astute as he was, countering every move he made that didn't suit her purposes.

"These are his reports to Lord Salisbury, then Foreign Secretary of your country, and later ones to Suffolk and Weymouth. My English is not very good. I would like you to translate what you think of interest and write it down for me in French."

"I'd be glad to try," I said and, taking the book, hoped I was dismissed. I got up from the bed.

"Oh, there is no hurry. Sit down on a chair if you're uncomfortable," she said rather crossly. Her sharp eyes mocked my embarrassment. "Let's talk—I get so bored sometimes. I can't, as you see, move around much. Our Holstein has a very damp climate and the fogs and miasmas of the Schwarzensee are enough to cripple anyone with rheumatism.

No matter. At my age one must expect deterioration of one kind or another. Of physical pleasures I have few left, except for food and wine. Pour me some Schnapps—the bottle's over there—and help yourself." I obeyed. I was by then, in the hot and scented atmosphere of the room, spellbound by this fascinating, if monstrous, old woman.

"The body wears out. Fortunately the brain lasts longest. Even if mine becomes occasionally clouded, I can still enjoy studying the lives of others, such as that of Catherine the Great."

I felt the moment had come to mention my mother's interest in the same subject and to enquire about the letters Alexander had spoken of.

"*Tiens,*" she said, leaning on one elbow and readjusting her robe. "I didn't think that Englishwomen were interested in history. However, if there have been any new books about the Empress and her times that your mother knows of I would be glad to have them. Though really, thanks to the amount Catherine wrote herself, one is—except for matters she considered too private to mention—fully informed about her life."

"My mother," I said tentatively, "when she heard of Schwarzensee's Russian connection and how generously the Empress rewarded your ancestor, wondered if there weren't documents or perhaps even letters here that she wrote to Count Plevke? They would, of course, be of great historical importance."

"If they existed," she said in a less amiable tone of voice. "I suppose Alexander encouraged you to think so. That boy will invent anything to please. There are no letters—and if there were, I would have too much respect for the Empress to let them be seen by anyone. However, there is something I will show you that was once hers." From under her pillow she drew a gold box studded with what I took to be diamonds. Inset were the initials of Catherine the Great.

"Just one of her gifts to Count Plevke." She put the box in my hand.

It was heavy and very beautiful. I expressed my genuine admiration of it as best I could, to be rewarded with a smile of satisfaction. I handed it back and she replaced it under her pillow.

"It will go to Alexander, of course, as will everything else after my death. How were the lessons?" she then asked and, without waiting for an answer, "No doubt you found that there is not much you can teach him that he doesn't know already."

I had to admit that to some extent that was true.

"Why only 'to some extent'?"

"Because he as yet knows nothing of the modern world."

"And who needs to," she growled. "The more one can ignore it, the better."

"Strange you should say that."

"Why?"

"Because you so much resemble the Empress Catherine and she certainly was interested in everything progressive. She would never have turned her back on the spirit of her time and age nor kept her grandson, Alexander, from doing so."

It was the best I could do and it was effective.

"True, I suppose," she pondered, staring at me. "Harris, you have reason. And you think him very intelligent, capable of a great future, perhaps?"

"Yes," I said firmly, with more conviction than I felt, "but only if he was allowed a twentieth-century education."

From then on I repeated more or less what I had said to Elaine.

"Oxford? Where my son, Paul, went. It didn't improve his mind much but then he wasn't very clever."

"Well, of course, you might prefer a German university. There is one even in Kiel I hear."

"No gentleman has ever gone there as far as I know," she said tartly.

"Then perhaps Bonn—that has a great tradition."

"Yes, of Prussian Junkers slashing each other's faces and swilling beer like pigs. We Holsteiners dislike Prussians."

She heaved herself up, dropping cushions right and left and sank back, breathing heavily.

I started to pick up the pillows.

"Leave it, leave it," she gasped.

"Are you all right?" I asked anxiously. "Shall I fetch someone?"

"No." She swallowed a pill that she took from a bottle secreted, too, beneath the cushions and her face which had grown very red gradually turned pink once more.

"In any case, Harris, it doesn't matter very much what happens to me. But to ask me to give up Alexander, who is the only real joy I have left—isn't that demanding too much?"

"Of course," I said, "though it would only be for part of the year. He could come back for all his holidays. Forgive me for having upset you. I just thought he merits being given a chance to know a little more of the world beyond Schwarzensee. He has, you see, inherited your intelligence.

Ashamed of my devious flattery, I nevertheless watched for it to take effect. It did.

"His mind is certainly more like mine than that of his timid, feather-brained mother—yet physically he resembles her. I was never as pretty as she is but I had all the fire, courage and determination that she lacks. And I could transform myself, becoming ever different persons according to what served my purpose best, as Alexander can."

She sighed. "Don't think Elaine hasn't been a good and obedient daughter-in-law to me, such as Catherine was to the Empress Elizabeth, but she has no sense of humour and she bores me. If only you could persuade her to go back to England."

"But I have the impression," I said carefully, "that the main reason for her staying here, except of course for her not wanting to part from Alexander, is her affection and concern for you."

"For me? As if I needed her help. All my life I have depended on men for advice and comfort and I still do.

"I will think over everything you said but now I am tired. Please rearrange my pillows, take away this heavy tray and cover me up—I want to sleep." She heaved her vast bulk sideways.

I followed the orders she had given as best I could, finally drawing the scarlet and gold bedspread over her gross body.

She was not as unconscious of my ministrations as I thought.

She raised her bonneted head with its absurd baby-blue bows and smiled.

"I have always loved young men," she said in French, then snuggled back into her cushions once more.

As quietly as I could I escaped from her room.

On the passage outside and suspiciously close to her door I found Alexander waiting.

"You talked about me?" he asked anxiously.

"As I suppose you overheard?"

"No," he said, then quite unabashed, "I tried to, of course, but that door's padded. She says it's to keep out the draught.

I could hear nothing. Oh, Eddie, will she let me go to England?"

"I did my best to persuade her but I don't know her well enough to be able to judge if it was effective. She did say she would think it over."

"But that means a lot from her," he exclaimed, looking delighted.

"Well, don't be too hopeful. Besides, there is still Beck to convince."

His face fell. "Perhaps if I told him that I know that he sleeps with the Tsarevna?"

"Alexander!" I exclaimed angrily. "How dare you say a thing like that about your grandmother."

"Because it's true. If I threatened to tell Mummy—I don't think he would like that."

"Stop it, Alexander!" I said, disgusted and shocked at the boy's imaginings and at the revolting picture he had conjured up in my mind's eye. "If you want us to be friends, please never mention that again."

"As you like," he shrugged. "I just thought it might help. Oh please, Eddie, don't look so solemn. Come, you haven't seen my room yet."

It was a charming sunny room, blue and white striped cotton on the walls and canopying the small four-poster bed. There was no carpet, the wide beechwood floorboards not polished but scrubbed almost white. There were toys everywhere. A large rocking-horse with red and gold trappings, an exquisite doll's house, obviously eighteenth-century, and a quantity of wooden soldiers standing in rows on shelves.

"My grandfather's regiment," Alexander said. "All in Prussian uniform. It seemed he played with toys even when he was grown up. I don't any more, of course. The doll's house and the horse belonged to the Tsarevna when she was a child. I don't know why I keep it all in my room, except they are rather pretty and one grows fond of things one has seen for years. But I'll show you two things I really like. My English granny sent them. She always asks me what I want for my birthday and Christmas."

He showed me a large puppet theatre complete with scenery and dolls. "I will put on a play for you when I can get hold of Fritz and Ivan," he said. "They work the puppets and I do the voices. Look, in that mirror there I can see what goes on." There was indeed a large looking-glass on the wall facing the little theatre. I examined the puppets. They were the usual kind with papiermâché heads—king and queen, prince and princess, witch and devil.

"You'd be surprised how many plays I can do with them. But Fritz and Ivan much prefer it if I make up one about Schwarzensee. How they laugh then—that's the Tsarevna, of course," he held up the queen. "The devil is Beck, the princess Mummy and the prince is me."

Though I would have much liked to see this play, common decency forbade it, I felt. "You shouldn't make fun of your family in front of the servants."

"But they know us better than we do ourselves! Still, if you prefer I can do *Faust* for you one night."

This gave me an idea. "I'd like it even more if you wrote me an essay on the play as homework."

"Why?"

"Because I'd like to know how far you have understood it," I said. "Acting," I added—sanctimoniously I knew and probably incorrectly—"demands great depths of understanding of the part played."

"Oh really? I thought that it came to one quite naturally through the words one speaks. But I'll try, Eddie, though I don't think I write very well. Now come and look at the most precious of my presents from Granny." It was a gramophone with a large horn-shaped attachment and a handle by which to wind it.

"It's a bit old-fashioned but since we have no electric light nothing else would have worked here," he exclaimed, "but I have plenty of modern records: foxtrots, tangos and waltzes."

"Any classical music?"

"Oh yes, but I can't very well dance to that. I love dancing, don't you?"

"I'm not very good at it," I confessed.

"Then I'll teach you."

"How did you learn?" I asked.

"From Mummy mostly. The rest I make up myself. Shall I show you?" He wound up the machine.

He put on a record. I seem to remember it was "Every little whisper seems to cheer me, every little whisper brings you near me," or something of the kind. Without any embarrassment or affectation he started to dance and with perfect balance and grace too.

"Come," he said, stretching out his arms. "I need a partner. It's silly to dance alone."

"And even sillier if we danced together."

"But why?" he asked, looking disappointed and puzzled.

"Because we are men."

"And what difference does that make?" he asked, wide-eyed. "Look, I'll put on a tango and teach you the steps. They are quite difficult."

"Leave it," I said. "Have you done the homework I gave you?"

"I'll do it tomorrow, I promise, if you dance with me now."

"Alexander, I won't and that is final."

"I'll fetch Mummy then if you prefer her to me."

"Oh, for goodness' sake!"

But he had left the room.

A few minutes later he reappeared, dragging in a resisting but laughing Elaine.

Remembering our last encounter and embrace I didn't dare look at her.

"I hear you want a dancing lesson," she said, rather shyly.

"I never would have ventured to suggest anything of the kind, but Alexander—"

"Don't think I don't know how tiresomely insistent he is when he wants something."

"Let's show Eddie what we can do," Alexander said, winding up the gramophone once more and giving me a triumphant look.

Though they danced expertly, as far as I could judge, for there was much complicated criss-crossing of feet and bending and turning, I did not much like the performance. It seemed unsuited to Elaine somehow to sway with Spanish abandon in her son's arms and Alexander seemed to have lost some of his light aerial grace that had so enchanted me when he had danced alone. It was as if he had become suddenly heavy, earthbound, as he guided her steps.

"Now it's your turn, Eddie," he called as he let her go.

I don't think it was intentionally that he chose to put on the "Merry Widow Waltz", at least I hoped it wasn't, but how mischievous he could be I knew by then.

Elaine did not seem to notice.

"I suppose we must oblige," she said. "He won't give us any peace if we don't." And then to Alexander, "Just once and no more, darling, then I have to see about dinner."

"And Alexander must do his homework," I said.

"I talked to the Tsarevna," I whispered as we revolved at first slowly, then faster to the time of the waltz. "I think there is hope." I had been holding her politely, well away from me, but at my words she drew closer, though perhaps it was only the speed of our dancing that forced her to press against me for support and her fair hair to brush against my cheek.

The gramophone needle scraped into silence.

"You're a liar, Eddie," Alexander exclaimed indignantly. "You said you couldn't dance."

"My mother taught me to waltz as yours did," I said, looking with some concern at Elaine who had dropped into a chair, her hand pressed to her forehead.

"Anything the matter?" I asked.

"No, only rather dizzy. I'll be all right in a moment." She got up, gave me a rather forced smile and left the room.

Dinner was informal compared to the meal of the night before. Neither Beck nor the Tsarevna appeared. There was cold meat and a salad, followed by a pink jelly that Alexander told me was called Rote Grütze. Elaine was rather silent and absent-minded but she looked happier and more serene, I thought, than she usually did as she stared dreamily into the flickering candles. I hoped it was due to the hopeful news I had been able to whisper to her while we danced.

Alexander talked mainly to Fritz who was serving, laughing and joking with him in German. This, though I had grown accustomed to the familiarity with which the servants were treated in Schwarzensee, I resented, the more so because they were both using the Holstein dialect and I could not understand what they said.

"It's about finding a gun for you," Alexander—who must have noticed my lack of comprehension—explained. "He thinks he can borrow Beck's as he's gone away for the weekend; living it up in Hamburg, no doubt, as he often does. Have you ever heard of St Pauli and the Reeperbahn?"

"No. What is it?"

Alexander looked at Fritz, who looked back at him. Both laughed. "I'd better not tell you in front of Mummy."

"Darling, I don't know what you are talking about but you are not being very polite. I think you have forgotten to bring the cream, Fritz," she said to the servant, which obliged him to leave the room.

"But why should I have Beck's gun?" I asked.

"Because we are going shooting tomorrow at dawn and I need my own. Beck won't mind lending his. He asked Fritz to tell me that there is a good roebuck out in one of the clearings."

"Darling," his mother said, "perhaps Mr Livingston doesn't shoot."

"I've never shot anything larger than a pheasant or rabbit," I confessed.

"Well, all the more fun," Alexander said. "It seems this roebuck has a fine pair of horns. It will be something nice for you to take home."

I thought of the grim trophies in the corridor in front of my room and shuddered, if not visibly.

"But darling, what about lessons tomorrow?"

"Mummy, have you forgotten that it's Sunday?"

"Why, so it is," she looked startled. "I really don't know what you must think of us, Mr Livingstone," she said, "for not going to church, but the truth is it's a long drive from here and, except for asking Beck, who doesn't attend, to take us by car, we can't get there in time. As for shooting on Sunday—"

"It's my only free day," Alexander protested, "and you know there's no more meat. Perhaps we can get some ducks too. Mummy, I have an idea. Couldn't we have a picnic lunch near the lake as we used to and afterwards we could all swim?"

"And what about the Tsarevna? She will hardly enjoy being left alone all day."

"Well, she can come if she wants to. Fritz and Ivan can get her downstairs and wheel her along the drive in her chair in time for lunch."

"I don't know if Mr Livingstone likes picnics," Elaine hesitated.

"I've loved them ever since I was a child," I said, thinking with nostalgia of the big wicker basket and all it had so surprisingly contained. "Things taste so much better out-of-doors somehow."

"And we could make a fire and roast potatoes and trout,"—Alexander's eyes sparkled with delighted anticipation.

"Are there trout in the lake as well as eels?" I asked.

"No. It is much too muddy, but there's a clear stream that flows into the lake. Mummy's very good at tickling trout."

"You must think it very unsporting, Mr Livingstone," she said, having noticed my puzzled look, "but we catch them by hand from under stones. It's quicker than fishing for them. You see, in the war there was so little food and even now we have to depend on what lake and forest provide, like game and fish and what we used to call toadstools in England, and berries that I collect for jam and jellies. Alexander and Beck do the shooting and I the picking. You see, nearly everything the farm produces has to be sold. Only rarely are we spared any pork or beef, even potatoes are scarce. I grow some vegetables in the garden but it's never enough."

"I hadn't the impression that things were as bad as that," I said, looking at Elaine with sympathy. "The food has been so good and plentiful."

"That's because the Tsarevna told Beck that you must be properly fed if we don't pay you for teaching me," Alexander said.

"But I never expected—you're doing me a favour by letting me come here. Please don't go to any extra expense for my sake. I don't mind what I eat."

"But the Tsarevna does and is glad of the excuse," Alexander laughed.

"You must forgive me if I took too much for granted," I said to Elaine, still worried at what I had heard. "My only excuse is that this house is so beautiful that one has the impression of living in another more splendid century."

"In the days of Catherine the Great?" Alexander asked, smiling mischievously.

"And there's all the valuable furniture, the pictures and books—that make one think—"

"Riches indeed," Alexander snorted, "and nothing the Tsarevna would allow us to sell, while we forage for food in the forest in order to survive."

"You are upsetting Mr Livingstone, Alexander. It's not as bad as he makes out," Elaine said, turning to me, "but the Tsarevna is rather demanding and won't understand that times have changed and that it is not easy with only three servants to keep this big house clean, the horses attended to, wood cut for the fires, parts of the garden at least cleared and all the other odd jobs that have to be done."

I thought of the lack of plumbing, the water that had to be carried from the kitchen and buckets that had to be emptied and wondered how much I could afford to tip Fritz and Ivan.

"I think it's marvellous how you manage," I said, "but surely it's more than should be expected of any single woman? Still, it won't be for long now," I added. Her eyes held mine. It was a deeply searching look.

I did not quite know how to answer it, unsure if it didn't ask for more than I could give.

Deliberately or not—how could one tell—Alexander came to my aid.

"Eddie's convinced he can get me to Oxford, Mummy, and then a new life begins."

If she accepted this with more certainty than I myself felt, I don't know, but she gave me a warm smile as she got up. "Now don't stay out all night, Alexander," she said as she kissed him. "Sleep well, Mr Livingstone—and don't think I'm not grateful."

"Have some more wine," Alexander offered after she had left, pouring himself a glass. "We don't get it very often."

"Not if I have to be up at dawn," I said, rising from the table.

"What are you going to do now?" he asked.

"Translate the letters of Sir James Harris into French for your grandmother and I hope you will write me that essay on *Faust*."

"I'll do it tomorrow night ready for Monday. Does that suit you?"

"I suppose so, but why not now?"

"Because I rather feel like going to that girl I told you about. Beck insists that the house must be locked up every night, so will you let me use your window to get in and out? There is still some light and I'll be back at dawn. It's nearly a kilometre's walk through the forest to the village and not so pleasant in the dark."

"But where will you sleep?"

"Why, with her, of course."

I contemplated the beautiful, innocent, child-like face, as sexless as I imagine those of angels are, and tried not to laugh.

"Alexander, aren't you making all this up? It's not that I mind. I had such fancies too when I was your age, but how about occasionally telling me the truth?"

"The truth," he murmured, flicking a crumb off the tablecloth. "You don't really want to know it, do you? No one does." He straightened in his chair. "Mummy always says she can read in my eyes when I'm lying. Can you?" He looked at me with eyes as clear and as cold as a mountain stream.

"Yes," I said. "You invented the story of the girl, of course, and all that nonsense about Beck and the Tsarevna too."

"All right," he said, with a shrug. "Believe what you please. It might reassure you if I told you that I go out to lay lines to catch eels in the lake after dark and that I have to pull them in before dawn."

Though relieved that he was at last telling the truth, concern for him made me exclaim: "That means you are out almost all night in the wet and the dark. Doesn't it worry your mother? Where do you sleep then? In the forest?"

"Mummy's quite accustomed to my nights out. But so as not to wake her when I come and go I sleep downstairs with Fritz or Ivan."

"Well, I think it is high time you went to a decent English school, though of course you won't have quite as much freedom as you seem to have here."

"I suppose freedom is something one has to fight for wherever one is. I think I will manage, especially if I have friends there like you," he added, smiling.

He followed me down to my room.

It was a warm night and I had left the window open and forgotten to extinguish the candle I had lit when I dressed for dinner. A cloud of insects buzzed around it.

"Mosquitoes," Alexander said. "They breed in the mud of the lake. I've become quite immune to their stings but I doubt you are. I'll lure them out—shut the window after I've gone but leave it unlatched so I can get back in the morning. Good night, Eddie." Holding my candle high he walked out, his head as if encircled by a halo of shimmering flying creatures. Within seconds he and the light he carried were gone, absorbed into the darkening night. Gone too I noticed gratefully were the mosquitoes. I lit another candle and went to bed.

# Chapter Six

When Alexander came to my room next morning he wore the same sort of shooting uniform Beck did. He had on a green felt hat and carried two guns.

"Hurry up," he said. "I've been through here before but you didn't wake. Now it's high time we started or we won't find him."

"Find whom?" I asked, still half asleep.

"The roebuck, of course."

"Take this gun," he ordered, after I had dressed. "It's Beck's rifle. Do you know how to use it? No—don't fiddle with it now, it's loaded." He adjusted the strap. "Keep it pointed down as we walk. If you should stumble, I'd rather you shot the ground than me. My gun's only good for birds," he added, as he shouldered his.

It was dawn when we left the house but the forest was still dark, the dense undergrowth shutting out all but the faintest light. Alexander led the way, walking soundlessly in spite of wearing heavy boots. He followed a track so narrow that it only allowed for one person at a time to pass between the trees. Now and then he would bend and carefully pick up a dead branch and lift it out of the way. I only understood why when I stepped on one—it cracked under my foot.

"For God's sake, don't make such a noise," he whispered. "You don't know much about stalking, do you?"

Ashamed of my incompetence I tried to be more careful but even the slightest sound seemed magnified by the deep silence of the forest.

Alexander paused in a small clearing, spat on his index finger and held it up.

"Why?" I whispered.

"Testing the wind. We will have to change direction a little so he doesn't get our scent."

He dropped on all fours and crawled through some bushes, then held them aside for me to be able to pass. I was growing less clumsy and moved almost as soundlessly as he did, except that my heart was beating so hard that I feared he might hear it. Not from exertion but with excitement: the most primitive instincts alerted a mixture of fear and daring that I suppose our early forefathers had known when they went out to kill some dangerous beast.

Alexander gripped my shoulder. "Look," he whispered, standing up. Though we were still concealed by trees, we could now see through them. We had reached the edge of a sunlit meadow bright with flowers. Grazing peacefully was a small graceful animal, its body copper-coloured in the rays of the rising sun.

"Wait," Alexander whispered. "I'll bring him nearer. Be ready with your gun."

He took a blade of grass, held it to his lips and whistled softly. The animal raised its head. It had short spiky horns like those I had seen on the skulls hung in the passage that led to my room.

Closer and closer it stepped on its delicate legs, seemingly compelled to do so by the sound Alexander was making. Then it was so near that I could see its eye, large and gentle, fringed by velvety lashes.

"Shoot," Alexander hissed in my ear. "Aim for the eye or shoulder."

"I can't," I said.

"Well, then, I will." He had put down his own gun and had snatched mine within seconds. The buck, alarmed at last by our voices, turned as if preparing to flee. Alexander fired. It leapt high in the air, then fell to the ground and lay there, twisting and turning.

"It's not even dead."

"I always make sure," Alexander said. "I've never yet lost a wounded animal." He took out a hunting knife, knelt beside the struggling deer and cut its throat. It lay still.

"Not a bad shot considering I wasn't prepared," he smiled at me, having examined its bloodstained side. "It wouldn't have got far."

He slit open its stomach and pulled out the entrails, tied them into a patterned handkerchief and cleaned his hands and knife on the flowering grass.

"In this hot weather the meat spoils if one doesn't take out the guts immediately," he said calmly. He lifted the dead animal's head. Its eyes had glazed over. "The horns are well worth keeping. Come and look."

I felt totally incapable of doing so; in fact I felt sick.

"I'm sorry, Eddie," he said as he returned to me.

"For what?"

"For not having let you shoot." He must have mistaken the distaste he read in my face for disappointment. "But your hands were trembling. You would have missed. I was just the same," he said confidingly, "when Beck took me out to shoot for the first time. I simply couldn't pull the trigger. Of course I was only nine then. I must have shot over a hundred deer since.

"Come, let's join Mummy for lunch. Fritz can take the game to the kitchen later." We crossed the meadow side by side, he swinging his narrow hips a little, his sunlit face expressing nothing but satisfaction in a job well done. But though I knew it was just that and no more, and that he had every right to pride himself as a hunter and that, in all he had done so coolly and efficiently and mercifully even, there was no guilt, I could not get over my disgust.

He broke a small branch from a pine tree we passed, shortened it with his knife and stuck it in the band of his green hat.

"It's a German custom," he explained. "It shows I got my roebuck. Oh, don't look so glum, Eddie. You will have better luck next time."

We reached the lake. Near the water's edge on a small rock platform shaded by willows, a white tablecloth had been laid and Elaine in a short cotton dress, her arms and legs bare, was bending over a wicker basket just like ours at home, taking out cutlery and covered dishes, bottles and glasses. Beside her enthroned in a wheelchair was presumably the Tsarevna. All that was visible was a large straw hat from which fold after fold of what looked to me like common mosquito netting descended, entirely covering her face and body.

From under this tent her voice boomed, if somewhat muffled. "You've had *Waidmannsheil*," she called in German, probably having caught sight of Alexander's adorned hat through the netting. "Bravo! And Harris, nothing?"

I was bareheaded so how could she tell? Elaine looked at me with sympathy. I wondered if it was because she knew what I had witnessed or because she was sorry for me for not having killed.

"It was all my fault," Alexander said loyally. "I didn't leave Eddie time to shoot."

"Most impolite, since he is a guest," the Tsarevna grumbled behind her veil. Then, drawing it apart, she peered at me: "You're probably better at hunting foxes, Harris—" then hastily covered herself up again.

"Elaine," she screamed, "one of them has got in. I knew it would. It's your fault for making me sit so near the lake. Help me—it's buzzing all around me."

Most of Elaine vanished under the netting and there were sounds of a scuffle, moans from the Tsarevna and giggles from Elaine.

"I got it," she said, re-emerging flushed and triumphant, squashing a mosquito between her fingers.

"I'll light the fire, Tsarevna," Alexander called. "The smoke will keep them away."

"And get into my eyes—how I dislike *le pique-nique Anglais* and being stung by these brutes. It's nothing to laugh at—I can hear you."

Elaine was indeed trying to stifle her laughter.

"Just because they prefer my blue blood to yours," came indignantly from behind the netting.

Elaine stopped laughing.

"Did you catch any trout, Mummy?" Alexander asked.

"Yes, three. They are in the bucket there. Will you please see to them, darling? They are still alive."

Alexander took them out, one by one, by their tails and clapped their heads against a tree, then started to gut them with his knife as he had the deer.

"You'd make a good butcher," I couldn't help exclaiming. "Do you enjoy your work?"

He looked at me with grave surprise. "Of course not. Would you? But someone has to do it if we are to eat."

I watched him as he neatly wrapped each spotted fish separately in leaves and trussed them with string which he took out of his pocket. I felt ashamed of my remark and of my unmanly squeamishness. "Let me help."

"All right. Rake the fire and lay the fish carefully in the hot ashes. The potatoes are in already. I've got to get out of these clothes."

Squatting beside me he unlaced his boots, then discarded everything but a brief pair of bathing trunks.

"What a relief," he said, standing up and stretching. His body was covered with a sort of golden down, like there is on peaches.

"We can swim after lunch," he said. "Did you bring your bathing suit?"

"I forgot," I said, "but in any case I'm a bad swimmer."

"Then perhaps you'd better not try here. The lake is treacherous. There is only about five feet of clear water. Below there is deep mud that would suck one down if one got one's feet stuck in it. I try never to touch ground. When I think of my grandfather, I wonder how his body ever reappeared."

"Don't you mind bathing here because of it?"

"It's nearly fifty years ago that it happened. Several other people have drowned in the lake since. I'm careful, but I don't think of death, mine or others, all the time."

"And the Tsarevna?"

"She doesn't like coming here much," he laughed, looking back at the extraordinary net-enclosed figure, "but that's, I think, more because of the mosquitoes than because of my grandfather. I have to work here almost every day when I'm not studying: shooting ducks, fishing for eels, spearing pike or carp; and swim for them too, since I don't have a dog any more. Beck murdered mine."

"But why?"

Alexander stared into the fire. "Two years ago Granny sent me a black Labrador puppy from England. I trained him all by myself, teaching him to hunt and retrieve. I was supposed to keep him in the stable but he was lonely and so was I, so I sneaked him into my room at nights. One day I forgot to shut the door. I had trained him not to bark but he must have heard Beck prowling around the house. I suppose he bit him, but I don't know. Next morning when I went searching for my dog Fritz told me Beck had shot him, saying he had become too dangerous to keep."

Something sizzled in the glowing embers.

"Quick, Eddie, the fish are cooked. Hand me that dish." He forked out charred fish and potatoes from the ashes and placed them in the pan I was holding. "I'm starving, aren't you?"

Elaine, whom we joined, had put out plates. There was cold duck and salad and hard-boiled eggs, cake and a bowl of wild strawberries she had picked.

The Tsarevna had thrown back some of her draperies. They framed her round heavy face like the austere veil of a nun, but there was nothing austere about her appetite. She devoured the largest of the trout, two baked potatoes drenched in butter and several pieces of cake with unconcealed enjoyment. All of us drank wine.

Afterwards we helped Elaine to put things back in the basket. The sun was beating down on the platform and it was very hot.

"I'm going in now," Alexander said, standing poised at the water's edge. "Are you coming, Mummy?"

"I'll join you in a minute."

He dived almost flatly, skimming into the water like a fish, then swam around waiting for her. She had unbuttoned her frock and emerged from it in a blue bathing suit that, if modest, revealed more than her dress had. What I only dared glance at briefly was of pleasing proportions. She sat down on the ledge, letting her feet drop into the water.

"Hurry up, Mummy, don't be such a coward." He swam up to her and started to splash her, then took hold of her feet and dragged her in. What with her protesting cries and his laughing encouragement, they made a lot of noise.

"And I was trying to sleep," the Tsarevna complained, throwing back her veil once more. "Look at them showing off. All for your benefit, I suppose." They were ducking each other like children. Elaine's hair had loosened and floated all around her. "Both competing for your attention. Well, which do you prefer?" She looked at me, her eyes as black as the lake, sparkling with amusement.

How could I answer? I didn't know. So I said nothing.

"Which of them is it you want to rescue so gallantly by taking them to England?" the wicked old woman teased. "Is it Elaine? If so, you will have to marry her. She is a romantic prude; she'll never be satisfied at just being your mistress!"

"Frankly I don't know what you are talking about, Countess Plevke," I said angrily. "Elaine is years older than I. Why, she might almost be my mother!"

"As if that mattered," she chuckled.

"I respect her; I feel sorry for her; I like her. I'd never dream of thinking of her in any other way. As for marriage—why, it's absolutely ludicrous—I won't be able or ready to marry anyone for many years and if I do, it certainly won't be Elaine." I had talked myself into a fury of indignation and, pausing for breath, thought I heard a slight sound. Turning I saw Elaine was sitting at the water's edge, drying her hair in the sun. How long had she been there, I asked myself with horror? How much had she heard?

The old woman too had seen. "Elaine," she called, "I've been waiting for you. Have you been sitting there long?"

"I've only just got out of the water," she said, pushing back her hair.

I saw that it was almost dry.

"Come here, I need you."

Obediently Elaine rose. She had legs as long and straight as Alexander's, I noticed, and she did not look much older than him either in that damp and clinging bathing suit.

She bent over the Tsarevna, who whispered something. Then she started to push the heavy chair.

"Let me help," I said, jumping up from where I had been sitting.

"No thank you, Harris. There are some things I prefer to do without a gentleman's assistance," the old woman said.

Elaine managed to turn the chair half-way round, intending I suppose to head it for some bushes. She had obviously not noticed how steeply the ground there sloped towards the water's edge. The chair gathered speed. I saw she couldn't hold it; in fact, it was torn from her grasp. In a matter of seconds I knew it and the Tsarevna, helplessly entangled in her netting, would plunge into the lake. I heard Elaine's wild scream. There was no time for thought. Only instinct made me throw myself on the ground in front of the chair. Its wheels ploughed into me with grinding force, but the weight of my body stopped it, if only inches from the water's edge.

"What are you doing there, Harris?" the Tsarevna asked, looking down at me. Though her face was very pale and her lips trembled, she managed to smile. "I seem to have got rather close to the lake."

Elaine came running, tears streaming down her face; so did Alexander, though his was only drenched with the lake water from which he had just emerged. Both bent over me. "Are you all right, Eddie?"

I felt faint with pain and thought every bone in my body was broken, but I managed to gasp: "I might be if you pushed the chair off my back." They did, pulling it and the Tsarevna to safety. I lay still for a moment then, assisted by Alexander, managed to get up. He looked at me anxiously as I tested my limbs. Though bruised and sore, there seemed to be no serious damage.

Elaine was sobbing. "It was all my fault," she stammered.

"Nonsense," the Tsarevna said. "In any case I'm not easy

to kill as long as I have brave young men around me. Thank you, Harris—I won't forget.

"I'm tired now. Take me home," she said to Alexander. He wheeled her out on to the drive that led to the house. I looked after them until they were out of sight.

"What courage."

"I don't think she realized the danger she was in," Elaine said, still in tears.

"Oh yes she did."

"And to think you both might have been killed through my fault," she sobbed.

Suddenly she clung to me, as if for support. Though I still ached all over I knew that more was demanded than merely friendly comforting. I have always heard that proximity to danger and death stimulates the reproductive urge. I found it to be true.

Yet after I had drawn her behind some trees and lain with her, I thought how much more real to me was the gross old Tsarevna with her coarse and earthy jests, compared to this feeble creature trembling in my arms and murmuring words of love to which I had no answer.

Never could the sound of voices and approaching footsteps have been more welcome than those that excused my withdrawing from Elaine's clinging embrace. Through the screening shrubs I could see Fritz and Ivan. They had come to collect the picnic basket. Ivan carried the dead deer, tied by its four feet to a pole. Its head hung low. So did mine.

They did not see us. After they were gone we walked the short distance back to the house in silence.

When I had reached my room, I lay down on my bed, totally exhausted, aching in body and soul. What had I done? Why?

Suddenly there was Alexander, holding a tray.

"Mummy thought you might like some tea." I drank it gratefully.

"You were so brave," he said, looking down at me, "and I thought you weren't man enough, even to shoot a deer." He bent and kissed my forehead. "Now sleep," he said, drawing the sheets up around me.

Eventually I did.

# Chapter Seven

In the week that followed I spent my mornings with Alexander; in the early hours watching him shoot duck, or fish in the lake or stream, and then studying with him in the library until lunch time. I enjoyed teaching him. He was a good pupil, alert and attentive, if at times rather impatient.

I had not approved his essay on *Faust*; it seemed to me that its deeper meaning had escaped him. The fact that Faust had sold his soul to the Devil in exchange for earthly pleasures, and having found them unsatisfactory felt he had made a bad bargain, had been clearly put by Alexander but he seemed to see in Faust's final redemption no more than a clever ruse to get his soul back.

"Surely there was something more to it than mere opportunism from beginning to end?" I protested.

"Well, I don't think so," Alexander said, "but then I don't understand the second part very well and all those bits about Helen—do explain."

"I think she is a symbol of the female element in all of us, gentler, kinder than what is male. Also, if you like, of the eternal mother who because of her compassion and mercy can intercede for us with God. That's at least how I understand it."

"But I thought Helen of Troy was merely very beautiful. Lots of men died fighting for her but it doesn't say anywhere that she saved their souls."

"Just by being beautiful perhaps—I think what Goethe meant is that even mere physical beauty is a reminder of heavenly beauty—recalls something eternal—through the centuries artists have tried to express that. Sculptors, painters, writers, musicians."

"And actors?"

"They too transmit and translate it through their art. In the ancient world the Gods spoke through the mouths of actors."

We had many like discussions on diverse subjects, though I

66

noticed that it was generally I who defended moral concepts and more abstract ideals.

Frequently he would get the better of an argument by simply quoting from books instead of putting his own thoughts into words, though it was not parrot-like as I had at first feared but always very much to the point. He had understood what he had read and learnt. If he disliked explaining anything or writing down his ideas it was, I think, because he had a great respect for words and a distaste for expressing himself inadequately. Though he showed no more than average aptitude for mathematics and science—in fact, nothing that he could not personify or mirror himself in interested him very much—his knowledge of history and classical literature in three languages, four with Latin, was amazing for a boy of his age.

Studying these subjects with him was immensely rewarding and in these I learnt from him at least as much as I could teach him.

My respect for the Tsarevna grew when he told me it was mainly she who had awakened his interest in literature, teaching him first to read, then to recite, repeat and re-enact what he had understood. I had not seen her since the accident. Alexander said it had rather shaken her, that she said she wanted to rest and only admitted the servants, himself and Beck, who had returned from Hamburg.

Beck was as friendly and benevolent towards me as usual when he came to dine, but seemed rather silent and less cheerful as if preoccupied with something. Probably money problems concerning the estate, I thought. Sometimes as if lost in thought he would stare at Elaine. I had been avoiding her as much as politely possible, fearful of being held responsible for my brief lapse at "le pique-nique Anglais". I did not know how to respond to her timidly questioning and, I feared, demanding glances. Then again, Beck would turn to Alexander's bright face, as if with regret.

So did I, if probably for different reasons. Mine was that I had asked Alexander if I could make a drawing of him that afternoon. He had seemed delighted.

"What shall I wear?" he asked. "The Tsarevna's uniform of the guards or shall we make something up? I can borrow some of Mummy's clothes."

"I only want your face."

"Oh." He looked disappointed. He watched me pinning a

large sheet of paper to a board and laying out charcoal and crayons.

"I didn't know you were an artist, Eddie."

"I am not, but I try. Now sit still for a moment; it won't take long."

It didn't. Had I laboured more I would have overworked the sketch. What I had hoped to express I had caught; that fleeting moment of child-like innocence on the brink of change. After I had left it as incomplete and beautiful as is youth itself, I handed it to Alexander.

He contemplated it with grave interest.

"You haven't got my hair quite right. Surely it doesn't wave so much? Still, is that really like me?"

"Yes, don't you think so?"

"How should I know? I only look into the mirror when I act and then I am other people." He distorted his face in a series of grimaces, comic and tragic. He inspected my drawing once more. "Am I really as pretty as that?"

"Perhaps I flattered you. In any case, it won't last."

"Why?"

"Because as you get older your face will change, will express what you really are."

"Like in *The Picture of Dorian Gray*?"

"I didn't know that was in the library here."

"Oh yes, among the Tauchnitz novels."

I tried to remember the book. "Wasn't it a rather turgidly romantic repetition of the story of Faust?"

"In a way, I suppose, except that Faust was saved. Dorian was not because of his picture. It told too much."

Before I could hinder him he had pulled my drawing off the board and torn it into bits.

"How could you!" I exclaimed, startled and angry.

"Because I'd rather stay as I am." Then gently: "I'm sorry, Eddie, perhaps you could draw Mummy instead. I'm sure she would like it."

It was about the last thing I wanted to do.

"What's gone wrong between you, anyway? At first you chummed up so nicely."

"Nothing, except that I've been rather busy with our studies and the translations the Tsarevna gave me."

"And with learning to shoot and fish with me too." Having favoured me with one of his most dazzling smiles he had left.

I thought of Elaine, knowing I had hesitated too long to clarify whatever there was between us. Then next evening, before dinner when we were alone together waiting in the drawing-room for Alexander to appear, I found the courage to speak.

"Elaine, I want you to forgive, if you can, and to forget what happened—I had no right—but you were so upset about the danger the Tsarevna had been in I quite simply wanted to comfort you, and then when we embraced I lost my head."

"Forgive you, Eddie?" she asked, with an unmistakably tender smile, "when it was all my fault and I deliberately allowed it to happen."

Probably I looked as surprised as I was.

She blushed slightly.

"Let me explain. You see, even in the short time you have been here I thought I had reason to think you were growing rather—well—fond of me. Then that afternoon I overheard the Tsarevna talk so coarsely and cruelly about me to you, saying I was a prude and that you'd have to marry me if you wanted me and you protesting that I was old enough to be your mother; and that's not quite right, Eddie, because I'm only thirty-five; and that in any case you had never thought of me except with anything but respect."

It was now my turn to blush.

"Oh yes, I heard every word," she continued, "and, of course, you were right in saying what you did."

Relief flooded me. Though ashamed and penitent at perhaps having hurt her feelings, at least she now knew the truth.

"Right," she resumed, "to deny what you really felt for me to that gross, inquisitive old woman as best you could. It was the gentlemanly thing to do. And do you know, Eddie, for a moment you almost convinced me. I doubted you loved me and I wanted to make sure. And then you proved to me how much you did."

I tried to force my features into some adequate response but I could not. I felt numb with shock.

Perhaps she noticed.

"Of course, it was very wrong of us," she said. "It must not happen again, not here. However difficult it will be to control our feelings, we must—if only for Alexander's sake. He's still a child. He would not understand."

A brief respite.

"That's exactly what I felt," I said, trying not to sound too enthusiastic. "It wouldn't be decent, would it? Not in this house—" and then, believing I could risk it—"that's why I haven't dared come near you all this week."

"But I understood that, Eddie. We will simply have to wait a little longer, even if I seem to have waited for you all my life. Now that I know you love me I don't mind. And once we are back in England and Alexander at school, we can get quietly married."

"Elaine, darling," I said, wondering why I didn't choke over the endearment, "I'm afraid it will be ages until we can marry. Surely you must realize that it will be years until I can support a wife."

"Don't let that worry you, Eddie. I've thought it all over. My parents are quite well off and we could live with them at first—the house is big enough."

I visualized myself being immured in the Vicarage with this pathetically obtuse woman; and I thought of Alexander as my stepson. I did not doubt that given the opportunity he would play even Hamlet off the stage.

I was appalled by it all but how to find the kind and proper way out? I felt like a hapless fly enmeshed in a spider's web, ever more inextricably entangled as Elaine revealed more of her hopes and plans.

"The Tsarevna can't live forever. Her health and mind are rapidly failing. Once she's gone, I don't think Beck can hinder us from selling all or part of Schwarzensee and then Alexander and I will have no money worries at all."

I don't know what prompted me to say what I did, except that my nerves were on edge, that I deeply resented the way she was disposing of my future and that I felt irrevocably trapped.

"So really it would have solved all difficulties if I had let the Tsarevna drown?"

I by then so disliked looking at Elaine's face that only when she bent towards me did I see she was rather pale.

"Eddie, there must be no secrets between us." I was suddenly reminded of Alexander's having used the same words when telling me of one of his imaginary adventures. "The truth is I was so upset and angry by what I had heard the Tsarevna say to you about me that for a moment I didn't care what happened to her if I let the chair go. The provocation was too great. You do understand, don't you, Eddie?" she pleaded.

Never for a moment, though I had witnessed it all, had I

thought the wheelchair had been intentionally released by Elaine.

"Of course I understand," I said, though I felt cold with horror. Then relief swept over me. I was free. The trap was sprung. I had no moral obligations towards this creature who was capable of murdering a helpless old woman in order to get what she wanted. Well—it wouldn't be me.

Now there was only the Tsarevna and, indirectly, Alexander to protect.

"Why, has the Tsarevna said anything to you?" she asked, alarmed at my expression I suppose.

"No, but I haven't seen her since then."

"Neither have I; she hasn't even asked me to come to her room."

"Perhaps she fears a second attempt."

Elaine looked at me, her big blue eyes wide with fear.

"But, Eddie, surely you don't think—?"

"I don't know what to think, except that I wouldn't be able to defend you if anything like that happened again."

"But I didn't mean to kill her, I really didn't," she sobbed.

I left her to her tears. I had had enough of comforting the fair Elaine.

■

Next day I was called to the Tsarevna. I took with me the translation I had made of Sir James Harris's dispatches. They had interested me more than I had expected. There were amusing descriptions of political intrigues and diplomatic manoeuvres and fascinating accounts of the barbaric splendour of Catherine's court, of the profligacy of her favourites, of Potemkin's long domination over her in spite of her having other lovers, of her remarkable intellect and total lack of morals.

Lying in her vast bed the Tsarevna listened to what I read to her. Now and then she would smile or frown in approval or disapproval at something or say: "Harris, you got that wrong," or "You are quite right about that." But often she would sink back among her cushions and close her eyes, seeming to pay no attention to what I was reading. However, as soon as I stopped, because I thought she slept, she asked me to continue. After half an hour she told me to put the book away.

"Talk to me, Harris."

"About what, Tsarevna?"

"Ah, you've come to call me that too! About anything—your home, your family, your future prospects."

As I did, I thought how much she had changed. The shock of having been so near death must have had a sobering effect on her. She listened to me quietly without interrupting, there were no lewd remarks, no laughter, no teasing references to Elaine; in fact, she never mentioned her.

Finally she said, her dark eyes seeming to have lost all their wicked sparkle, to have become deep and sad: "A life for a life, isn't it so, Harris? Was that what the lake wanted?"

"I'm afraid I don't understand."

"No matter—yet you saved mine, though it was scarcely worth the trouble. It has been forfeited for many years. Still, I owe you something in exchange for your gallant effort. I will permit Alexander to go to school in England if you still feel that would be best for him and will look after him there. I have come to trust you, Harris, more than I do others."

I bent and kissed her old hand.

"I will have to tell Beck, of course, since he is Alexander's guardian—he will make difficulties. *Mais après tout c'est moi qui est maîtresse*," she said. "Now go, Harris."

How glad I would have been to have brought the good news to Elaine only a week ago. But it was certainly not I who was going to tell her about it now. Once Beck had decided, Alexander could inform her. I dreaded even the slightest involvement with her and her future plans. As for the boy of whom I knew I had grown absurdly fond, he should have all the help and friendship I could give him once he was separated from his mother and at school in England.

Fritz had left the mail in my room. The postman on his bicycle came only once a day to Schwarzensee. There was a parcel of books I had ordered from Hatchard's for Alexander, mainly plays, Chekhov, Ibsen, Shaw and Wilde, and some modern English poetry. There was also a long letter from my mother, thanking me for two of mine. To my surprise, she wrote from home. She said she had returned sooner than she had expected because she had missed her work so much. Knowing my mother, I felt certain that nothing but boredom would have forced her to change her plans and that she must have found staying with her aged relations in Ireland extremely dull. Also she admitted it had rained all the time and that she had not been able to leave the house. She is not the sort that goes for walks in gumboots and mackintosh and is only an outdoor person in fine weather.

Then there followed a long and, to me, incomprehensible list of questions. Not that they were not clearly written, but their purpose was totally obscure to me.

They asked for the first names of all Plevkes down to Alexander; the dates of their marriages, births and deaths. Also the dates of birth of everyone in the house, even those of the servants and Beck. How could she expect me to go around asking such questions? Nor could I understand what it had to do with her work. "Try and get at the letters," she said, "they may explain a lot." What did Alexander look like? Had I some snapshots? Was there a concealed staircase that led into the Tsarevna's room? Were there any more portraits besides that of Catherine the Great? ("Note: duplicate or copy of one by le Toque still in, what is now, Leningrad.") Did Elaine have a photograph of her husband?—and more equally pointless-seeming questions and remarks, the last begging me to be careful.

What could she possibly mean? My mother, if of Irish descent, was not the seventh child of a seventh child but the only daughter of intelligent and enlightened parents. She had never been fey or psychic as far as I knew. How could she have guessed of Elaine's attempt? I tried to remember what I had said to her in my last letter. Certainly about the Tsarevna's believing she was Catherine the Great. That I felt Alexander's gifts would be wasted if he remained here much longer. That both Beck and the Tsarevna objected to his going to school in England and that only Elaine was on my side—certainly no more about her.

Even if my mother had somehow guessed at my involvement with the fair Elaine, she could not have foreseen its consequences, nor believed that a respectable parson's daughter would attempt murder because of me.

I came to the conclusion that, what with her liking for detective stories and solving mysteries, she must have read something that coincided with what I had told her about Schwarzensee and confused one with the other.

I wrote to her rather briefly, saying that I foresaw nothing ominous happening, that I was having a very pleasant time and that I would try to find the answers to some of her questions, though it would not be easy. I also said the Tsarevna had at last given her permission for Elaine and Alexander to go to England, that there was now only Beck left to persuade and that I would probably be home soon. I enclosed a small drawing I had made from memory of Alexander.

# Chapter Eight

Next day Fritz came to say that Beck wished to see me in his office whenever it was convenient to me, as he would be working there all morning. That he lived in one of the two lodges I knew, since his car usually stood in front of it. So at eleven I sauntered through the enchanting courtyard of which I thought one saw much too little, because most of the windows of the living-rooms overlooked the lake and the garden instead, and knocked on the door of Beck's lodge.

A very old woman, the only female servant ever to be seen at Schwarzensee crossing the yard occasionally, though never in the house, opened the door. There was a hall; I could see a kitchen beyond and a staircase. The woman—she wore the usual blue and white flowered Holstein peasant dress and apron—indicated I should go upstairs.

I entered a large and pleasant room. It was panelled as those in the main house were, cupboards built into the walls and a bed recessed into one of them.

Beck rose from a desk at which he had been writing. There was the inevitable Germanic handshake, then he sat down once more, indicating a chair that faced his desk, poured me and himself a glass of Schnapps, crossed his booted legs and leant back to contemplate me with evident amusement.

"You must excuse me for taking up your valuable time, Mr Livingstone."

I could not accept this remark as being intended to be anything but sarcastic.

"Less important than yours, Herr Beck," I nevertheless said politely.

"I have asked you to come here because there are some things better discussed in private."

"I quite agree."

The next move I thought was his, but he just stared at me as if taking my measure. Resenting this, I looked around the room. It was well furnished, though here also, as in my passage, stags' antlers and the horns of roebucks and several stuffed birds, presumably of a rare species, hung attached to the walls. Standing around on tables and chests were a lot of framed photographs.

"May I look?" I asked, getting up.

"Certainly," he said.

There were several of Alexander in shooting dress, holding up the horned heads of dead deer. There was a miniature of the Tsarevna which must have been painted many years ago—a slim, dark woman with a vivacious, lively expression on her rather plain face, and a photograph of a young man in uniform, also dark-haired, with features slightly resembling hers, except that they lacked her laughing mouth and determined chin.

"Alexander's father?" I asked.

"Yes, and my best friend."

"The boy doesn't resemble him much."

"Neither in looks nor character. Paul was not as clever nor as handsome, but more reliable. Yet, I honour his memory and it is for his sake that I take my responsibility to his son so seriously. Please sit down again and listen to what I have to say with attention." I did as I was told.

"I know you have managed to persuade the Tsarevna to let Alexander go to school in England." I did not like his tone of voice.

"Do you object?" I asked, defiantly.

"Absolutely. Mr Livingstone, I must confess that you have rather disappointed me. When I agreed that a young Englishman should be engaged to teach Alexander, I did not expect him to so far exceed his duties as to dare mix in family affairs which are none of a tutor's concern."

He waved away whatever protest I was ready to make and continued. "Besides, wasn't your quite ingenious act in seeming to save the Tsarevna from the lake rather transparent? It is to me. You must have known that afterwards it would be easy to persuade a frightened, mentally and physically weak old woman that she had been in real danger and that she must prove her gratitude for your gallant rescue by letting Alexander go. Quite a clever manoeuvre, Mr. Livingstone, but then I'm not a bad tactician myself. However, you went too far when you allowed the Tsarevna to suspect, as she now does, that it was Elaine that let go of the wheelchair, when we both know that it was you who gave it a push."

"Did Elaine say that?" I was furious, but rather frightened.

"Not in so many words," Beck admitted, "but she is a good simple woman; what she thinks is easy to read. A loyal one too. She must have feared for you and wished to protect you since she said no more. But you showed no such scruples in spite of certain intimacies that have taken place between you, so I am told. But you never really wanted her, did you—only the boy?"

I could not contain my anger.

"How dare you, Beck—not a word of this is true."

"Can you deny it then?"

How could I, without exposing Elaine and telling the whole sorry tale of my physical lapse? After all, she had given herself to me and done what she had because she thought I loved her. I was as guilty as she, if not of what Beck accused me; and if she hated me now, knowing I would not marry her and, frightened perhaps by Beck, had insinuated I had been responsible for the near tragedy—could I blame her?

"It was not at all as you seem to imagine, Herr Beck," I said lamely.

From then on I was at his mercy. There was very little of it, though after his third glass of Schnapps his tone became somewhat more conciliatory.

"I understand your interest in Alexander only too well. I know that in some ways his mind is as brilliant as is his appearance. I understand too why you wish him to have an English education and go to university. And I can't deny that he might benefit from it had he more moral stamina. But have you considered that because of his physical beauty and desire to please, he might become a victim of vices prevalent, I have heard, in English public schools and universities? Paul, you perhaps know, was at Oxford and afterwards complained to me about these perverse customs."

I was too angry to find a suitable answer.

Beck saw. "Forgive me," he said. "I was, of course, not suggesting that you had such tastes—Not that I think," Beck resumed after a significant pause, "that the boy, though he lacks all moral sense, will become a pederast. In spite of all my care and surveillance he has seduced a peasant girl and she is now pregnant."

"I don't believe it," I exclaimed. "It's just one of those stories he makes up."

"So he told you?"

"Yes, but I knew it wasn't true. How could he father a child when he is still one himself?"

"Well, unfortunately, I know better, since the girl's parents came to me for payment. And he has been seen creeping into the village at night and leaving her room at dawn. Not that it matters very much, only these things have become more expensive and cause scandal these days. In the past it was considered an honour for a girl to be with child by one of the Plevkes. In the village of Schwarzensee are many related to Alexander, if born on the wrong side of the blanket. I hope you will not repeat this, but Fritz and Ivan are his half-brothers. That's why the Tsarevna is so attached to them and took them into the house to work. They were born before Paul married Elaine, of course."

"Does she know?" I asked, shocked.

"No, Paul kept it from her."

"Alexander?"

"He may suspect, as he does other things with less reason. But you may have noticed by now how secretive and deceitful he can be, always putting on an act to conceal what he really thinks and feels."

"Many sensitive and lonely children do that."

"A child?" Beck questioned. "Have you found him mentally underdeveloped?"

"Of course not."

"Well, neither is he physically, as he has proved. But as he has grown into manhood he must now learn discipline and self-control and he must be protected from himself by someone who knows his family's history and the weaknesses inherent in his blood."

"In fact by you."

"Certainly—I stand in his father's place since he appointed me guardian and must uphold the family's honour. Such as Alexander is, I dare not let him leave Schwarzensee before I have moulded him into shape, developed his conscience and made a good German out of him—a personality worthy of inheriting this place that I've worked to improve for so many years now—for his sake."

"And what about his mother? Is she to have no say at all in the development you plan for him?"

Beck shrugged. "The poor good woman. She doesn't understand him at all. The only thing she does is spoil him, whereas he is in need of the strictest discipline instead."

"Thank you, Herr Beck, for your explanations," I said stiffly. "And I hope you will excuse my having interfered in so far as to wish a better future for a boy as gifted as Alexander is, and for him to be allowed to develop his talents in a more intellectual atmosphere than in this stagnant one of decay and madness. Without companions of his own age, without the stimulant of intellectual competition, even deprived of competitive sport—" I looked around the room—"Though you have taught him to shoot well, Herr Beck, I don't consider killing harmless animals with a gun sport."

Beck rose. He was a tall and powerfully built man and towered above me.

"It seems we don't understand each other, Mr Livingstone. So be it. But let me warn you that my decisions concerning Alexander are final. I have to leave for Hamburg again tomorrow early, but I will be back in the evening. Meanwhile I will have to ask you not to meddle any more with what you obviously don't comprehend or I fear your stay at Schwarzensee will be brief."

"Are you threatening me with dismissal?"

"Oh no," he said—then with an unpleasant smile—"but circumstances might arise that would make you want to leave of your own accord." He opened the door, politely bowing me out.

Had the circumstances not already come, I asked myself as I returned to my room? Would it not be best to leave before there was more unpleasantness either from him or Elaine? And though much that Beck had said about Alexander had angered me, there was, I knew, enough truth in it to make me uneasy. After all, Beck knew the boy from his early childhood: I for only ten days.

I had been shocked at hearing about the girl but I had to grant that Alexander had not lied to me and only when I refused to believe had invented the story of catching eels at night. I remembered other things he had told me. Of Beck's sleeping with the Tsarevna—of his grandfather having been murdered—of his nights spent with Fritz and Ivan and their games together—of Beck's being in love with him. Was it perhaps all true?

I shuddered at my thoughts.

But even if it was true, what chance was there left of my helping him escape from this house of iniquity? None! To what purpose to continue teaching him when his future training was already determined by Beck? Why stimulate the boy's mind, raise hopes that would never be realized, because by the time he came of age it would be too late. All that was still now fluid and malleable would be forced by Beck into the form of his choosing.

How utterly I had failed in everything, I told myself. I had cruelly misled Elaine—to the extent that she had almost committed a crime. I had allowed the boy to believe that his fervid ambition to become an actor would be fulfilled. There must be no more deceit, I knew, except one last. I would say my mother was ill and had written to ask me to come home.

It was only a short while until Alexander came into my room, his face radiant.

"The Tsarevna says I can go to school in England," he sang out. "Oh, Eddie, isn't it wonderful? Of course, she did say Beck would have to agree," he added, with less enthusiasm.

Though it pained me almost as much as I knew it would hurt him, I had to tell him Beck had refused, that he had called me to him and left me in no doubt as to his intentions. "It wouldn't be fair not to tell you, Alexander," I excused myself, seeing disappointment and anger cloud his bright face. "He made it quite clear that nothing would change his decision."

"But why, Eddie, why?"

"He gave many reasons, but I think the main one is that he found out about the girl—and thinks you're not responsible enough to leave his care."

Alexander looked very frightened. "How did he find out?" he stammered.

I told him.

"And I promised to pay her parents as soon as I could—I would have sold my father's gold watch. Eddie, he won't tell Mummy, will he? She would never understand that I didn't love the girl—you know how romantic she is—that it just happened and that I can't marry her even when I'm grown up."

"No. I don't think she would understand," and with sudden shock knew I was speaking from experience.

"Oh, how can I stop him from telling her?"

"Only, I'm afraid, if there is no more talk about your going to England. In fact, he warned me that if I continued to encourage you in the hope of a future there, I would have to leave Schwarzensee."

"He dared? Oh, how I hate him; hate him." The boy started to sob desperately.

"I think you wrong him, Alexander. He has your welfare very much at heart. He is very fond of you and that he feels responsible for you is surely natural, since he's your guardian. You are very young. You have all your life in front of you—who knows if you won't become a famous German actor one day?"

"But I want to be an English actor—" Alexander stamped his feet as if in a frenzy of childish temper.

"Come, calm yourself," I said, putting an arm round him. He snuggled up to me, raising eyes flooded with tears.

"Let's run away together, Eddie. I will get Fritz to drive us to Kiel on some excuse and there we can take the train to England. Please, please—"

"Alexander, you know it's impossible. What about your mother and the Tsarevna, they would go mad with anxiety if you were missing?"

"We could telegraph them as soon as we arrived in England."

"And have Beck come to fetch you back? He has every legal right to do so and to accuse me of having abducted a minor. Be reasonable, Alexander. Be a brave boy and accept what can't be helped."

He tore himself free from me. "I would rather drown myself in the lake and then you'll all be sorry."

"Oh, come, you swim too well for that."

It brought no smile to his face. He ran out of my room and I heard him patter upstairs to his own and slam the door.

Neither he nor Elaine came to dinner. Only one place had been laid.

Fritz said the English lady begged to be excused as Alexander wasn't well and she had to stay with him.

Poor, bitterly disappointed child, I thought. Still, he was safe in his bed with his mother to soothe and comfort and pity him.

I read a while in my room, mainly the books I thought I would take to him next day, since I did not quite believe in the permanence of his illness. Then I sat for a long time staring into the candle flame, thinking that there was only one cowardly way out and that was for me to leave Schwarzensee as soon as decently possible. I would give it a week, I thought, until I announced my mother's illness, not wanting Beck to think that I had instantly fled because of his threats. Calmed by my resolve, I slept.

# Chapter Nine

The sound of Beck's car driving out of the courtyard woke me at dawn. So he had left for Hamburg. I remembered my interview with him with distaste, yet I had to admit to myself that in some ways if all he had said was true he was, from his point of view, right to have refused to let Alexander out of his care.

Then I went back to sleep. It cannot have been much later that Alexander crept through my window and woke me once more.

"Take your damn gun and let me sleep," I said, not opening my eyes. He had been keeping it in my room, since it was more conveniently at hand there for his early morning shooting expeditions.

"Anyway, I thought you were ill and in bed." Then I opened my eyes to see with consternation that he was very pale and that he shivered as if with cold. "You certainly don't look at all well. You shouldn't have gone out. Go back to your room."

"I need your help, Eddie. Get up. And please hurry, for God's sake." He threw my trousers on to my bed. There was something so strange and urgent in his tone of voice that I obeyed and dressed.

"What on earth's the matter, Alexander?"

"Come. There's no time to lose. You'll see."

I followed him out of the window. "Don't make any noise," he whispered, as he led the way into the forest. I wondered what unfortunate beast he was forcing me to help him stalk, then realized he had not taken his gun. We broke out into the drive that edged the lake where we had picnicked. Beck's big black Mercedes was parked there and on the rocky promontory that had seen near-tragedy and witnessed my taking of Elaine, Beck lay. He was dressed in town-going clothes but wore his green shooting hat. In fact it entirely covered his face. His gun was beside him. I bent over him.

"You don't have to look," Alexander said. "He's dead. I made sure. His head's an awful mess so I covered it up."

Suicide? Poor old Beck, I thought. What secret guilt could have led him to it, perhaps partially revealed and drawn forth in our talk the day before?

"We will have to call the police," I said. "Obviously he has shot himself."

"He didn't. I did."

I looked at Alexander's pale but composed face, trying to comprehend what he had said. "It was an accident then?"

"It was self-defence. Eddie, you must believe me now. Have I not always told you the truth, though you wouldn't accept it before?"

I thought of the girl. Cold with fear I waited for what he would have to say next.

"Beck tried to strangle me. Then he would have thrown me into the lake for the eels to devour. Look at my throat!" There were indeed some purple bruises. "He tried to kill me."

"But why?"

"Oh, I provoked him, I suppose. I called him a thief—and a murderer—after all, he shot my dog. I said I knew everything and all about the secret staircase by which he crept into the Tsarevna's room at night and that if he didn't let me go to England I would tell all; that the moment I came of age and Schwarzensee was mine I would see to it that he was held to account for all he had stolen from us. He just laughed! And do you know what he said then? That Schwarzensee was his if he so chose after the Tsarevna's death. Then his big hands were around my throat. 'I will have to shake some sense into you, young puppy,' he said. I knew he intended to kill me. Somehow I managed to tear loose. I picked up the gun and shot straight into his ugly, sneering face. And that is the truth, Eddie. Please believe me."

Though horrified at what I had heard, I did.

"Now for God's sake help me lift him into the car. I couldn't do it alone. I'll tie him into it. Look, I've got my eel-line ready." From under some shrubs he drew a coil of tarred rope with smaller pieces and hooks attached. "Then I'll drive him into the lake, swim free and no one will ever find him in that mud."

"But you don't understand, Alexander," I protested. "We daren't touch him. We must go back and send Fritz for the police."

I looked at his pale and suddenly frightened face. "Come,

nothing will happen to you, since you did it in self-defence."
I glanced at the marks on his neck. Weren't they already fading? "Besides, even if it came to the worst, you are under age. You wouldn't be held responsible."

"And the scandal? I'd have to tell all that I told you, and much more that you don't know, that I've kept secret for years. Think of what it would do to Mummy, to our family's reputation, to the Tsarevna! They would find out everything—Oh please, Eddie, there's so little time. If you don't help me now, we are all lost."

He looked at me piteously, his beautiful young face a mask of despair. "I didn't want to do it—but I didn't want to die either."

"But why were you here at all, Alexander? And with his rifle?"

"I took it with me in case I met some deer."

"But did you know he would drive past?"

"Of course I did. I waved him to stop and he got out."

"Why?"

"I wanted to plead with him not to tell Mummy about the girl—Oh, Eddie, can't these explanations wait until we have more time?"

What finally compelled me to help him I can't explain to myself even now. Pity, love, fear—for this desperate child at the end of its strength, for now he was trembling and sobbing uncontrollably—and concern for Elaine. Together we lifted Beck's body into the back seat of the Mercedes, with some difficulty since it was very heavy.

Then, to my horror, Alexander tore off his own clothes and, naked, squatted over the dead man, trussing him and his gun with the eel rope and tying its ends securely to the side of the car; then leapt into the front seat, accelerated, and drove straight into the lake. There was a loud splash, water fountained several feet high, then subsided into ripples, only a few bubbles rising from the muddied surface where the car had plunged into unknown depths, taking with it both murderer and victim.

Or so I feared. So shocked was I that I only saw Alexander's head as it re-emerged quite near the shore. He was clinging to the rock ledge. "Help me out," he gasped, "I'm nearly done." I dragged him up. He lay quite still for a moment except for panting for breath.

"The car overturned when it reached the mud," he said when he could speak, "and nearly buried me too. For a moment I thought Beck had got me after all." Then he sprang up, went to where his clothes were lying, dried himself with the large coloured handkerchief he used when shooting and dressed hurriedly.

"See if everything's gone," he ordered. Except that the water was more opaque than usual, there was no sign of its having been disturbed. Then I saw Beck's green shooting hat bobbing jauntily towards the shore. Horrified I watched it approach. Was Beck under it?

"Alexander," I screamed and pointed.

"Good you saw it," he exclaimed. He picked up a dead branch and leaning far out hooked the hat out of the water. "I should have remembered that it might come off, but I didn't want you to see his face." He took the hat, which was only stained with water. He looked around, then finding a rotting tree with a hole in it, he thrust in the hat as far as his arm could reach—then carefully washed his hands in the lake. "You had better check if there's any blood on you, Eddie."

I shuddered.

"There might have been some when we lifted him into the car. Still, you could have cut yourself shaving. I don't have the same excuse yet." And he actually laughed. "Look me over carefully."

Feeling sick with disgust I did, but there was not a spot nor a stain on him. "Now see if there are are tyre marks—" he handed me the stick. "It doesn't matter if there are some on the drive, since he passed by here almost every day, and there won't be on this rock, but there might be when I turned the car off the road." There were and I scraped them away, wondering how he could suddenly be in such complete control of himself after all that had happened—and of me. On returning I found him rubbing earth and ashes from the picnic fire into the ground where Beck's head had lain. Once more he washed his hands, even cleaning his nails with a twig.

"One might as well be careful," he said calmly, "though in a few days' time they will probably search for him in Hamburg. I doubt they will here." Then he peered into the lake in which even the cloud of mud had subsided. He looked around once more. "I think we are all right, Eddie, now let's hurry back. If we should meet anyone we've gone on one of our morning strolls. How long have we been?"

I looked at my watch. "About half an hour. It's seven now." We reached my room unobserved.

"Now go back to sleep, Eddie, and I'll get back into bed. Not even Mummy will know I've been out. If I'm still rather ill this morning, don't worry. I have to think things over."

"You seem to have done so pretty well up to now," I exclaimed, amazed at his cold-blooded competence.

"Oh please, Eddie, don't look so upset. I know it was all dreadful and I shouldn't have involved you, but I had no other choice. You're the only real friend I ever had. I've never been able to trust anyone else before—you'll keep our secret, I know." He smiled at me and was gone.

I sat on my bed, my face buried in my hands, but I could not shut out the vision of Beck's dead body. I had never seen anyone dead before. My father had died when I had been thought too young to be shown his corpse—and as for killing—I remembered I had not even had the guts to witness the death of a deer without feeling sick. I thought of the marks on Alexander's white neck. What if they faded before there was any investigation? What proof would we have then that he had been attacked? Only if I asked for the police to come now was there any hope of saving him from being accused of murder. And how strong the motive for it had been I could not conceal from my awakening mind, nor what might be revealed and become public news even if Beck was proved to have been the main culprit. And what about myself? Suspect, as foreigners always are, in a country not their own. How to explain why I had complied? Should I go to Elaine now, confess all and would she not, in order to save her son, implicate me inextricably? Perhaps only anxiety for myself recalled me to reality. And then I realized how remarkably clever Alexander had been.

There was no body, there was no murder weapon, the black lake had covered it all and Beck was known to be on his way to Hamburg. All it needed was for me to keep quiet and behave as usual. And so, though I knew I could eat nothing, I went to the dining-room for breakfast.

Neither Elaine nor Alexander appeared. Fritz brought the coffee as he always did. I glanced at him surreptitiously. Though much coarser featured, he did somewhat resemble Alexander.

"How is the invalid?" I asked.

"Not so good. He has a high fever and the English lady is

worried. She wants to speak to you in half an hour in the *Bibliothek*."

Fear gripped me. Could he be really ill? It would be no wonder if he was. What if he became delirious?

I made a semblance of rearranging books in the library but my hands shook too much for me to hold them. I looked out of the window. It had started to rain. It would wash away any traces we might have left, I thought, disgusted at the relief I felt. Over the black lake a few ducks rose into the lead-coloured sky.

Then Elaine was in the room. She was still in her dressing-gown, her hair in girlish plaits but she looked pale, tired and old.

However she smiled at me. "Sorry I'm not even dressed yet but Alexander has a fever. What do you think could be the matter? He doesn't have a cold or a tummy-ache. I can find no spots except that his neck is a bit swollen. Perhaps it might be the beginning of mumps?" She looked at me anxiously.

"He hasn't had them?"

"No. Do you think I should call the doctor?"

"Of course, if you are worried, but he probably couldn't tell either. It's too soon to know what it is. Perhaps if I could see him," I ventured.

"He's asleep now. Later perhaps, but I want to keep him very quiet. It might be just a nervous reaction. He was so dreadfully upset yesterday, poor baby, after you had told him that Beck had refused to let him go to England. But then I never thought Beck would permit it," she sighed. "Well, one becomes resigned to many things. But Alexander is so young, he won't understand that one can't have everything one wants. I do by now, Eddie—I've learnt my lesson." She looked at me humbly. "Let's at least be friends."

"You are very generous, Elaine."

"I've done penance for my sins too. I went to the Tsarevna and told her the truth: that angered by what she said I had let the chair go and I asked her to forgive me."

"It must have taken a lot of courage."

"It did rather, but she's a strange woman. She wasn't at all upset. She said she would have done the same if she had been in my place and she apologized for having hurt my feelings. She said she knew I had never really meant to harm her— that I was not the murdering kind—so I've got just a little of my self-respect back," she added with a wintry smile. "Well, I'd better return to Alexander now. Yesterday he cried himself to sleep, poor child. I went into his room several times in the night. He seemed very restless. He asked for some hot lemonade; after that he slept soundly. This morning he wouldn't touch his breakfast. Said he was much too ill and showed me his thermometer. It was a hundred and two."

"He should have plenty of warm drinks with such a high fever," I said, greatly relieved that Alexander was allowed to take his own temperature. There is not a child that doesn't know the trick of dipping the thermometer into a glass or cup containing warm liquid. Probably Elaine had been a very good little girl or her mother had taken her temperature for her, I thought, wondering how I could still feel amused at anything.

I sat on in the library after Elaine had gone, now sure I need not worry about Alexander becoming delirious. Touched by what she had told me and certain from now on she would expect only friendship from me, I felt all the more committed to protect her from knowledge that might destroy all she had left: her love for Alexander.

I recalled the whole dreadful scene once more. Had he really been clever enough to think of everything? Was every trace gone? Then it struck me with sudden fear; what if someone had heard the shot or shots? The picnic ground was not far from the house. Still, if Beck's gun was missing, might he not have taken it with him in the car and aimed at something in the forest? But then, where was the game? That nothing Beck or Alexander shot at was allowed to escape I knew by then.

All one could do now was wait, I told myself, and be ready for any eventuality. Of one thing I was certain, that I wouldn't go home until I felt assured that Alexander was safe. I owed that much to Elaine.

Three uneventful days passed. I was told that Alexander's temperature was still high and that he was best kept very quiet, that when it was suggested a doctor be called from Kiel he went into a tantrum and threatened to get out of bed. However, no mumps had developed and the swelling on his throat had gone, Elaine told me.

"I think it's a sort of malaria," she said. "Who knows if among all the mosquitoes that breed in the lake there aren't some which are carriers? I'm giving him quinine. If you see very little of me," she excused herself, "it's because I have two patients now. The Tsarevna is not at all well and worried about Beck. It is rather queer his not having returned. His housekeeper came over two days ago and said she had prepared his supper since he had said he would be back in the evening, but he didn't come. Do you think anything could have happened to him?"

"Probably he is detained in Hamburg," I managed to say quite casually.

"Yes, but he didn't even take a suitcase with him, his housekeeper says. Could he have had an accident?" Elaine asked anxiously. "He drives that powerful car very fast—I've always been terrified of going with him. And he is an old man in spite of his vigour, and a heavy drinker."

"I suppose it's possible, but surely he and the car would be found and the police would let you know? I'd wait a day or two. News doesn't seem to travel very fast in Holstein. Don't worry, Elaine. Sufficient unto the day is the evil thereof." It was, I knew, a rash quotation under the circumstances, but it seemed to please her.

"You're right, Eddie. My father always said that—but if anything has happened I wouldn't know what to do. You see, Beck saw to everything. I'm hopeless at dealing with things, so is the Tsarevna, and Alexander is ill. I'd most desperately need your help if anything had happened to Beck.

"I don't like him because he is so possessive about Alexander," she added, "but he's a good and decent man. Without his efforts to keep everything going, Schwarzensee would have had to be sold long ago. It would be disastrous for all of us if he'd had an accident. Still, thank God Alexander's better and he wants so much to see you. But perhaps it would be best not to mention that Beck is missing. In spite of everything he was fond of him and he might worry. Let's go up."

In his canopied bed, curtained in blue and white lawn billowing around him, Alexander lay looking as still, pale and beautiful as a marble angel on a tomb.

"Do you feel worse, darling?" Elaine asked, bending to stroke his head.

"Oh, Mummy, I'm so thirsty," he moaned. "If only I could have some more lemonade."

"I'll see if there are any lemons left," she said, and then whispered: "Don't let him get excited," as she left the room.

Alexander sat up. "What news? Has Beck been missed?"

"Yes."

"How soon do you think the police will come?"

"Certainly in a couple of days. I may have to call them in myself since your mother has asked for my help." I told him as quickly as I could what she had said. "Alexander, what about someone hearing the shots? Did you think of that?"

"Eddie, I'm not a fool. Beck's car backfired as he left. But perhaps you had better check the lake once more before the police come. I think I will lie low for a few more days.

"Oh, thank you, Mummy darling." She had brought the lemonade and he had sunk back into his pillows. She held the glass to his lips. He sipped slowly while she supported his curly head.

"I think we need some sleep now, darling." He raised his blue eyes to hers gratefully then, as if utterly exhausted, closed his lids as she rearranged sheets, blankets and pillows. "Comfortable now, my angel?"

"Thank you, Mummy," he whispered; then turned on his cushions in my direction, opened one eye, winked at me, then closed it again.

Two more days passed. Much as it had revolted me to do so, I had gone to inspect the place where Beck had died, had looked down into the dark lake and searched its surface, but except for a frightened moorhen skittering across the water there was nothing unusual to be seen. Nevertheless, I felt uneasy. All sorts of possible dangers passed through my mind.

How long would the ropes hold? Probably forever since they were tarred. But how would Alexander explain their loss? A fishing accident? They had sunk, if anyone questioned their disappearance at all. And with sudden dreadful apprehension, what if parts of Beck's decomposing body should come loose and drift to the surface? And then, with disgusted relief, that Alexander had told me that the eels devoured any corpse that had fallen into the mud. He seemed, indeed, to have thought of everything.

# Chapter Ten

On Saturday I agreed with Elaine that the police must be called. A group of labourers who worked on the estate had gathered in the courtyard demanding their wages and asking for Beck. Ivan had been sent down to explain that he had not yet returned from Hamburg. There had been some angry murmurs but finally they had dispersed.

"I don't even have the money to pay them if Beck doesn't come back," Elaine complained. "He sees to all our accounts, even the household ones. Oh, I do wish he would return to deal with things."

I could not feel the irony of this, since it was the complications caused by his death that he was supposed to deal with.

"Oh, what am I to do, Eddie?" Elaine exclaimed plaintively. "I'm so helpless about everything. Please advise me."

I saw to my relief that there was not a trace of coquetry in her appeal any more; it was just that of a very worried woman who had never learnt to think for herself.

"Why not ask your lawyer's advice?"

"But we haven't any. Except for Beck's, and I don't even know his name."

"Your bank manager then? He might be able to help."

"Beck did all our banking with the Hamburger Bankverein."

"Well, that's something. At least his accounts can be checked if he doesn't reappear."

"Eddie, surely you don't also believe what Alexander thinks, that he has bolted, taking all the money he has amassed through the years with him?"

"It's a bit far-fetched."

"That's exactly what I said, but then you know how imaginative Alexander is." She got up. "I'd better go to the Tsarevna now; she is not at all well and very worried, of course."

I remained in the library to gaze regretfully at the books I had never been given time to put in order.

After a while Elaine returned. "I told the Tsarevna we must send for the police. It seemed to upset her rather. I asked her if she wouldn't like the doctor to come but she said it would be no use. She wants you to visit her. Try not to excite her. I've given her her heart tablets. They always help for a few hours."

Once more I entered that overheated, overscented room and approached the great crimson and gold bed in which the Tsarevna lay. I was shocked by the change in her appearance. She seemed to have shrunk to half her former size. Her face was grey and drawn and her dark eyes had lost all their former sparkle. She seemed to have difficulty in breathing.

"Harris, I need your help."

How often had I heard this plea in the last week? How much more was expected of me from this terrible family?

She tried to raise herself then sank back with a grimace of pain. "It takes a while for the medicine to work," she gasped. "I will be stronger in a few minutes." I waited, seeing her lips slowly become less blue, her colour return to normal and her breathing easier.

"Beck's dead," she then said quite calmly.

"But surely he may still be detained in Hamburg?"

"I spoke to his housekeeper. He took no luggage and in fifty years he has not left me one day without news as to his whereabouts."

"He might have had an accident?" I ventured.

"Yes, a fatal one. No matter—I'll see him again soon." Was her mind wandering, I wondered? When she told me to go to the icon that hung on the wall close to her bed I was certain it was. Did she expect me to say a prayer for Beck? The oil lamp underneath the picture was lit and faintly illuminated the silver frame and ornamentations that partially covered the little picture, revealing only the dark-complexioned faces of mother and child looking out from under tall golden crowns, both seeming to stare straight at me out of enigmatic Byzantine eyes.

"Take it down," the Tsarevna said impatiently, "there isn't much time. Underneath the icon you will find a sort of handle. Push it." I did as she ordered and to my amazement an entire wall panel slid sideways revealing a spiral staircase that descended into darkness.

So once more Alexander had told the truth and I had not

believed him. But how could my mother possibly have known? I was given no time to ponder this.

"Hurry!" the Tsarevna urged, now in a voice almost as strong as when I had first met her. "Bolt my door. We do not want to be disturbed. Take that candle—" there was one already lit near her bed—"Go down the stairs and you will find a passage that leads under the courtyard to Beck's lodge. At its end you will find a wall that opens and shuts as this one does. Once in Beck's room go to his desk and in one of its drawers you will see a small red leather case. I know I can trust you not to examine its contents. Bring it back to me as soon as you can and be careful to leave everything else untouched. The police will certainly search Beck's room, so make no disorder."

"And what if I meet the housekeeper?"

"I don't think you will. Though she has a key to the room, she locks it after she has tidied up and when he is away. But even if you did, just tell her you've come from me. She's a loyal soul; even if threatened she would never reveal anything to the police. Now go."

With some trepidation I climbed down the stairs and found myself in a narrow, dark passage built of rough-hewn stone. It smelt of damp and mould and was so airless that I feared my candle would go out—and what then? Something soft and furry leapt from under my foot. It was a large rat. For a moment I believed my heart had stopped but then it started pounding at double its usual rate. I thought of the length of the courtyard above and of how much further I must go. Then at last, to my relief, I saw more stairs and a glimmer of daylight from under a panel that easily opened. I was in Beck's room.

It was empty, except for his disembodied presence, or so it seemed to me as I opened his desk, fearful that he was standing behind me with the mocking laugh with which he had dismissed me from this room on the day before his death.

The numerous drawers were full of tidily stacked folders. I only glanced at them briefly. On their covers were neatly inked "Forestry," "Farm," "Household," with different dates on each in the simple copybook writing of a conscientious schoolboy. Far back behind the folders I finally found the red case. I returned safely with it the way I had come.

I put it on the Tsarevna's bed. She clutched it as if I had brought her something infinitely precious. She even managed to smile at me though I could see she was again very short of breath.

"Just one more thing, Harris," she gasped, "then it will all be over. Now go to that chest over there. Here is the key." From underneath the folds of her neck she detached a small chain—a key was suspended from it. "I keep what is of value in the chest. Don't bother about the jewels. Bring me only the packets of letters you will find."

I did as she asked me to, removing and then replacing the many large and small velvet-covered jewel boxes and cases after I had found several bundles of letters underneath them. Tied with faded ribbon they had no envelopes, were just folded over and sealed with scarlet wax bearing the Imperial stamp of Catherine the Great of Russia. The seals were broken. The letters had yellowed with age and the ink had faded so that "Le Comte de Plevke" was only just discernible. There was no further address. They would at the time, of course, have been delivered by some hard-riding, trusted servants of the Empress by hand. I re-locked the chest, returned the key to the Tsarevna, and placed the letters on her bed. She put them on top of the red case.

"Now stoke the fire," she ordered. "Make it burn high and bright so I can see it from my bed and throw all this in. I want it destroyed."

"But Tsarevna," I protested, "I can't." It was impossible for me not to recognize what those letters were. "How dare I burn them? They may be of the greatest historical importance. To destroy them would be a crime."

"No greater than the crimes they reveal. Do as I say, for the love of God."

I looked at her desperately-jerking old face and thrust the whole lot into the fireplace.

It flamed up, the letters curled and twisted as if alive, small slips of paper with pencilled writing, which I recognized as the Tsarevna's, floated, raised by the heat, long enough for me to distinguish a few words on them. They were in German and they were words of love. There was a document of stiffer paper which unfolded as it burnt and I saw it was a marriage certificate drawn up by the Diocese of Hamburg in the names of William Beck and Grafin Katerina Plevke geborene von Zerbst and the year 1876. The red case was the last to be consumed.

"Is it all gone?" she asked after a while. "I can't see properly from here."

"There is nothing left but ashes."

She sighed deeply and sank back into her pillows. I bent over her, fearful she might have fainted, but she opened her eyes, as dark and opaque as the lake itself.

"I trust you not to speak of this, Harris. No one knows of the stairs, except perhaps Alexander—he bumped into the panel as a child—but even if he remembers, he won't tell." She looked at me intently as if trying to read my thoughts. "Believe me, I know your stay here has not been an easy one. No doubt you will be going home soon."

I murmured something about my mother's not being very well. She fumbled among her sheets and drew out the golden box she had once shown me. "I want to give you this, Harris. Take it."

"But I can't," I stammered.

"Why?"

"Because it is much too valuable."

"Not more so than your services have been, *gentilhomme Anglais*. Besides," she added, with a faint flash of her former spirit, "Catherine always rewarded her favourites generously. Take the box and ask Elaine to make me ready for the night."

As I went in search of Elaine I tried to fathom the meaning of it all. But there were mysteries I knew I could not solve. What had been among those papers that the Tsarevna had feared the police might find? Why had she compelled me to destroy all evidence of her marriage to Beck? And why had he been obliged to creep into her room through the dark, rat-infested passage at night when she was his legal wife? Above all, why had she married him? An uneducated man of such humble origin. Passion? I thought of my first impression of her, as a woman of gross appetites, of her coarse and suggestive jokes, of her admitted fondness for good-looking young men; a woman who would surely have had no moral scruples in taking a lover. Had it all just been part of her impersonation of Catherine the Great? An act, while she had been Beck's staid and faithful wife for over half a century?

I found Elaine in Alexander's room. They were playing chess on his bed. He looked up, seemingly delighted at my entrance and put the board down on the floor.

"It's not much good going on, Mummy, you would have been checkmate in three moves."

"It's the fifth game he's won," she sighed. "How did you find the Tsarevna?"

"Physically very frail; mentally quite alert. She is certain that Beck's dead."

"But how could she be?"

"I think because he has never yet left her without news when he was detained anywhere." I took the gold box out of my pocket and put it on Alexander's bed. "She gave me this. Of course, I can't take it."

"But why not?" Alexander exclaimed. "I'm so glad she gave it to you. It's lovely, isn't it?" He turned it round and round, making the diamonds sparkle as they caught the light. "I so much wanted you to have a nice present, only I had nothing precious enough to give you."

"Of course you must have it, Eddie," Elaine said. "You saved her life and you have been so good to us in all this bother about Beck too—I'll go to her now and tell her how glad we are that she gave it to you."

After Elaine had left Alexander leapt out of bed and thrust the box back into my pocket. "You've deserved it, Eddie." He looked angelic in his long, old-fashioned white nightgown, frills at neck and sleeve. He gave me a radiant smile.

"Oh, I'm so happy," he exclaimed. "Do you realize, Eddie, that I'm free now, that I can come to England whenever I please and go to school and Oxford and become a great actor?"

"You already are," I said coldly. "I feared you were really ill."

He laughed.

"Besides, it seems a bit early to triumph. The police haven't even been here yet."

"And what can they find? Nothing. Besides, I'll talk to them. I'm sick of staying in bed. I will still be rather weak, of course—" he tottered and supported himself on the back of a chair. "I wonder if I walked with a stick?"

"I think that would be rather overdoing it."

"Oh, just leave it all to me. I'm ready for any questions."

"Alexander, I must ask you this once more. Did you deliberately plan to kill Beck?"

He looked at me with wide-eyed amazement. "How can you ask when I told you the truth about everything. Should I have let him kill me?"

I searched the lovely child-like face for a trace of guilt and saw only innocence. Nevertheless I said firmly: "I will be going home shortly."

"But, Eddie, you can't leave us now! We need your help!"

"I will only stay long enough to see you're safe and then I will spend the rest of my days trying to forget Schwarzensee."

"But surely not me, Eddie? You are my friend. I am counting on you for help and advice in England."

Next morning, when I went to have breakfast in the dining-room the table was not laid and there was neither coffee nor anything else. Surely the impending visit of the police could not have so frightened Fritz and Ivan that they had fled? I thought I would go up and ask Alexander what had happened and met Elaine on the stairs. She was sobbing.

"It's the Tsarevna," she said. "She's gone."

"Gone where?" I asked, startled.

"Fritz took up her breakfast this morning and found her dead. She must have died in her sleep. I've just been there with Alexander. She looks quite peaceful, as if she hadn't stirred at all since I put her to bed. Oh, why did I leave her?" Elaine moaned. "Perhaps if I'd stayed with her it wouldn't have happened."

I was surprised at the shock and distress I myself felt. I had grown strangely fond of the Tsarevna. Meanwhile I knew it was my duty to comfort Elaine as best I could without overstepping the lines friendship had, I hoped, securely drawn between us. So I repeated all the soothing words I had so often heard that supposedly comfort the bereaved—"died peacefully"—"blessed release"—"after all she was very old", and so on. The familiar triteness of it seemed to calm Elaine. Finally I said: "No one could have done more for her than you did through the years."

Elaine blew her nose. "I did try to be a good daughter to her but she was so strange, so—well—foreign. I don't think she understood how difficult it all was for me here after Paul's death."

So much so that she had even searched for an English tutor of pleasing appearance, I thought, but said: "I had the impression that she was deeply grateful for all your care."

"Her last words when I gave her her medicine last night were 'Thank you, Elaine, for everything.'" She started sobbing once more.

Suspicions one scarcely dares to confess to oneself afterwards can nevertheless momentarily pass through one's mind. Had Elaine on an impulse, as sudden as letting the wheelchair go, given her mother-in-law too large or too small a dose of medicine?

"Did Alexander go and say good night to her?" I asked.

"No," she said, "she didn't want to see him, she was too tired. Poor darling. He's desperately unhappy. He loved her in a way perhaps more than he does me. They were somehow more alike."

"Elaine, I do think you should call a doctor. Even if it's too late, there are certain necessary formalities in establishing the cause of death."

"I know. I sent Fritz to the village to telephone Doctor Broderson who always attended her. He will be coming from Kiel by car and should be here in half an hour. I'd like you to be here when he comes, Eddie." Could she have sensed my suspicions?

"Can I go to Alexander meanwhile?" I asked.

"Of course. Try and comfort him as much as you have me," she smiled through her tears.

It proved not quite so easy. I found him lying on his bed, not crying as he so readily did when he thought it opportune. He was staring at the ceiling and his face made me feel that he too would one day be old. He seemed hardly to notice me and when I clasped his hand he withdrew it.

"I'm so sorry, Alexander," I said, "but after all, these things are inevitable. Your grandmother was very ill. It had to come one day."

"It wouldn't have if I hadn't killed her."

"But Alexander, how—why?" I scarcely dared ask, so appalled was I by the prospect of some ghastly new revelation. That neither my nerves nor my judgement were very sound by then is perhaps comprehensible.

"By shooting Beck," he said. Relief swept through me.

"How was I to know that it would break her heart? Even if he had been her lover I thought she was too old to care any more."

"I don't think she did. I think her heart just stopped beating because it was tired. There is no need to dramatize a quite normal death, however sad it is, or to feel guilty about it."

"I loved her more than anyone. She was such fun," he added, rather oddly, and then: "If only I could atone somehow. Eddie, I have decided to give myself up to the police and to take my punishment for her sake." Fearfully I looked at him. Was he breaking up? If so, I realized that his suddenly awakened conscience was even more dangerous than his former lack of it. His face expressed nothing but a sort of calm resignation.

I said as firmly and decisively as I could manage: "It's too late, Alexander. All you can do for the Tsarevna now is to keep her secrets and your own. It is what she would have expected of you now that you are head of the family. It would only bring shame and dishonour to you all if you confessed now and it certainly won't absolve you from your inner guilt. That is something you will have to live with as best you can without the Tsarevna being remembered as having had a grandson who murdered her lover and your mother knowing what you have done. Besides you might also consider me. I would certainly be accused of complicity and as you are under age it is I who would be sent to prison for many years for having helped you conceal a crime."

"I hadn't thought of all that," he sighed. "I suppose it's foolish to want to confess and be punished."

"Especially since the marks on your neck are gone, so you couldn't even prove that Beck had attacked you."

He fingered his throat. "They might hang me," he said calmly. "And yet, you know, Eddie, I wanted to do something good and brave for the Tsarevna's sake. Like standing up and saying to the police 'I killed Beck, now do with me as you will.' Do you understand?"

I did, with infinite pity, but I knew I must not weaken. "You didn't think how many other people you would punish by your touching act of contrition?"

"No, I suppose not."

"In any case, it's too late," I repeated. "You have more important duties than self-indulgence now. Pull yourself together, Alexander. You owe it to the Tsarevna to be brave, not weak, and to shoulder the responsibilities that will fall upon you. There will be a funeral and many other things you will have to deal with from now on."

"Oh God, yes, I'd almost forgotten the funeral." He sat up in bed. "All the neighbours will come, all the people she never wanted to see, and expect food and drink afterwards. Hundreds of them."

"Can't you put something in the local papers? They will have to be advised of her death anyway. You could say 'Only close friends and relations.' "

"We haven't any relations. The Tsarevna's are all dead and I'm the last of the Plevkes. We never had any friends. Besides, it's the custom here that anyone can come to a funeral if they want to." And then he suddenly smiled and leapt out of bed. "What about making it a really splendid, almost royal, affair. She would have liked that, don't you think?"

"Yes, I'm sure she would," I answered, profoundly relieved that he had found some alternative to appease the Tsarevna beyond confessing his guilt.

"All the best silver—the Sèvres dinner service with the Imperial coat of arms—a band from Kiel, perhaps to play the Volga Boat Song—lovely flowers—delicious food." He seemed completely recovered and delighted at the coming prospect and I felt slightly shocked at his sudden change of mood.

Then his face fell. "I don't have a decent black suit. The one I had for my confirmation is much too small. I will have to ask Beck to take me to Kiel in his car to have a new one fitted." He had, in his excitement, totally forgotten where Beck was.

"Perhaps we might order a taxi," I suggested.

He had the grace to blush. "Of course—and you will come with me, Eddie. We should go this morning though, since there isn't much time to have the suit made."

"But can't you just buy one off the peg?"

"A ready-made thing? What would I look like, Eddie? After all, this is an important occasion on which I will have to meet the public. I'll go to my father's tailor. I'll ask Fritz to telephone from the village for a taxi immediately. And perhaps when we are in Kiel we can order the flowers and the band too." He rushed down the stairs. I followed, more slowly.

# Chapter Eleven

Elaine was in the drawing-room and called me in. I needed no introduction when I saw the small black bag all country doctors carry. He was a very old man, thin and spare and somewhat rusty; the brown spots of age marked his face and frock-coat. He gazed at me solemnly through gold-rimmed glasses that perched on the bridge of his nose. I think they were what is called pince-nez.

"A very sad occasion," he said, and shook hands. His were small and dry.

"Doctor Broderson has been upstairs," Elaine said, also speaking German.

"She did not suffer at the last, of that you can be assured," he said, looking out of the window where the dark lake was visible beyond the weeping willows. "Thank you for leaving everything just as it was," he bowed to Elaine. "Death must have been instantaneous, since she had not moved in her bed. A rare blessing. But then she was a rare woman. We won't see the like of her again."

He looked once more towards the lake. "When I had to attend the inquest on her husband, so tragically drowned, she controlled her emotions enough to sympathize with me—I was very young then—at having had so dreadful a duty to perform as the autopsy. And what courage she had. When her son, Paul, was born three months later, bereaved as she was and the birth so difficult that I feared she would not survive it, she never cried out once and later even overcame the puerperal infection, usually fatal, thanks to her indomitable will to live—and my assistance," he added modestly. "Nevertheless her heart was weakened. I warned her repeatedly to be careful. She wouldn't listen. She rode as fiercely as a cavalry officer, drank as much as a dragoon and—excuse me," he bowed to Elaine—"ate as much as a pig. Even in her old age, when I tried to explain to her that she might die at any moment if she over-indulged as she did, she laughed at me. 'Doctor Broderson, there is no less pleasure in the day enjoyed because it might be the last.' Well, it has come and later than I dared expect, thanks, I think, entirely to your excellent care, Frau Gräfin. Between us two we have kept her going for years," he added with a chuckle. Then looking solemn once more: "I have heard of Herr Beck's disappearance, at such an unfortunate moment too, just when his help would have been most wanted."

"I know," Elaine said. "I only realize now how entirely we depended on him."

"If I can be of any assistance? Has the coffin been ordered?"

"No. I didn't know where," Elaine said.

"I will see to that then. First class I imagine?"

"Is there any difference? I thought it was only in trains."

The doctor made a note in a grimy prescription book. "And to lay out and wash the corpse?"

Elaine shuddered. "Beck's housekeeper and a woman from the farm have, I think, seen to that."

"And where is Graf Alexander? Fritz told me he has not been at all well lately."

"He's still in bed. He had a fever for some days and the moment he was better this happened. Of course, he is terribly distressed."

"Loved the old lady, I know. But then they were so alike, old or young—branches of the same tree rooted in Schwarzensee. Oh dear, he was almost as difficult a patient as his grandmother. Always joking and playing tricks. Never will forget when I was called in and measles were suspected. I went up to his room. Unfortunately, I had that day broken my glasses. I bent over what I took to be his round, pink face on the pillow shrouded in sheets. It was measles all right, but on his little bottom!"—and the old doctor cackled with laughter.

I tried not to laugh too, seeing Elaine's face, but I did.

She rose with dignity. "Thank you, Herr Doctor, I think that will be all," and escorted him to the door.

"Rather a vulgar old man, I'm afraid, though he's a good doctor," Elaine said as she returned to me. "Where is Alexander?"

I told her about our planned expedition to Kiel, and the reasons for it.

She seemed pleased. "Perhaps he will forget his grief for a few hours and I'm glad he is trying to take over some responsibility already. How I dread this funeral! I've never even been to one in Germany. And it seems the guests expect to be fed afterwards. I have nothing left in the house."

"Well, wouldn't there be some catering place in Kiel? Where you could order it all?"

"Perhaps Holst's Hotel would do it. You might stop by and ask. But won't it be very expensive? Where shall I get the money to pay for it?"

"I wouldn't worry about that, Elaine. No doubt Alexander will be given all the credit he wants since he, presumably, is the owner of Schwarzensee now."

I was not far wrong. When we had arrived in Kiel he was addressed as the "Herr Graf" wherever he went. The news of the Tsarevna's death had evidently spread fast. Alexander played his new role to perfection, accepting condolences with grave dignity.

At Holst's Hotel the manager came to offer his sympathies too and soon arrangements were made for a uniformed brass band to play the Tsarevna to her last resting place in the family crypt in the village church at Schwarzensee. Then the menu for the funeral feast was discussed.

"Borsch, of course to begin with—she was so fond of it," Alexander said, "and, I think, caviare would be most appropriate."

"Alexander," I warned, "one simply can't be so extravagant if you expect a hundred people. This isn't Russia."

The manager looked relieved at my protest. "It would indeed be almost unobtainable in such quantities at short notice. As for the expense—" He gestured expressively.

Finally Alexander was persuaded to agree to cold chickens in aspic, lobsters with mayonnaise and several cold roasts.

"Smoked eel?" the manager suggested.

"I rather think not," Alexander said, giving me a brief glance. "It's so indigestible." And then a choice of salads, desserts and cakes were decided on.

After that we went to the bar and Alexander stood me and himself several rum punches for which he did not pay, only asking me to tip the barman generously, which I did.

At the tailor's, obviously a smart establishment of repute displaying royal arms and panelled in oak, not only was Alexander measured for the black suit and assured it would be ready in time for the funeral, but encouraged to order three more outfits after he had consulted me as to what would be most suitable for England. Ties and socks were also chosen in some quantity.

The shoemaker came next. In the flower shop Alexander ordered a wreath from his mother as a tribute to the Tsarevna. "It should be of roses and perhaps with some forget-me-nots and broad blue ribbons with just 'Elaine' printed on them in gold," he decided. For himself he chose one of white lilies and then, to my shocked amazement, spelled out the name "William Beck" to be put on the ribbon of the third wreath which was to be of evergreens.

"But you can't, Alexander," I whispered.

"Why on earth not? It's what he would have wanted to do and surely she would have liked being remembered by him? Won't you choose a wreath, too, Eddie?"

"No," I said, "but I'll take her a flower now." I chose a perfect dark red rose.

"What a good idea," and Alexander gathered up the rest of the flowers in the shop and had them put in the waiting taxi.

There was a car standing in the courtyard when we arrived. "The police, no doubt," Alexander said, gathering up his flowers and then telling the taxi driver that an account would be opened with his firm and, asking me to give him a liberal tip, ran into the house. We were late for lunch. Elaine met us and apologized for its not being served as usual since the police were questioning the servants downstairs.

"Have you spoken to them?" Alexander asked, rather anxiously I thought.

"No, not yet, but I saw them arrive. Two policemen and a man in plain clothes. Ivan brought me a message: if not inconvenient, might the inspector call on me in half an hour? Of course I said he would be most welcome to do so."

"Here, take these flowers, Mummy." Alexander thrust them into her arms. "They are for the Tsarevna. I've got to get dressed." He hurried upstairs. Puzzled, his mother looked after him. So did I.

When he reappeared shortly afterwards I understood. He had put on his black confirmation suit. It was indeed too small for him and too tight. But it made him look much younger than he was and with his pale face and sad expression he looked the very picture of a beautiful bereaved child. Still, I felt slightly nervous. On the way back from Kiel he had been almost excessively exuberant, talking and laughing all the time; if not drunk, certainly intoxicated by the first independent shopping spree of his life and he had, I remem-

bered, downed three rum punches too. How would he react
when confronted by the police? Assert his newly-found importance and say too much, or even confess all, carried away
by his sense of the dramatic?

What I took to be the inspector was shown in by Ivan, the
welts on his damaged cheek standing out scarlet against his
unusual pallor. No doubt he had been rigorously questioned.
Yet there was nothing at all intimidating about the inspector—a big, cheerful man with a rather nondescript but
certainly not brutal face.

He clicked his heels and bowed. "I could not regret more,
having to disturb 'die Herrschaften' at such a bad time. May
I offer my condolences?" Both Elaine and Alexander bowed
their thanks. "But when we were alerted before the sudden
death of the "Gnädige Frau Gräfin," he continued. (I have
given the polite addresses in German as they sound too absurd in English.)

Elaine sighed deeply. "We were so worried about Herr
Beck's disappearance. I did not realize that anxiety for him,
once she heard there was reason to call in the police, might
endanger my mother-in-law's already very frail health. She
was very fond of him."

"So she feared he might be dead?"

"I think so." Elaine stammered. "She believed we would
not have called you otherwise."

The inspector looked at her thoughtfully. "And you have
this suspicion too?"

"I don't know what to think by now," Elaine said. "He has
been gone for ten days and not a word from him."

Alexander had been sitting quietly on the sofa, occasionally
glancing from the inspector to his mother from under lowered lashes. Now he got up. "Do be seated, Herr Inspector,"
he said politely, drawing forward one of the black and gold
Chinese lacquer chairs. "Can I offer you a glass of
Schnapps?"

"Since this is merely a courtesy call I think I might—thank
you, Herr Graf."

As Alexander poured the Schnapps with a steady hand the
inspector watched his graceful young host with appreciation.

"I hear you have not been able to leave your bed for the
last week?"

"Just a slight fever," Alexander said, bravely.

"A hundred and two is more than that," Elaine exclaimed.
"I'm sure you shouldn't have gone to Kiel, darling, you're

very pale." She turned to the inspector. "It was his first outing. To make arrangements for the funeral."

"And have you any idea, Herr Graf, what might have delayed Beck?" The inspector smiled at Alexander. "Young heads are often better than old and I must confess I am puzzled. Have you any theory that might account for his disappearance?"

But Alexander did not take the bait, if that is what it was. "I wish I had. His absence just at this time is very awkward for my mother and me. He saw to everything. But perhaps if he reads of my grandmother's death in the newspapers he will return?"

"Perhaps," the inspector said. "One should only presume the worst when all other possibilities have been eliminated. Still, it is rather strange that his housekeeper maintains that he took no luggage with him at all and that his gun is missing."

Alexander looked duly surprised, "But couldn't it be somewhere in the house? He often leaves it here. I frequently use it when I go for roebuck since I've only got a shotgun."

"Yes, we know that. Yours is in Mr Livingstone's room." So he had found out my name and searched my things already.

"I have been trying to teach Eddie to shoot," Alexander said; then with a sudden giggle, "Not with much success," and more seriously, "You think that Beck took his rifle with him to Hamburg?"

"The servants seem to think so. They believe he took it back to his room weeks ago and since it can neither be found in the house nor there, the most plausible explanation does seem that it went with him."

"Perhaps," Elaine suggested, "he took it to shoot us something on his way through the forest since he knew there was no more game in the larder—it has been empty since Alexander became ill."

"So you provide for the household, Herr Graf?"

"I have to," he admitted.

"Of course, it is quite possible that Beck took his gun for that reason. Still, do you think he had any enemies or that he might have been afraid of being robbed? On occasion he could have taken large amounts of cash to deposit in the bank in Hamburg—after sales of farm produce, or timber, or, as now, after the harvest?"

"I don't think Beck could have had any enemies, not at

least round about here. Everyone liked him," Alexander said. "But he was always rather afraid of thieves. He insisted the gates and the house be locked at night."

"Well, for the time being we must concentrate our search in Hamburg," the inspector said, "since Beck's housekeeper and the servants, both separately and yet unanimously, declared that they had either heard him, or—in the housekeeper's case—even seen him leave in his car in the early morning of the fifteenth for Hamburg. Did you hear anything, Frau Gräfin?"

"No, my room is on the other side of the house—so is Alexander's. I was up all of the night with him."

"And you, Mr. Livingstone?"

"I heard the car leave," I said. "My room looks on to the courtyard. It must have been at about six, I think."

"Thank you. I will have to seal up Beck's room, of course, but I don't think that will be an inconvenience to anyone. We have only made a cursory inspection of it but if he doesn't reappear his papers will have to be thoroughly examined to see if they prove any irregularity. Meanwhile, I don't want anything removed from there."

"Might it not be possible," Elaine asked, "that since Herr Beck managed all the finances of Schwarzensee something went wrong? That he speculated perhaps and then, not being able to face up to it, fled somewhere?" I had no doubt as to who had instilled this thought in her mind.

"It is an idea, of course, but it does not quite agree with Beck's reputation for integrity and honesty throughout Holstein. But if something so disastrous should have happened, I think he was the sort of man who would rather have shot himself than escape."

"The gun," Elaine exclaimed with horror. "Is that why he took it?"

"There is no need at all at present to fear anything of the kind, Gnädige Frau Gräfin," the inspector said soothingly. "There may be much simpler explanations and Herr Beck may be alive and well. It is just a question of finding him. We will check all the hotels in Hamburg where he might have stayed, the hospitals for any casualties delivered round that date, the morgue, even St Pauli," he added, with a smile.

"But isn't that the red light district where the sailors go?" Elaine asked, looking shocked.

"Yes, but many a gentleman has been known to do so too in search of a bit of fun—a night out, so to speak. It seems

Beck was quite a heavy drinker, at least so the servants admitted. Well, perhaps a glass or two too many in a district like that—he might—er—" the inspector looked slightly embarrassed, "but please be assured that we will do our best to find him and let you know the moment we have any news, good or bad." He bowed himself out.

"What a nice, polite man!" Elaine exclaimed. "You were very silent, darling. Tired?"

"Just a little."

"Why did you put on that awful old suit? It's much too small for you. You look even more childish in it than you are."

"Because it's the only black one I have, Mummy. After all, we are in mourning," he said reproachfully.

"Oh dear, I'll have to see to mine. I think I still have the black veil and dress somewhere I wore after your father's death. I'd better go and look."

■

After she had left Alexander turned to me. "How did I do Eddie?"

"Not a bad act. At least you underplayed instead of overplayed." I touched his cheek. My finger came away as white with powder as I knew it would. "Poor little orphan."

He grinned. "The inspector is not as stupid as he looks. And perhaps better so. It's always difficult to deal with fools. How can one tell what they will think or do? With a clever person one knows."

"He seems to have questioned the servants very thoroughly," I remarked.

"Which made it all the easier for him to be polite and lenient with us."

"Why did he believe Beck had taken his rifle with him?"

"Because I asked Fritz to look for it quite a while ago and since he couldn't find it in the house he believed Beck had taken it back to his room, which Fritz probably told the police."

"And where was it?"

"It might have been under my bed. One can't have a loaded rifle all over the house. I have often kept it there."

"And that night?"

"Really, Eddie, how can I remember. Probably yes. Since I went out shooting with it in the morning."

I let it go. "But why is the inspector so interested in the gun?"

"Firstly, all Germans always are. Secondly, because he can't discount the possibility that Beck shot himself with it. It would solve everything nicely for the inspector if it could be proved."

"But how? There is no body and, above all, no car. A large, expensive, black Mercedes can't suddenly vanish into thin air. It will be searched for in Hamburg, then all over Germany of course, even the frontiers will be checked—a man, dead or alive, can disappear; not a car like that."

"You see, the car's the point of it all—think it over, Eddie." I tried to.

"I suppose he couldn't have committed suicide without leaving it somewhere," I admitted.

"Of course not. So they will have to give up that theory very soon. Then they will suspect murder. That it happened on the way to Hamburg seems the most probable. Someone who knew he was carrying money stopped him, threatened him, shot him, either with Beck's own gun or with a revolver, or just hit him over the head, dumped the body in a wood or lake and drove off. But however far the murderer went, he would eventually have to leave the Mercedes somewhere in order to clear himself of suspicion."

"And then, if they find no car? Won't they search here?"

"Probably they'll comb the forest in a last hope of finding Beck's body and even consider the lake, but I don't think our inspector, intelligent as he is, will imagine that Beck committed so spectacular a suicide as to drive himself right into it, car, gun, and all. And even if he did, everyone knows that a dead body floats."

I shuddered. "They might drain the lake."

"The Schwarzensee? It's three miles long and half a mile wide. It would take years to sluice away its waters and then they would be left with mud of unknown depth to dig up. I doubt the province of Holstein could afford it. All because of one man whose death wasn't even proven. No, Eddie, don't worry—as for us, we are all absolutely in the clear. Even questioning us would be an absurdity. What motive, even if it had been physically possible to do so, could any one of us have had for killing Beck?"

"You for one," I said, more and more incensed by his cold, logical and heartless analysis of the case.

"And why?"

"Because you were afraid he'd tell about the girl. They may question the villagers and find out all about it."

"Eddie, you must be joking. Now that I practically own Schwarzensee I have so much more to offer than the police. Besides, the peasants hereabouts loathe and fear them. They won't talk. And even if it was all revealed, I'd be more admired than blamed for my nightly adventures. No one in their right mind could believe that I murdered Beck to conceal something so unimportant."

"And what about me? Foreigners are always suspect. I might have had some sinister motive."

"Political assassination perhaps?" Alexander laughed. "It's quite an idea, Eddie. Shall I suggest it to the inspector? But can't you understand," he added, more seriously, "that whatever our motives, none of us could have killed Beck."

"And why not?"

"Because four people heard or saw the car leave the courtyard that morning with Beck in it and there was no one else with him. I was in bed with a high temperature. Mummy by my side all night—she doesn't even know that she dropped off to sleep before dawn. The Tsarevna unable to move from her bed. Fritz feeding the horses and Ivan cleaning the courtyard at the time Beck left and you in your room."

"But I might have crept out of it earlier and ambushed Beck. I knew he was going to Hamburg. Shot him with his own gun, made it look like suicide, and run back to the house."

"And a nice mess you would have made of it. Fingerprints all over the gun and the car. The gun left in a position from which no one could have shot themselves, provided you could have wrested the rifle from Beck at all, which I doubt, and then breakfasted calmly half an hour later."

"I grant I'm not an expert at murder," I said bitterly.

"Indeed not. The car would have been found the same day with Beck's body in it and you would be in prison, since no one would have believed in the suicide you had staged. Come, cheer up, Eddie. There's nothing to worry about, I promise. Shall I tell you what really happened to Beck and what will finally be accepted as the only possible explanation of this disappearance with the car?"

"I would be most interested to hear it."

"Well, listen. I have got it all worked out." He looked pleased with himself. "On one of his frequent visits to Hamburg, Beck bought a seaman's pass, papers and identity card, easily done in a port if one is ready to pay enough. He also found a ship, probably a foreign freighter, one of the hundreds that dock there, ready to take him and his car, with no questions asked or answered, to South America."

"And why should he wish to go there?"

Alexander smiled mischievously. "He sometimes spoke of relations he had in Patagonia—sheep-farmers, I think—and complained that things were so bad in Germany that he would like to emigrate."

"Strange," I said. "I had the impression he loved his country and that his life's interest was Schwarzensee."

"It may have been so for a time, but he might have had grave financial difficulties and even if his accounts are found to be in order, which I very much doubt, he had a vast fortune in hand with which he could start a new life elsewhere whenever he chose to. You needn't look so surprised, Eddie. Don't you remember I told you that he had the Tsarevna's jewels copied and told Mummy he had been obliged to sell them or we would have lost Schwarzensee? How do we know that he really did? He sold off a good bit of land too at the time, I've since learnt, to pay off some of our debts. Might he not have kept the jewels for himself?"

"And is this what you will finally suggest to the police?"

"I won't have to. I will just hint it to Mummy. She is so wonderfully suggestible—besides she would much rather accept that Beck was a thief than she would that he killed himself or was murdered. She's really squeamish about violence and death."

"You certainly are not," I said, disliking him intensely for his cleverness.

"Why should I be? In all the great dramatic plays, whether by Shakespeare, Goethe or Schiller, Racine and Corneille or in Greek tragedies, there is plenty of murder and death."

"On the stage."

Aptly he quoted: "All the world's a stage and all the men and women merely players. They have their exits and their entrances and one man in his time plays many parts."

"As you know so well how to do." I was still incensed by his callous explanation of Beck's disappearance.

"Look here, Eddie," he said, "I know what you are thinking, but if you consider that I have been obliged to shoot living creatures ever since I've been nine years old, taught to do so by Beck, why then should I feel guilty about having killed him? He savagely attacked me. No animal I shot ever had."

I tried not to be moved by this reasonable excuse. I must, I knew now, somehow detach myself from Alexander and all that concerned him. If I could not hate, I must at least learn not to love. I thought of the rifle, perhaps deliberately hidden under his bed in preparation for the murder and of the, thanks to my assistance, faultlessly executed crime and the fiendish intelligence that had allowed him to foresee, step by step, what course all investigations would have to take, ending finally—I didn't doubt for a moment—in Beck's being believed to be in South America. I tried to accept the fact that I had been ensnared by the beauty and intelligence of a boy of fifteen and become the willing slave and accomplice of a monster in the most beguiling of human forms. I could not. If the boy was guilty, how much more so was I who had raised his hopes, convinced him he would have a brilliant future if he came to England and tempted him to free himself of Beck. Why, he was no more than a child! And he had been ready to give himself up to the police when his conscience suddenly woke, and I had persuaded him not to confess. For the Tsarevna's and Elaine's sake, or because I feared for my own safety as much as for his?

Suddenly I longed for my mother. Only she with her clear, logical mind and sense of proportion might be able to help me understand my problems and face my guilt without its destroying me. Common decency and consideration for both Alexander and Elaine demanded that I stay for the funeral, but immediately afterwards I would leave for home.

A little later Alexander came to my room. There were tears clinging to his long lashes and a catch in his voice as he said: "Come, Eddie, you too must say good-bye to the Tsarevna. She was fond of you. I put the red rose you got for her in her hand. Mummy and I have made her look lovely. Mummy found her wedding veil and thought she might like to be buried in it. They are bringing the coffin any minute now." Bravely he stifled a sob.

I went with him to enter the Tsarevna's room for the last time. Its windows were wide open, flowers were banked around the bed. Everything looked clean and tidy. The books had been removed, the fireplace cleared of ashes. A veil of fine lace was draped round the Tsarevna's face and shoulders and her waxen hands were folded over my red rose. Her features, firmed and narrowed, had acquired in death the austere dignity they had somewhat lacked in life.

Under the great crimson and gold canopy of her curtained

bed her still face and form were like some carved effigy on a royal tomb. I stood in respectful silence next to Alexander and Elaine, their hands folded as if in prayer, then I turned away from the dead face. It seemed to me in no way to resemble that of the lusty, forceful woman I had known. I looked instead at the icon, remembering my last service rendered to the Tsarevna, and the secret stairs. Probably no one had thought of refilling the lamp. Then while my eyes were fixed on it, it flamed up brightly and went out. Was it her last greeting to me? *"Eh bien, Harris, gentilhomme Anglais."* I seemed to hear her say with that rich throaty laugh of hers.

Quietly I left the room, strangely comforted. It was as if the spirit of this strong woman, who had feared neither life nor death, had spoken to me and renewed my courage to face both with greater equanimity.

Not even the sounds of the coffin being nailed down later disturbed me.

■

For the following two days I helped Elaine and Alexander with the funeral arrangements as best I could. Something, perhaps the fact that I was resolved to leave for England immediately it was over, had already somewhat detached me from Schwarzensee and its inhabitants. They did not seem quite real any more. This feeling was augmented by the, to me, quite unfamiliar ceremonials of a German funeral. On the day itself, several stalwart men from the village came and carried the Tsarevna's coffin, covered with a silver-fringed black velvet cloth, downstairs and lifted it into a farm cart to which the two big roans were harnessed. The cart was decorated with green branches and flowers. On the coffin, much to my surprise, was a little cushion; on it a pair of white kid gloves and a fan.

"Why that?" I whispered to Elaine.

"It's an old custom they have here. It's a sign of rank. Like they put an officer's sword and his helmet on his coffin, I think."

Fritz was driving the cart. He wore a mourning band on his hat and sleeve and so did Ivan, who opened the big gates wide for the Tsarevna to pass under the Imperial Eagle of Russia for the last time. Alexander and Elaine were both in sombre black; Elaine with a long veil covering her face, Alexander in his smart new suit looking handsome and grown up. Behind them, keeping a modest distance, both from the chief mourners and the servants, came I; then the old cook supported by a stick and Beck's housekeeper. Ivan joined them after he had closed the gates.

The horses went at a snail's pace. We walked behind the coffin. In the forest we passed the spot where the drive adjoined the picnic ground. I saw Alexander turn towards the lake, raise his arms as if trying to aim. Startled ducks rose from the water to circle high in the sky. A joke in poor taste, I thought, but I heard Ivan laugh, though he had been wiping tears away only minutes before. It was almost a mile that we had to walk until the village was reached. There, all around the red brick church, were cars and carriages and people dressed in black. Many pressed forward to shake hands with Alexander and Elaine and to express their sympathy, giving me, however, only puzzled glances since I was not in mourning.

Alexander's acting was at its most perfect. Though I did not doubt for a minute that the Tsarevna's death had greatly distressed him, having witnessed his first agonizing sorrow, I think in the excitement of playing to so large an audience he had forgotten her for the moment. His golden head bare, his face expressing just the right combination of amiability and reserve, he moved gracefully from one group to the other, speaking to people with youthful deference yet leaving no one in doubt as to his being the new lord of Schwarzensee.

I found myself watching him appreciatively but with curious detachment, admiring his performance as I would that of any good actor on the stage, and with a sudden pang, almost painful, I realized that I watched him as I might have a stranger who meant nothing to me any more. Something had burnt away all that I had felt for him in the past. When had it happened? Had it been when the small lamp underneath the icon in the Tsarevna's room had flamed up so brightly and I had seemed to hear her strong, laughing voice encourage me before it went out? And I remembered how strangely reassured and comforted I had left her room. Guilt or innocence, Alexander's, or Beck's, or Elaine's, or the Tsarevna's did not seem to concern me any more. As for myself, I hoped I would find the courage to face my own conscience in the future.

The Tsarevna's large domed coffin, like an Egyptian sarcophagus with its silver handles and what I supposed were angels decorating its corners but looked more like Sphinxes, was placed in front of the altar. It was surrounded by wreaths, the names of the donors clearly printed on different coloured ribbons.

"Hamburger Bankverein," I read, "Kieler Kulturbund. Schleswig-Holsteinischer Jagdtverein. Dorf Schwarzensee," and then many with aristocratic-sounding names, presumably those of neighbouring families, and several ones with royal titles—Prince of Prussia—Duke of Schleswig-Holstein. However, in place of honour on the coffin were only the three wreaths of the chief mourners, Alexander's, Elaine's and Beck's.

With cynical amusement I wondered if Alexander's rather touching gesture in providing Beck with one was not perhaps part of his subtle way of implying that the man was still alive.

We sat close to the altar in what I assumed was the Plevke family pew. Other notables, perhaps of equal distinction, had their own. But the aisle too was crowded, the front rows with people clad in black, then came the villagers sitting in the rear.

There was a long speech delivered from the pulpit by the Pastor of Schwarzensee. It could hardly be called a sermon since it scarcely mentioned the Almighty or His Son, but in great detail the generations of Plevkes who with their military prowess had played so important a part in the history of Schleswig-Holstein. The Tsarevna's eulogy towards the end was, I thought, rather brief.

"One of the last of her kind. A great personality of outstanding culture—speaking three languages fluently. Deprived so tragically of both husband and son, bereavement and illhealth made it impossible for her in later years to play her part in the community as she would have wished. Though no doubt now," and the Parson's voice rose sonorously, "our young Herr Graf whom you see standing so modestly before you, my devout pupil, whom it was a pleasure to teach so great was his interest in religious matters and an honour to be finally allowed to confirm, will prove fully worthy of the great responsibilities awaiting him. Firm in his faith, ready, as his ancestors were, to fight for God and country, surely he too will declare as our great Martin Luther did '*Hier stehe Ich—Ich kann nicht anders. Gott helfe mir.*' "

Indeed, I thought with secret delight, how well these words could be applied not to Alexander's religious beliefs, but to his faith in himself.

All eyes were fixed expectantly on his beautiful solemn

young face, but though he stood up very straight he kept his head modestly bowed.

Prayers for the dead and the bereaved were then intoned. A hymn was sung. Suddenly Alexander nudged me. "Do you see a girl in a funny hat," he whispered, "sitting far back among the villagers?"

As a matter of fact I had noticed her because her upturned gaze had never left our pew and because her black feathered hat, perched on top of her tow-coloured frizzed hair, amused me.

"It's her," Alexander said. "She used to be prettier."

I looked once more. Her face was round and flat, her features coarse and undistinguished. She looked the peasant girl she was but she had a lovely complexion like strawberries and cream. Of her condition there was no doubt. Her large work-reddened hands were primly folded as if with resignation on her extended stomach.

Finally the Tsarevna's coffin was carried out of the church. The uniformed brass band from Kiel had assembled outside and played doleful music. There was no grave dug to receive her but the iron doors of a sort of lean-to built of brick against the church wall had been opened. Coffins of former Plevkes stacked one on top of the other were revealed to the curious gaze of the forward-pressing crowd. The Tsarevna's was heaved in and the doors closed. The funeral was over.

We did not have to walk back to the house. The taxi service from Kiel, now at Alexander's disposal, had provided him with a smart car.

The feast prepared in the white and gold ballroom was impressive. Long trestle tables, assembled from boards by Fritz and Ivan, were covered with white tablecloths and decorated with flowers and baskets of tropical fruit. The green and gold Sèvres dinner service with the Imperial arms shone with rich lustre. There were huge soup tureens full of purple Borsch, platters heaped with scarlet lobsters, or dark-larded venison, pale chicken in amber jelly, pink smoked hams, succulent asparagus, various colourful mixed salads and cakes decorated with whipped cream or sugar icing as ornate as the plaster ornaments on the ceiling of the ballroom. Waiters from Kiel's Holst's Hotel hurried here and there, directed by a chef in a tall white bonnet. "Bowle" was served in great jugs, a punch-like mixture of champagne, white wine and soda water. So was beer and Schnapps.

Alexander proved a perfect host, finding chairs for old

ladies—since there were not enough of these the more youthful had to eat standing up—seeing to it that everyone was served and urging people to eat and drink. Not that much encouragement was needed. It looked rather as if the feast was the main reason why all these people who knew neither Alexander nor Elaine had come at all. Conversation, at first subdued, became quite animated after the "Bowle" had taken effect. A strong smell of mothballs permeated the room, emanating from the black clothes probably stored in chests and cupboards and only aired on solemn occasions. There were, I thought, not quite the hundred people Alexander had expected, but there certainly were more than enough and they seemed to take up more space than the inhabitants of other countries. Big, heavily-built men and women with white-blond hair and their offspring equally large. Pimply, inarticulate youths and fat, giggling girls crowded round Alexander in the hope I suppose, that good-neighbourly relationships would now at last be established between Schwarzensee and the rest of the country. No one spoke to me. Perhaps it had got around that I was merely the English tutor.

With proud disdain, the Tsarevna looked down on it all from her picture, brandishing her sword, the white stallion ready to break into a gallop and carry her far from the common crowd to Imperial glory.

After the feast had ended and the guests had left I asked Alexander how he had enjoyed himself. He looked quite shocked. "Really, Eddie, I had to be polite—but what dreadful people! So utterly provincial, uncultured, uncivilized and ugly. All the women looked like Holstein cows and the men like brawny prize bulls. And to think they expect me to live here among them! I can't wait to get to England. Mummy and I have decided to sell Schwarzensee as soon as it's possible. Now that Beck and the Tsarevna have gone it seems senseless to keep it. Besides, I'd like to forget—well—all about everything."

"I hope you will," I said.

He gave me an uneasy look. "You are not really leaving me, are you, Eddie?"

"Yes, the day after tomorrow. I ordered the taxi that took us back from the funeral to come and fetch me."

He was silent. It still moved me when he looked unhappy. I knew he was fond of me. Was it cruel to leave so soon? "What are you thinking of, Alexander?"

"That I ought to come with you to Kiel. Those suits should be tightened in the waist. Look at this one." He got up and pulled the coat round his slim figure. "It's much too wide— I'd have to grow a Holstein paunch to fit into it."

# Chapter Twelve

On the day before I left, two opulent-looking chauffeur-driven cars entered the courtyard, one after the other, within an hour's interval. The owner of the first was announced as Beck's lawyer. He sent up Fritz with a polite enquiry if he might call. We were in the drawing-room.

"Don't go, Eddie," Elaine begged, as I tried tactfully to leave the room. "We have no secrets from you."

"Indeed not," Alexander said, looking amused. "Wonder what the man wants?"

"Perhaps the Tsarevna made a will after all and Beck deposited it with him."

I knew Elaine had been searching for one in the Tsarevna's room, if in vain.

Herr Stein—pronouncing his name as he introduced himself in Hochdeutsch—was obviously not a native of Schleswig-Holstein. A dapper, dark-haired and dark-complexioned man, whose alert eyes and vivacious gestures had none of the phlegmatic stolidity of those of the North Germans.

He expressed his sympathy at the Tsarevna's death, politely kissed Elaine's hand, shook Alexander's, then mine and sat down. "What I have come to discuss is rather private," he said. "It really only concerns the family." I saw his eyes resting on me.

Once more I got up to leave.

"Please stay," Elaine said. "We have nothing to conceal from Mr Livingstone." She turned to the lawyer. "He is a dear friend."

"Ah, well then—" I could see by his smile what conclusions he had drawn from this.

I sat down again. I was curious at what he had come to say.

"I am in a rather difficult position. I was—" he hesitated—"that is, I suppose I still am, Herr Beck's lawyer. Also, in many years of working together in matters concerning Schwarzensee, such as sales of land and timber for which I drew up the contracts, William and I grew well acquainted and, I might say, became close friends. I gained his confidence and he had mine. So his death affects me personally as much as from a business point of view." He passed his well-kept hand over his forehead in a gesture indicating grief.

"But surely you don't think, Herr Stein," Elaine said tremulously, "that Herr Beck could be dead?"

"I did not mean to shock you, Frau Gräfin," he apologized, "but what other conclusion can one come to? As Beck's lawyer I have, of course, been in touch with the police ever since his disappearance. Their investigations in Hamburg, I am sorry to say, have proved quite fruitless. And surely, had he been alive and heard of Countess Plevke's death—every paper in Germany carried the news—he would have returned. In fact, he had every reason to do so."

Neither Elaine nor Alexander seemed to note the significance of the last sentence. I feared I did, since Beck had been her legal husband.

"That is exactly what I thought," Elaine exclaimed, "that once abroad he would not have heard of her death. Especially not on a ship."

Herr Stein's distinctive black eyebrows rose. "I am afraid I don't quite understand—why a ship?"

"My mother has this idea that Beck might have—well—left the country," Alexander said, looking at her with an indulgent smile.

"But what reason could he possibly have had to do so?" The lawyer's astute dark eyes went from mother to son.

"We have been in financial difficulty for years, in fact ever since my husband's death and Beck took over managing the estate. We have had to live extremely frugally, constantly warned by him that stringent economy was necessary. So I thought that something might have gone wrong and that he preferred to leave instead of admitting it," she added, hesitantly.

"But did Herr Beck never inform you, Frau Gräfin, that with careful management through the years he has paid off two-thirds of the mortgage, plus interest, and that by the time the young Graf Alexander comes of age he would be free of all debts?"

Though Alexander looked startled at this he said: "Herr

Beck only discussed estate business with my grandmother, never with us."

"I see—so it may come as a pleasant surprise to know, as I am informed by the police who have by now checked Beck's accounts in the bank and gone through his private papers, that everything is in perfect order and accounted for and, thanks to William's unflagging efforts, it looks as if you will inherit an almost unencumbered estate of considerable value, Herr Graf.

"Except, of course, for the rather serious loss of the twenty-five thousand marks. Ah—perhaps my information is more recent than yours," seeing Alexander's look of surprise. "It was the annual payment Beck made to the bank, always on the fifteenth of August after the harvest, which is the day on which he disappeared—and which he probably had on his person, mainly in cash, since the local farming people don't pay by cheque."

"That's a lot of money," Alexander exclaimed. Momentarily his gaze wandered to the window from which the lake was visible.

"And I fear untraceable if the murderer is not found. A serious loss indeed but, of course, as nothing compared to the loss of Beck himself."

"Have they found his car?" Alexander asked.

"Not yet, but except for the thief's having discovered some most unusual method of disposing of it, they certainly must in time. Which brings me to a question I hope you won't think impertinent. Did Gräfin Plevke by any chance leave a will?"

"I have gone through all her papers," Elaine said, "and found nothing. We thought if there was one, Beck might have perhaps deposited it with you."

"Certainly not. However, did you perhaps come across other documents, records of births, deaths and marriages, as they are usually kept by families such as this? Or letters?"

"No," Elaine said, looking puzzled. "I suppose it is rather strange, but then so was my mother-in-law. She may have just thrown them away if there were any. Is it of much importance?"

The lawyer shrugged. "Not really." He contemplated the small black hairs on the back of his hands. He then said: "I rather doubt Countess Plevke made a will at all. Though I did not have the honour of knowing her personally, I knew through Beck what a remarkable woman she was. And in spite of her lapses into history, extremely shrewd. Well, if there is no proof to the contrary there will be no difficulties with the inheritance."

"But how could there be?" Elaine asked.

The lawyer gave her a rather searching look. "Bequests to others, relations, friends—perhaps even servants—that was all I meant."

That he knew of the secret marriage I was by now convinced, also that Alexander had told me the truth once more when he spoke of Beck's having said that Schwarzensee could be his if he so chose. Had Beck lived it was he who would have inherited Schwarzensee. Had the lawyer, even if he knew this, any proof other than the papers I had burnt, I asked myself anxiously? The Tsarevna had trusted me with her secret. I desperately wanted it kept.

Perhaps so did the lawyer. Besides, as Beck was dead, what point was there in disclosing what would only cause scandal?

Surprisingly the lawyer said: "Beck deposited his own will with me several years ago. I do, of course, know its contents. If I had any hope of his still being alive I would not mention this, but as matters are I think I can disclose that everything he died possessed of, after Countess Plevke's death, would go to Graf Alexander."

Elaine, looking moved, said: "Poor Beck, what a kind thought. Not that he could have had much to leave, except for his few personal belongings or perhaps what he saved from his wages?"

"Herr Beck," the lawyer said with a rather ironic smile, "did not receive wages. For many years he worked entirely without remuneration for the good of Schwarzensee and in order to deliver it free of debt to you, Herr Graf, on your coming of age."

Obviously some appreciative answer to this was expected from Alexander. I felt curious as to what he would say; if he would be hypocritical and callous enough to proclaim his affection or gratitude for the man he had murdered, or say nothing, which might perhaps rouse suspicion in the mind of this sharp-eyed, intelligent lawyer.

"You make me feel very guilty." The expression of regret on his beautiful young face was quite genuine. "Herr Beck was my guardian, you see, and rather strict, which I sometimes resented. I'm sorry now."

Perfect, I thought, and even true.

The lawyer looked at him with sympathy. "How often is it

so—that only when someone dies do we realize how great is our loss."

"I still can't believe that Beck is dead," Elaine exclaimed. "It seems too dreadful that he might have been murdered. I'd really far rather think that he had taken that money himself and escaped somewhere."

"A very feminine point of view," Herr Stein smiled, "but praiseworthy in that it shows a tender heart."

Elaine flushed with pleasure, unaccustomed to masculine compliments as she was.

"But what did Herr Beck live off," she then asked, "if he was paid no wages? His trips to Hamburg—that big car?"

"Necessitated by his work. His few expenses will, I'm sure, be found meticulously listed in his accounts which he kept very carefully. Perhaps just because Countess Plevke trusted him so absolutely, giving him a free hand in everything. If Beck had ever wanted to leave the country or enrich himself he could have done so long ago, since all the estate brought was at his disposal. But he was not that sort of man. I have every reason to believe that whatever profit he could make went back into Schwarzensee.

"However," Herr Stein straightened in his chair, "if you wish a careful investigation of this I am at your disposal, Frau Gräfin, Herr Graf. Also in the matter of the inheritance, though it seems to me a clear case, there are certain legal formalities. Since Graf Alexander is not yet of age, his mother will have to be declared his guardian and by law he will need a co-guardian. Have you anyone in mind? A relation perhaps, a trusted friend?"

"You, Eddie," Alexander exclaimed, delighted.

"No thank you," I nearly said, but was spared doing so by Herr Stein explaining that it must be someone of German nationality.

"I can think of no one," Elaine confessed. "Would one of the servants do?"

"Well, not quite. I believe it would have to be someone of more responsible position. A man of the Church, or the law, or perhaps your bank manager?"

"Would he have to come and live with us?" Alexander asked, and I could sense with what distaste and fear this new threat to his freedom filled him.

Perhaps so did the lawyer. "Of course not," he said. "All he would feel bound to do is to call on you once or twice a year and proffer advice when asked for it. He would have no wish or right to interfere in your private life in any way. A co-guardian is only there to assist in case of important decisions concerning property, such as gross mismanagement of the estate or sale of land and he would have no power of decision contrary to yours, Frau Gräfin, or your wishes, Graf Alexander.

"I would, of course, consider it both an honour and a privilege to be allowed to serve you in whatever capacity you might choose," and he looked directly at Elaine.

The man, I noted, had considerable masculine charm and her response to it was immediate.

"We do rather need help, don't we, darling?" she appealed to Alexander. "All this tiresome business with the police too."

"In that I can certainly be of assistance. The inspector and I are on the best of terms. Even if they do now have to concentrate their futile search around here, since Beck could not be traced in Hamburg, I can persuade the police to respect your privacy." He paused to clear his throat. "No doubt you will need time to consider carefully whom to choose as a suitable guardian, but meanwhile if you saw fit to accept me as your legal adviser I would try to be of service. And if later you should find me worthy to act as your co-guardian, Gräfin Plevke, in case there is no one more suitable, I would consider it an honour to do so and serve you with as much disinterested devotion as Beck did."

"I'm sure we could find no one better," Elaine said, completely won over.

"And you, Herr Graf? Would this meet with your approval?" the lawyer asked in a rather patronizing tone of voice, as if talking to a child.

It was a mistake. Alexander raised his luminous eyes, bright as searchlights and focused them on the dark ones of the lawyer, holding his gaze until Herr Stein's lids fell and he seemed to be contemplating the frayed Oriental carpet at his feet.

"You are very kind, Herr Stein," he then said, "and I am grateful for your offer, but I think there are certain things you should know before we come to any agreement. It was my grandmother's wish, as it now is my mother's and mine, that I should complete my education in England. First at a public school and then at Oxford."

The lawyer could not quite conceal his surprise, whether at the cool maturity with which the boy expressed himself or at what he had been told, I could only guess.

"My mother has not seen her parents for fourteen years and we have decided to settle in England, probably permanently. Would you, if we accepted you as co-guardian, have any objection to this? If so, I fear we will have to choose someone else."

Herr Stein moved rather uneasily in his chair, then said after brief thought: "The form your education should take is entirely, as far as I might be concerned, for your mother to decide. Personally I can well understand a young mind reaching out beyond the intellectual limits of Schleswig-Holstein. I have always heard an English education is the very best preparation for life. I only wish I had had the same opportunity in my young days.

"I suppose Mr Livingstone will be able to assist you in finding a good school?"

"I was thinking of Eton," Elaine said.

"*Ach*, Eton!" He looked impressed. "I have heard of it, or course. But is it not very difficult to get into?"

"Not if one is as gifted as Alexander is," his mother said proudly. "Besides, my parents put down his name when he was born—Alexander is English by birth, you know."

The lawyer looked surprised. "Strange, Beck never told me that!"

"He didn't much like it mentioned. He wanted Alexander to be a real German."

"Yes, one can understand that. Beck was a great patriot. So when you are twenty-one you will have the choice of one or the other nationality. How fortunate you are," Herr Stein sighed. "Have you made up your mind yet?"

"How can I," Alexander asked tersely, "before I have lived there?"

"Very wise."

"But if I want to settle in England permanently, would there be any difficulty in selling Schwarzensee?"

"But, Herr Graf, surely you would never want to do so," the lawyer exclaimed, deeply shocked. "I can well imagine that the recent sad events might make you wish for a change, but to sell this beautiful house with all its historical associations, and a property now almost clear of debt, would be sheer folly and I must warn you, whoever your future guardian might be, he could never agree to that. Why, you might change your mind and could hold the man who permitted you to sell responsible. Of course, when you come of age you can do as you please, but in such an important matter no one in their right senses could allow it while you are still a minor. I doubt even the law could be bent far enough to permit it." He looked at Elaine for help. "Surely you don't want to sell Schwarzensee, Frau Gräfin?"

"Tell the truth, Mummy," Alexander ordered.

"Yes, I would," she stammered. "I have, since my husband's death, always felt a stranger here. I do very much want to go home and live a normal life among normal people once more."

The lawyer gave me a quick, searching look, presuming, I suppose, that this was due to my influence.

"Besides," Elaine continued, "how could I possibly, without Beck's help, be supposed to manage this big estate? Alexander, though he's clever and does his best—" she looked at him fondly—"is still a child and if we can't sell Schwarzensee, how will we pay for his education and live decently in England?"

"But my dear Frau Gräfin!" the lawyer exclaimed, "don't you realize that your son is due to inherit one of the most valuable properties in Holstein, that the contents of this house alone are worth a fortune, that the income the place brings—which, of course, will be yours to dispose of through the years of Graf Alexander's minority—will be quite large and that if it should not be sufficient, Schwarzensee could well carry another loan now the mortgage is almost paid off?" He looked at her almost tenderly. Perhaps he thought naïveté in a woman endearing and no doubt also noted that it might prove advantageous to himself. He remained silent for a moment, as if in deep thought, but his well-manicured fingers moved as if ticking off item after item.

Then he turned to Alexander with a smile. "Herr Graf," he said, "though I cannot in all honesty promise to be of assistance in the sale of Schwarzensee before your majority, I can, should you decide to accept me as your guardian, offer certain suggestions that might be of help now that I know your plans. I am too busy a man to be able to look after the management of the estate personally, but if you entrusted me with the responsibility of being in charge of your and your mother's interests, I would suggest the following: rent out farm and agricultural land to a reliable tenant for the next six years, which will give you a secure income if the harvests prove good or bad and which you can depend on receiving wherever you choose to live; place the forest under the care of the Holstein Forestry Departments who, probably at no expense to yourselves, provided they have the right to cut the matured timber, will replant and if allowed to cull a certain amount of game see to it that the deer are protected."

"But what about the house and the garden?" Elaine asked.

"Why, all that would be needed is to close the house and to keep Fritz and Ivan as caretakers. They do, if I may venture to say so, deserve some consideration since Schwarzensee is their only home. They think of themselves as almost members of the family."

So Beck had informed the lawyer, as he had me, that they were Alexander's half-brothers. My respect for the man's astuteness had been growing all through the long discussion. His discretion had been faultless and his desire to serve Alexander and Elaine was probably as much sincere as it was the product of self-interest. That he would finally make a nice profit out of it all I did not doubt. But why not? Neither Alexander nor Elaine would care as long as they got exactly what they wanted from him.

After the lawyer had left, thanked warmly by both of them and assured as to his future position as their legal adviser and co-guardian, Alexander confirmed my impression.

"Of course he will cheat, but who cares as long as he proves amenable?"

"But I thought he seemed very decent," Elaine protested.

"You rather fell for him, didn't you, Mummy? I think the sooner I take you to England the better. Though I liked Herr Stein, I don't really fancy him in the position of stepfather."

Elaine blushed. "But we don't even know if he is not married."

Alexander laughed. "How typical you are, Mummy. What did you think of him, Eddie?" he then asked me.

"I think his suggestions well worth considering. I believe you could hardly find anyone better suited for what you want."

"Exactly what I felt," he admitted.

Charles Hlumberg                                    123

express to yourself, provided they have the right to cut the
planted timber, will remain and if allowed to cull a certain

# Chapter Thirteen

"Well, now all we still need is money," Alexander said.

"I thought the lawyer implied the bank would be ready to
offer a loan as soon as the inheritance is settled?"

"And God knows how long that will take. We need it now.
We will simply have to sell something." He looked attentively
round the room. "That desk is very valuable, so the Tsarevna
always said." It was, indeed, a magnificent piece of Louis
Quinze furniture, a *bureau plat,* with finely chiselled ormolu
mounts. "Why not sell it?"

"But you can't, Alexander," Elaine protested. "It's not even
really yours yet and it's so spectacular everyone would notice
that it had gone."

"Perhaps something smaller would be easier to dispose of,
but I can't think of anything of real value."

"Would you like the gold box back?"

"Of course not, Eddie. I'd be dreadfully hurt if you didn't
keep it. But it's a pity about the Tsarevna's jewels, they
would have been just the thing."

"I don't know at all what to do with all her stuff," Elaine
complained. "Her many dresses—yards and yards of valuable
material—but they would hardly be of use to the village
people and yet it seems a waste to burn them or throw them
away. And she was so proud of her clothes too. She designed
them herself, some are exact copies of those of Catherine the
Great."

"Why not present them to a theatre for historical plays?" I
suggested.

"But wouldn't that be rather unfeeling? Some ridiculous fat
old opera singer or actress wearing them?"

"Not at all," Alexander said, evidently pleased with my
proposal. "After all, she was a great actress herself."

"And let them have the jewels too? Well—why not?"

"But wouldn't you like to keep them, Mummy? Even if
fakes, they are very pretty."

"I rather prefer the pearls your father gave me," she said, fingering the modestly-sized single strand she was wearing. "At least they are real."

"Perhaps after all we should keep the Tsarevna's fakes until the police have seen them," Alexander thought. "If they take them to a jeweller he can probably assess what their real value would have been when genuine."

"I'm sure Beck never told me how much he got for them," Elaine said, "but then it's very long ago. I may have forgotten. But surely if Beck kept his accounts in such good order, as it now seems, there would be a record of the sale? Except if, as you think, darling, he stole them—though one would believe with twenty-five thousand marks he would have had enough to start a new life with."

Alexander looked at his mother as fondly as he might have at a well-trained dog, but then meeting my eyes quailed somewhat. "What's wrong, Eddie?"

"Only that I think this constant talk about Beck in very bad taste." It was as far as I dared to go in warning Alexander that I could not tolerate his callousness much longer.

"You are quite right, Eddie," he readily admitted. "If the man's dead, let him rest in peace. If he's alive, well good luck to him! I'm quite satisfied with what he has left behind. Besides, I too am getting heartily sick of hearing about him all the time. How good a man he was, when all he did was to make life difficult and unpleasant for us in every way; or how bad he was when, even if it is proved he was a thief, he left our affairs in such good order." Alexander looked at me for approval.

I was spared having to express what I thought. Ivan came to announce that a Herr Bankdirektor from Hamburg wished to be received.

He was a less attractive type than Herr Stein, a fat, elderly, pompous little man, dressed immaculately in a morning-coat, striped trousers, a large pearl pin in his cravat and a heavy gold watch-chain stretching across his rotund stomach.

After having expressed his condolences briefly, he made it quite clear what a concession it was for a person of his importance to have travelled all the way from Hamburg to call and offer his assistance. He said he was an extremely busy man but that he felt the disappearance of Beck with the twenty-five thousand marks which he was to deliver to the bank as the annual mortgage repayment might have left the Frau Gräfin in difficulties?

Elaine admitted it had.

"I scarcely knew your manager," he then said, "but we had to show the police his accounts and they seem in order. Still, since Countess Plevke allowed him such a free hand, even having given him the right to write cheques for her, who knows how much he might have stashed away? In my position one learns to be mistrustful and I cannot help wondering if the temptation was not too great for a man of such humble origin."

"I think Beck was a very honest man," Alexander said loyally, his eyes on me.

"You say 'was,' so you too presume him murdered?"

Alexander shrugged. "Well, what else is one to think?"

"Has it then not struck you that he might still be alive, abroad somewhere?"

"You see, Alexander!" Elaine exclaimed triumphantly. "The Herr Bankdirektor thinks as I do."

"So you too have suspicions, Frau Gräfin, that he fled? After all, twenty-five thousand marks is not a mean sum to start a new life with, as I have told the police. They were most interested in my theory. Alas, if it proves correct there is little chance, I fear, of ever finding him or the money since he might be anywhere by now, living under a false name. Did he ever speak of wanting to go abroad?"

"Oh, he would complain sometimes about the bad state German politics were in," Alexander said, which I knew was true since I had heard Beck ranting against the new Republic several times.

"And he had some relations in South America, I think," Elaine added, obligingly.

"Well, that might be a clue, though to trace him there would be virtually impossible, I'm afraid."

"But if he left, surely he would have had to leave his car somewhere?" Alexander asked.

"Perhaps he could have taken it with him on some ship?" Elaine suggested.

"Exactly! I must compliment the Frau Gräfin on her keen intelligence."

Elaine looked pleased.

"Mummy," Alexander said, "I thought we agreed that we would talk no more about Herr Beck. It's not a very pleasant subject and I'm sure we are wasting the Herr Bankdirektor's valuable time. Is there anything else you wished to discuss?"

"Well, yes," the banker said, looking slightly embarrassed

at being called to order by a boy of fifteen. What followed then I still remember with amusement. The banker asked Elaine if she had found legal advice and before she had time to answer offered his own lawyer, as well as himself as co-guardian, obviously well-informed as to the necessity of Alexander having one.

"I think I could just spare the time," he said, "and would be only too glad to accept this honorary position. And it would be of considerable advantage to you since my seeing to the estate being well run would greatly facilitate the repayment on the mortgage that my bank holds."

"Oh, I thought most of that was paid off?"

The banker flushed. "May I ask who your informant is?"

"Our lawyer, Herr Stein, and my future guardian," Alexander said, with impish delight.

"Oskar Stein?"

"I think so. Do you know him?" Elaine asked. "He comes, like you, from Hamburg."

"Of course I know him. Who doesn't by now, though he is certainly not a Holsteiner by birth—different race, different creed altogether—almost a foreigner."

"But then so are we, being half English. That's probably why we thought him so sympathetic."

"Mind you, I have nothing against Oskar Stein," the banker scowled. "He has managed in a few years to build up a formidable law practice and there is no doubt that he is very clever."

"Which is surely no disadvantage?" Alexander asked innocently.

"We in Holstein do not entirely trust clever men," the banker said, and then: "I confess I am slightly disappointed as I would like to have been of service to you." He grinned unconvincingly at Alexander. He had rather long, fang-like teeth and I was reminded of a wolf snarling at a lamb that was just out of his reach. "However, since I hope you will continue to bank with us, I may still be of use to you. I think I might even see my way to grant a small loan if you should be in straitened circumstances now, due to Beck's disappearance and, of course, once the inheritance of Schwarzensee is secured it could well carry another mortgage.'

"We do rather need some money now," Elaine said shyly. "The workmen are clamouring for their wages and the funeral will have to be paid for."

"If a few hundred marks would help," the banker said, taking out his wallet.

"A few thousand would be more useful," Alexander said.

"But I'm afraid I couldn't," the banker stammered, "since there is as yet no collateral."

"That's strange," Alexander said. "Herr Stein was certain the Kieler Bankverein would lend us as much as we needed. Oh well, we will just have to transfer our account to them."

The banker flushed an unpleasant red. He took out his cheque book and placed it on the desk. "How much?" he asked and his hand holding the fountain pen poised above it trembled visibly.

"Three thousand would do, wouldn't it, Mummy? Make it out to my mother, please."

"I could scarcely do otherwise since you are still a minor," the banker said sourly, but he wrote out a cheque and gave it to Elaine.

"And now," Alexander said, smiling enchantingly at the banker, "I have to pay a few urgent debts for Mummy in Kiel tomorrow and as you so rightly observed, I'm too young to cash a cheque and she is too busy to leave Schwarzensee just now, so we would be grateful for a few hundred in cash for our most immediate needs," and he looked pointedly at the fat wallet on the desk. "Three or four hundred will do."

"This is most irregular," the banker protested, "it will have to come out of my own pocket."

"Indeed!" said Alexander.

With a sigh the banker took out notes to the value of three hundred marks, then scribbled on a piece of paper. "You will sign for this, Frau Gräfin, if you please."

Elaine obediently did.

The unfortunate banker, depleted of much of his former pompous self-importance, bowed himself out.

"Got him!" Alexander exclaimed. "As slippery as an eel too—what an awful man. I think if he had become my guardian I would have shot him."

"You are clever, darling," Elaine said, looking at her son with admiration, "but what about the Kieler Bank? Was it quite true?"

"Well, almost, but it certainly did the trick," and he started to laugh so uproariously that Elaine and I could not help but join in.

Next morning I packed my belongings, all except for the books I had brought. I was leaving those in Schwarzensee's library where I might have spent so many happy studious hours, given time and leisure and peace of mind. Carefully I folded into a rather colourful silk scarf my mother had once given me, and which I had never ventured to wear, the heavy gem-studded gold box and put it in my suitcase. I counted my money and traveller's cheques. There was enough for the journey and, in spite of Alexander's having somewhat depleted my ready cash on our expedition to Kiel, sufficient to tip the servants generously. I thought with pleasure of their surprise. No doubt they had never been tipped before by anyone nor even paid regular wages, being members of the family so to speak.

I looked around the charming pale green panelled room, at the French window through which so much had entered and gone, at the ruined Greek temple behind which I had been able to discreetly dispose of, without the servants' assistance, the contents of my bucket every morning, and at the lake beyond and remembered what its dark depth concealed.

For the last time I passed through the passage that led from my room to the hall with its bleached skulls of countless dead animals. The taxi was standing ready in the courtyard. Fritz and Ivan put my luggage into it. I handed them the folded notes I had prepared.

Smiles broke out all over their faces. "But this is not necessary!" Fritz exclaimed, nevertheless pocketing the money. "It was a pleasure to serve the English gentleman and it is sad to see him go."

Elaine kissed me chastely on the cheek but I saw there were tears in her eyes as she bade me goodbye. "Thank you for everything, Eddie. Above all, for bringing me back to my senses—we will miss you though."

"No doubt we will soon meet in England," I said, with false cheerfulness.

Alexander was already in the car. "Hurry, Eddie," he called. "There's a shop or two I have to stop at before I take you to the station."

"Your tailor's, no doubt," I said resentfully. He did not seem in the least disturbed by my leaving.

"Oh, I can do that later."

As we drove out of the enchanting courtyard, I looked back once more at the house, so perfect in its architectural symmetry, at the stables and lodges and sentry boxes, at this royal toy domain shut off for so long from the rest of the world behind its dense forests and great armorial gates. I could have wept because of its mysterious beauty which no doubt would be desecrated and exposed to the greedy eyes of strangers and dealers as soon as it was up for sale.

"Don't you feel you belong here and that it would be a shame to lose such a unique place?" I asked Alexander.

"Not at all," he said airily. "Imagine having to contemplate the lake for the rest of my days."

Once in Kiel he made the driver stop at various shops, coming back loaded each time with parcels. I stayed in the car.

"Have you spent all the money you squeezed out of the bank manager?" I asked.

"Well, not quite all," he laughed. "I've kept some for the girl. Maybe I will soon have a son."

The train was already in the station when we arrived there.

"See if you can find an empty compartment, while I get my ticket. There isn't much time."

Having deposited my second-class fare for the journey, I found him waving at me out of the window of a first-class compartment. On the purple plush of its seats lay hothouse grapes, a basket of peaches, a bottle of wine and one of Cognac, a large box of chocolates, smoked Holstein sausages and a loaf of black bread. Also a bunch of red roses, a travelling rug and a matching pillow, all carefully unwrapped.

"So that you can travel in comfort, Eddie," he said, looking delightedly from me to his surprises.

"*Alle einsteigen!*" the train conductor called.

I didn't know how to thank the boy, except by drawing him close in a final embrace. He clung to me, suddenly bursting into sobs. "I can't bear it, Eddie," he cried, "let me come with you. I have enough money to pay for the ticket now."

The doors of the compartment were slammed shut and there was a loud whistle.

I wrenched open the door, lifted him out and deposited him gently on the platform. For a moment he stood staring at me, his face pressed against the closed window and I thought of the first time I had seen it like that through the glass of my bedroom door, watching me, strangely distorted and wet with rain, as it now was with tears and grief, and of the premonition of evil I had then had before his radiant beauty had dispelled that first impression. Then the train started and he turned away.

# Chapter Fourteen

On my return home, warmly welcomed by my mother, back in reassuringly familiar surroundings, what had happened at Schwarzensee seemed a nightmare best forgotten. I tried to forget, but I could not. Finally I had to accept that the strain of the last weeks and its sudden relaxation had brought on what I supposed was a sort of nervous breakdown. I felt depressed, ill, confused and I could neither eat nor sleep.

No doubt my mother noticed the disturbed state I was in. After I had told her briefly of the Tsarevna's death and Beck's disappearance she refrained tactfully from questioning me further. Instead, with maternal solicitude, she ordered all my favourite dishes, had the maid bring me up a large breakfast in bed, advised me to rest and even offered me some of her precious sleeping pills. She has been hoarding them for years in case she is stricken by some painful, terminal disease and becomes a burden to herself and others, as no doubt my father was in his last years.

It was all to no avail. My appetite decreased every time food was set before me and though, for her sake, I forced myself to eat I was inevitably sick afterwards. Sleep? I did not dare lest Alexander's or Beck's face or even Elaine's should confront me in my dreams.

After a week of this I knew that only in confession might I hope to find some relief. So one night I went down to the drawing-room, knowing my mother always stayed up late, preferring those undisturbed hours to the frequently interrupted daytime ones.

I found her sitting in front of a bright fire, intent on *The Times* crossword puzzle.

"Here's something I want to show you," I said, and handed her the golden box.

"Why, it's lovely," she exclaimed. "What workmanship." She turned it here and there. The firelight was mirrored in the precious stones and shone on the initials of Catherine the Great.

"The Tsarevna gave it to you?"

"Yes, on the night before she died."

My mother opened and shut it thoughtfully. "Pandora's Box?" she questioned with a slight smile. "How much evil escaped?"

"A lot."

"I thought as much. Would it not be best if you told me about it, Eddie?"

So I did. I left nothing out, neither my involvement with Elaine nor my love for Alexander, both of which had had such disastrous results. I recounted event after event as accurately as I could remember them, terminating in the deaths of Beck and the Tsarevna, blaming myself for both. I told her all I had done to help conceal Beck's murder, my burning of the letters, of my proof of the secret marriage and about the interviews with police and lawyers and my final departure.

My mother listened quietly, only rarely interrupting to ask a seemingly rather pointless question. But how could she understand it all anyway, I thought? Sufficient that she listened, her clear grey eyes fixed on me with tender sympathy, and allowed me to unburden myself.

"I feel so horribly guilty," I said finally. "If I had not gone to Schwarzensee none of this would probably have happened."

"Perhaps not, but don't blame yourself too much, my poor boy. You were merely the innocent catalyst that brought it all to a head. Even if you had heeded my warning and answered my questions sooner, the tragedy might have been delayed but not averted, since one crime is inevitably punished by another. The mills of God may grind slowly but they grind exceedingly fine."

"But, mother, Beck was not a criminal, nor was the Tsarevna and Elaine, I am by now convinced, did not really intend to let the wheelchair go."

"No, I don't think she did. She wouldn't be the killing kind."

"Strange, that is exactly what the Tsarevna said."

"She was a very perceptive old lady, I think."

"Then only Alexander and I were really guilty."

"To the extent that you were instruments of justice—yes."

"Mother, you seem to know much more about it all than I do," I exclaimed, puzzled.

"I think so," she said calmly, "but only thanks to your father's book and the *Almanach de Gotha*. When you didn't answer my questions I sent for the latter. In it, of course, the Plevkes are listed with dates of birth and death and so is the Tsarevna's family. I will tell you what I discovered. I had started to wonder at the cause of Countess Plevke's identifying herself with Catherine from the moment you wrote to me about it. Great as the Empress was, she seemed to be scarcely the type of person a virtuous woman would want to be like. Then the Gotha revealed that your Tsarevna was born Katarina von Zerbst and that she was, through a morganatic marriage concluded by one of her forebears, directly descended from the princely house of Anhalt Zerbst, Catherine's family. So from her early youth she would have been interested in the real Tsarevna and later all the more so when she married Count Peter Plevke."

"But," I exclaimed, "I had supposed her delusions were all due to the connection Schwarzensee had with the Empress and perhaps the letters she found? I'm sorry about them," I added, "but what else could I do but burn them?"

"Nothing. Much as I regret their destruction, the Tsarevna had no alternative but to see to it that they were burnt before her death."

"She said they revealed a crime," I remembered.

"Yes. The murder of Catherine's husband, the Tsar, by the first Count Plevke. You see," my mother said, smiling at my surprise, "it is nowhere stated that it was Orlov who actually killed the Tsar, though it is generally believed that he initiated the murder. Plevke was a member of his guards regiment and probably one of Catherine's early lovers too. He was less important than the Orlovs and no doubt they induced him to carry out the assassination. After that it would have been safer for him to return to Holstein where he had originally come from. Catherine rewarded him for his loyalty to her with the estate of Schwarzensee.

"The letters probably revealed most of this and for the sake of the family honour, as well as other reasons, your Tsarevna kept them secret and finally saw to it that they were destroyed before her death."

"Other reasons?"

My mother looked at me thoughtfully. "Did it never strike you as odd the names Peter, then Paul, then Alexander?"

"Well, I knew they were the names of Russian Tsars, but I thought it was because of Schwarzensee's history."

"I think the name Peter, which Alexander's grandfather was called, was a mere coincidence, unless some member of the Plevke family had had a very wry sense of humour, but did you never ask yourself why your Tsarevna chose to call her son Paul and her grandson Alexander?"

"I suppose not."

"It might have given you a clue, how concious she had become of her life developing much on the same lines as that of Catherine the Great, though her Empire was only Schwarzensee, not Russia. Did they speak at all of Alexander's grandfather? Of what sort of man he was?"

"Oh yes. Most unpleasant, I gathered. A drunkard, cruel to animals and he forced young men from the villages at gun point to obey his orders."

I was surprised at the pleased smile on my mother's face. "It all fits," she exclaimed. "And he was murdered?"

"Alexander and Beck thought so. It seems he was extremely unpopular on the estate."

"And you never thought that it might have been Beck himself who killed him?"

"Really, Mother," I protested, "isn't your imagination running wild? Beck told me that he barely knew him. He was a stable boy when it happened and not much older than Alexander is now."

"Yet even Alexander has managed to make a girl pregnant. You needn't look so surprised. Just imagine a girl of fifteen, which was the Tsarevna's age when she was married off by her parents who, no doubt, what with the Russian connection, thought it a most suitable alliance. Probably her husband proved to be just as mad, bad and impotent as Peter the Third was."

"But isn't all this just guesswork?"

"Not really. Have a little patience. Accept for the moment that I've guessed right. What would this unfortunate young woman—lonely, frightened and neglected, yet of a passionate nature—have done but seek comfort with someone else?"

"But, Mother—a stable boy? You don't know how class-conscious the German aristocracy is. Besides, how would they ever have met? In the hayloft? It's absurd."

"She rode, I suppose?"

I remembered the Tsarevna's pride in her former horsemanship. "Well of course."

"And wouldn't she have been accompanied by her groom?"

"I suppose so." And suddenly I seemed to see Schwarzen-

see's dense forest and the tree-enclosed secret glades covered
in fern and soft pillows of moss and the impassioned embrace of two young creatures, and felt that what my mother
had suggested might well be true. I remembered the miniature of the Tsarevna I had seen in Beck's room, the laughing
wilful young face, the slim figure in its riding habit and also
the portrait of Catherine the Great in the ballroom, their costumes almost as identical as their features. The same dark
flashing eyes, the same determined chin.

"When your Tsarevna knew herself pregnant and started to
fear that she could no longer conceal her condition from her
husband, believing that ruthless as he was he would probably
kill her since he could have no possible reason to believe the
child to be his, she asked Beck to save her—which he did by
murdering Peter Plevke."

"But, Mother, how can you know all this?"

"Because her problem was not at all unlike that which the
real Tsarevna had to face. She too found herself with child
from a lover and knew her husband might not recognize it as
his. But contrary to your Tsarevna, she lived through years of
anxiety, always threatened by her husband to be sent to a
convent or even killed, and it was only when the Tsarevich
Paul had reached the age of seven that the Tsar's increasing
madness allowed her to rally sufficient support to have Peter
eliminated and proclaim herself Empress of Russia. Your
Tsarevna had only one loyal subject: young Beck. Paul was
born three months after his father's death. The legitimate heir
to Scwharzensee, yet Beck's son."

"But then," I stammered, "but then—if all this is true—
Alexander killed his real grandfather."

"Yes, but I rather hope he will never know," my mother
said, "and thanks to you why should he? All proof of it is
presumably burnt? Your Tsarevna had no Imperial Crown to
gain by her husband's death," my mother continued, "only
safety and security for herself and her son and, of course,
Schwarzensee—which may have seemed to her as of much
importance as ruling all of Russia was to Catherine the
Great."

"But why did she have to marry Beck?"

"Was your impression of him that he was a stupid man?"

"No, though evidently lacking education and inflexible in
his reactionary Germanic beliefs, certainly not stupid."

"Well then, surely he would have known that, as his wife,
the Tsarevna could not testify against him, as she might oth-

erwise have done had she tired of him as a lover? And almost certainly too he aspired to become complete master of Schwarzensee."

"But why the secrecy?"

"Mainly, from his point of view, because the marriage might have indicated a motive for murder."

"And from hers?"

"Surely no arrogant, proud woman descended from a princely family would have liked it known that she was now plain Frau Beck, married to her former groom? So it was in the interests of both to keep their secret. And even if she loved him, the fact that she was tied for life to an inferior must have rankled. It seems to me no wonder that she escaped more and more into fantasies of grandeur, identifying herself with her famous ancestress whose lack of morals and even crimes had been forgiven by history because of her greatness."

"Do you think she had other lovers, like Catherine?"

"Only in imagination. I believe Beck would have been less tolerant than Potemkin to whom Catherine was secretly married, but he also had to creep into her room at night through a hidden staircase—as did other favourites."

"So that's how you suspected there was one! I suppose she had it built for exactly the same purpose." I thought over all my mother had told me.

"But if Beck was a murderer," I then asked, "and had always wanted Schwarzensee, perhaps he would not have stopped at anything to get it? Perhaps the tale of how he so bravely tried to save Elaine's husband when he was wounded in the trenches is not true? Perhaps he just let him die? And then when Alexander became difficult, tried to kill him too?"

My mother sighed. "My dear boy, you must believe what is easiest for you. After all, Beck is dead and we will never know the real truth. But I doubt he was so much of a monster as to have wanted to kill his own son and grandson too. As you told me, he seems to have been devoted to both. What I think is that he merely wanted to frighten Alexander into submission and warn him that if he revealed what he must have seemed to Beck to have guessed, he would suffer the same fate as his grandfather."

"But Alexander never told me that he threatened Beck with that, only with his sleeping with the Tsarevna and embezzling the family fortune."

Then I thought of the dog Beck had shot and that Alexan-

der might have accused him of murder. After that he may
have seen no alternative but to kill the boy.

"So Alexander shot him in self-defence after all!" I exclaimed with infinite relief.

"It's quite possible," my mother said, but I thought I read
doubt on her grave face. "I want to show you something."
She picked up a book and pointed to the coloured reproduction of a painting. It was the portrait of a young man in the
tight-fitting uniform of Napoleonic days, his proudly beautiful
fair head held high, his eyes widely spaced, large and very
blue and his mouth curved in an enchanting smile.

A shudder went through me, so remarkable was the
likeness.

"Alexander the First, just after his father's assassination.
Though he did not take an active part in the murder himself,
there is no doubt that he knew of the plan. For a while all of
Europe was under the spell of this dazzlingly beautiful young
Emperor. He was intelligent, cultured and generous. His
charm and fascination made him irresistible to men and
women alike. He is said to have been equally fond of both.

"He was all things to all men and a genius at deception,
the most accomplished actor on the European political stage
of his time, misleading his enemies by sweet words and false
promises, betraying his friends and allies as well if it so suited
him."

"And was he finally assassinated like his ancestors?"

"Oh no. But, when he finally died normally, it was
rumoured that he had even been able to cheat death and he
was seen all over Russia appearing in different disguises."

My mother smiled. "Now go to bed, dear boy, I think you
will sleep better tonight. And don't blame yourself any longer," she added. "What happened was not your fault. It had its
roots in past evil out of which what you witnessed grew. A
tragedy reenacted by almost identical characters as the
historical ones, even if the stage was only Schwarzensee and
not the Imperial Court of Russia. Why you were called
upon to take part in it, I think I know."

"Why, Mother?"

"To save an entire family from shame and disgrace. The
Tsarevna from having her complicity in her husband's death
revealed, which no doubt her letters to Beck might have
proved had you not destroyed them; Elaine from killing the
Tsarevna and, what would have been almost as horrible, marrying you; and a child of fifteen, who as yet doesn't know

right from wrong and has a whole life in front of him in which he may learn it, from being condemned for murder."

"And Beck?"

"A life for a life—justice was done."

"You are a surprisingly ruthless person, Mother."

She laughed. "Let's say I am a realist. Now, take your box. I think most of its evil spirits have been laid to rest. Sleep well, my darling," and she kissed my brow.

I took the box but perhaps my hand trembled. It slipped from my grasp and fell to the ground. It burst open unfolding a double lid. My mother picked it up. Curiously she looked at the small painting it had disclosed. She was not the sort of person who blushed easily but she did then. She handed it to me without comment. It was painted in the manner of Watteau, every exquisite detail distinct—trees, a lake, a shepherd and a shepherdess lying in a close embrace, their partially nude bodies leaving no doubt as to their intimate contact.

"Your Tsarevna and the real one evidently didn't only have the same tastes but an equally frank sense of humour," my mother remarked drily.

Once more I thought I heard the old woman's rich laughter. Of course, she had known what the box contained and that one day I would discover its secret. *"Après tout c'est naturel quand on est jeune—et même après,"* I remembered her saying.

I slept soundly that night, strangely free of all thoughts of guilt, thanks to my mother's wisdom and the Tsarevna's wit.

■

Though I heard from Alexander occasionally in the years that followed I made no effort to see him or Elaine.

His first letter had arrived when I was already at the Foreign Office and living in London. He wrote from Eton. He said that he had passed the entrance exams with ease and was popular with most of the masters, but there had been certain difficulties with the boys at first.

"Many of them coarse, stupid oafs with nothing but brute strength to prove their superiority. Of course I soon found several ready to be my protectors, but their demands in exchange for this seemed somewhat excessive. Still, I learnt to play one against the other and so escaped some of the rigours imposed in the first months. I am all right now and have become quite popular, thanks to my gifts for acting and miming. From the headmaster down to the newest boy here, I ape their voices and gestures to perfection and make everyone laugh."

Concerning Schwarzensee he wrote that the police had finally given up the search and that Beck was believed to have fled overseas. This piece of news had not surprised me much, but the next did.

"Imagine, Eddie, our amazement and delight at being told by the police that the Tsarevna's jewels were real! They had taken them to a jeweller to assess what the originals might have been worth. Just think—if we had given them to some theater with her old dresses as we had planned to do! They are, it seems, worth a fortune. So we are quite rich now and it doesn't matter that I can't sell Schwarzensee until I'm twenty-one.

"Herr Stein, who is proving both useful and amenable, explained it all. When Beck returned after the war had ended and found the bank was ready to foreclose on the mortgage and that we might lose Schwarzensee, he told Mummy the jewels would probably have to be sold and the Tsarevna would, I suppose, have had to agree. But it seems that all he did was to deposit them in the bank for several months as security, sold some land to meet the necessary payment and returned the jewels. Considering how attached he was to the Tsarevna and our family it was really foolish of us to think he could have brought himself to sell our heirlooms. I'm afraid it must have been me who invented the story of the fakes. I hated him even then for having shot my dog, but since both Mummy and the servants believed my tale and Beck didn't deny it, I came to believe it was true. Beck had a very good reason not to refute my tale. It was at the time when one fears a Russian-type revolution and he thought we might be robbed if it were known we kept such a treasure in the house. Later it suited him, frugally as he forced us to live, that we should not know what readily convertible valuables we still had!

"Mummy is staying at the vicarage getting involved with parish work, but has also started to hunt again. She looks years younger, has found many old and made quite a lot of new friends and is perfectly happy. So am I, dearest Eddie, and all thanks to you."

I had been appointed to our Embassy in Rome and had been living there for almost a year—my mother staying with me through the winter months in my flat in the Via Con-

dotti—when Alexander wrote once more to tell me that
Elaine had married.

"Would you believe it, Eddie, a country parson like my
grandfather Hollington. As if one in the family wasn't
enough! Really, if they put too much pressure on me to wear
the collar too—and there are ominous signs—I'll become an
RC just to spite them. In any case I am rather drawn to it.
Those lovely vestments, the candles and incense, the divine
music and the Latin chants! All so much grander and more
mysterious—besides, so many obliging saints to intercede for
one whenever one has sinned!

"Meanwhile my new stepfather doesn't interfere with me
much. He is quite harmless really. Elderly, scholarly and pi-
ous. What Mummy sees in him I don't know except perhaps
that he's rather good and kind. Like those Chinese mon-
keys—he speaks no evil, hears no evil and sees no evil. He is
a widower with two virgin daughters. The younger one is
quite pretty and growing rather fond of me."

My mother, to whom I was reading the letter, could not refrain from commenting: "She won't be for long!", though
whether she was referring to lasting affection or virginity I
didn't dare ask. In any case I was scanning the next sentence
which I thought wiser not to read out. "I am not in the least
in love with her because there is a person here to whom I am
almost as deeply attached as I was to you, Eddie."

"Nice to think that the fair Elaine has found so eminently
suitable a husband," my mother remarked.

"He sounds rather dull and humourless."

"Well, wasn't she?"

Past physical pleasure leaves almost no memory, I thought.
"She was a very attractive woman, just the same," I nevertheless said defensively. "How can you judge? You refused to
meet her when she called on you. It was only polite that she
tried to once she was back at the vicarage."

"I did not refuse," my mother said with asperity, "I only
excused myself for having to join you in London where you,
too, were keeping out of her way. Besides, my dear boy, what
would she or I have had in common, except you? It seemed
to me a connection best forgotten. What more does Alexander
write? I find his future development of considerably greater
interest than that of his mother. Quite a significant sign that
he is already becoming drawn towards the true faith, if at
present only for aesthetic reasons. Still, it may be the thin
edge of the wedge—well, go on reading."

"I have joined several debating societies. I act in all the plays we put on here and quite often direct them. I have become quite good at athletics too, which makes even the fools respect me, though I have my own little circle chosen from the more intelligent. I couldn't be happier. With love and gratitude always."

"I'm glad he remembers how much he owes you. Where would he be except for you?"

Perhaps safer under Beck's care, I could not help but think.

Then our correspondence practically ceased, except that several years later there was one more letter from Oxford. Alexander seemed almost ecstatically happy there, revelling in the beauty and tradition of the ancient colleges, relishing their almost monastic atmosphere of learning which nevertheless permitted so much youthful light-hearted freedom.

"I drink deeply from the font of wisdom," he wrote, "as well as unlimited amounts of champagne with my friends. I have rather grand panelled rooms, decorated according to my own taste with peacock-blue velvet hangings and purple cushions, where we dine sumptuously by candlelight. I am doing Mods. I have joined several clubs and, as you surmised I one day might, I have become an important member of the OUDS."

He seemed to have succumbed blissfully to all the temptations that had beset me in my years at Oxford. If I had not been able to indulge them fully, it had not been from lack of inclination. However, a meagre purse and natural timidity had enforced restraint.

"You can't imagine, Eddie, how popular I am here and how large my circle of friends."

Indeed I could. With his dazzling looks, intelligence and fortune—no wonder!

Yet his resolve to become an actor still seemed firm. He wrote he had been promised acceptance at Stratford after graduation and that he had had several offers to work in films already.

And that was—since I did not answer—the last I heard from him directly. Much to my relief.

# PART TWO

# Chapter Fifteen

In 1932, after two years at our Embassy in Rome, I was transferred to Copenhagen. Certainly an advancement on my climb up the diplomatic ladder but a post I did not particularly enjoy. After Italy, the grey north, with its seemingly endless dark winters and brief summers in which contrarily the pale sun never set, did not appeal to me. Copenhagen, except for its excellent restaurants and surprisingly diverting night-clubs, seemed provincial after the Eternal City. Though I made friends with several Danes and was invited to their country houses—kind, jolly and hospitable people and very pro-English—I missed the quick wit, vitality and charm of the Latins that I had grown accustomed to and the sophistication of Roman society.

My mother, who came to stay with me occasionally, thought much as I did about Copenhagen. On one of her journeys north she had not been able to resist viewing Schwarzensee. She told me its present owners, rich German industralists, had modernized it beyond recognition—electric light, bathrooms, new furniture, if appropriate in style certainly not in century. The park was no longer a dense wilderness, the undergrowth cleared, many of the great trees felled; the black lake no longer darkened by its overhanging weeping willows, but a bright expanse of limpid water. In my once derelict Greek Temple, now repaired and restored, she had been served tea.

"They were very nice people," my mother reported, pleased by my interest in Schwarzensee's history—of which they, though totally unconnected with it, seemed quite proud.

"I was shown the ballroom. That at least has remained intact and the Tsarevna's portrait is still there—she bestrides her prancing stallion as before. They seemed to know very little of the Plevkes, or perhaps did not want to speak of them. Neither did I, explaining my visit as merely one of historical and architectural research. What a gem of a house—

even if its interior is rather spoilt, the courtyard and the great gates are still as when you knew them. How could Alexander ever sell it!" Then seeing my face she changed the subject.

"I have sent these people your father's book on the Tsars" (she had finally completed it) "to thank them for their kindness."

We did not speak of Alexander any more, though no doubt her interest in him persisted. She would of course, because of gossip at home, have been better informed about him and Elaine than she dared admit, believing that I did not want to be reminded.

I did not, even if I could not refrain from occasionally scanning the theatre reviews in the newspapers. Frequently his name was mentioned and his performances praised. He had indeed come far. He had worked at Stratford and with Reinhardt in America and even starred in two films in Hollywood. I could not help wondering what he would look like now after so many years. That so innocently angelic child's face must have changed beyond recognition. True, his good looks were often commented upon, but what would the constant use of greasepaint have done to the radiant golden complexion; and hair, nightly covered by wigs or dyed to whatever colour suited his role, now grown sparse no doubt. Perhaps I thought with distaste, he had even grown a beard. And would not maturity have hardened and coarsened his features, dissipation marked them, revealing his true self at last, no matter what mask he assumed on the stage? I hoped so. If he only entranced his audience from behind the footlights no harm was done.

In 1935 I was transferred to Vienna and remained there for the next three years as first secretary.

The beauty and charm of Vienna is too well-known for me to add adequately to its praise. Truly the city of song and laughter, whatever the circumstances; and most of them had been grim after the First World War. Not only had the monarchy collapsed but so had the krone, the Austrian currency. Inflation, followed by unemployment, political unrest, poverty to a greater or lesser degree affected all classes. Yet the unquenchable optimism, good humour and *joie de vivre* of the Viennese persisted unchanged.

Socially the aristocracy, in spite of Austria being a republic, still ruled supreme. Even if deprived of former privileges and political power, and their fortunes somewhat depleted, its members still lived in their baroque palaces built by Fischer von Erlach or Hildbrandt—if on a reduced scale. Frequently only one or two flats would be occupied by their owners, the rest left empty or rented out. But the great stone stairways, wide enough for horses to ascend as they had in the past, still rose between banisters of elaborate ornamental richness. Gods and goddesses, nymphs and satyrs and plump-bottomed *putti*, coats of arms and heraldic emblems of the families one was visiting, were in spite of being covered in dust impressive enough. And usually, after having ascended with a certain trepidation through so much ancestral grandeur, one found a small flat crowded, it is true, with good pictures and works of art and fine furniture, but above all with people of irresistible charm.

Having had from necessity to forget the Imperial past, a lost empire and to ignore what the uncertain future might bring, they lived entirely for the moment and its pleasures. Devout Roman Catholics as they all were, never missing mass on Sundays, as long as certain rules were observed there seemed no conflict between their consciences and their morals. The grace of God was still theirs in the Imperial sense and, because of it, the conviction that they could do no wrong. The men—good-looking and well-groomed—if extremely civilized as to manners were rarely intellectually inclined or much interested in the arts except for that of the theatre and music and the art of living, in which sport was very much included. In the country they shot or rode; in town they womanized. Trying to earn a living was considered ungentlemanly, so few of them did. If destitute there would always be some uncle or cousin in that closely-knit clan who could be depended upon to provide in the end—so why bother? Needless to say that the attractive women of that society shared their men's light-hearted attitude towards life.

"The Austrian aristocracy is a pit into which every young English diplomat inevitably falls," my chief had warned me when I first arrived in Vienna—and fall I did, thanks mainly to Marie Therese.

My ambassador was a rather strange man whom I only gradually learnt to like and understand. He was an elderly bachelor and, except for his absolute conviction that only he was right and all foreigners wrong, very un-English. He did not look like an Englishman either; small, delicately-limbed, swarthy of complexion, very dark too, as to eyes and brows,

though his head was entirely bald. Perhaps the fact that he
had been born in India, if of English parents, explained his
odd appearance and his looking rather like a Buddhist monk.
His habits, too, were monastic. He ate sparingly, meat rarely,
never drank wine or spirits, and what was served in conse-
quence at the Embassy table, was frugal to say the least.
Nevertheless, in spite of his faddishness about food and his
rather spinsterish liking for economy, he was diplomatically a
man to be reckoned with. For one thing he was a brilliant
linguist speaking French entirely without an accent, rare in
an Englishman, and German fluently, even if Berlin had been
his last post before Vienna.

He had risen only very slowly to his present position; the
main reason probably his celibacy and the undoubted fact
that wherever he had been he was unpopular with his staff.
Hardworking himself he expected the same of others, was a
hard taskmaster and did not suffer fools gladly. Cold sarcasm
instead of humorous tolerance did not endear him to those
who worked under him. Nor had he ever become well-liked
in any of the various countries in which he had represented
His Majesty's Government. He lacked social graces and de-
tested entertaining; though many of his colleagues came to
admire his political astuteness and insight, he had made few
friends, a few intellectuals; he was well-read, mentally extremely alert, very intelligent, but a certain aridity in his personality always finally repelled more than attracted.

If in time he came to befriend me more than others of his
staff, and even took a certain interest in my welfare, it was I
believe more for my mother's sake than mine. She had come
to live with me in Vienna and had gradually made herself
indispensable to him. She was exactly what he needed, a
perfect hostess whenever he entertained, a competent housekeeper which he had never been, and too old a woman and
too respectable as to background for there ever to be any
doubts that their friendship was anything but platonic. In
general he disliked women, especially young and pretty ones,
believing them to be obsessed by sex. However, he had come
to value my mother's quick wit, charm and tact and the way
she dealt with his guests, keeping from him those he considered insufferably boring and bringing him those she knew
would interest him.

"It's all very well your playing ambassadress," I told my
mother. "I suppose you think it rather fun—but surely you
cannot really like such an odd, cold fish of a man?"

"A fish that perhaps needs greater depth than the surface on which you swim," my mother said. It was, I knew, a mild reproach. My private—well—even my public life, had become far from exemplary in Vienna.

There had been so much going on ever since I had arrived. It was the opera season and that of theatrical performances in the Burg Theatre, and balls, some still in private places: many public, such as the Künslerfest, the Jöger Ball and the Gnaschfest to most of which men and women went masked and in fancy dress. They offered opportunities of brief contacts and occasional consequential adventures to those of all tastes, preferences and classes. Artists and their models, shop-girls and their friends, Viennese intellectuals and the bourgeoisie as well as the aristocracy all found equal enjoyment and escape from reality in these festivities.

There were the Heurigen where rich or poor drank the new wine in trellised arbours at Grinzing, just outside Vienna, singing folk-songs together and eating *Backhändel* or *Wiener Schnitzel*.

Finally, there were the night-clubs, the elegant ones set apart for society, the more dubious ones where ladies of the demi-monde could be seen and the dark haunts where gypsies played their violins, their music more intoxicating than wine.

Bleary-eyed, having escorted Marie Therese often until dawn, I would arrive at the embassy late for my work and not very efficient at it until one of the office girls took pity on me, reviving me with strong black coffee. Sir John knew of my affair with Marie Therese of course, as did most of Vienna by then, but except for occasional sarcastic remarks as to my unpunctuality, there were no personal reproaches. Perhaps he felt that my private life was my own business or shared my mother's opinion—though this, too, never expressed in so many words—that as the lover of a securely-married woman much older than myself I could come to less harm than I might have otherwise.

Besides, since Marie Therese was the avowed queen of the society in which we all moved, certain advantages in my association with the Hohenturns could not be ignored by someone as shrewd as my chief was. Though he rarely spoke of her, he showed a rather curious interest in her husband, Prince Heinrich, questioning me occasionally as to his political opinions. I had to confess that I did not think he had any and that he was only interested in sport, as were most of his class. His interest, however, brought him almost into the orbit of international affairs, as he was head of the Austrian Jockey Club, sponsor of motor racing in many countries, and his polo team was well-known all over Europe. He piloted his private plane the "Falcon" himself. His shooting parties to which people from all over the world were invited were famous.

Prince Heinrich was a handsome man in his early fifties when Marie Therese first introduced me to him. Yet it seemed to me that he lacked the casual grace of manner so typical of the Austrian aristocrat. There was something rather stiff and arrogant about him, perhaps because of his having been brought up in Prussia and later becoming an officer in the Imperial *garde du corps*. Due to the quite unexpected deaths of several of his relations of another line of the family, he had come into a vast inheritance. I did not like him. Perhaps it was my guilt that forbade me to do so but also the realization that he considered the fact that I was one of Marie Therese's lovers of little importance. Their marriage—an arranged one—had been a marriage of convenience. Two great princely families had been suitably allied; they were second cousins and, as far as their different temperaments made it possible, loyal to each other, each leaving to the other his chosen sphere of interest without interference—united, however, when it came to representation and above all charity. For there was no doubt that both never neglected either obligation. If Prince Heinrich gave the most splendid parties in Vienna and in the country, there was not a youth club, sports club, swimming club or ski club that he did not support or help organize in Austria, Czechoslovakia and in the Sudetenland, where he had large estates.

As for Marie Therese it was well known that no appeal to her would ever go unanswered. She was as generous with her husband's money as she was with her charming self.

At first I had suffered agonies of jealousy when I found out I was not the only man she favoured but gradually I learned not to care—even taking a certain pride in being united with others in worshipping this generous pagan goddess of plenty, for that is what she seemed to me. If her lack of morals was occasionally laughed at in her own circles, she had no enemies. It was generally accepted that certain sacrifices had to be made to her by lesser women. Loans of sons, husbands and lovers were the tribute she demanded as her right. If often unwillingly given by wives and sweethearts, everyone knew that no harm ever came to those whom Marie Therese briefly embraced. In fact, quite the contrary. Renewed, the life force rekindled, men would be returned to their families more capable of affection than before.

With gratitude I thought how utterly she had swept away all my puritanical inhibitions about sex and had taught me that what had seemed to me a rather shameful animal act, could be one of reciprocal joy and tenderness. To me she became everything, not only a superb and experienced mistress but mother, sister and friend. In fact, all women in one!

Though her beauty was famed in Vienna, it certainly was not classical nor was her figure what fashion then demanded. If not exactly fat, Marie Therese was definitely plump. "Mollet" they call it in Austrian dialect, but then I and probably most of her admirers thought the more there was of her the better. I knew she was forty-nine, thanks to my mother's reading her up in the *Almanach de Gotha*. Yet her charming face was quite unlined, her complexion flawless, her brow unmarked, as pure and untroubled as that of a happy child. If tiny wrinkles crept around the corners of her large golden-brown eyes, laughter had drawn them, not care or sorrow or age. Two engaging dimples graced her round cheeks when she smiled, which was nearly always.

Intellectually, I must confess, she was extraordinarily limited. She had had only the most rudimentary education and had never been to school. Various governnesses had taught her to read and write and to speak foreign languages, but that was all. Nor had she made any effort to improve on this. If she read at all it was some fashionable magazine. If she wrote a letter it was typed by her secretary, only bearing her large scrawled signature and frequently crosses for kisses. But stupid she was not.

Her instincts were more sure than knowledge, her judgement of people unfailingly accurate. If she exclaimed in her impetuous way "I do not like him or her—" which was rare because she was usually tolerant of others—one could be sure that sooner or later it would be proven that there was something wrong with the person involved. One would have expected her conversational capacities to be limited; oddly enough, they weren't! She prattled happily in every language, exploiting her naïveté to amuse and certainly succeeded in doing so, making people laugh and relax. She spread warmth wherever she went. Was it her essential goodness that had this effect, I wondered? I knew her to be incapable of an evil thought. She was totally devoid of envy or malice.

She knew all about "sin" in the Catholic sense, of course,

especially the sins of the flesh to which she was prone. She
was very devout. She must have been somewhat of a problem
to her confessor. There was not a charity to which she would
not generously subscribe if asked by him to do so, but the
fact that she gave herself as readily to all and anyone who
appealed to her for other reasons, must have troubled his
conscience perhaps more than it did hers. Often in the afternoons when I called on her in the palace, at an hour when
most men were at their clubs or enjoying themselves in similar pursuits as I, I would find her alone, her ample form
inadequately draped in a loose tea-gown of lace or satin
edged with swansdown, assiduously telling her rosary, its
beads rapidly slipping through her plump beringed fingers.

"Just one more *Ave,* darling," she would say, interrupting
the prayers she was murmuring to look at me tenderly, "or
Father Ignatius will be cross again."

Why her affection for me, which at first could not have
been more than a whim to seduce a shy and still rather awkward young man, had persisted for nearly a year I do not
know. There were interruptions when, of course, the demands
of her other friends became too urgent or she had had to leave
for the country or travel with her husband. Nevertheless ours
had become as permanent a liaison as I knew she was capable of. Was it perhaps only because I was English?

From the last half of the past century everything English
had been very much the fashion in Austria, Hungary and
Czechoslovakia and not even the war had changed that. To
speak the language was considered as smart as speaking
French had been in the past. To keep English horses, trainers
and grooms essential in the sporting world. Dogs came from
England, guns from Purdey in London, Harness, saddles and
riding boots were still made in Vienna by English craftsmen
who had been allowed to continue working undisturbed all
through the war, since their services were indispensable to
court and society. Coyle and Early still made everyone's
shoes and all gentlemen's clothes were tailored in Savile Row.
In the palaces, the fine silks and velvets that had covered furniture and walls had been replaced by bright and gaudy flowered English chintzes and from the bedrooms the big
tapestry-hung four-posters, that had seen centuries of copu-
lation, birth and death, were discarded, brass beds taking
their place.

"So much more hygienic and modern," Marie Therese had
said with pride. "I ordered this one from Maples—feel how

soft the mattress is, and how strong." To demonstrate its qualities she had bounded up and down on it with childish delight.

Also, doubtlessly, I had become useful to her as an escort. Not that she could not have found many of her own set willing to do so, but certain conventions had to be observed due to her husband's position. For a married woman to be seen too often in public, no matter what she did in private with one of the other males of her own society, might cause unwelcome gossip and surmises; or so, at least, Marie Therese had tried to explain to me.

"And me, I suppose I am of no account?"

"Not to me, darling, you know how much I love you," and she caressed me tenderly. "But you see, they don't understand. They believe all Englishmen to be gentlemen no matter what class they come from and much too moral to endanger a married woman's virtue.

So it was I who was privileged to take her to expensive restaurants, public or private balls, concerts and theatres when her husband was away. If the demands she made on me nightly, calling on me at all hours if a sudden fancy to be taken here or there struck her, were exhausting, her indefatigable zest for life, her capacity for enjoyment were so catching that all she asked was as nothing to what she gave.

On my modest salary I could never have afforded to take her out. She only drank champagne and plenty of it and ate voraciously, as far as I could ascertain, only what was the most expensive on the menu in whatever restaurant she made me escort her to.

"But don't you like caviare, darling?" she asked, puzzled when I refused to share in the large amounts she was greedily consuming. "It is so healthy!"

Even when I learned that neither she nor I were ever to be presented with a bill; the bowing head waiters all recognized her and murmured discreetly—"The secretariat, as usual, Durchlaucht?" And she would smilingly assent.

Tickets for the theatre and opera were all paid the same way through the Hohenturn offices that employed more secretaries than our embassy.

However, I was still responsible for tips, for taxi fares and for supplying Marie Therese with cash—she never carried any—whenever we met a beggar, and there were still many in the streets of Vienna. I am sure she never knew how often I had to walk all the way back to my flat after having parted with her at the palace, with not even enough for a tram fare left in my pocket.

Nevertheless, my self-respect suffered at having to accept what after all would finally be billed to her husband and when the first Christmas came along, after we had been friends for nearly a year, I searched all of Vienna for something of such beauty and value that it would, to a small extent, repay all I had accepted. Needless to say, I found nothing that pleased me which was not absolutely beyond my means. Besides, I could not really give a jewel, though I saw one which I liked at Paltscho. Such a gift would have indicated our intimacy too obviously; nor would it, I think, have really pleased her—she had so many. I was in despair.

# Chapter Sixteen

As usual, after I had confessed my problem, my mother came to my rescue.

"Why not the Tsarevna's box?" she asked. "It is certainly valuable enough to repay even a princess for her favours."

I looked at it where it lay as always on my desk, glittering with its emeralds and diamonds, and realized I had become so accustomed to it through the years that I scarcely noticed it. The memories it held had faded, though its beauty had not. I thought of the hidden compartment and the lovers embracing on the miniature painting inside it and realized it was exactly what I wanted to give Marie Therese. Something so splendid that even her husband would be impressed, yet containing a secret that was ours alone.

"But do you think the Tsarevna would mind?"

"I think she would laugh," my mother said, drily.

So, carefully wrapped, the box was delivered at the Hohenturn Palace on Christmas Eve. The effect it made there was beyond all my highest expectations. Marie Therese called me immediately.

"Eddie, it is the most beautiful object ever given to me in my life. Heinrich says—he knows this sort of thing—that it is Russian and must have belonged to the Great Catherine herself. He says it is immensely valuable and told me to ask you where you got it. In England, I suppose? Some Russian must have stolen it in the revolution, he thinks, and then sold it not knowing its worth. All our guests are admiring it now. Oh darling! I cannot thank you properly over the telephone, but come for tea tomorrow."

I did—and showed her how to open the secret compartment, which added to her delight, as I had known it would. From then on the box was always on the table beside her bed and she kept her rosary in it.

Even her husband thanked me, on one of the rare occasions on which we met, for my Christmas present. Generally he was away. He travelled a lot of the time to Berlin and Munich where preparations were being made for the Olympic Games. Often, too, he was on his estates in Czechoslovakia or Hungary or the Sudetenland; or he flew to whatever race courses at which his horses were running. Occasionally Marie Therese had to go with him, but typically Viennese as she was, she disliked leaving the city. She had no fondness for outdoor life and showed a great dislike for any form of exercise except dancing.

"Heinrich is quite simply killing himself with all this sport," she complained.

"Dr Koritschoner says he can die of a heart attack any minute if he is not more careful. It worries me dreadfully, but what can I do?"

"Heinrich looks perfectly healthy to me," I said reassuringly. Indeed he did. "Your doctor is probably quite wrong. They are not infallible, you know."

"But he is the best doctor in the world. Even I, though I am rarely ill, would not feel and look as I do except for his care. He does wonders for my skin. He is a magician."

And also one of the most famous plastic surgeons in Vienna, I could not help remembering, looking at her still so remarkably youthful face. The doctor was the Hohenturn's *Hausarzt*. In spite of his large practice in town, I had met him quite often in the corridors and anterooms of the palace but though we bowed to each other politely, no one had ever introduced us. He was a shadowy figure, hurrying by, dressed in black, a greying beard obscuring part of his face, and strong glasses distorting what was visible of his eyes.

"The Koritschoners have been our family doctors for centuries. His father even brought me into the world."

"But socially there seems no contact at all."

"What do you mean?" she asked, looking surprised.

"Well, he never seems to mix with your guests or to be invited for a meal here or come into the drawing-room."

"But of course not, darling, he is a Jew; don't you know they crucified Our Lord Jesus?"

"Rather more theirs than yours," I could not help remarking.

Though I loved her and her absurd naïveté in general amused me, the realization that as to knowledge and education she still lived and thought as if in the Dark Ages occasionally irritated me. It did so now, but there was worse to come.

"And, you know, there are still those dreadful ritual murders, especially in Poland."

"Horrible pogroms, I suppose you mean?"

"Oh no, that is only because the Jews there still slaughter innocent Christian children every Easter and drink their blood and eat their flesh, as we do Our Lord's flesh and blood symbolically when we take the host, in some dreadful mockery of our beliefs." I looked at her aghast.

"Besides, even if I could invite Dr. Koritschoner to dine, what could I give him to eat under the circumstances?" There was no possible answer.

"And does your husband feel like you about all this?" I asked at last.

"But of course, all of us do. But we are very fond of old Koritschoner. We have even employed a niece of his in the secretariat because he asked us to. She is a tall, thin, very ugly girl, very dark. Perhaps you have met her? She speaks perfect English." I was not sure. "Not that she needed the work—her family in the Sudetenland are rich industrialists. They have a large factory there and have built a modern villa in the mountains near our castle. They are under our protection, so to speak—they are our Jews."

"But why do they need it in Czechoslovakia? Surely there is no anti-Jewish feeling there?"

"There is in the Sudeten. Our people there are Germans after all, feeling like their brothers in the Fatherland. One cannot blame them. Sudeten Germans are cruelly exploited by Czechs and Jews."

"And where do you hear all this nonsense?"

She shrugged. "It does not matter, but it is true. In any case we will always see to it that Dr. Koritschoner's relatives are safe as we cannot do without him, Heinrich could die just like that," and she flicked her fingers, "except for his constant care. You see, Heinrich works much too hard and there is no stopping him."

"Works!" I exclaimed in amazement. "I thought he only lived for sport."

"Well, so he does in a way, but it comes to the same thing," she added. "You see, he loves children and we have not been able to have any, not from the want of trying I assure you, but by now we have to accept that we never will. It has been a great disappointment to him as it is to me. He wanted a son and heir whom he could bring up as he was in the Germanic tradition—strict discipline, devotion and loy-

alty to Emperor and Fatherland—all that. He has never really accepted the Austrian way of thinking and feeling, that the
past is past and why worry about tomorrow.

"Heinrich still looks to the future and believes its only
hope is to inspire young people with his ideals. And what
easier way than through sports organizations? He thinks, you
see, that the day will come when all the youth of Europe can
be united. Of course, it is all rather secret," she added hastily,
"but he told me he did not mind if your ambassador knew
about it. Heinrich does so hope England's young people will
join one day. They are so good at sport. Most of Austria is
already organized into groups headed by young leaders Heinrich has trained; so is the Sudetenland and Hungary. Only in
Czechoslovakia are there still difficulties. The Czechs are so
foolishly anti-German—still, that will have to be changed."

"What are they supposed to do, these young people?" I
asked, amazed at what I was hearing.

"Oh, work together and march together."

"Like the young fascists and the Hitler *Jugend*?"

"More like your Boy Scouts, I think, but this will be a
much bigger movement."

"And their aims? Or those of their leaders?"

"To strive for peace and to be prepared to fight for it."

"Rather a contradiction in terms," I could not help saying.

"Well, I do not really understand much about politics or
sport," Marie Therese shrugged. "Where shall we go tonight,
Eddie?"

When I informed my ambassador of what I had heard, he
listened with considerable interest.

"Do you know if Hohenturn works with young Prince
Starhemberg and the home guard he is forming?"

"I do not think so, at least Marie Therese did not mention
it and well, you see—" I paused rather embarrassed—"he
only rarely speaks to me. We hardly ever meet."

"So you do not have much idea of what goes on in his
mind?"

"No, I'm afraid not."

"But have you the impression he might possibly be somewhat deranged?" I pondered this.

"Not really—a bit strange, perhaps, but certainly not
mad."

"Do you think he is any way involved with Hitler and his
gang? I hear he is often in Berlin and Munich."

"Yes, but I believe only in connection with sport. I really

do not think he would associate with a man like Hitler. Heinrich is too arrogant and proud. He would think it below his rank and dignity to do so—even if he may have accepted some of Hitler's ideas."

"He is still a monarchist, I would imagine?"

"Oh yes, I am certain of that, and as devout a Catholic as is his wife."

I noticed the slight twitch of amusement that flitted across Sir John's face before he looked down at some papers on his desk, shuffling them until he had found the one he wanted. I saw with surprise that it was in my mother's writing.

"Thanks to your mother's kind help and study of the *Almanch de Gotha* on my behalf, I find that Prince Hohenturn has enough royal blood to be eligible for the Austrian throne if there are no competitors."

"But surely Archduke Otto is the legal heir, even if in exile, should it ever come to a restoration?"

"Ascending the throne has, in past history at least, often depended more on force of arms than on legality of succession."

"Sir, I think Prince Heinrich much too loyal to the Habsburgs ever to contemplate such a thing as usurping the throne."

"Well, he might want to keep it warm for them until they return—as Regent perhaps, like Admiral Horthy in Hungary or General Franco in Spain.

"Sitting pretty, meanwhile."

"Quite so; still one can only surmise at present, but a youth organization of such size as he seems to aspire to assemble would certainly be a source of future power."

"But it is a peace organization."

"Which war has not been fought in the name of peace! However, I may be entirely wrong about Prince Hohenturn's motives and intentions. Only time will tell. In any case, I will report what he obviously wished me to, to His Majesty's Government; though I doubt they will show much interest, just as they did not even when Dollfuss was murdered," he added with some bitterness. "Well, thank you Eddie, keep me informed." I felt myself dismissed.

# Chapter Seventeen

Soon I forgot all about my interview with Sir John. Something of infinitely more personal importance to me happened. Something I had feared, dreaded and evaded for years. I met Alexander again.

I had escorted Marie Therese for the opening night of a play by Molnar in the Burg Theater. It was a light comedy in the French manner about matrimonial infidelity, the elderly husband pursuing the pretty chambermaid all through the first act. Only towards its end did his wife's lover appear on the scene. I heard Marie Therese gasp, and then audible to all the audience—she had never learned to keep her voice down in public when enthusiastic—she proclaimed loudly: "He is beautiful!"

It was Alexander. He heard her. We were sitting in the front row. He paused momentarily, glanced down and then saw me. He smiled in recognition; I sat as if frozen in my seat. Flushed with mounting excitement beside me, Marie Therese watched with avid attention the inevitable development of the play—the seduction of the wife, and then that of the chambermaid too. So did I. It seemed to me that he was playing entirely for me as he had in the past. His voice had deepened, become more musical, his diction more perfect, but the unconscious grace of his movements were still those of the slender boy I had known. He played it with such delicate understatement that it was he who seemed the guiltless, innocent victim of the two women he had seduced.

"He is absolutely marvellous," Marie Therese said in the interval, "and so young." She sighed and searched for his name in her programme. "Alexander Plevke," she told me, "an odd name for an actor to take."

An usher approached us and handed me a folded note. I had no doubt whom it was from. I hastily thrust it into my pocket.

"Herr Plevke wants an answer," the man said, waiting.

"What is it, Eddie?" she asked. "You look funny—show me that letter."

In a second she had it out of my pocket and read it. So did I, since she had spread it open on her lap.

"Eddie, darling. At last, at last! Come to my dressing-room after curtain call. Alexander."

"Tell Herr Plevke we will," she told the usher imperiously.

Thens he turned to me. "You really might have told me that you knew him," she said reproachfully, "and rather well I would think, considering this." She gave me back the note.

"Actors are always rather effusive in their way of expressing themselves. It means nothing."

"But why was it in English?"

"Well, they do have to learn languages if they are to be any good; besides, he has always spoken it. He has an English mother."

"Anyway," she said, "since he has invited you, let's go."

"I will not," I said, "and you definitely cannot go without me. As a matter of fact, not even with me. What would Heinrich say if I took you to an actor's dressing-room?"

To meet an actor I knew was socially unacceptable for an Austrian lady. Mainly, I think, because so many actresses were kept by their husbands. Vienna loved the theatre and the opera and took interest and pride in the quality of its productions, but more intimate association with the players was frowned upon.

"You don't have to tell Heinrich," Marie Therese pleaded, "after all, you tell him nothing about us either. But how does it happen that you know this Plevke?" she queried.

She will find out in the end anyway, I thought despairingly. Just as she was by nature incapable of keeping anything secret, my fondness for her made me unable to withhold from her anything she really wanted. So I told her that long ago I had tutored Alexander in a Schloss in north Germany when he was still a child.

"A Schloss!" she exclaimed. "But then he must be—"

"Indeed, *Hochwohlgeborn*," I said sourly. "A German count, if you really want to know."

"Oh I do, Eddie," her eyes had widened with delight, "then I can meet him and ask him to our house?"

"That is up to you. I do not want to see him again."

"But why?"

What could I say? "Because I was rather unhappy at Schwarzensee. I don't like to remember that time."

She looked at me closely. "Was it because you fell in love?" It was always the first thing she would think of.

"Yes," I said, then added hastily, "with his mother."

"No wonder, if she was as beautiful as he is—and her husband made difficulties?"

"No, she was a widow and now she has been happily married to an English parson for some years."

"Poor Eddie," she said, stroking my wrist. "Obviously she was not kind to you. Was she your first love?"

"In a way. Look here, I'd rather not talk about it."

"I quite understand, but surely that is no reason not to want to meet the boy again, if he was only a child."

In silence we watched the last act and Alexander's faultless performance. There was much applause and calls for "Plevke, Plevke". He bowed modestly several times, then stood proudly erect, looking directly at me and smiling, his old irresistible, triumphant smile once more.

We found him in his dressing-room. He was draped only in a towel, as he had been on that first morning after he appeared at my window in Schwarzensee and then had thrown himself on my bed. He had cleaned the greasepaint off his face which shone with the same golden lustre as in the past; so did his hair and body. He leapt up to embrace me, kissing me on both cheeks, as I suppose actors do. Embarrassed I disengaged myself hastily.

"Still the same shy old Eddie," he laughed delightedly. *"Eh bien, Harris, gentilhomme Anglais."* It was the Tsarevna that spoke in her deep booming voice once more through him. "Do you remember?"

"Everything—only too well," I said.

He shrugged his naked golden shoulder. "Is that why you never answered my letters?"

"I tried, but some things are best forgotten."

"But surely not me, Eddie," his luminous eyes pleaded. "Besides, I've changed a lot, you know, since then."

"I very much doubt it."

"Look here, I only accepted to play in Vienna because I knew you were at the Embassy here. I thought it was time we met again. It is not my kind of play but was I good, Eddie?" How often he had asked me that in the past.

"Wonderful!" Marie Therese exclaimed.

I had totally forgotten her presence and I do not think Alexander had even noticed her, because he turned as if surprised. She had sat down on a bench near the door. She wore, as was usual in Vienna on opening nights, evening dress and jewels and looked both regal and lovely.

"A friend of mine," I said, "Princess Hohenturn. She very much admired your acting and wanted to meet you."

"Oh, I am so glad." He bent and kissed her hand, tightening the towel round his waist modestly.

"Rather like the Tsarevna," he chuckled, as he turned back to me, "before she grew too old and fat."

And suddenly I knew it was true and that perhaps in embracing Marie Therese I had also embraced a memory.

"Come and join us for supper at the palace," Marie Therese said. "We can go there together now, my car is waiting."

"Thank you, Princess, but I am afraid tonight I cannot. After the opening of a play we always have a party for all the actors. Any other time, if Eddie will take me and guide me to your house as I do not know Vienna at all, having only just arrived."

"Eddie will," she said, almost fiercely.

"Gracious, it's high time I got dressed," he exclaimed, looking at his gold wrist watch. "I will call you at the Embassy tomorrow morning, Eddie."

"My chief does not like us being interrupted at work," I said.

"Oh nonsense—now that I have found you, you won't escape me any more."

Marie Therese was very silent on the drive back to the palace, did not invite me in, or suggest any prolongation of the evening. She did, however, ask me to come to tea the next day.

Arriving at my flat I found my mother still up doing a crossword puzzle.

"You are early for once," she said, looking pleased. "Where did you dine?"

"I didn't. I want to the Burg Theatre with Marie Therese."

"But then you must be hungry. There is some cold meat in the fridge if you want it."

"I would rather have a cup of coffee."

She made some and poured one for herself as well.

"Play any good?" she asked.

"Quite, since Alexander was playing."

Though her face remained impassive, I noticed the cup in her hand trembled slightly.

"Marie Therese insisted on meeting him after he had sent

me a note. He had recognized me from the stage. I could not refuse, so we went to his dressing-room. She invited him to the palace after she had wormed out of me that he was a count. There is nothing I can do about it except keep out of his way. He has not changed, at least not in looks, and his acting was superb. He was delighted to see me."

My mother was silent for a long time. "Of course, you must do as you think best," she said at last. "How long is he going to be here?"

"As long as the play is on, I suppose."

She sighed. "Have you never considered how deeply attached to you he may still be—just because of what happened at Schwarzensee? You were his only friend and protector then. And for years now you have denied him all affection, never answered his letters, never tried to meet him again. Well, now you have—and if you cannot at least compromise and feign friendship, even if you do not feel it, there may be disastrous consequences."

"But what do you mean, Mother? What harm could he possibly do me even if he wanted to?"

"I don't know. But then neither did anyone ever know what Tsar Alexander the First, whom he so closely resembles, would do to his friends or enemies. It was always a surprise and not always a pleasant one. Your Alexander is just as brilliant an actor as he was, so be on your guard."

Had I only needed her warning. Next day at the Embassy, while I was with Sir John, a blushing girl secretary came into the room, apologized, and said there was an urgent call for me from a gentleman called Alexander Plevke, would I take it? I refused to do so, saying I was working.

My ambassador looked at me with some surprise. "Really, Eddie," he said, "I can very easily spare you for a minute or two or even longer. All the papers are full of this young actor's performance—obviously he must be a friend of yours. He is half English, I gather, Eton and Oxford and all that. I would rather like to meet him myself. Do ask him to the next of our tiresome receptions."

The same day I went to the palace for tea, to find Marie Therese's small private sitting-room so full of roses that one could scarcely move about and their scent so overpoweringly strong that one could not breathe freely either. Some were in bud, some had unfolded into full bloom and I knew their fragrant pink lushness resembled that of Marie Therese.

"What's happened? Surely it's not your birthday?"

"Oh no," she said, dimples marking her cheeks enchantingly. "It's that beautiful young actor friend of yours. Generous, isn't he? I have been sent as many roses afterwards, but never before."

"Before what?"

She had the grace to blush slightly. "Before dinner, of course. I have invited him for tonight. Heinrich is here and wanted very much to meet him. Imagine, the boy's father, Count Paul Plevke served in the same regiment in Germany as did Heinrich—we looked it up. You are asked too, Eddie. Alexander said he would be too shy to come without you."

"Said? Have you spoken to him since last night?"

"But of course. How could I have invited him otherwise? I asked the secretariat to find out where he was living. He is at the Sacher—for a young actor he must be very well off." She looked at me questioningly.

"I really wouldn't know," I lied—then added—"Look here, I can't possibly come tonight. I have to work late on some dispatches that have to go in tomorrow's bag."

"But Eddie, I promised you would be here. Please don't fail me when I need your help!"

"For what?" I asked bitterly. "You seem to be managing quite well on your own."

She touched me appeasingly but it neither reassured nor stirred me and I left her abruptly—none of the usual tea-time diversions enjoyed.

For the next weeks I did not hear from her. Obviously she was offended. No more telephone calls in the morning to plan for afternoons or nights out. Neither did Alexander contact me. Had he understood at last that I did not want him to re-enter my life! I should have been relieved but all I felt was fear. If I had managed to be rid of him, what about Marie Therese? She had been unfaithful to me before and probably would be so again, and I had learnt not to mind, since it was usually with young men of her own society and to me they seemed somehow of as little account as I was to them. But Alexander? I suffered pangs of jealousy I had thought myself immune to.

Meanwhile the invitations for what Sir John called the "Annual Wash Up" had been sent out. Many hundreds. To the Hohenturns too, of course. But members of the Austrian aristocracy rarely came to our Embassy receptions.

"Darling," Marie Therese had explained to me, "I really can't! Your champagne is always too warm and your food too cold. And besides, who would want to meet the sort of people you invite? Dusty intellectuals with their frumpy wives, shopkeepers and Jews and politicians. Not to mention members of our own present government, totally uneducated and uncivilized peasants. Still, I prefer them to someone like Schuschnigg, a bourgeois intellectual even if he did marry a cousin of mine. And after both had been divorced too!" I knew by then now she felt about divorce and remarriage.

"My ambassador likes and admires Herr von Schuschnigg very much," I remembered having said.

"A weak man always trying to compromise."

"A brave man, since it can't be very easy for a patriotic Austrian to deal with Hitler."

"Well, Heinrich seems to manage."

"I often wonder why and how? They can't have very much in common."

"Darling, surely you being English should understand. We lost our empire piece by piece after the war, now you too are losing yours. We want to re-create ours in all its former glory. The Holy Roman Empire."

"Under Hitler?"

"No, of course not!" she had exclaimed indignantly. "But he has his uses for the moment, rather like John the Baptist preparing the way for the Saviour."

"And who will that be?"

"A noble ruler elected by the young, for theirs is the future," she had declared sententiously.

So I knew I would not see Marie Therese at our reception and had not expected Alexander to come without her. Enough kind friends had pointed out to me that they had become inseparable and that he had been seen escorting her to dances and nightclubs, as I had in the past.

After I had greeted Sir John, shaken hands with various diplomats and Austrians, I went in search of my mother, finally to find her in a small, remote drawing-room talking to Alexander. They were sitting together and very closely so on a sofa. He was resplendent in white tie and tails, she modestly but as always suitably dressed for her age in a gown of grey—chiffon I think it was—and wearing her pearls, the large beaded bag without which she never went out in the evenings on her lap. It contained, as I knew, neither money nor cosmetics but a pad of writing paper and a pencil in case she wanted to make a quick and surreptitious note of something that had aroused her interest.

It was Aleander who saw me first.

"Oh, Eddie!" he exclaimed, his eyes sparkling with wicked amusement, I felt. "It seems extraordinary that this is only the first time I have met your charming mother. We have found so much to talk about, mainly you of course and Schwarzensee. She told me she had been to see it and she knows all about my family's strange history."

I gave my mother an angry look, muttered something about having to see to the guests and rudely stalked out.

After talking to various friends I saw how late it had become and went in search of my chief. I found him with Schuschnigg: a tall, thin, distinguished-looking man.

"Sir John, have I your permission to take my mother home? It's after two, most of the guests have left."

"I had no idea it was so late," Schuschnigg said. "I enjoyed our talk, Sir John, and I am grateful for your advice." He bowed and left.

"Really, Eddie, was it polite to chuck out the Chancellor?" But he looked more relieved than angry. "I am weary," he said, "of trying to solve unsolvable problems. By the way, I met that young actor friend of yours—your mother introduced him to me. What a combination of physical beauty and intellect, it does so seldom go together. Well, it probably won't last—one will eventually destroy the other. Take your mother home, Eddie, she must be exhausted. Thank her for all her help this evening."

"Quite a good party, didn't you think, and the buffet somewhat better than usual. Did you try the fresh liver pâté? My recipe—I lent it to the cook," my mother said in the taxi. For a while she talked on, remarking on this and that aspect of the evening and then, because I barely answered, fell silent.

But on arrival at our flat I confronted her. "So you have fallen for Alexander too!"

"Fallen?" she smiled. "What inappropriate language you use. I thought the word was only applicable to a certain unfortunate kind of woman."

But I was not to be so easily diverted. "And you thought him irresistible, I suppose?"

"Well, he is! But then so was Alexander the First."

"A murderer, too!"

"If it's the Tsar you are speaking of he was only indirectly guilty and, even because of that, was later to suffer years of remorse."

"That is one thing Alexander will never feel. He has no conscience," I exclaimed.

I wouldn't be so sure of that. You behaved very foolishly tonight," she said. "It was unnecessary to be so rude to him."

"I had my reasons."

"Yes, I suppose so. I can think of several." She passed her hand through her close-cropped grey curls as she did when she pondered for the right word when writing or solving one of her puzzles.

Then, as if she had come to a sudden decision, she opened her evening bag and, to my amazement, took out the Tsarevna's golden box.

"He asked me to return this to you. I suppose he wanted to give it to you himself, but when you walked out so abruptly he handed it to me instead, saying you would understand."

I looked at the lovely object, the diamonds sparkling coldly like icicles, the emeralds winking like small evil green eyes, and at the untarnishable gold that still shone so warm and alive.

I shuddered. Its message was clear. Had Marie Therese just given it to him, I wondered, only because he asked for it; as readily as she gave herself? Or had he told her that it had once belonged to his family and that he wanted it back? Or had he simply taken it from beside her bed?

Perhaps my mother read some of my thoughts. "You should not have hurt his pride by denying him your friendship. For what else can he think now—than that you have evaded him so long because of what happened at Schwarzensee? No one likes to be reminded of past guilt. Yours, Eddie, was greater than his—as he must know. He was a child, you a grown man. If his beauty seduced you into weakness and crime, was it not you who seduced him first, if indirectly, into committing it?"

"*Werd ich zum Augenblicke sagen Verbleibe doch, Du bist so schoen, dann darst Du mich in Ketten schlagen, dann will ich gern zugrunde gehen.*" I remembered he and I quoting blissfully together from Goethe's *Faust* so long ago at Schwartzensee. But the chains had become mine, not his.

Mercilessly my mother continued. "Don't you realize that by having evaded him for so many years you have merely been trying to escape your own guilt?"

I knew it was true.

"You didn't speak like that," I nevertheless protested, bitterly resentful of her knowledge, "when I first told you the whole sorry tale! You said I should forget and that I was not to blame myself."

"I thought it best at the time. I don't now, because obviously you have never been able to do so." She laid her hand on mine in one of her rare gestures of physical tenderness and I felt how much I was still the child to her that she had loved and cherished, encouraged and sustained, far beyond the financial sacrifices my schooling and university had cost her. I owed her everything.

And when she said, gently but firmly, "Try to make it up with Alexander, forgive yourself and him at last," almost imploringly, I knew that was what I had to do and said I would telephone Alexander the next day.

However I overslept and had to hurry to the Embassy and only at noon was I free to call the Sacher Hotel. It was too late. They told me Alexander had left and that they did not know his address.

But how could he leave if the play was still running, I asked myself? I telephoned the Burg Theatre and was assured it was still on.

"And Alexander Plevke?" He needed a rest, his understudy had taken his place for the present, was the only information I got.

What on earth could have happened? Was he ill? I knew I must call Marie Therese; surely she would know. I was told, "The Prince and the Princess have left this morning by plane for Schloss Hohenturn."

"And did Count Plevke go with them?"

"Yes."

"How long will they be away."

"A couple of weeks, I think. The *Hirschbrunft* has started," the secretary said.

So that was it.

Last autumn it had been me Heinrich had honoured, by inviting me to shoot a stag. I had gladly accepted, hoping it would give me more opportunity to be with Marie Therese than I usually had, and I was right. I even managed to get a stag, thanks to her calling me a cissy and laughing so heartily when I confessed to my squeamishness about killing animals that in my anger I shot the poor brute dead.

Hohenturn was in Czechoslovakia in the Sudeten mountains, a turreted neo-gothic castle that looked rather like Balmoral. It was surrounded by dense forests through which I had stalked stags every morning with a gamekeeper; whereas in the evenings Marie Therese would have us driven by car to as near one of the platformed stands as was possible—she hated walking—and there, screened by fragrant pine branches, we would make love while the stags roared their primeval challenge through the autumn-tinted forest.

Of Heinrich I had seen little. "Doesn't he shoot?" I had asked.

"But of course. But only at our big shoots when we have a lot of guests. He hasn't time for the *Pütsch*. We don't come here very often and when we do he has to see to the estate. It is immense, you know, and we are responsible for the upkeep of the villages and churches on it and for their repair."

For dinner Heinrich had usually joined us wearing a green velvet smoking jacket. The food had been good and plentiful, so was the wine. Marie Therese, if she did not bother much about anything else, saw to that. Conversation was very much more frugal than our meals. She made no effort to enchant and amuse as she did in Vienna, when she had an admiring audience of worshippers around her; perhaps because her husband had heard it all before; perhaps because she was too hungry and tired after so many hours in the fresh air. She only opened her mouth to eat or yawn.

Except for polite enquiries as to my shooting prowess, how many stags had I seen and so on, and occasional remarks about the weather, Heinrich did not speak much either. My few efforts to raise the conversation to a level of what was of interest to me, Austrian politics and the danger of the German-oriented National Socialists taking over, brought no response.

You know, Eddie, we never discuss politics in our society," Marie Therese warned me next day. "It's too boring!"

"Well then, what should I talk about? Literature, art, music? Neither you nor Heinrich would, I imagine, be interested in any of those subjects either?"

"No, of course not. That is as bad as politics."

"But why?"

"Because," she said, with one of her usual flashes of perception, "we have been steeped in the arts for so many centuries and all of it was created for us in the past under our patronage and guidance and that of the Church. Well, who wants to be reminded that that is all over? And it's the same with politics. We have no power to influence events either any more. So we just live from day to day and try to forget the past. It is not that we don't care, we still care too much,

especially Heinrich. All the more does he dislike an Englishman like you, who after all can't possibly understand much
about our arts or politics, talking about them."

After that I did not even try. After dinner Heinrich read
the papers sitting by the fire, his long elegant green-clad legs
stretched out, and Marie Therese and I played dominoes, the
frequent contact of our hands more important than joining
the stones correctly. Stalking next morning gave me a welcome excuse to go to bed early.

Now, just a year later, Alexander had taken my place—no
doubt enjoying the shooting more than I had, since he was so
adept at it, and probably also Marie Therese.

I did not like to think about it—if my resolution to befriend him once more was to stay firm.

# Chapter Eighteen

I missed Marie Therese as week after week passed. Every night I came home early, disturbing my mother who had started to write a book of her own after the success of my father's *Life of the Tsars*. Its subject was Rudolph the Second, a Habsburg Emperor of extreme eccentricity and very esoteric tastes as far as I could make out. I paced our rooms restlessly. I played the gramophone; Strauss waltzes that so nostalgically recalled Marie Therese. I tried to read and could not and drank half a bottle of whisky every night.

If only she returned I knew I must forgive her. But would Alexander give her back to me, as he had the golden box, I wondered?

Then one morning at breakfast my mother looked up from the Viennese paper she had been studying. Her German had become quite good but she still had difficulties in reading it.

"Perhaps you had better look at this," she said. Then I saw how pale her face was.

"What's wrong?" I asked. "Has Hitler declared war on us? Mother, what's the matter?" I repeated, now deeply concerned as I saw tears gathering in her eyes. But she left the room without answering.

I scanned the headlines.

"*Near death of famous actor!* Graf Alexander Plevke, who was a guest at Schloss Hohenturn in the Sudeten, was seriously hurt in an accidental fire that destroyed a nearby villa belonging to the rich industrialist, Herr Koritschoner. In a heroic effort to save the lives of the old couple who were alone in the house. Graf Plecke fought his way through the flames, but it was too late. Both Koritschoners are dead. When other help finally came, Plevke was seen running from the house, a flaming torch from head to foot. When he could be approached he was found to be mercifully unconscious, but miraculously still alive. He was carried to Schloss Hohenturn, where the village doctor did for him what he could and he was then flown to Vienna by the Prince himself in his plane, the Falcon.' He is now being cared for in Dr. Koritschoner's private clinic. By a strange and tragic coincidence, the famous plastic surgeon is the brother of Herr Koritschoner who died in the fire. We wish heroic Count Plevke rapid recovery."

I re-read it once more; only then did the full horror of it penetrate beyond the socially chatty and sensational.

I sat and stared out of the window at some sparrow for whom my mother had spread crumbs on the sill. "Not a sparrow falls . . ."

I knocked at my mother's door. She opened it immediately. Her face was still very pale but calm and composed. "I've looked up the telephone number of Dr Koritschoner's clinic," she said.

"Give me the address. I must go there immediately. It's the least I can do for the sake of Alexander's mother and the Tsarevna."

"Or for his? Eddie, he may already be dead. Let me telephone," she said. "I have every excuse. I will use the Embassy as authorizing me, an Englishwoman, to be told the truth. After all, we will have to let his mother know one way or another and I can honestly say that she has been my neighbour at home for many years."

She went downstairs to telephone in the hall.

"I couldn't speak to Dr Koritschoner," she said when she returned, "but the matron was quite obliging and seemed grateful I had enquired. He is still alive! She thought there would be no use in sending for his mother since he is unconscious and even the slightest disturbance or emotion might wake him into a state of shock, which he could not survive.

"Absolute quiet and no visitors, the matron said, is his only chance now. Be reassured—he is in good care. In a couple of days we will know more."

"Did you ask how bad his burns were?"

My mother hesitated, then squared her shoulders. "Yes— third degree mostly. He will need skin-grafts and probably some bonegrafts too." With difficulty she forced herself to continue: "They don't know as yet how much brain damage he may have suffered after having been unconscious for so long. Nor if he will ever speak again—his vocal cords are, it seems, totally destroyed. Also he may be blind. Well, that is all."

"It's enough," I said.

"Oh, the pity of it!" my mother exclaimed and then, losing all composure, buried her face in her hands and sobbed. I had not seen her cry like that since my father's death. Could I only permit myself the same relief, I thought.

The telephone rang. I went downstairs and took it. It was Heinrich Hohenturn. "You will have heard," he said. "A tragic accident."

"Yes."

"Poor boy. He was so handsome. Well—Koritschoner will probably patch him up. But what foolish bravura to rush into a burning house to rescue two old Jews who were probably dead already."

"Yes."

"Hello? Are you still there? By some chance he was the first to see the fire—we were all asleep. And even if we had not been, there are so many bonfires in the hills at this time of year it would have been mistaken for one."

Why was he telling me all this, I wondered, in that cold, impassive tone of voice.

"The local police have fully established the accident happened because of a faulty chimney. Unfortunately, the Koritschoner's servants lived in separate cottages in the grounds of the villa and only saw the fire when it was too late."

Then, somewhat impatient, "Look here, Eddie, what is over is over. I've called you only because Marie Therese has totally collapsed. I need your help. She won't even eat."

"That is indeed ominous," I said, glad I had the strength left to match his hateful callousness at least with irony.

"She asked me to fly you to Hohenturn, so please be at the airport punctually tomorrow at half past eight and ask to be taken to the 'Falcon's hangar where I'll be waiting. That's an order!"

What right had he to order me about, even if Marie Therese had?

"If my ambassador gives me leave—I'll have to ask him first."

"No doubt you are not as indispensable to him as you seem to have become to Marie Therese." But there was neither reproach nor accusation in his level tone of voice, rather the contrary, then it suddenly warmed into, "Come on, old boy, we all have certain responsibilities."

"If I can I will be at the airport tomorrow," I said. "If it is impossible I will let you know, after I have seen Sir John."

I hung up. A feeble gesture of futile defiance, I thought. If Marie Therese needed me, of course I had to go.

My chief, after having looked at me closely, his dark un-English eyes as inscrutable as those of Orientals, granted me leave.

"It seems your young friend will survive," he said. "I called the clinic."

"Better he should not," I said. "What has he left?"

"Only I think the unknown source from which such courage springs," Sir John remarked. "I'm sorry, I know how you feel." How could this cold ascetic old spinster of a man, detached from all human passion, understand? And yet I knew he did. The moment passed.

Resuming his usual manner he said: "There are some aspects of the tragedy that might be worth looking into more closely. Keep your eyes and ears open once you are in Hohenturn. The Sudeten too is becoming a hothouse of rapidly growing unrest, thanks to Herr Hitler, and these unfortunate people were Jews."

"But surely, sir, you can't think there is any connection?"

"Probably not. But I will want a full report of not only what you hear in the castle but also in the surrounding districts. You can walk, can't you? Take a rucksack with you; act as if you were a British tourist."

"British?"

"Well, why not? Your German accent is not perfect."

I knew his was. Somewhat nettled I took my leave.

Next morning early I left for the airport. My mother had packed all I might need, including my old rucksack.

"*Coraggio,*" she said, trying to smile. "*Avanti Savoia!*" recalling happier days in Rome in a feeble effort to humour.

But when our eyes met we knew that there was no laughter left for us both for a long time.

The "Falcon" was a small private plane. Heinrich was already sitting in the cockpit wearing goggles and a kind of helmet. "Here—" he threw me some similar equipment—"put your suitcase in the back and climb up beside me. I'm ready to take off."

Once in the air I was grateful that I had brought a heavy coat. I had never been in an open plane before and in spite of the transparent shield in front that gave some protection, the pressure of what seemed like gale-force wind roaring in my ears and pressing against my uncovered mouth deafened me and left me speechless.

We circled partially over Vienna. Soon the Stephansdom with its tall spire grew as small as a toy. Even the curving Danube, never blue but brown, shrank to the size of a small snake as we gained altitude. It was the last landmark I recognized. Then forested hills and green valleys, plains, golden with the stubble left after the harvest. Towns and villages only faintly discernible as the "Falcon" rose higher and higher. Then we were among white clouds, shining and radiant like angels' wings, followed by dense menacing black ones. Finally they intermingled as if in a great silent battle, then the white ones, victorious, floated triumphantly free into the clearing sky.

I looked at Heinrich. Only so slightly did his hands rest on the controls that I wondered if planes, once airborne, fly themselves. Perhaps he felt my gaze, because he turned and to my surprise smiled. I remembered how rarely he laughed or even condescended to smile. What transformed his arrogant mouth now was an expression of proud satisfaction, certainly not intended for me but presumably due to his skill as a pilot and the performance of his plane. Or perhaps even more. Mighty not one be tempted to feel like the all-seeing Almighty, so far above the earth?

We plunged quite suddenly and unexpectedly. My stomach heaved and I thought my eardrums would burst.

I did not even have time to wonder if this was death before we were skimming over mountains at tree-top height and had landed quite gently in a narrow valley with the crenellated towers of Schloss Hohenturn in sight.

"Do you feel all right?" Heinrich asked, after we had climbed out of the plane and had taken off our goggles. "There was quite a lot of turbulence in the lower regions so I had to climb rather high and descend a bit abruptly."

"It took my breath away," I managed tò gasp and then saw that he, too, seemed to have some difficulty in breathing and that his face was pale and his lips rather blue. The cold, I thought; but then, in the car which had been waiting for us, he took out a small bottle and swallowed some pills. I remembered Marie Therese having told me he had a weak heart and of having heard that flying at high altitudes could, under such circumstances, be dangerous.

And high indeed we had flown. I realized with shocked surprise that in the brief hours of our flight I had neither thought of Alexander nor Marie Therese for one moment. I had experienced such strange detachment from all earthly matters as I had only known at sea; seemingly the air gave the same relief from all mundane preoccupations.

"Now about Marie Therese," Heinrich said. Both his colour and breathing had, I saw with relief, returned to normal. "I must leave her in your care for a couple of days. I have to by back to Vienna this afternoon."

He must have noticed the anxiety I suddenly felt for him, because whatever he was, he was a brave man and if he really had a bad heart he was pushing himself beyond reason.

"It was merely some indigestion tablets that I took. Nevertheless, these days have been somewhat strenuous. I am flying back with one of our young local pilots I have trained, so don't worry. But about Marie Therese—what happened has of course shocked her. She had grown very fond of Alexander. So had I. I had plans for him. Well, it's too late now. I will be busy here for some hours," he said, "then I am off again. You know the house—make yourself at home."

If familiar, there was nothing homelike about the castle. Though its exterior, seen from a distance, was at least impressive and convincing, even if most of its outer walls had been constructed of cement, its semi-medieval interior was not. The castle had been built on the site of a former one that had fallen into ruins. Heinrich had inherited it from his uncle who had built and decorated it according to his tastes.

There was a galleried *Rittersaal,* full indeed of ancient armour and family portraits, but that was all that was authentic in it. The stained-glass windows with their inset coats of arms were modern and so were the frescoes, imitating tapestries, on which an artist had depicted in the most garish colours courtly life of medieval days, neither certain of the dress of that time nor the correct proportions of the human body.

The adjoining chapel too was elaborately painted and decorated, if with more religious motifs, by the same artist.

In total contrast was the little private theatre with pseudo-rococo décor, brightly gilt, with red velvet curtaining and seats. It was almost a replica of one of Vienna's smaller night-clubs. Perhaps intentionally, because the ageing prince had built it so the singers and dancers could entertain him at home without his having to travel.

There were several drawing-rooms curtained and hung with either green, yellow or pink damask, the furniture covered in the same material, and many pictures perhaps of merit but so darkened by age and neglect that only an expert eye could have discerned their value.

The footman took me to my room. It was the one I had occupied a year before. It was small and papered in dark green. A large print above the bed depicted Christ expiring on the Cross and the other walls were ornamented—as the passages in Schwarzensee had been—with antlers, horns and the tusks of long-dead animals. It was a depressing room that had only had one advantage; an adjoining winding iron staircase led up into the passage on to which Marie Therese's apartment opened.

"Did Graf Plevke sleep here?" I asked the servant.

"But of course. It is the room always given to unmarried young gentlemen. We have just packed his luggage for His Highness to take back with him to Vienna."

"Did they bring Count Plevke here after the accident?" I managed to ask, looking at the bed in which whatever was left of Alexander may have lain writhing in agony only a day ago.

"Oh no, His Highness flew him straight to Vienna on a stretcher. If I might presume to enquire, sir," he added, "since you come from Vienna, is there any hope? Such a charming young gentleman and so handsome, generous and so brave."

"He is still alive," I said, "that is all I know."

"Oh thank God. We feared he would not survive the flight." Why was his smile of relief so unconvincing?

"How did it happen that only he noticed the fire?" I asked, as casually as I could.

"The young Herr Graf must have gone out for a stroll after the party. Some of us were still clearing in the house and saw nothing and the Herrschaften had gone to bed. It was after two o'clock. But here I am talking when I should bring the Herr his breakfast," and he hurried out of the room—to return some minutes later with a heavy-laden tray.

"Her Highness would like to see you as soon as possible," he then said. "She is in her bedroom."

Hastily I gulped some coffee, but eat I knew I could not. How I dreaded what was awaiting me, yet it had to be faced and the sooner the better.

I found Marie Therese's maid seated in the anteroom of the apartment. She rose as I entered and laid down some sewing. I knew her, of course, having often seen her but except for "good morning" or "good evening" we had never spoken. She was a stern-looking woman with sparse white hair and a face as if carved in wood by some primitive artist.

"You wouldn't think she was my milk-sister by her looks and manner," Marie Therese had laughingly once said.

Seeing her puzzled expression: "We were fed from the same breast—her mother was my wetnurse. I always think I must have taken all the cream and left her only sour milk. But she is a devoted and loyal servant and has been with me ever since we grew up." I recalled my astonishment then, when I had realized that she and the aged maid must have been born in the same year.

"How is Her Highness?" I asked.

She did not answer but just opened the door, standing well back to let me pass, then closed it firmly behind me. I was alone with Marie Therese. She lay in her chintz-hung brass bed. Though I dreaded to, I approached it—but what came then was infinitely more horrible than anything I had feared. I had expected tears and despair, but not a smiling woman who stretched out her naked arms to me.

"Hold me, Eddie, please hold me. I've been so miserable for weeks and now I am ill." Then I saw her face more clearly as it emerged from the shading curtains. It seemed to have lost its former firm contours, to have shrunk and withered and crumpled like a dead flower.

Only pity compelled me to bend and kiss her brow, smoothing back her tangled matted hair. Beneath the auburn curls grey roots showed.

"You are all I have left now," she whispered, as I gently laid her back on her pillows. "Alexander's gone and it is all your fault."

What could she mean?

Then a change of light from the only partially-curtained window revealed her eyes, large and golden-brown as before, except for pupils shrunk to mere pinpoints. I realized then that the effect of the drugs that they had given her had not worn off and that she probably did not know what she was doing or saying.

Hating myself for it, nevertheless I asked: "Why my fault?" It was too vital a question for me to spare her an answer.

"Because you were his friend and when he saw the golden box in my bedroom he knew, of course, that you loved me and I couldn't deny it. So I gave it to him to prove that I loved him more. Forgive me, Eddie!"

"And then?"

"Oh, Eddie, I'm so tired. Nothing—he came here with us,

shot stags with Heinrich, play-acted in our theatre for Heinrich's boys and now he's gone."

"So you were not lovers?"

"No, but I will still win him, you'll see. I always get what I want in the end. But oh, why do I feel so ill and confused now? If only Dr Kortischoner were here! Why hasn't he come? Heinrich promised he would send him."

Did she then know nothing of what had happened?

"Will I die?"

"But what nonsense, Marie Therese. You are perfectly well. You have had a shock, that's all, it will pass." In my effort to reassure her I had said the most disastrous thing I could.

She sprang up in bed, her nightgown falling away from her breasts.

"A shock, what do you mean?" Then she giggled. "Of course, I was cross and upset when the gamekeepers suddenly carried a skinned charred deer into the hall instead of into the kitchen or larder. It was a disgusting sight. I asked them to take it away and then—someone said, yes someone said—" Her eyes widened and she screamed again and again. Her maid was by her side instantly. She held the tousled head and poured something into the horribly gaping mouth, then laid Marie Therese back into the pillows and gently tucked the sheets around her.

"Go now," she whispered to me. "I will meet you outside when she is asleep."

It took only minutes until she joined me in the anteroom.

"What did you tell Her Highness?" she asked, looking at me severely. "The doctor said she must not be excited in any way."

"All I said was that she wasn't ill but only had had a shock."

"Oh, you should not have reminded her of what she must forget if she is to remain sane. Not even as a child could she bear to look at a broken doll. She is so tender-hearted."

"But surely she will have to know the truth in time?"

"Better she believed Count Plevke dead. She is religious, her faith would give her the strength to bear that. She could pray for his soul and forget what happened to his body."

"He may indeed not live."

"Well, that would surely be best for her and for him," she said drily. "Dr Koritschoner will be here tomorrow, so His Highness telephoned to say. He will have to decide what she can stand being told. She knows nothing about the fire, you see, and the death of his relations. We have kept all that from her. Go now, she will not wake for hours after the medicine I gave her and, if she should, I will be here."

I went back to my room, saw the breakfast tray had been removed and my bed made. I had only one urge left, to get out of the castle and breathe some fresh air.

■

I shouldered my rucksack and walked into the hazy sunshine of a cold crisp autumn day. There must have been a night frost, the ground felt hard under my feet.

I walked fast, in fact I almost ran as if in so doing I could escape my thoughts—but it was no use. I still seemed to see Alexander's beautiful mischievously-smiling face as it had confronted me last at the Embassy party. He had known he would win me back one way or another. His returning the golden box had only been a subtle warning of his power over Marie Therese should he wish to take her from me, and he had not.

Well, she was mine once more, untouched by him. She had been of no value to him except in connection with me. I knew that then for certain; and also that I would never want her again myself either.

Pity for her I could still feel, but not desire.

I thought of his last and final act of reckless heroism. Had he wanted to prove to himself and perhaps to me that, even if he had taken a life so many years ago, he was now willing to risk his own to save those of others? I remembered my mother's warning not to remind him of his guilt by denying him my friendship. Was it I who had destroyed him? To what purpose his life now; voiceless, sightless, horribly disfigured? Better dead; I repeated what the maid had said and I too hoped he would die.

I walked on. I knew the surroundings of Hohenturn well and suddenly realized where I was, close to where the Koritschoner's chalet-type villa with its fretted wooden balconies and gay display of flowers had stood. Now all there was left was one lone chimney, some blackened foundations and a mass of charred timber, some of it still smouldering. A uniformed policeman barred my way as I tried to approach the ruins. *"Es ist verboten,"* he said.

"Why?" I asked in German.

"Too dangerous," he said. "It might flame up once more."

"How did it happen?"

"They think the chimney caught fire."

I looked at it. It was the only part of the house that still stood intact. Perhaps he noticed my unbelieving expression. He was a young man with a pleasant open face, Germanic as to build, features and colouring.

"But then these wooden houses catch fire so easily. It might have been a spark carried by the wind. It was *Allerheiligen* when there are bonfires and fireworks all through our mountains."

I then remembered the date. It had indeed been the night of Hallowe'en.

"I am staying at the Schloss. The young Englishman who tried to save the unfortunate owners of the house was a friend of mine."

"I'm sorry," he said. "Will he live?"

So he knew. "Probably not," I said. "How was it that only he saw the fire?"

He looked down, kicking a stone. "I don't know," he said. "Many things can be seen from the height of Hohenturn which are not seen in our valleys. In any case he was too late, the old Jews must have died in their sleep long before he tried to save them. What was left of them is in the mortuary now."

He gave me a cheerful smile and I knew he would say no more. He lifted his hand in the Hitler salute.

"*Grüss Gott,*" I called back as I started on the road that I knew would take me to the nearest village. I saw he was staring after me, a puzzled and perhaps suspicious expression on his young face.

I walked for another mile and reached the village. Welltended houses and small neat gardens ablaze with dahlias and chrysanthemums. I was hungry and thirsty and entered what was obviously the local inn. The taproom was empty. I looked at my watch—it was two o'clock. No doubt the landlord was having his afternoon nap. Nevertheless I knocked on the counter. After a while a squarely-built elderly man appeared. His wide, high-cheek-boned face, above all his eyes, small, dark and somewhat furtive, proclaimed his Slavonic origin.

He looked me up and down, at my rucksack, my flannel trousers and duffel coat.

"What do you want?" he asked gruffly.

"A glass of beer, please, and if possible something to eat. I am on a walking tour."

"Indeed," he said. "One does not expect foreign tourists at this time of year. You are English, are you not?" He poured me a beaker of frothing Pilsen.

"Yes," I admitted.

"Would bacon and eggs do?" he then said to my surprise in quite good English.

"I would be grateful!"

"I will just tell the wife."

When he returned he sat down at the table beside me.

"How does it come that you speak English?" I asked.

"I learnt it from my children, helping them with their homework. An English lady gave them lessons. They are grown up now. My eldest son is doing well in America and the younger one is at the university in Prague."

"You are Czech?"

"Yes, though my wife is Sudeten German."

"Won't you have a beer on me?" I asked.

"Thank you, not at this hour. It's too early or too late, like most things in life."

A buxom woman with a face that must once have been pretty came in carrying a tray which she placed before me. *"Guten appetit,"* she said. I thanked her though her encouragement was quite unnecessary. I was very hungry.

"I wouldn't have thought they fed you so little at the Schloss," the landlord said, watching me eat.

The fork nearly dropped from my hand.

"Don't let it perturb you. It is part of my job to know what goes on here," and his small eyes narrowed with amusement. "But why make yourself out to be a tourist?"

I thought it was best to be honest.

"Because I hoped to gather some information which I don't think would be given me if it was known I came from the Schloss. It's about the accident," I added. "You see, Count Plevke was a great friend of mine. He is very ill now and may die. It's for his sake and for his English mother's sake that I must know what really happened."

"But surely they told you at the Schloss?"

"The Princess has had a great shock and is ill. She doesn't even know that there was a fire and she believes Count Plevke had to leave suddenly for Vienna."

"And the Prince?"

"He told me the same as the policeman did who guards

what is left of the villa; that a chimney must have caught fire
and that the old people probably died in their sleep. He did
what he could for my friend, flew him straight to Vienna.
Count Plevek is now in Dr Koritschoner's clinic."

"Are you a detective?" he suddenly asked.

"No, of course not. What makes you think so?"

"Because Mrs Koritschoner was English by birth certain
aspects of the tragedy might have been thought worth investigating. The Koritschoners were very wealthy."

The sudden directness of his at first rather shifting and
evasive gaze startled me.

I knew I had to tell the truth. "I am an attaché at the
British Embassy in Vienna."

He evidently pondered this. "And whatever I might tell
you, how far would it go?"

"If it was of political importance I would have to report it
to my ambassador, but he is neither indiscreet nor talkative.
Otherwise I can give you my word that whatever you can tell
me will go no further."

"Your word as an Englishman?"

"Yes."

He went and bolted the pub's entrance and sat down again
beside me.

"Please understand that what I will tell you might cost me
my livelihood here, or even my life, since I am a Czech.
They might choose to set fire to my inn any day, as they did
to the Koritschoners' villa, if they believed I had become an
informer.

"It was arson, of course, and deliberate murder."

"But who on earth would do such a terrible thing as to
burn two old people to death in their beds?"

"They were not in their beds. What was left of their bodies
was found near the window of the top floor, where their bedrooms were, from which they must have called for help in
vain except for your actor friend who heard and saw them,
but by then all the ground floor must have been aflame. He
himself tried to reach them, but it was too late and the boys
who had started the fire, terrified at what they had done, escaped."

"Boys? Have they since been arrested?"

"But no, what would be the good? They are children,
mostly all under age and naturally their families, even if they
suspect the truth, will reveal nothing."

"But how do you know all this?"

"Because my wife's nephew was one of the gang. I forced him to confess. He is quite a good lad really and was frightened and upset. He said none of them had known the house was occupied, which is probably true. The Koritschoners have of late mainly lived in Prague and only came here for occasional week-ends. Those youngsters were only partially guilty; the real guilt lies somewhere else."

He wiped his forehead. I saw he was sweating.

"If I tell you all this it is for Mrs Koritschoner's sake, who saw to it that my sons got a good education. She was a very kind and charitable lady. The couple were well liked in this district, before things changed. Suddenly it was remembered that they were Czechs and Jews, and said to have exploited poor Sudeten Germans by whose sweated labour, in the three textile mills they owned, the Koritschoners had enriched themselves. Now no doubt the factories will pass into German hands."

"Had they no children."

"Only one daughter—she lives in Vienna. Probably she will be glad to sell out after what happened here." he shrugged his broad shoulders. "Often I feel like doing the same and returning to Prague, but all my wife's family—to which she is much attached—lives around here and this inn is her inheritance. I would have to start all over again and probably without her. Living here is not easy these days, at least not for a Czech, thanks to Hitler and his stooge, Konrad Henlein."

Sympathetic as I felt about his problems, I did not want him to diverge from a subject that was of greater interest to me.

"And so you think someone told the boys to burn down the Koritschoners' villa?"

He hesitated. "Not in so many words I believe, but there was a big rally at the Schloss that night. Prince Hohenturn, whenever he is here, has these gatherings of youths. He does a lot for them in our lands as I hear he also does abroad. They call themselves the Young Falcons. Well, this was a rather special occasion. Count Plevke recited in the theatre parts out of Schiller's and Goethe's plays. I am not a very educated man but I've read some of them. It's rousing stuff. Also I hear much beer was drunk. The boys, intoxicated by words as well as drink, only left the castle after midnight planning to make a bonfire before they went home, so my nephew says. A servant gave them two cans of fuel to light it with. They then thought it more fun to burn down a Jewish house instead.

"Even if anyone had noticed the fire it would have been thought just one of many in the hills that night. Only your young friend the actor, perhaps suspicious by something he had heard or seen, went out to investigate. You know the rest."

We stared at each other in silence. "I have your word as an Englishman?" he asked once more.

Since he believed it was as binding as I knew it would have to be; I said: "You have. Thank you for your confidence." We shook hands. His gripped mine with such force that I winced.

To ask for my bill seemed somewhat of an anticlimax. He must have felt the same. "It's on the house," he said then, his small eyes twinkling with sudden laughter, "it's so rarely we see a British tourist these days."

I walked back to the Schloss. The big iron gate was barred. I rang and the manservant that let me in was the same who had brought me my breakfast. He looked at me reproachfully.

"Lunch had been prepared for you, sir. I had to take it back to the kitchen."

"I'm sorry," I said. "I completely forgot. How is Her Highness?"

"The village doctor came and said she should not be disturbed. She blessedly sleeps and will, one hopes, through the night. Her maid is with her.

"Is there nothing I can bring you, sir?" My legs were tired and I had sat down on one of the benches in the hall. I shook my head. "Did you have a long walk?" he asked, hovering and staring at me curiously.

"I went to look at the house that was burnt down," I said.

"A sad sight and such a waste too, a fine big house like that which could have benefited others more worthy to own it than those people." He grinned, malignantly.

Suddenly I lost all self-control.

"Ignorant fool!" I exclaimed angrily. "You don't know what you are saying."

"I am only a servant, sir," he muttered with cowed humility. "I'm simply repeating what everyone says around here."

I felt deeply ashamed of myself. What on earth come over me to insult someone in his position?

"I'm sorry I was rude," I said. "It has been a rather tiring day. I apologize."

He grinned. "No harm done, sir. I may be an ignorant fool, but I have a thick skin. And no doubt a gentleman would be tired after such a long walk and several hours spent over beers in an inn."

How did he know? Then I remembered that from the heights on which the castle stood anyone watching from it could overlook the entire district and check all comings or goings."

Obviously someone had mine.

"If I'm needed I will be in the library."

"Shall I bring the gentleman's dinner there then later?"

"Yes, please," trying to give him a friendly and appeasing smile, yet thinking what an odious face his was, at once so obsequious and yet slyly mocking.

# Chapter Nineteen

I knew the library from my last stay. It was seldom used, and no wonder. Except for the German classics and some old Tauchnitz novels, the shelves were filled with elaborately bound and tooled volumes of ecclesiastical and legal treatises written in past centuries, which could not have been of much interest to anyone any more.

On the large table in the middle of the room piles of old magazines were stacked, mainly *Tatlers* and *Das Salonblatt* which was about all Marie Therese ever read; but also some books that must have been recently taken in from the shelves. One was Goethe's earliest play *Goetz von Berlichingen*.

Was it here that Alexander had refreshed his memory before his performance? And why had he chosen to recite from *Goetz* which neither he nor I had liked very much? For the most obvious reason, it struck me—Goethe's drama written in his youthful *Sturm and Drang* period would still appeal to youths.

The other volume was *Faust*. It was open on the page that contained the dedication, surely some of the most profoundly beauiful verses ever written.

Was this inadvertently Alexander's last message to me?

As I re-read the poem all the horror of which I had seen and heard in the last three days receded. It was like a calming cool hand laid on a fevered brow. There was still pain, but who is not born to suffer, either through the self or because of others? I thought of the German word *"Mitleid"*, untranslatable because its meaning is neither mercy, compassion nor love; it quite simply tells us that we must take upon ourselves the pain of others as if it were our own.

I thought of Alexander and of Marie Therese and of the innocent people who had died and I felt neither indignation nor anger nor pity. Only the absolute commitment of *Mitleid*.

The servant came in with a tray. A steaming onion soup aroused my appetite. But big chunks of meat swimming in blood-red sauce among potatoes did not appeal; I left it because of the strong flavour.

"What is it?" I asked.

"Goulash," he said. "A stag that Count Plevke shot."

I pushed it away with disgust.

"We servants don't mind, but usually stags shot in the rutting season do not appeal to the taste of gentlemen. Still, cook thought that you being English it didn't matter." He placed a bottle of wine, one of whisky and a jug of water beside me and watched me as I ate some fruit with an expression of sly amusement.

"You don't have to wait. Thank you," I said, "you can take the tray now. I will need nothing more. Good night."

He went. I poured myself some whisky and returned to the books on the table, then saw to my amazement that the third was Hitler's *Mein Kampf*. It had been concealed under the other two. I recognized the cover as we had a copy of it in the Embassy. Sir John occasionally urged his staff to read it, but none of us ever did, and it had become a sort of joke. When someone or other vanished to go to the lavatory and Sir John irritably asked what he was doing for so long. "Studying Mein Cramp" was the answer. Not as inappropriate as it might seem, since we all drank too much cheap sour wine at night and often suffered from stomach cramps in the mornings.

But what was the book doing in the Schloss *Bibliothek* and why had Alexander read it? I opened it and saw the dedication. *"Meinem Freund und Mitarbeiter Fürst Hohenturn— Sieg Heil!—Adolf Hitler."*

What did it mean? I remembered my ambassador's request that I should remain alert to what was happening in Sudeten.

*"Mein Freund."* It seemed impossible. I thought of Heinrich's proud arrogant face and of Hitler's undistinguished weasel-like features. No more could a royal falcon make friends with a stoat, one circling the sky ready to plunge on his prey and carry it high in powerful beak and claws to his eyrie, the other earthbound, sneaking from hole to hole, mesmerizing helpless creatures into submission and acceptance of death, as does a snake.

Nevertheless *Mitarbeiten* means collaboration. Had they started to hunt together, one having agreed to take what the other left? Falcons are not scavengers, neither are weasels; both live on fresh meat and blood. Would the supply suffice for them both?

If not, would not a final battle between them become inevitable?

"*Sieg Heil*, indeed," I repeated, and went to my room. But sleep had evaded me for so many hours that I slept far into the morning.

To be told by the servant who brought my breakfast that Dr Koritschoner was now attending the Princess, but would be grateful if he could speak to me in the library in half an hour.

I dressed hurriedly but found him already waiting, examining the same books as I had the night before.

We shook hands. I remembered to murmur some words of condolence.

"Thank you," he said. "I am here to make the funeral arrangements. The remains will be taken back to Prague to be buried in the Jewish cemetery there, where for centuries we Koritschoners have had a family resting place." He spoke entirely without emotion and what I could see of his face, partially concealed behind beard and spectacles, showed none either.

"How is Alexander?" I asked.

"He may live or he may choose to die, the final decision will be his. I am a doctor. It is my duty to do everything my skill has taught me to keep him alive and even more so, since it was in trying to save my family that he became what he is now. One slight ray of hope—he has not lost his sight as we first feared. He is conscious now and he can see as well as hear—and though still in considerable pain, his mind does not seem affected."

"And speak?"

"No, alas, and probably never will again. Some things are almost beyond repair, though I will try. Yet with time I may be able to give him back something resembling a human face."

"Better dead," I said. "You can't know what he was; not only one of the most beautiful of human beings to look at, but a great artist in his chosen field as an actor. What future has he now?"

"None, if you put it that way," the doctor said coldly.

He looked down on his hands, small, narrow-boned, immaculately clean, the hands of a skilled surgeon.

"But it is the Princess who needs our help now. Her fear that Alexander had thought her too old to desire her and had therefore left without even saying goodbye was, to her, infinitely more painful than if she heard he could not do so because he was dead! So for her own peace of mind I told her he was."

"But how could you?" I protested, deeply shocked, "when he's still alive."

"Prince Heinrich, whom I attended in Vienna, agreed with me that it was for the best. She is a deeply religious woman and she can accept death with greater resignation than she could wilful desertion or what he has become."

"That's what her mind said, too."

"Peasant wisdom is often profounder than ours. Besides, the maid has known the Princess since they were infants together and has never left her since. Due to her care and the Prince's protection, Marie Therese has been allowed to remain a happy innocent child of nature, knowing nothing of evil or cruelty or what men can do to men."

He caught my rather sceptical look.

"Is it a fault to love too much?" he asked. "Even her Church absolves the sins of the flesh. I had to tell her about what happened to my brother and his wife," he resumed, "she would have heard about it anyway. She grieved, of course, for my sake. But never must she know that it was anything but an unfortunate accident, nor should anyone else."

"So you know it was murder?"

I had startled him out of his composure. "Yes, but how do you? Who told you?"

"I can't tell you—I gave my word."

He pondered this. "Prince Heinrich assured me his young scouts were sworn to silence about anything connected with the castle and would not talk; that the police would obey his orders as well as the rest of the population of these realms of his do. You see, it is as much in his interest as mine that no one should know the real truth."

"But why yours? A horrible crime was been committed. Two innocent people have been burnt to death, only because they were—" I hesitated—"Czechs nor Germans."

"Jews is what you want to say, is it not?"

I could not answer.

"Because whatever anger and resentment I personally might feel, I am responsible for the welfare of others. As a doctor, for that of my patients, as a Jew for my people's safety as a whole. Oh, we have known persecution before and have learnt how to deal with it. A small fire, if not dampened early, can ignite others and end in a general conflagration. We have to keep our own counsel, we Jews. Violence begets violence, one crime leads to another, for such is the nature of man; easily led like sheep, yet wolves in sheep's clothing, ready to rend, tear and destroy if their leaders encourage them to do so.

"So to keep quiet about what happens and to suffer in silence has become our policy, not to show resistance or resentment and to wait patiently till the wolves turn into sheep once more. Fortunately they always do."

"I don't understand," I said. "Surely, if a crime such as this was given publicity it would shock the world? Will you at least let me speak to my ambassador about it?"

"Any publicity would do more harm than good."

"But don't you want justice, revenge? I thought you believed in an eye for an eye and a tooth for a tooth, as the Old Testament teaches, not in turning the other cheek."

"Christ was a Jew, too, you know," he said mildly, "and taught submission to God's Will. We believe in an all-knowing Deity, infinitely just. A Father who, if He punishes us, does so for our own good; and that to decide our destinies is not our right, but His. So for my people's sake as well as for the Prince's sake, will you not speak of what you have heard or seen here?"

"But why for Prince Heinrich's sake?" A horrible thought struck me. "Do you mean he was in some way responsible for this murder?"

"No. It is not the weapon used to kill that one can blame, sometimes not even the hand that wielded it, but the instigator who puts it into the hands of others—in this case of children. Naturally for the sake of his young scouts, who if guilty of arson certainly didn't intend murder, Prince Heinrich wants it all hushed up. But you are totally wrong in thinking he could have deliberately inspired the crime against my family. The royal falcon would disdain such lowly prey. Other predators do not and there are many in the Sudeten German party."

"Have you seen the dedication in this?" I pointed to *Mein Kampf* on the table.

The doctor smiled. "Yes, but it doesn't mean he is a friend of Hitler's. As a matter of fact he hates him. Not because he persecutes Jews; Prince Heinrich is above such minor matters." I heard the bitter irony in the doctor's voice. "But because a common little man is usurping the power he wants to wield himself. Prince Heinrich has fantasies of grandeur and conquest quite as excessive as Hitler's."

"Is he mad too?"

"With such aspirations only history decides in the end who is mad or sane. But Prince Heinrich is not an evil man. He is proud, arrogant—yes, restricted by the aristocratic prejudices of his class. But, like all of them, he has courage and obeys the rules of Christian chivalry. In short, he is a gentleman. Herr Hitler is not.

"Well one can only wait and see who wins." The doctor sighed, then looked at his watch. "I will have to go soon. I still have some things to attend to here and this afternoon I must leave for Prague."

He stared at me through his glittering glasses. "Why is it that we Continentals always believe the English can be trusted more than others?" He shrugged impatiently. "I may be entirely wrong in telling you so much. Yet I see no alternative to trusting you, since I will need your help.

"Firstly, I must ask you to leave here after the Prince has arrived. Any comfort you could give the Princess now would be merely of a physical nature and remind her too painfully of what she has lost. She is quite calm and resigned now and her mental balance is restored. She mourns Alexander's death, of course, but finds comfort in his heroism and as time passes she will become her old cheerful self once more. I trust I have been able to erase from her mind forever what she saw. I have certain hypnotic powers and for the sake of her sanity I used them."

I gazed at this small insignificant-looking man, his face masked by beard and glasses, whom I had only met on the back stairs and passages of the Hohenturn Palace as he went his humble way and who now spoke with such compelling and absolute authority. Was he going to hypnotize me too, I wondered, fearful as he continued with his extraordinary demands.

"Have you, too, not wished Alexander dead, rather than what is left of him should survive?"

So he knew. I made a gesture of assent.

"Still, surely you must accept it is my duty as a doctor to keep him alive?"

"I suppose so."

"Then the beautiful young actor must die so that Alexander can live with a different face and under a different name."

"But why? I don't understand."

"It will cause you pain, I know, but I must tell you the truth. Though I am a skilled plastic surgeon, I cannot restore a face—as disfigured as his—to anything like what it was before. His scalp was so badly burnt that his hair will never grow again. He has no eyelids left. Even his lips—well, I will spare you further details. But I wanted you to know that although I will do my best for him, people will from now on look at what Alexander Plevke has become with pity, perhaps, but also with disgust and fear. His friends and admirers will forsake him. Even those who formerly loved him will turn from him in horror. Is that what you wish for him?"

"Let him die," I cried out in agony. "What has he left to live for?"

"His inner self. Would you not say that he had a remarkable mind, was in fact highly intelligent and gifted? Even if his exterior beauty is destroyed there has been no damage to his brain."

"But if he will never speak again? Acting was his life."

"He may be able to learn to write plays instead of acting in them, since he knows so much about the theater. He may even find happiness living quietly somewhere where there is no need for anyone to see him or pity him or turn from him."

"All alone! Locked in some room, shut away from all human contact. You can't be serious!"

"The room could be a beautiful one, full of works of art, books, newspapers, music, shaded lights, a few sympathetic friends. Who knows?"

"And is he supposed never to go out of that room?"

"And why not? Many people go about with a bandaged face and cause no horror. But that is all in the future. At present he is well cared for in my clinic in the private ward. He has a nurse whom I trust absolutely and whom he seems to like. As a matter of fact she is my niece, Esther Koritschoner, and after what he tried to do for her parents she would gladly give her life for him. Perhaps you met her. She has been working in the Hohenturn secretariat."

Vaguely I remembered a tall dark girl.

"He will, for the next months, still have to suffer a certain amount of surgery," the doctor resumed, "but he is brave and too intelligent not to realize it is necessary. He is now listed in my clinic as Mr Henry Stanley, an Englishman, since he is that by birth, who suffers from a contagious skin disease and must be kept in isolation. He chose the name himself."

"But what about his mother and stepfather?" I said bitterly. "Surely if you have faked his death there must be a body?"

"My niece speaks perfect English. She will write to his mother on my behalf expressing my sympathy, announcing his death and explaining the circumstances that led to it, that he has been cremated and that the urn with his ashes will be sent to her through the British Embassy. That is where I need your help."

"But I can't, I really can't!" I protested. "What ashes, anyway?"

"They all look much the same, even those left in fire-places," the doctor said, "and I'm sure the poor woman will be much relieved that she doesn't have to travel all this way to take her dead son home." And remembering the fair, highly emotional Elaine as I knew her so long ago, I thought so too.

"I will not collaborate with you in this monstrous deception without seeing Alexander," I said angrily. "How can I know, otherwise, that what you are so high-handedly planning is what he wants himself?"

He sighed. "I thought you might demand that. All right, you shall see Mr Stanley next week. By then he should be stronger. But remember, Alexander Plevke's death will be in all the papers tomorrow."

"I don't know what gives you the authority to do all this."

"Only gratitude towards your young friend and my knowledge as a healer of men."

"Do you know how rich he is?" I asked, with sudden suspicion. "Well, under these circumstances his entire fortune will revert to his mother and not to Mr Stanley."

"Even if I am a Jew, I am not a very mercenary one," he said mildly, "and in this case all my skill and my entire fortune are his. But things are becoming difficult. Although I am a famous surgeon and have many important and influential clients, a day may come when I will have to pack my small bag and be forced to leave. If Mr Stanley is to survive in the future, handicapped as he is, he will need money. So Alexander Plevke will bequeath his entire fortune to you, and I know you will return it to him when he demands it."

"But why to me? Why not leave it to Mr Stanley?"

"Because it might cause publicity and his mother might

even feel she had to contest the will. Knowing of your great
friendship for her son and his love for you, she will not."

How could he know so much? I made my last protest.

"I will have to tell my mother all this. I couldn't keep it
from her anyway. It is a terrible responsibility you have
forced upon me. I can only take it on if she agrees. Do you
understand?"

"Oh, only too well," he said, looking at me with a faint
smile that rose surprisingly above his grizzled beard. "I foresaw that, when I met her, and since I thought her both highly
intelligent and trustworthy I took her into my confidence, because we might need her help too."

"And she approved your plans?" Probably she would have,
I thought angrily, knowing her adventurous trend of mind.

"More or less. In any case she showed much understanding."

"Even the best of women have no conception of what is legally right or wrong," I said. "It is not in their nature."

"But compassion is—and God bless them for that."

He laid his fine-fingered hand on the *Faust* and quoted
from the *Chorus Mysticus*:

> *Alles Vergängliche ist nur ein Gleichniss*
> *Das Unzulänliche heir wird's Ereigniss—*
> *Das Unbeschriebliche hier ist as gethan—*
> *Das ewig Weibliche zieht uns hinan.*

"What do these words mean to you?"

Hesitantly I said, "That all that is mortal, transient, incomplete will be brought to fullness of life: that it will achieve its
true form of which we see only a distorted shadow."

"You have read your Plato, I see—go on. What do you
think Goethe meant by the eternal feminine? Mother
Nature?"

"Perhaps," I said. "Or love or tenderness. Perhaps just
beauty."

■

After he had left I was called to Marie Therese. Though still
in bed she looked tidier, younger and more composed and
spoke quite calmly, if sadly, of Alexander's brave death.

"On that last night," she told me, "he recited so wonderfully to Heinrich's boys, all about courage and chivalry, and
then went out to prove it himself. He looked like an archan-
gel, so beautiful and fair, and now I am sure he is one. No

need to pray for his soul in purgatory, because all the heavens must have opened to receive him back."

I could not answer.

"I know how you feel, Eddie, you loved him too. But believe me, he is not lost to us. We can pray to him now and he will intercede for us with God and the blessed mother of God."

"I've come to say goodbye," I stammered.

"I understand, Eddie. The temptation is too great when we are together. But even if we must suffer restraint, I think for a while we should just remain friends. It would not be right, somehow, now—do you understand? After all, we lived in sin and this perhaps is our punishment."

Relief swept over me. "Farewell, Marie Therese." I bent and kissed her hand. She stroked my hair gently then looked up, the dimples forming enchantingly as she smiled.

"Who knows what the future will bring?" she asked.

Next morning I only saw Heinrich briefly.

"Our doctor will have told you about our young friend the actor's death."

"Yes, he did." I could read nothing further in his impassive face, or how much he knew.

"Better so, don't you agree? Even a crippled or wounded beast is allowed the mercy of death, either by man's hand or God's."

I told him I had to leave for Vienna. He did not seem at all surprised.

"Ask my valet about trains and the car will, of course, take you to the station whenever you want to leave. Meanwhile, thank you. You have proved yourself as true a friend to Marie Therese and me as you could, and I hope will continue to be so in the future."

We shook hands in the Germanic manner and I knew I was dismissed.

The train journey seemed endless compared to the one by air, if more reassuring. Hills and valleys, villages and small townships, had regained their normal terrestrial proportions and aspect and the comfortably rhythmic chugging of the train lulled me into sleep.

It was late at night when I arrived at our flat, rather hoping that I would not have to confront my mother. Nevertheless she had purposely waited up for me.

"Dr Koritschoner telephoned me to say you would arrive tonight. I have grilled some veal kidneys with mushrooms and made a cream sauce—just let me see to some toast. Do you want a salad?"

"Mother, I don't want anything. I'm not hungry."

However, when she set the prettily arranged tray before me I ate avidly and drank the white wine she had carefully chilled. When she handed me my steaming black coffee with its dollop of whipped cream on top, such as she knew I had learned to like in Vienna, I answered her unspoken question.

"All right. It was awful. But then, you know all about it by now." I could not keep the resentment out of my voice. "The omnipotent doctor has no doubt informed you about everything and, I know, persuaded you to connive with his plans."

"As to information, yes. As to conniving, certainly not. Whatever I might think and believe, I will accept your decision. The doctor, though a wise man, is not omnipotent. It is entirely up to you to make up your mind. You have evaded responsibility for Alexander successfully for many years and indeed, of what use now to resume it when he is a poor crippled creature and no longer the radiant being he was? You have no obligation to be burdened with Mr Stanley's future. Alexander is dead. I would quite understand if you now hoped finally that you had done with him forever and left it to others to deal with his welfare as far as that is possible. Even if I agree with the doctor's opinion that, if he survives, he must learn to live in another way, with another face, why should you be involved and become responsible for him?"

"Mother, you simply don't understand. I would do anything in my power to help him, except become involved in this monstrous deception which the doctor has so cleverly planned and with which you seem to agree."

"And if it is Alexander's only chance of resurrection, as I believe it is?"

"How can I be sure? Do you realize that my whole future career would be at stake if all this was discovered?"

"So would it have been if what you did at Schwarzensee had been revealed. However, I don't blame you in the least, my dear boy," she mercilessly continued, "if you want no part in all this. Like your good father you have a strictly Protestant conscience. I suppose being of a different and more flexible and forgiving faith that accepts we are all fallible, I can't really understand your scruples."

Miserable as I felt, I could not help but laugh at this and I had not laughed for weeks.

"Mother, you have tried to reduce me to nothing with utterly unfounded and cruel accusations and have insulted me as no other human being would dare to do," I nevertheless protested.

"Except a mother." Now she too was laughing.

"But to find excuses for your not knowing right from wrong because of a religion which you haven't practised for years is really too much!

"Now look here," I added as sternly as I could. "I am seeing Alexander next week. If I can ascertain that this monstrous masquerade is what he himself wants, I will agree to all the doctor's requests. Otherwise I won't. Is that quite clear?"

"Of course, dearest boy. I never would have expected you to decide otherwise." But she was laughing.

With whatever dignity I hoped I still possessed, I bade her good night and left the room.

# Chapter Twenty

All through the following week I waited fearfully to be called to the clinic. Meanwhile I had read a brief notice of Graf Alexander Plevke's death in the Vienna papers, in which his aristocratic German background was stressed more than was his career on the stage, and an obituary in *The Times* which contrarily mentioned his English birth and education and his having been a member of several famous theatre companies and regretting that so greatly gifted and promising a young English actor had been called from life's stage. So convincing did it all sound that I asked my mother to ring the clinic dreading, yet somewhat hoping, the report of his death might be true; to be informed by her that Mr Stanley was as well as could be expected and that I could visit him the following Tuesday.

The day after my arrival back in Vienna I had, of course, reported at our Embassy. Sir John, much to my relief, perhaps warned not to do so by my mother or because he himself wanted to spare my feelings, had not questioned me about my stay in Hohenturn. Though generally uncompromisingly brusque in his manner, he could on some occasions show rare tact. He merely expressed conventional regret at Alexander's death, then moved on to subjects only vaguely connected with Hohenturn. He told me that his Prague colleague, passing through Vienna on his way to the Foreign Ofce, had informed him that Konrad Henlein, SDP leader, was asking His Majesty's Government to intervene on behalf of the Sudeten Germans with President Benes. Even more concessions than had already been granted were demanded, though Henlein still declared himself a loyal subject of the Czech republic.

"A devious man, this Henlein. By all accounts playing two sides against the middle, because it is well known that he has contacts with Hitler too. Is he a frequent guest at Hohenturn?"

"I doubt it. Heinrich likes to dominate his own roost."

"Of Royal Falcons. That is what the young members of his secret society are called, aren't they?"

Sir John did not seem to expect an answer.

"Well, back to work" he then said. "It is still the best cure for the tribulations all of us have to suffer at times. I would like you to check these reports for me—" handing me a large sheaf of them—"and mark what you think of interest."

I carried them into the adjoining room where I usually worked.

On Tuesday I drove to the clinic. It was situated on the outskirts of Vienna—a large building of modern construction, though in the Empress Marie Theresa's style, painted pale yellow, its doors and window frames white. High stone walls enclosed the well-tended grounds shaded by large trees, evidently much older than the house.

At Reception I asked, as I had been told to do, for Nurse Koritschoner. I did not have to wait long. A tall slim girl, very dark in contrast to her starched white uniform and cap, came hurrying up to the desk.

She glanced at me briefly. What a stern, unsmiling young face, I thought.

"My uncle apologizes for not being able to meet you," she said in perfect English, "but he is in the operating theatre this morning. However he asked me to give you any information you might need and take you to Mr Stanley."

"Why 'Stanley'?" I asked.

"What's in a name," she shrugged. "Besides, it was his choice."

"But I thought he couldn't speak."

"He can't. But fortunately his hands are almost undamaged. He can communicate by gesture and to some extent even by writing down a few words. His hearing is not impaired."

"But that is good news!" I exclaimed.

Her lids veiled her dark eyes momentarily, as if to shut out the sight of something. When she opened them again I saw how deeply shadowed they were; not by cosmetics, but as if by grief and pain. Hers or of others? Then I remembered.

"I am so sorry about your parents."

"So am I," she said curtly, and I knew how trite my remark had been.

At her touch the door of a lift slid open. I followed her inside.

"I suppose I need not warn you that he must not be excited in any way," she said.

We ascended through several floors.

"He is still very weak. Also I cannot allow you more than ten minutes with him."

"I will do anything you say."

The semblance of a smile curved her lips.

"Then above all, calm yourself. It is natural that you should be nervous and frightened at what you might find, but don't let it show when you are with him. Pity and sympathy is the last thing he wants now or, I believe, ever will."

I hesitated. "And does he know—well, about his death?"

"I read him his obituaries several days ago."

"And he doesn't mind?"

"No. By now he trusts my uncle absolutely to decide what is best for him."

"Dr Koritschoner has among other gifts that of hypnotism," I said.

She stared at me and I saw her pale face flush with indignation.

"How dare you think he would ever use it except for the good of his patients."

In silence we walked through a long corridor smelling of disinfectant. Everying looked very clean. Polished floors, white-painted walls, big sunny windows overlooking trees on one side, on the other a series of numbered doors. Uniformed nurses hurried by, some pushing trolleys with jars or glasses or instruments concealed by a white cloth; other women, also capped but wearing aprons, carried trays of what presumably was food under silver covers.

"What a pleasant place this is," I said, in an effort to appease.

She turned to me. We were so exactly of the same height that our eyes met on an equal level.

"The clinic is my uncle's life work. Come."

She pushed open a door. We entered a room that was large but rather dark, daylight only filtering through shutters. In its centre was a tent of what looked like white mosquito netting. Why was I suddenly reminded of the diastrous picnic so long ago at Schwarzensee and the netting under which the Tsarevna had hidden? I do not know, except that my mind was trying to escape what I might see underneath it. I felt the nurse's hand grasp my wrist firmly. Was she surreptitiously trying to feel my pulse or just wanting to reassure me?

She drew me closer to the tent. Dimly I could discern a bed underneath it and what looked vaguely human as to shape, even if swathed from head to foot in gauze. Nothing but a pair of dark glasses visible through the curtaining assured me that there must be eyes beneath those bandages.

"Mr Stanley," the nurse said, "your friend is here."

There was a sudden stirring of what lay there and an eerie scraping squeaking sound.

The nurse bent and took something out from under the covers. It was a child's school slate. Awkwardly pointed on it in chalk but quite legible was "Doctor Livingstone I presume?"

"That silly old joke," I exclaimed. "Really Alexander!" And I was back at Schwarzensee again when he had first entered my room, a shining rain-drenched apparition, and had used the same words to greet me. Tears gathered in my eyes. I rubbed them hastily so the nurse would not see. She did though and gave me a warning look.

"Have you any questions you want Mr Stanley to answer?" she asked, then wiped the slate clean and passed it back under the curtaining.

I pulled myself together.

"Yes," I said. "Alexander. I must know for yours and your mother's sake, and for my own, if you agree with everything Dr Koritschoner has decided for you. I simply will not accept this deception otherwise. Is it really what you want?"

The chalk scraped again. "Yes," emerged in large capital letters.

"But why did you risk your life so rashly?"—and then, seeing the nurse's shocked face, knew I should not have asked.

There was a sort of movement behind the netting and a horrible croaking gasping sound. I shuddered. What had I done? The nurse partially vanished underneath the curtains to reappear seconds later. "It's all right," she said, "Mr Stanley is only laughing," and handed me the slate once more.

On it was written firmly, "Because of you" and then only faintly traced and almost illegible, except to me, *"Gentilhomme Anglais."*

Then I knew that whatever had happened to Alexander's body, his laughing, mocking, teasing spirit was unchanged.

"Time to go," the nurse said.

"Just one more question," I pleaded, because suddenly the netting not only recalled the Tsarevna's protective covering from mosquitoes, but also Alexander's little bed in Schwarzensee equally canopied and hung with muslin, behind which he had lain for so many days successfully faking a non-existent illness as an alibi for murder.

Are you just putting on another act to fool me? I wanted to ask and then knew I could not. "May I come back?" I asked instead.

A hand and part of a bandaged arm emerged from under the curtains and groped helplessly till I took it in mind. It clung to my fingers feebly. It was very cold and yet when I looked down I saw it was bright red and covered with blisters. God knows what the nurse must think of me, I thought, but nevertheless I bent and kissed it.

"I will be back," I repeated as the nurse, now looking very anxious, compelled me to leave the room with her.

Once outside she said, "We took a great risk in allowing you to see him, he is still very ill and your questions cannot have helped. Further, your having touched him may have even more serious consequences. He is in that sterilized tent to protect him from germs and infection. His whole body is still one open wound—he is only lightly bandaged since anything heavy would cause acute pain. As it is he suffers enough. We dare not drug him too much lest his will to live weakens. Do you realize he still has to be fed intravenously, since he cannot swallow anything solid and that he would not be able to sleep at night at all if it were not for my uncle's dubious, as you seemed to imply, hypnotic gifts? There are at least three operations ahead of him—he will need all his strength."

I think she read in my face how much her reproaches had unnerved and shattered me. When I made an effort to apologize, her smile was almost friendly.

"Do you know, in spite of everything I think seeing you did him good. He has not laughed before."

"You seem to care very much about him."

"Naturally, he is my patient."

"But you must have many."

"None of them tried to save my parents from burning to death."

As we descended in the lift I suddenly knew I had seen her before.

"Haven't we met somewhere?" I asked.

"But of course, frequently, on the back stairs of the Hohenturn Palace. I worked in the secretariat there for the last half-year. But I trained as a nurse under my uncle before and now he needs me here."

The lift door slid open.

"I have to return to my patient. He has incredible courage. I trust you have some too. These next months are not going to be easy but don't despair—we will pull through somehow and your help may be all-important. If I call you back, will you come?"

"Day and night."

"Night and day," she echoed, "not a bad song!" and then laughed quite frankly. The stiff stern nurse's manner was suddenly gone and she looked almost pretty and very young.

She gripped my hand in a sort of boyish comradely way and left.

I returned to my flat and found my mother busily writing at my desk which, since I rarely needed it, she had acquired for her own use. On it lay the golden box, its gems coldly sparkling in the already wintry sunlight.

"I am writing to Alexander's mother," she said. "I felt I should."

"What?" I asked.

"Oh, just the ordinary letter of condolence."

She did not look at me but kept her eyes fixed on the sheet of paper.

"Did you see him?" she asked.

"Not his face."

She turned towards me, startled. I told her everything then, except what I felt, since she would know that even better than I did.

"Certain responsibilities, however unpleasant, must be accepted," she said.

"Indeed."

"By the way, this letter was delivered by hand just before you came. It's from the clinic."

What now? I thought and hesitated to open it. "You see what it says, Mother."

As she read her eyebrows rose as if in puzzled amazement. There was, I saw, a typewritten note and one on which I immediately recognized Alexander's handwriting. I snatched it from her.

Even if rather shakily penned it was clear enough.

"I, Alexander Plevke, being of sound mind bequeath in case of my death my entire fortune to my beloved friend, Eddie Livingstone."

Witnesses: Jacob Koritschoner, MD
              Esther Koritschoner, Nurse

It was written on the clinic's notepaper and bore the date of a fortnight previously. I took the other note.

"Dear Mr. Livingstone. Before his death Count Plevke made this will in your favour and left it in my keeping. Permit me to advise you to get in touch with your lawyers soonest, so that all matters concerning the deceased's estate can be satisfactorily settled. Count Plevke's bank is Barclay's DCR of London. His legal advisers are—" a name and address followed—"Yours sincerely, signed Jacob Koritschoner."

"He simply can't force this upon me," I exclaimed, wiping the sweat from my forehead.

"Alexander told you of it?"

"No, the old witchdoctor planned it all. Mother, I cannot accept this inheritance. It is simply too dishonest and besides—"

"Besides what?"

"Don't you see that if I do, I'm tied to Alexander for life?"

"You have always been that anyway," she said drily. "But of course I understand your scruples at accepting what must be a very large fortune."

"But Mother, surely you can't think that even if I did, I use a penny of it for my own benefit?" I looked at her with horror.

"Not really. But if not, I can't quite grasp the reason for your qualms of conscience. Alexander, quite rightly confident in your integrity, has charged you to administer for him a fortune for his benefit. Helpless and handicapped as he is, who else could he trust to provide him in the future with all the security and comforts his money can still bring?"

"All plotted by that old witchdoctor."

"And what reason could he have had to do so? Certainly not any advantages for himself. If he was that kind of man, would he not have persuaded Alexander to make a will in favour of his clinic, and so himself? Many grateful patients have been known to do so for their doctors."

As always her calm logic irritated me as much as it reassured me.

"Alexander must have written that—" she touched the will—"today after your visit. Did he seem to you of sound mind?"

Because of you, *Gentilhomme Anglais*, I remembered.

"Yes, very much so," I admitted bitterly. "There is nothing wrong with his brain or memory."

"Well then, surely you have courage of sorts." I thought of the sad young nurse who had said almost the same when she asked for my help.

"You had better take this and have it sent to London through the Embassy to Mathews & Ward—" our lawyers— "It will travel more safely that way."

It was not the only thing that was to travel care of His Majesty's Government that day. At the Embassy I hung up my coat in the clothes closet provided for that purpose and stumbled over a wooden crate.

"What on earth is this?" I irritably asked a young colleague who was divesting himself of his mackintosh.

"Ashes," he grinned. "There is a funeral urn in it. We didn't know where else to put it. It is what remains of that poor actor fellow, Plevke. It's to be flown home to his family in England this afternoon."

I did not see Sir John that day.

Several weeks passed. I was not called to the clinic. On telephoning the nurse she told me Mr Stanley had been operated on successfully but that he needed rest. She promised to call me when he asked for me.

Marie Therese had returned to Vienna, but she no longer telephoned me to make plans for the day or night, neither was I asked for tea as before. However, I was occasionally invited to dinner parties over which she presided in semi-mourning, black lace off-setting her fairness, her gaiety perhaps somewhat more restrained, her manner more befitting her age, even if her looks—I wondered if with the doctor's help—were quite ravishingly youthful once more.

If we talked it was only casually and I would note with secret amusement how her glance would stray to rest on one or another of the handsome, well-groomed young men invited. Soon she would choose another lover, I knew, and why not? I did not mind at all. I still felt warm friendship, affection and gratitude, but nothing else for her any more.

I rarely saw Heinrich. Marie Therese told me he was now more often in Hohenturn and also in Prague than in Vienna.

"He is trying to make our palace in Prague habitable."

"Another palace!" I said.

"Yes, and really beautiful, though rather fallen into neglect since we have never used it, both of us preferring Vienna."

"And now he wants to live there?"

"Oh, I hope not. Prague is so dull and provincial. Still, one can never tell with Heinrich."

After a fortnight a letter from our lawyer came.

"My dear Eddie—" he had been a friend of my father's and had known me since I was a child—"I will spare you the verbosity of our legal language. Firstly I would like to express my sympathy at the loss of your friend, but also congratulate you on your gains. You are now, I have ascertained, very rich indeed.

"Your income alone amounts to twelve thousand pounds a year! Count Plevke's family was satisfied that the will was genuine and will not contest it. But there are certain formalities and decisions which make it imperative that you come to London. The deceased banked with Barclay's DCR. The bank naturally want to know if you will continue with them.

"The fortune is invested at present in safe securities. Count Plevke rarely touched capital, living off his income and his considerable earnings in films and on the stage. However, he supported several charities such as a home for impecunious old actors and schooling for young aspiring ones. The bank wants to know if you will want to continue contributing to these charities; also if you agree to a certain sum paid up to now annually to a Frau Margarethe Reinecke living in the village of Schwarzensee, Schleswig-Holstein.

"Further, if you will want one thousand pounds transferred to you monthly as was to Count Plevke, or prefer other arrangements.

"If I can advise in any way . . . etc."

I laid down the letter.

How could I answer or decide anything before seeing Alexander and knowing what he wanted. Twelve thousand pounds a year seemed a fortune beyond belief, considering what I had to depend on, and I knew nothing of business or finance. Why had this awesome responsibility been thrust upon me?

*Eh bien, gentilhomme Anglais,* I seemed to hear the Tsarevna boom reassuringly once more and then I knew, whatever the cost to myself, I must accept this new burden too.

A letter from Elaine answering my mother's brought home to me once more the monstrousness of the deceit in which I was conniving.

"We have placed his urn in a niche to be walled in later in our parish church. A bronze plaque will commemorate him.

My dear husband read the prayers for the dead and then spoke most movingly about Alexander's achievements and the brave final act that led to his death. How proud I am of my boy you will know, since you too have an only son, and how much I will miss him. Though we have not seen much of him these last years, it was only his work that kept him away, not lack of affection. Yet my dear husband and stepdaughters have convinced me that God was merciful in taking Alexander to Himself, since the doctor wrote he would have been disfigured and crippled for life. Tell Eddie that I am glad Alexander's fortune should have fallen into such good hands and that he must accept it without the qualms of conscience to which he was rather prone in the past—" was there a trace of irony in that last sentence?—"We are quite well off and would probably have only donated it to charities." There followed the usual "Yours," etc.

"A thoroughly good woman," my mother said, "if perhaps slightly limited."

I saw Alexander once more before I decided on leaving for London.

The nurse received me at the desk. "He has had several grafts," she said, "and they are healing well. He is more comfortable now and really, considering everything, remarkably cheerful. He is looking forward to your visit."

She ushered me into the room but stayed outside herself. "If you need me, call me," she whispered, closing the door.

He was still shrouded in tent and bandages but, as far as I could ascertain through the netting, was sitting up, his bedhead having been raised.

Beside him was a table with a radio, books and to my surprise an English Scrabble board.

"How are you, Alexander?"

A hand emerged from under the netting. It seemed less red and swollen and clasped mine with almost reassuring strength. Then it pushed the cardboard box with its laid-out lettered sentence towards me.

"Amuse me, Eddie, I'm bored," I read.

"Good idea, the Scrabble," I said.

He rearranged the blocks. "Clever nurse," he spelt out. "How is MT. Got her back?"

"Marie Therese?" The bandaged head nodded. "No, she doesn't want me any more, nor do I want her. She is mourning your death."

"What a laugh!" he set out on the board.

"Alexander, be serious for a moment. I think you should see this."

"Henry," he spelt out.

"All right, Henry then. Can you read it?" I handed him the lawyer's letter. He took it. I heard it rustle under the tent.

"What do you want me to do about it?" I asked, after some minutes' silence. "Should I go to London?"

"Yes." His hand reappeared.

"Then what are you instructions to the bank?"

"Investment to remain. Take monthly income. Pay clinic and doctor."

"But Dr Koritschoner told me he does not want to be paid."

"I do. Need cash too to tip nurses. And for me."

"All right, that is settled then. And the charities?"

"To continue—girl had son."

For a moment I could not think what he meant, then recalled his nightly exploits at Schwarzensee.

"Then there is this letter from your mother to mine too. I don't know if it will upset you," I said hesitantly, but he had grabbed it out of my hand by then.

"Poor silly Mummy," he spelt out after a while.

"Isn't that rather heartless?" I asked, shocked.

He rearranged the lettered blocks.

"Can't afford to be sentimental now. My ashes?" With his finger that trembled slightly he drew a question mark in the air.

"Out of Dr Koritschoner's fireplace, I imagine."

Though he made no sound, his whole bandaged body seemed to shake as with laughter.

"Look, when will you get out of that tent? I feel all the time that you are simply hiding underneath it to fool me."

"Have a lot to hide."

"Well, what shall I bring you from London," I tried to ask cheerfully after that.

"Cash, large Xmas hamper, books and presents," he spelt out.

Only then did I remember how near Christmas it was.

"And a domino."

"The game?"

"No, Venetian, with hood and bauta."

I pondered this. "But what for?"

"Tired now." He pushed the box away and it clattered to

the floor, gave a sort of weary wave, switched the back of his bed flat and lay quite still.

I walked out of the room as silently as I could to find the nurse waiting outside.

She saw my worried face. "I'm afraid I may have tired him too much," I said.

"Just a moment, wait here."

"It is all right," she reassured me when she reappeared. "He is feigning sleep but he will always test his strength to the utmost possible, that is our difficulty. Also he is still quite an actor."

"As if I didn't know," I said. "That Scrabble board was a bright idea of yours."

"I suddenly remembered it and had it sent from Prague. It belonged to my mother and as a child I spelt out words on it as he does now."

"Is Prague your real home?"

"Except for the villa in the Sudetenland, which we only used in summer, I was born and grew up in Prague in a very old house that has always belonged to my father's family. It's on the river. Once, long ago, it was a mill. It's mine, now, I suppose—but since my parents are gone it would seem so empty, so I don't know when I will go back, if at all."

I knew she was not demanding pity. Nevertheless, looking at her narrow, tired young face, I asked: "Do you never get out of here?"

"There is not much time to do so. But he is better, don't you think?"

"There is certainly nothing wrong with his mind," I said, "or with his sense of humour either."

"Wicked, isn't it?" And she actually laughed.

"Look here," I said. "I won't be in London for more than a few days. When I'm back and you have an hour or two to spare, won't you come to my flat for tea?"

"Tea?" she repeated, giving me an odd, startled look.

"Yes, don't you like it?"

"Not quite as much as Princess Hohenturn does."

So she knew, as probably did the whole secretariat, about Marie Therese's tea guests. I felt acutely embarrassed.

"I live with my mother," I stammered. "I simply thought you might like to meet her, yours having been English too. And you have other things in common. She is as concerned for Alexander as you are and just as involved as all of us have become."

Her dark eyes held mine for a moment. She could not
have read in mine anything but the wish to befriend her,
which was all I felt.

She smiled, blushed a little and looked almost pretty.

"Forgive me for my silly remark," she said. "Of course I'll
come to tea."

# Chapter Twenty-one

Next day I flew to London. I took a room in a small family hotel off Pont Street that my mother had recommended. I ate an indifferent evening meal in its restaurant among old colonels and their wives and next morning took a taxi to Barclay's DCR in Cockspur Street.

I asked to see the manager, giving my name and showing my passport and diplomat's card. Expecting a long wait I sat down on a bench, but within minutes I was escorted to a sumptuous office. Obviously I had become a person of importance.

Since I could quite clearly and decisively repeat the instructions Alexander had given me, there were no difficulties. In fact I thought I read relief in the manager's face that I demanded no changes.

"Then we can open an account in your name?"

"Certainly," I said. I had thought it over in the night. I must have two separate accounts. I had banked with the Midland for years, and would continue to do so, since I knew I must keep Alexander's money separate from mine if I was to administer it according to the small amount of conscience I felt I still had.

"I will need a cheque book," I told the manager and noted slight surprise in his expression. "I have been posted abroad for so long that I have had to bank wherever I was, or depend on traveller's cheques."

"Of course," he said. I was handed a most luxurious-looking cheque book, gold embossed in a blue leather cover.

"Can I draw a thousand pounds cash now?"

"Naturally."

"Thank you."

"Always at your service, sir." He ushered me out as if I was royalty.

At the counter I wrote a cheque, pocketing one thousand pounds.

What now, I thought. I had not been in London for so long that I doubted I had any friends left worth contacting. Alexander's Christmas presents, I remembered. I walked to Fortnum and Mason and enquired about hampers. The attendant looked me over.

"The cheapest we have contains a bottle of port, some packets of assorted teas, biscuits, several small jars of jam, a tin of ham and, of course, a Christmas pudding."

"And the most expensive?"

"Vintage champagne, Beluga caviare, pâté de foie gras, marrons glacés, assorted pralines and, of course, all the usual other English Christmas food, all packed in a large willow hamper."

"I will take the expensive hamper," I said.

His eyes widened with surprise. "Sir, have you an account here?"

I wrote out a cheque—my own—for a staggering sum.

"Will you see to it that it is delivered to the airport tomorrow morning?" I wrote down my name and my flight number to Vienna.

"Certainly, sir. But do you realize, sir, that it must all be kept cool to remain in good condition?"

"They must have facilities for that in the airline," I said, hoping it was true.

I walked on, looking occasionally into shops glitteringly decorated for Christmas, wondering what else I could bring Alexander. Books? I would go to Hatchard's later, I thought. I tried to remember what he had liked best as a boy. Jewels, costumes that enhanced his beauty, I recalled. What use now, I thought sadly. I passed a shop that sold oriental wares. There was a kimono in the window patterned with apple blossoms printed on a blue background. I went in and asked to see it. Very rare, almost a museum-piece, I was told. I fingered it. It was silk, very soft, thin and light. It could not have laid any weight even on the most suffering of bodies. I bought it—also an embroidered shawl for my mother—again paying with my own cheque. That I must keep the thousand in my pocket untouched I knew.

I was hungry by then and remembered that the Ritz was within walking distance. In the past I had known it well. Not that I ever could have afforded to have more than a drink there had I not been invited to share meals with more affluent friends. After all I had spent, what did a little more or less matter? At least I would have a good lunch. I did not go into the Grill but went straight to the big dining-room, still one of the most beautiful rooms in London with its mellow old-fashioned décor and its tall windows overlooking Green Park.

I studied the menu placed before me. I ordered smoked salmon, filet mignon with sauce Bearnaise, assorted vegetables and crème à la coeur with strawberries. I also ordered a bottle of burgundy recommended by the wine waiter.

I ate and I drank, vaguely contemplating the other tables to see if there was anyone I recognized. Except for some shy-looking honeymooners, there was no one young; mostly elderly ladies very smartly dressed and well turned out, with enamelled faces and blued and lacquered hair, obviously Americans. There was a large flower-bedecked empty table in a corner with champagne bottles in coolers. Some birthday party was expected, I thought.

Then something surprising happened. Several youths sauntered in wearing black shirts. But they were certainly not Italian fascists or they would have strutted with more self-assurance, not were they booted like the German SS. They wore quite ordinary flannel trousers and the defiant embarrassment on their young faces was unmistakably English. And leading them to the large flower-decked corner table was Heinrich Hohenturn.

I heard the popping of champagne corks. I did not dare look round fearing to embarrass Heinrich if he recognized me.

"Will you please serve my coffee in the hall and bring me my bill there?" I asked the waiter and walked out unnoticed.

What on earth did it mean? I knew about Mosley, of course, but what was Heinrich doing among what were obviously his followers?

Was he a member of the British Union of Fascists as well as an adherent of Hitler's? Or had the Royal Falcon flown to London merely in search of fresh prey hoping to incite these boys away from their leader? In spite of all I knew about him, Heinrich's real motives remained a mystery to me.

I took a bus back to my hotel. But the dreary indifference of my bedroom depressed me. I noted the amount I had spent that morning and was shocked. Had the mere fact that I had carried a thousand pounds in my pocket, even if they were not mine, stimulated me into such folly?

Then I thought of Alexander and remembered the domino he had wanted. But where was I to find that? I scanned the telephone book and finally found "Theatre costumes, Fancy dresses, for sale and for hire." I noted down the address and set out once more by taxi.

It was a small dingy shop in the theatre district, though it contained a remarkable assortment of costumes, masks and headgear.

"Would you have anything like a domino?" I asked the old woman, by her make-up and speech obviously an ex-actress.

"But of course. It is in frequent demand. We have several sizes and kinds. Is it for yourself, sir?"

"Yes," I said. "I would like the lightest you have got, preferably silk."

"I will see. It is not often to be found in that material, but we might just have one left. A lady had one specially made for a fancy-dress ball and she returned it, but she was tall and it might just fit." She went to another room and brought back a black garment on a hanger.

"Try it on." She adjusted it over my shoulder and drew the hood over my head. It was indeed quite light, covered my entire body and obscured most of my face.

At last, with a pang, I understood Alexander's request.

"I look like a member of the Ku Klux Klan," I tried to joke.

"Oh no, straight out of the *Commedia dell' arte*. But for perfection a *bauta,* the mask, is still needed."

"Of course," I said, remembering.

She brought it. It was black with small slits for eyes and a long nose. I tried it on before the mirror. Except for my mouth I was totally unrecognizable. A sudden thought struck me. "Do you sell false moustaches?"

"Certainly. And every kind of wig." I remembered Alexander's golden hair.

"Black," I said, and I bought all that she had brought me.

While she was wrapping everything I said: "I have not been in London or to the theatre for a long time. Anything good on now?"

"A fine production of *The Seagull*. But then, perhaps I am partial to it. Madame Arcadina was my last role four years ago. I played with that wonderful young actor who recently died, Alexander Plevke. He was Constantine—I have never known a better."

I wrote out a cheque and she handed me the parcel.

"I hope you enjoy your fancy-dress party," she said.

As I walked back past the theatres I saw *The Seagull* was playing at the Aldwych. I went in and rather to my surprise found tickets were still available, if at some expense. I got one in the third row.

I then went to Hatchard's and fingered the latest novels. Of what interest to Alexander now, I thought. I chose biographies of famous actors and actresses and, with the help of an obliging assistant, whatever he could find concerning theatrical history and several books I thought would interest my mother.

In the evening I went to the theatre.

Though I knew the play, this was a very modernistic production. There was none of the cosiness and fustiness so characteristic of its usual stage décor. The interiors contained nothing but a few chairs. The lake was just a painted line of blue. All effect depended not on scenery but on perfection of speech and gesture. And that seemed to me somewhat lacking as the play progressed. All three women indulged in loud hysterics most of the time. The men were more coherent, except for Constantine, a swarthy youth whose shrill screams of righteous anger and frustration fell unpleasantly on the ear. I remembered Alexander's perfect diction, his subtle insidious restraint of voice and gesture, and I was sorry I had come.

Next morning I flew back to Vienna with all I had accumulated at such rash cost to myself in two days; but Alexander's thousand pounds were still intact in my pocket.

After my arrival in Vienna I called at the Embassy.

"Everything all right?" I asked Sir John.

"Here? Need you ask? It never is," he said sourly. "The police have evidence of a Nazi *Putsch* being planned for early next year, so Schuschnigg told me. He hesitates to crack down on the agitators for fear of offending Hitler. Well, London must have been a pleasant change, though it didn't take you long to be back. Hardly worth the expensive air fare, one would think. What did you do there?"

"I had some business to settle, some Christmas shopping, went to the theatre, lunched at the Ritz."

"Dear me! How grand we have become. How much did your lunch cost?"

"About five pounds, I think."

"Well, no doubt you can afford that sort of thing now, since you have come into such a large fortune."

"But sir?" I felt myself blush. "How did you find out?"

"Quite simply. Bequests of importance are noted in *The Times*."

"Do the staff know?"

"I presume they can read, though sometimes I doubt it."

He stared at me, his expression far from friendly. "I suppose I should congratulate you, if not myself, since I will obviously have to dispense with your services."

"Do you mean I am to be dismissed? But why—what have I done wrong?"

"Nothing, I hope. But no doubt you will have more interesting future plans now than the drudgery of a diplomatic career, considering your income alone will amount to more than His Majesty's ambassadors are paid."

"But sir, you don't understand," I exclaimed in panic. "I still depend utterly on my salary, the other money is not mine to use."

"Indeed, I do not understand. But perhaps you will have the grace to explain."

How could I, without telling the truth? And with his compelling stern eyes fixed on me, haltingly at first and then with greater ease as I felt the relief of unburdening myself to a man who, if he seemed to me cold and inhuman, was nevertheless I knew utterly trustworthy, I told him everything. Of my early involvement with Alexander at Schwarzensee, of my guilt and how I had tried to escape it by evading him for years, of his reappearance in my life and its consequences and how, after the tragedy, I had been forced to concur with not only his doctor's but his own wishes to be believed dead.

"And those ashes that we had to fly to London? May I ask whose they were? The remains of one of Dr Koritschoner's other patients?"

"No. Out of his fireplace."

"Well, I'll be damned," Sir John said and to my surprise I saw he was laughing.

"But I still can't quite grasp why your young friend wanted himself believed dead?"

"I think because his pride forbade him to be still identified with what he had once been. Surely it is understandable, sir?"

"Since I have never been blessed with good looks such as his or fame as an actor, it is difficult to imagine—such an extent of vanity—because that is what it amounts to."

"Sir, if you knew what he has become and with what courage and humour he bears his affliction!"

"And so by trusting you with his future welfare and fortune, which he knew you would administer for his benefit, he has enslaved you once more, probably for life?"

"But how could I refuse?" I asked, knowing how desperately true Sir John's words were. "Would you have, sir?"

He hesitated and there was something unfamiliar in his expression. I thought I read sudden sympathy and compassion.

"No," he said at last. "Though not as sentimental as you, I would have known no alternative either. But you have loaded yourself with a great and difficult responsibility. May God help you to bear the burden, with courage as well as discretion. The latter you must realize is very important. Should all this ever be revealed, well it would certainly mean the end of your career—and mine if I was known to have been in any way involved. Is that understood?"

He seemed satisfied by what he read in my face.

"Now to the more practical aspects of this matter," he said briskly. "I suppose you realize that the news of this fortune you have inherited will spread far and wide—gain you friends and sycophants, but also secret enemies, especially among my staff. They might well ask resentfully why, rich as you have become, you have need to advance in the Service now, taking the bread out of their mouths so to speak—and I couldn't blame them.

"So we will have to deny firmly that you inherited at all. Maintain that what *The Times* printed was a mistake, that there had been a misinterpretation of the will and that Alexander Plevke's fortune had been left to his family. We dare not of course publicize this in the press, only by word of mouth. Though I may not inspire much affection in my staff, I hope they trust my integrity enough to believe what I tell them and you must, of course, say the same. In the tissue of deception in which you have so uncomfortably involved me, one lie more or less does not seem to count. Besides, in this case it is a half truth, since you are the only family Alexander has now."

He paused, looking at me thoughtfully. "I have for some time considered asking for an increase in your salary. You have worked well of late, in fact ever since you gave up your nightly excesses in the various haunts of pleasure to which you escorted a certain lady. I can, with a clear conscience as far as your work is concerned, recommend you for promotion now."

"Sir, I couldn't be more grateful. You see this strange situation I have had to accept has already brought personal expenses I could not foresee."

"Like lunching at the Ritz?" he asked, sardonically.

"I only mentioned that because I wanted to tell you that I saw Heinrich Hohenturn there with a lot of black-shirted Mosleyites."

"Really? That's interesting. Still, not entirely surprising since he tries to enlist recruits in every European country now, no matter what shirt they wear—black, brown or red. I hear he dressed his young Falcons in sky blue. But he will get into serious trouble one day, mark my words. Fascist as well as communist leaders do not like their prey snatched from under their nose and indoctrinated with different ideals from their own.

"Well, no doubt you have a lot to do. I will expect you for lunch on Christmas day as well as the rest of the staff. We will have the inevitable stuffed turkey with trimmings and Christmas pudding—one of the most indigestible of dishes." He sighed.

I went home, called up the clinic and asked to speak to Sister Koritschoner.

"How is he?" I asked.

"He will be glad you are back. He has been very restless ever since you left."

"Only for two days."

"The time seems longer to invalids. Have you brought his money?"

"Yes, and the hamper."

"And the domino?"

"That too."

"Well, he wants all that now. He is so impatient. Could you possibly bring it tonight? I know it's late and the wards will be closed, but they will let you in and I'll wait for you downstairs."

"I'll be there."

She hung up.

When an hour later she came to meet me I was startled by the difference in her appearance. She was still in her white uniform, but she was not wearing a cap and her head rose from her long neck strangely small and dark, the short cropped hair curling around her face neatly like some bird's blue-black feathers.

"Why, you have cut off all your lovely hair," I exclaimed.

"It was so heavy," she said. "This is much more convenient and hygienic."

"You know, I think it rather suits you," I said, "though

perhaps less feminine, somehow more attractive. Can I come and see him now?"

"I am afraid it is too late. We have certain rules that not even I dare break. And besides he only wants you on Christmas Eve. He is giving a party. That is, he hopes your mother will come and my uncle and me and you. That is why he wanted the hamper so much."

"There it is. It will have to go into your fridge immediately."

She looked at it with some concern. "It's much too large," she said and then smiled. "Perhaps we can keep it cool in the morgue. Have you brought the money?"

"Here," I said, taking the thick packets of notes that amounted to the thousand pounds and handing her them in an envelope.

"Good," she said, slipping it into her pocket. "He wants me to do some Christmas shopping for him. And the domino?"

I gave her the bulky bag.

She peered into it. "But what is this?" she asked, "some sort of fancy dress?"

"No, it's a domino."

"And I thought he had grown tired of chess and wanted me to play dominoes with him instead!"

She fingered the wig and moustache and mask. "Is this your idea of a joke?" she then said, indignantly. "Under the circumstances it is not very funny."

"I know it isn't, but it's what he wanted."

I saw understanding dawn in her face and then a look of the most tender compassion transformed it.

"Poor Mr Stanley," she said softly. Then, straightening her shoulders, she asked briskly: "How clean are these things?"

"I don't know. I bought them in a costume shop in London."

"Well, they will certainly have to be thoroughly disinfected before he even sees them."

"Will it take long?"

"No, we have these facilities here. He can have it all tomorrow. Look, I have to go back to him. He will sleep better for knowing you have brought everything he wanted. He is restless and impatient, being physically so much stronger now and it is difficult to keep him in bed."

"But can he walk?"

"Oh yes. He has therapy every day and his leg muscles are

much stronger. And now he is as excited about Christmas as any child and about his party. You will come with your mother, won't you?"

"Of course."

"Though I am Jewish, as were my parents, we always had a decorated Christmas tree every year and stockings. I will decorate a small one for him, candles and all, you'll see. Do you think you could manage the stockings? I don't have much time to fill them—just apples and oranges, nuts and raisins and silly little toys and things children like, and sweets and crackers."

I saw once more how young she was and thought that perhaps she, too, so tragically deprived of her parents, longed for such childhood pleasures.

"I'll do my best," I said. "We will have a happy Christmas Eve together, in spite of everything."

■

My mother and I had spent the day shopping, buying long black woollen stockings first, then the most varied oddities to fill them with; small weird animals of blown glass from Czechoslovakia, hand-carved wooden birds that opened their beaks to crack nuts, corkscrews with human heads, Christmas angels of all sizes and fruit and sweets.

"I don't think it's quite the right thing to put an angel in Dr Koritschoner's stocking," I remonstrated. "Isn't it too Christian?"

"Nonsense," my mother replied, "they had angels long before we did. As for that poor girl, shouldn't we think of something more exciting than nuts and raisins to put in hers? It can't be the most happy of Christmases for her."

"But, Mother, what?"

"The most dedicated nurses are the most feminine. Leave it to me—I will see what I can find."

"And for Alexander?"

"There are the books you brought and the kimono, and crossword puzzles would no doubt amuse him—" she would indeed think of that—"and then why not give him your father's book on the Tsars of Russia. I have a copy left."

Loaded with our heavy black stockings we entered the clinic on Christmas Eve. All the way there in the taxi my mother talked incessantly, as she is liable to do when nervous, of things totally unconnected with what she is nervous about.

At the clinic we were directed to go to Mr Stanley's room.

Esther received us at the door. To my surprise she was not wearing her uniform, but a long green evening dress that left her arms and shoulders bare.

"It's what he demanded," she said. "It is to be a night of masquerade."

I introduced her to my mother and we went in. The only light in the large dark room came from the candles that lit the Christmas tree. Though the netted tent was still there, its curtains were drawn back and there was no one in the narrow bed.

Out of the shadows rose a tall figure draped in black, hooded and masked. It swayed towards my mother and me, reaching out for her with a white-gloved hand. I would not have been surprised if she had screamed and fled in terror.

"Mother, it's Alexander," I said hastily. "He is in fancy dress tonight."

"And most authentic it looks, too," she said calmly. "I have never seen any of Goldoni's plays, but I know the *Longhis* in Venice well. The costume is perfect." And she clasped the outstretched gloved hand firmly. "Happy Christmas, Mr Stanley."

Dr Koritschoner got up from where he had been sitting and no doubt watching. He bent low over my mother's hand as if in homage, which indeed I felt her presence of mind fully deserved, and then greeted me.

"Mr Livingstone, open the champagne," Esther begged. "I can't quite manage—and help me serve the food. I have put everything on the trolley. You need only push it around."

Alexander had retreated once more into the shadows. All one could see of him that identified him as human were the pupils of his eyes, in which the candlelight flickered strangely, through the slits in the black mask.

"This is a splendid feast you have offered us, Mr Stanley," the doctor exclaimed, spooning caviare under his beard with obvious relish and then starting to devour most of the marrons glacés. There was no response nor sound from Alexander. The doctor might as well have been addressing a ghost.

I looked at my mother in the light of the candlelit tree. I could just discern that she was merely toying with the food on her plate. I was not very hungry either—thirsty, though.

"To your recovery, Alexander," I said, raising my glass to the still and silent figure in its black draperies. What horrible mockery, I thought.

"Shall we have the stockings now?" my mother asked, trying to sound cheerful.

"I rather think a little later," Esther said. "I believe Mr Stanley would be more comfortable if he went back to bed now, where he has been concealing all his presents. Just leave us for a few moments."

We went out into the corridor, evading each other's eyes and no one spoke.

The nurse returned. "He is more comfortable. Please will you come back?"

So in again we trooped. The black spectral figure was gone. Under the muslin curtains, not unlike those that shelter a baby's old-fashioned cradle or cot, Alexander lay swaddled once more in white bandages.

Esther bent under the tent. As she moved in the clinging silk dress, I noted the perfection of her slim young body with pleasure.

She drew out a tray piled high with parcels wrapped in Christmas paper, staggering under its weight.

"Let me help."

"No," she laughed, "I'm very strong. Some of my patients are much heavier to lift." And she set the tray on a table.

"Mr Stanley wrapped them all himself. He was most secretive about it, but I think this is yours, Mrs Livingstone."

It was small and flat. My mother unwrapped it to look with amazement and evident emotion at the small miniature in its gilt frame.

"But this is Tsar Alexander the First," she exclaimed, contemplating the beautiful young face, so like Alexander's once had been. "What a rare and unique treasure," she managed to say. "I don't know how to thank you, Mr Stanley," and she gazed helplessly at what lay so still under the netting. "I can't think of anything that would have given me greater pleasure." Or pain, I could not help feeling, seeing her face.

Dr Koritschoner was given his present next. It was a large and heavy book—ancient, battered and bound in vellum.

"It's the Talmud, Uncle," Esther said. "One of the earliest printed. In Latin, but that makes no difference to you. With Alexander's help I found it."

So evident was the doctor's pleasure and interest as he turned the tattered pages, pausing now and then as if he had found a favourite passage to re-read, that he seemed to have forgotten us all. Finally he closed the book and looked up from it.

"All the wisdom of our people it contains—and much of their folly too."

Esther had meanwhile unwrapped her present. It was a flat velvet-covered box. She undid the clasps. On a bed of white satin, yellowed by time, lay the Tsarevna's diamond and emerald necklace. She stared at it without comprehension, then looked at me as if for help.

"It belonged to his grandmother," I said. "Look, perhaps you had better read this." I gave her the note. She did—and then dropped it and averted her face, but I knew she was crying.

I picked up the piece of paper: "Dear Esther," I read, "Please wear this tonight. I want to see how well it suits you. I kept it thinking one day I might give it to my wife. Now I will never marry. But your care and devotion have been more than even the most loving of wives could have given. So please accept this Christmas present. It is of lesser value than what you have done for me. Alexander."

"But how can I take this," she said, turning back to me to look, as if entranced, through her tears at the shining gems once more. "Is it real? It's so beautiful."

As real as Alexander is, I thought. "Of course you must accept it," I said. "Put it on." When she hesitated I lifted it out of its case and clasped it round her neck. "It certainly suits you," I exclaimed, startled at her changed appearance. So obviously were my mother and the doctor—we all stared at her. And I had always thought her rather plain! Out of the great barbaric necklace that had once belonged to Catherine the Great of Russia, her long smooth neck rose proudly upholding her small close-cropped head. Her thin shoulders and girlish breasts, still not fully developed into mature fullness, were encircled by the gleaming regal gems. I suddenly thought of the Jewish virgin, whose name she bore, adorned to meet the King of the Medes and Persians: "She had neither father or mother but the maid was fair and beautiful—And the King loved Esther above all women and she obtained grace and favour in his sight more than all the virgins so that he set the royal crown upon her head and made her queen."

"Now show yourself to him," my mother said. Esther vanished under the netted canopy to reappear after a while, smiling.

"He is pleased," she said simply, "but I can't take it,

Uncle, can I? Not if it's valuable. My mother would never have allowed me to."

"If you were my daughter," my mother said firmly, "I would tell you to keep it and remember that there is often more virtue and grace in gratefully accepting a kind gift, whatever one's pride, than in bestowing one."

"I couldn't agree with you more, Mrs Livingstone," the doctor said, stealthily munching another marron glacé.

Esther, reassured, flushed with pleasure.

"Gracious," she exclaimed, "what with all this, I have forgotten your present, Mr Livingstone. Here it is."

I unwrapped it. Inside was the Russian icon I had last seen in the Tsarevna's room in Schwarzensee. Once more the inscrutable elongated Byzantine eyes stared from under their golden crowns. Attached was a note and a thick plain white envelope.

"Dearest Eddie" I read. "I couldn't think what to give you. Nothing seemed adequate. If I, like the phoenix, have been able to rise out of the flames, it is mainly thanks to your help. You are very good to me. I will tonight distribute between you and those equally kind and helpful, what I most treasure, things that remind me of the Tsarevna. I loved the wicked old woman. So I think did you, *gentilhomme Anglais*, almost as much as you have loved and feared me. Alexander. P.S. There is money in the envelope—certainly no gift, but just a small repayment for what you must have spent for me in London."

I stared at the canopied tent in which Alexander lay crippled and seemingly helpless and shuddered at the power he still had over me—over all of us I felt, because Esther was gazing at the bed as if under a spell, an unfathomable expression in her dark eyes while her hands softly caressed the Tsarevna's necklace. My mother, too, was looking fearfully towards it, still clasping the miniature. Only the doctor seemed quite unperturbed. He had switched on a small shaded light and he looked utterly content as he turned the pages of his ancient book.

The candles had burnt low and were starting to flicker. I snuffed out one after the other.

"I think Mr Stanley must have gone to sleep," Esther said, stretching and moving her head a little as if to dispel some dream on waking.

The doctor closed his book and rose. "It's time," he said.

"But what about our stockings?" my mother whispered.

"In the morning. Esther will distribute them. It's always good to have something to look forward to on the morrow," the doctor said.

Quietly my mother and I stole out of the room.

"Happy Christmas," I said once more, as we arrived at our flat, and kissed her good night. In spite of her gay flamboyant shawl, she looked old, tired and sad. For a moment she clung to me then straightened herself.

"Yes," she said, "we must not forget that it's Christ's birth-day and that He too rose from the dead."

Emptying my pockets when I got to my room I found the envelope. There were three hundred pounds in it.

Next morning, quite early, Esther telephoned to thank us for the stockings saying how delighted all three of them had been with their contents.

"You should have seen Alexander with his, just like a happy child as he pulled out one surprise after the other. As for me—what delicious scent! I get so tired of the smell of disinfectant. And the beautiful scarf—I will wear it all on my next day off."

"Which I hope you will spend with me. We will drive up to the Semmering and have lunch in the sun and snow. Do you ski, by any chance?"

"Oh yes, I learnt in the Sudeten mountains."

"And I, if only very briefly, in the Italian Tyrol. I may fall at your feet. Anyway, I nearly did last evening. You looked absolutely dazzling in that green dress and necklace."

"I think it must have been the jewels that dazzled you more than me." But she was laughing.

"Well, let me know when you have a free day."

"I will," she said and hung up.

# Chapter Twenty-two

The legend of my inheritance had reached wider circles, as I found out when Marie Therese called me up to invite me to a fancy-dress ball on New Year's Eve, and to thank me for the flowers I had sent her for Christmas.

"We will all be masked, wearing the costumes of figures in opera," she told me excitedly. "We are opening the entire palace." Her voice changed to a note of sadness. "I hope you don't think me heartless, Eddie, because it is only three months since Alexander died, but it is in a very good cause that we are giving the ball. It is for one of Heinrich's charities—*Milch fürs Kind*. It will mean that all the children and young people of the Sudeten will get free milk—though it seems to me there are more cows and goats than anywhere else in those mountains. Still, Heinrich says it's important, and so that people remember what it is all about, they will have to buy their wine in milk bottles. Isn't that clever? Heinrich has hired the Opera Ballet to perform and a famous soprano and we will have three bands. Won't it be wonderful, Eddie?" she asked joyously.

Without waiting for an answer she prattled on. "Of course, we expect a handsome donation from you, now that you are so rich. I was so glad when I read that Alexander had left you his fortune, though not surprised, since you were the only person he really loved."

"It is not true that I inherited, Marie Therese, please believe me and tell your friends that it was a mistake what *The Times* printed," I managed to say. "It all went to his mother in the end."

"Oh really? Well, all the better perhaps. Some people were even saying that you must have been *de l'autre côté*, you and he. Though I know it's not true, I couldn't really explain it to them without becoming too explicit about us."

"But what on earth does '*de l'autre côté*' mean?"

"Really, Eddie, I thought you were an educated man. In

English it is called after a flower, I think—could it be a pansy?"

My mother, too, had been invited to the ball, as was all of Vienna, but she refused to go.

"Of course, I might drape myself as Carmen in your lovely shawl," she joked, "but at my age I fear I would only be appreciated as a figure of fun. No, I will have a quiet dinner with Sir John at the Embassy. He is not going to the ball either and we will drink in the New Year with barley water, no doubt, and with no undue jollifications. I somehow feel the time for those is almost over. History has an odd way of repeating itself. While the Congress of Vienna danced, Napoleon was on the march. However, enjoy yourself."

She had helped me to choose my costume. It was the least conspicuous we could find at the hiring place, that of Mimi's lover in Puccini's *Bohème*.

Invitations were for ten o'clock. I walked to the palace. Snow had begun to fall and it was very cold. Cars and taxis came and went incessantly as I approached. The enormous double doors—usually closed, only a small side entrance giving access to the courtyard—stood wide open. Through them the costumed and masked crowd flowed up the great stone staircase, carpeted in crimson for the occasion. In arched niches at intervals stood liveried footmen with powdered hair, holding aloft flaming torches. They stood as still as statues, while the gods and goddesses that ornamented the baroque balustrade seemed to move in the flickering light and to have come alive, the grey stone of their scantily draped bodies glowing pink like flesh, their welcoming outstretched arms seeming to tremble and stir as light and shade intermittently touched them. Somewhere in the distance an orchestra was playing from *The Magic Flute*.

On the first floor, where most of the big reception rooms were, all the panelled white and gold doors stood open so that there was an unobstructed view from one end of the palace to the other. One could see through a seemingly interminable series of magnificent stuccoed rooms lit by thousands of candles in glittering chandeliers or silver candelabras. Their mellow light transformed the gaudy, tinselled costumes into beauty and authenticity.

At the very end of the enfilade of rooms was the large ballroom where Heinrich and Marie Therese were receiving their guests. Neither of the two was masked. Her costume was of the kind that suited her best. A wide pink and silver crinoline concealed her plump legs and thighs. Her waist was tightly laced, pushing up her fine breasts like ripe fruit offered on a tray. Round her neck was a beribboned wreath of tiny pink roses and more of them adorned her high-piled powdered hair. She looked enchantingly beautiful. It needed no explanation whom she was representing.

"Frau Marschallin," I said, bending over her hand.

I was masked, but I suppose by my voice she recognized me.

"Naturally, Eddie," she laughed, "and look behind me, I even have a Rosenkavalier." In the background hovered a slim figure, masked too, but not a girl; quite unmistakably male by the fit of his trousers and by the devoted attention I was later to see with which he followed Marie Therese all night, carrying messages, bringing her shawl and fan and frequent plates from the buffet piled high with food.

Meanwhile I had greeted Heinrich. Though taller and slimmer than the singers that usually play Baron Ochs, it was not difficult to discern whom he was representing. He did not recognize me. He shook my hand with the weariness royalty must know before he clasped the next hands of the onpressing crowds that came to salute him. Many hundreds of hands, I thought.

Later the ballroom was cleared for dancing. There was no end to the variety of costumes. Aïdas and Tosca's Butterflies, Lucias, Leonoras and Marguerites, fox-trotted, waltzed and tangoed with Toreadors, fur-draped Boris Godounovs, Don Giovannis and black-clad Mephistos.

I saw several buxom Carmens and felt my mother had been right in not having wanted to compete with them.

There were even one or two people who wore ordinary black dominos, presumably over evening dress. I might have borrowed Alexander's, I thought, had I know this was acceptable, instead of hiring an expensive costume.

At midnight nearly everyone unmasked. Great steaming bowls of punch were served by the powdered footmen and the year 1938—that was to prove so fateful for Austria—was joyfully welcomed in.

Afterwards, Madame K performed as Salome. It had been one of Jeritza's most famous operatic roles in the past. Not only her superb voice but the feline beauty in her dance as she discarded veil after veil was unforgotten in Vienna.

Unfortunately so, because though Madame K's singing, as she pleaded with Jokaanan to submit to her desire, was just as moving, her appearance was not. She was immensely fat and looked utterly ridiculous as, scantily clad, she squatted on the floor over the imaginary entrance to the dungeon where St John the Baptist (not unnaturally, one couldn't help but feel) elected to lose his head rather than yield.

There was stifled laughter. It was a relief when the Opern-ballet began their more graceful performance.

People dispersed. Some went downstairs where, in a room that had been tented and furnished with low couches, cushions and oriental carpets, gypsies played to amorously inclined couples in semi-darkness. In it I found Marie Therese with the Rosenkavalier. He was remarkably pretty, but so young that he might still well have been able to sing soprano parts.

Both were listening with that rapt attention which only Austrians or Hungarians give to those primitive, hauntingly sad melodies of a homeless people.

Marie Therese made room for me beside her on the couch holding her finger to her lips. Closer and closer to her the gypsy primas moved till he bent over her, his dark face inscrutable. Ever more softly and tenderly his violin sang, as if for her ears alone. I saw her eyes grow moist and widen as if with desire. She clasped my hand and that of the Rosenkavalier too, but was almost unconscious of doing so, I think, as someone drowning might reach out for help before sinking into the sweet death of oblivion. When I slipped away she did not even notice.

Across the hall the big dining-room had been hung with gaily-striped bunting and decorated with lattices. Rough benches and tables covered with chequered cloths transformed it into a sort of Heurigen Restaurant. I looked at my watch—it was four o'clock. Goulash was being served, hot sausages, *Kipferlen* and *Semmels* and coffee.

All the tables were occupied. There was much laughter and rather drunken bawling of Viennese folk-songs. I filled my plate and sat down with it on a bench in the more or less empty hall. I felt lonely and sad. *"Wien, Wien, nur Du allein, sollst stehts die Stadt meiner Träume sein"* they sang.

I looked up at the great baroque staircase. The torches that had brought it to life had been extinguished. A few meagre electric bulbs hanging here and there shone coldly on the grey stone. The gods and nymphs had withdrawn into dusty obscurity. Down the wide stairs people descended, but no one went up them any more. And with a kind of premonition, I felt no happy crowd of mummers, musicians, singers, dancers or guests would ever climb those steps again. It was as if a curtain had fallen on a final act, staged in the Hohenturn Palace. The magnificent pageant I had seen, that recalled all the centuries of wealth, luxury and privilege in which the aristocracy had ruled supreme, was over.

I'm probably sobering up, I thought, knowing I had drunk too much earlier, but not even the coffee and hot sausages could dispel my gloom.

One of the footmen came to stand beside me. Handsome, rather, his silk-stockinged legs were well formed. He was tall, broad-shouldered and his powdered hair gave him an air of distinction.

I looked more closely at his face and an uneasy feeling that I had seen it before in connection with something unpleasant came over me.

"Is the English gentleman feeling unwell," he asked, "sitting here all alone?"

"Thank you—I am quite all right." Surely it could not be so obvious that I was still slightly drunk that even servants noticed? He was looking at me with a mocking expression I suddenly recognized.

"We met, I think, at Schloss Hohenturn," I said.

"Indeed, sir. How kind you should remember. It was when the tragic accident happened to Count Plevke. What a beautiful young man—and now I hear he is dead." Was it an assertion or a question?

I saw he was swaying slightly. At least I hoped it was him, since I did not want to admit to myself that perhaps I was not seeing straight any more.

"Won't you sit down?" I asked. "You must be very tired."

"Yes—I have been on my feet for the last thirty-six hours, but it would not be right for me to sit here." He straightened himself.

"Mr Livingstone. Don't you need a valet?" he then asked, to my surprise.

"No. Why?"

"Well, surely a gentleman who has inherited so large a fortune should not remain unattended. I have served Prince Hohenturn in that capacity off and on for many years, to his satisfaction I believe, and I am thoroughly acquainted with what gentlemen, especially English gentlemen, demand of their valets."

There was nothing offensive in his remark, but there was in the almost conspiratorial look he gave me.

"I have neither inherited a fortune nor do I need a valet," I said coldly.

And then remembering that once already I had been unforgivably rude to him in Hohenturn—"Why? Do you want to change your job?"

"One has to look to one's future. Prince Heinrich is a sick man."

"But surely if anything happened to him the Princess would keep you on."

"Sir, I am a gentleman's gentleman, not a lady's maid."

"I am sorry," I said, "but I really can neither afford nor do I need anyone. Surely, if you applied to one of the embassies—what about the German? I hear Herr von Papen is increasing his staff every day now. You are Sudeten German, aren't you?"

"Yes, sir. But we are very pro-English. Our leader, Herr Henlein, is often in England and a close friend of your prime minister, Mr Chamberlain, so I hear."

"You hear a lot," I said, wondering why I disliked him so much. "Do you think you could find me my coat?" I handed him the tag.

He went and returned with my coat, helping me into it but smoothing it down over my shoulders with a sort of intimate solicitude that I resented. I shrugged off his hands, then felt sorry. Probably he was even drunker than I.

"What is your name?" I asked, "in case anything crops up?"

"Fritz Lang," he said. "Thank you, sir," smiling ingratiatingly once more.

I walked out through the courtyard, now dark except for the pale light of the dawning sky. The snow had melted and congealed into ice. There were sudden gusts of the wind that perpetually blows through the streets of Vienna at all seasons—its beneficence in having once dispersed the plague hundreds of years ago still recalled by prayer in all its churches. An icy blast struck me and, unbalanced by its sudden force, I slipped and fell. There was no pain until I tried to get up. My ankle must be broken, I thought, I could not stand on it.

So there I sat on the icy pavement wondering how long it would take until I froze to death. No one passed by, the street was quite empty. Then to my great good fortune a taxi, probably on its way home and at which I waved frantically, stopped. The driver open his window and peered down at me.

"*Besoffen*—drunk," he muttered.

I tried to get up but sank down helplessly on to the pavement.

"Look here," he said, "if you think I'm going to wait till you are sober enough to walk you are mistaken." He restarted his engine.

I would not have blamed him for driving away, but I knew I must not let him.

"*Fuss gebrochen*," I called as loudly as I could. "*Helfen Sie bitte.*" He heard. Evidently he was a kind man for he got out, though still looking suspicious. He bent down, put one of my arms round his neck and lifted me up. Though in extreme pain, I managed to get into the cab with his support.

"And where to now?" he asked.

I gave him the address of the Koritschoner clinic. It seemed the only sensible place to go to, because even my mother would question my sobriety if I crawled on hands and knees up the stairs to our flat.

Arriving at the clinic I paid the driver double what was on the meter and asked him to go in and seek help. He returned seconds later.

"They take no casualties here," he said. "They advised me to drive you to the Algemeines Krankenhaus."

"Then go back and ask for Sister Koritschoner to come down."

My large tip had been effective. "My name is Livingstone, in case they ask. I am well-known in the clinic."

He went; I waited. My foot ached insufferably and I felt faint.

What followed then has not remained very clear in my mind, except that I was lifted out of the cab, laid on a stretcher, wheeled through several passages, tried to explain to a uniformed nurse who looked rather like Esther what had happened and please to call my mother and to tell her why I had not come home—I seem to remember a darkly laughing face above me, then the stab of a needle, then nothing.

I woke up in a narrow hospital bed. I moved my foot. It was heavy, encased in plaster, but it did not hurt at all, not even when I put it down to see if I could walk on it. I was wearing pyjamas, certainly not my own.

"Well, I wouldn't try that just yet, Mr Livingstone. It has to dry. Go back to bed." It was Esther.

"But what happened?" I asked her.

"Merely that a drunken foreigner in fancy-dress was delivered by taxi at our door at five o'clock this morning. Thank goodness you remembered your name or you would not be here now."

"What have they done to my foot?"

"It's been X-rayed and my uncle set it. It is quite a simple fracture. You should be able to walk again in a few weeks, though you will have to rest it meanwhile and use crutches."

"But can I go home?"

"Oh yes, now that it is splinted and plastered, any time if you are careful and sensible. I talked to your mother and told her you would probably be back today."

I sighed with relief. "How is Alexander?" I asked.

"Tiresome and difficult," she said. "He kept me up all night."

Then I saw how exhausted she looked. "What with him, and your sudden arrival, I haven't slept at all."

"I'm sorry, Esther. I wasn't drunk, you know."

"Really?" she said, raising her brows. "We checked your blood, of course. That punch was very strong."

"But how could they know that it was punch?"

She yawned. "I did," she said. "I think we both need some rest now." She fluffed up my pillows, drew up the sheets and left me. Though puzzled by her last remark, I drifted into sleep.

I woke a few hours later feeling fit for anything. I was brought breakfast which I hungrily devoured, then asked for my clothes.

"I want to get up," I told the plump little Viennese nurse.

"That is for Sister Koritschoner to decide. She is still asleep."

"Well, could you find me some crutches or a wheelchair, so I can visit Mr Stanley," I asked.

"He is asleep too." She giggled. "Both he and Sister went to a fancy-dress ball and only came back in the early hours. I was on night duty so I know."

"But that is impossible," I said, unbelievingly. "Besides, I would have seen them. What were they wearing?"

"Oh, long black cloaks and hoods and masks. Quite unrecognizable, they were."

I suddenly remembered the people in dominoes.

"But I thought Mr Stanley was still much too ill to leave the clinic?"

"He?" And she laughed. "Well, I could tell you a thing or two, except that we are not allowed to discuss our patients, and perhaps I have already said too much.

"Do you want the bedpan? No need to blush, Mr Livingstone." She handed me a bottle. "Call me when you have finished. I will be waiting outside."

Half an hour later she ushered in my mother.

"I've got the ambulance, Eddie. I have been allowed to take you home. I talked to Dr Koritschoner—he doesn't expect any complications, though he might want his pyjamas back," she said, eyeing me with evident amusement. "I have brought you some clothes since you will, I imagine, hardly want to put on your fancy-dress once more. Were you very drunk?"

"Certainly not," I protested angrily, trying to struggle out of the pyjamas.

"Keep them on." Esther was standing at the door. "We will wrap you in a blanket for now. Good morning, Mrs Livingstone. He will be perfectly all right you know—don't worry."

"I certainly won't," my mother said coldly. "All his own silly fault." But I saw the grateful look she gave Esther. "Will you come and check the ankle now and then?" she pleaded.

"Of course."

Two men came in, covered me with a blanket and lifted me on to a stretcher. My mother and Esther followed in silence—as if I were a corpse, I thought.

I had to assert that I was still alive. I wriggled my head out of the blanket. "I saw you and Alexander at the ball, Esther."

"No doubt. Strong punch induces all sorts of hallucinatory fantasies."

I was lifted into the ambulance and when it arrived at our flat, into my bed. My mother made me comfortable and brought me some tea.

"Silly old boy," she said, stroking my head soothingly. "Now sleep."

After a couple of days I had learnt to hobble around quite competently in our flat on my crutches, but could not venture out; as yet my balance was still too insecure.

My mother had, of course, informed Sir John about my accident and much to my surprise he came to visit me.

He was not in the best of tempers—in fact even more irascible than usual.

"You could not have chosen a worse time in which to absent yourself from work. We need all hands at the Embassy just now and certainly feet." And he stared sourly at my plaster cast. "We may soon have to pack, you know."

"But what do you mean, sir?"

"Oh, just that Schuschnigg has had the courage to cònfront Hitler at last with what has been going on here. He is in Berlin now. It may bring things to a head—and very suddenly— Hitler likes surprises."

"You think he might march into Austria?"

"Frankly, I don't know, but it is best to be prepared. If he does do so, you realize that we will, of course, have to close the Embassy here? That there would be no possibility of His Majesty's Government's representatives remaining on in an Austria that had been annexed to the German Reich?"

"But, sir, surely that can't happen? After all, Austrian independence is guaranteed."

"By Mussolini." He shrugged. "We are not committed.

"But look here, I have not come to waste my valuable time in discussing what is at present still unascertainable, nor to sympathize with your having so foolishly incapacitated yourself, but there are some things I wanted to discuss with you in private. If anything happens here, I have good reason to believe—since my colleague in Prague is retiring—that I will be offered the Embassy there. Would you be willing to come with me as chargé d'affaires? After all, it would be promotion.

"But, of course, you might have other plans," he added. "It is not really very important, one way or another. I'll just have to manage without you, which of course I would regret; you have been quite useful at times."

So has my mother, I thought, and that it was in no way concern for me that had brought him to visit my sick-bed and to tell me all he had.

"I doubt very much that my mother would want to move with me to Prague, even if I went," I struck back. "She often says she would prefer to go home."

"Really? Strange—but then of course *la donna e mobile*, though I would not have expected such vagaries from anyone as sensible as your mother. She assured me she was quite willing to accompany you to Prague should it become necessary."

I quailed under his cold and level gaze.

"Sir," I said, "you know that I can't leave Vienna, whatever happens. There is Alexander."

"Oh that—I thought it might worry you." He gave me a wintry smile. "I have made certain arrangements. If anything happens here the Koritschoners know that they may have to leave at a moment's notice. I have discussed it with them both. They have a house in Prague where they will take Alexander who will still need their care for quite a while. One of the Embassy cars with the most reliable of my drivers will take them across the frontier into Czechoslovakia and to safety."

"But sir," I protested. "Surely Dr Koritschoner would not be in any danger, whatever happens? He is one of the most famous physicians and surgeons in Vienna."

"And what about those that were equally prominent in Germany? Where are they now?"

"But to have to leave his clinic! It's his life's work."

"Unfortunately so successful a one that there will be as many as anxious to take over as there were in the Sudeten to get his brother's factories. Many Jews have already fled this country and had to leave all they have worked for and achieved behind."

"But how do you know?"

"Because I spend most of my time signing entry visas for the United Kingdom for them, rather indiscriminately I must confess." He shrugged. "There is so little one dares do—or can. The rules of the Service are strict. Not to get involved in the internal affairs of the country we are accredited to, to learn to accept dispassionately and without taking sides, whatever happens, showing neither sympathy nor regret—those are more or less our inhumane orders."

And with venomous sarcasm, he added, "After all, it is none of our business what foreigners choose to do to each other, is it?" He stood up. "Well? If I am given Prague, will you come, Eddie?"

"I would be glad to, sir."

Next day Esther called, led into my room by my mother who, very properly, remained with us while Esther examined my foot or what she could see of it. She was not wearing her uniform and her small head, with its short curls, was bare.

"Does it hurt at all?" she asked.

"No, but it itches infernally."

"Do you have a knitting needle by any chance, Mrs Livingstone?" My mother brought one.

"This is not permissible in the clinic, nor should I allow

you to use it, but here—" she handed me the long needle. "Now slip it under the cast and scratch, but not too hard."

I did, and sighed with relief.

"I would say we can get you out of the plaster in a couple of weeks if the X-rays are all right and if we are not gone by then. Have you heard that we may have to travel?"

"Yes, Esther. I'm so sorry, especially for your uncle. It seems incredible that he might have to leave everything at a moment's notice."

"Oh, he is quite prepared," she said. "If a doctor could not face emergencies and a Jew exile and loss of property on occasion, we would hardly have survived so long as a people." But there was no bitterness either in her face or tone of voice.

"Besides, Prague is not really exile for him. It is where he studied, where he still has many friends and where he can practise again. We have a home to go to—in a way we are much more fortunate than others."

"And Alexander? Have you told him?"

"Of course."

"And how did he take it?"

She hesitated. "It's so difficult to tell with him since he can't speak and what he writes down is always carefully deliberated. But I know him so well now that I can almost sense what he feels or wants. I think he was rather frightened at first. Invalids do dread any disruption of familiar routine and environment. But when I assured him you would shortly be posted to Prague his relief was evident. I hope it's true, Eddie. You see, in a way you are all he has left." And her large dark eyes pleaded.

"Except for you. You love him, don't you?"

"Yes," she said firmly, "and I admire him. However broken the body, it is the spirit that counts. To lie down and die is easy, but to live, even under such adverse circumstances, is sublime. There is no need for you to worry about him," she added, and smiled at me reassuringly. "Since he knows you will come to Prague he is rather looking forward to a change. He gets very bored at times and then becomes mischievous and does all sorts of things he shouldn't."

"Like going to the ball?"

"I couldn't stop him, so I hired another domino and went with him. Before the unmasking came we managed to escape. I thought the Princess looked too lovely, didn't you? I still have friends in the secretariat. They told me that in case there is any trouble here, the Hohenturns will move to their Prague palace. So we will all be together again. Meanwhile I am teaching Alexander to read and write Czech."

# Chapter Twenty-three

We all fear our end, but since it is inevitable we ignore that it must come for as long as we can.

So did Viennese society. *"Glücklich ist, wer vergisst, was nicht mehr zu ändern ist!"* All through the *Fasching* they danced and sang.

On the night of 12 March, Austria as an independent and sovereign nation breathed its last. On the 13th it was proclaimed dead.

Nevertheless it had come as a shock to many. Even the large element of its pro-German and Nazi population woke from their sleep surprised to see Vienna occupied by German troops that morning.

German planes roared overhead, the cobble-stoned streets shook under booted feet and the old palaces trembled as German tanks entered the city.

My mother and I had stayed up all night listening to the various broadcasts. It had been like hearing a report of the constant decline of a patient's health. By morning there had been no doubt that Austria was beyond saving. Hitler's decision to strike with such lightning suddenness had left no time for any opposition to rally.

I looked out. German flags waved everywhere, at every window, even in our street. People were greeting each other with the Hitler salute.

"This is pretty bloody!" I exclaimed.

"That is just what I hope it's not going to be," my mother said, calmly buttering her breakfast *Kipferl*. "Long ago the Turks besieged Vienna with such superior forces that only by guile and patient diplomacy could they be held from destroying the town. In memory of this, the Prophet's half-moon is still baked. Who knows if one day we won't be able to eat Swastika-marked Hitler buns for breakfast too."

"Mother," I exclaimed impatiently, "I have to get to the Embassy."

She went to the window. "I doubt there will be any taxis," she said, looking down. "People are milling around like mad and you certainly can't walk. Shall I call the Embassy and commandeer the Rolls?"

"But Sir John will be furious."

"Not if it's me that asks for it. I will come with you."

Quite soon it arrived. It was a very old vehicle but kept so conscientiously tended and polished by the equally ancient sergeant who drove it, that it shone as new. We drove through the streets, not without some triumph. Not even a German tank could have advanced as impressively and as ruthlessly dispersed the crowd as the huge old Rolls did, guided by the impassive sergeant. There were almost as many cheers as jeers, but no one ventured to obstruct our passage.

I climbed the Embassy steps for the first time in many weeks. We found the ambassador at his desk sorting papers. He rose to greet my mother.

"But John," she exclaimed, looking startled and concerned. It was the first time I had heard her call him by his first name. "Are you ill? You are so flushed."

He was indeed strangely red in the face.

"No, only very hot and very tired. I have been stoking the fire all night. Since I don't know when we will be given orders to leave, I thought certain documents best disposed of. Not that I think they will dare investigate anything here. And they will avoid any provocative action for the time being at least, I hope."

"Sir, the Koritschoners?" I asked.

"They and your young friend reached Prague safely. The driver has since returned. They left two days ago."

I sighed with relief.

"And really only just in time. One of our contacts had reported considerable troop movements in southern Germany; it was obvious that they were on their way here.

"Meanwhile, there are already many arrests. Not only of Jews—and they don't shirk at jailing even the most prominent, Baron Rothschild is in prison—but of Christians too. Poor Schuschnigg has been held and many members of his government. Also quite a few aristocrats—the two Princes Hohenberg, Prince Carl Emil Fürstenberg, a Count Hoyos."

"But why?"

"They may have been monarchist, but the fact that they are patriotic Austrians is just as reprehensible to Hitler. Prince Heinrich Hohenturn has been arrested too."

"Heinrich? But I always thought he and Hitler collaborated."

"As indeed they did, as long as it suited either. It seems it did not suit the Führer any more."

"Marie Therese!" I exclaimed, "she must be desperate. I must go to her immediately to see if there is anything I can do."

"How, I wonder?" Sir John asked, contemplating my plastered foot. "Besides, they may not let you into the house, it's probably guarded by now."

"Oh, Eddie, you might get into trouble," my mother pleaded.

"As if that has ever stopped him," the ambassador said sourly. "But you'd better take the Rolls, I imagine it's still outside."

"He will be safer if they recognize where he belongs," he told my mother.

"Take your credentials with you and be careful as to what you say or do. I can't risk any member of my staff involving us in serious trouble. Do you understand?"

"Yes, sir. Thank you." Difficult as the old man was, it was not the first time that I had felt grateful for his foresight and help. I doubt I would ever have reached the palace except for the Rolls and the intrepid old sergeant.

By now the streets were jammed with screaming youths waving German flags. I saw several shop-windows being smashed or already broken. There was somewhat more quiet round the palace, but its gates were guarded by two armed men in brown uniforms with Swastika arm-bands.

The sergeant helped me out.

"Halt!" they called, as I approached the palace entrance.

"British Embassy," I said and proffered my papers. They scanned them—I doubt they could read English—looked at each other then back at me and then at the Rolls.

"*Heil Hitler,*" they said in unison, saluting.

I could only answer by raising my crutch instead.

"I won't be long," I called to the sergeant in English.

"Not with this lot, I wouldn't, sir," but I saw my feeble gesture of defiance had pleased him.

I was allowed into the courtyard and rang the bell. It was only after a while that a footman appeared; not in livery, but wearing a crumpled shirt, his hair dishevelled, pasty-faced, bleary-eyed, as if he had not slept all night. Nevertheless I recognized him.

"Aren't you Fritz Lang," I asked, "who offered to become my valet?"

"Sir. You must excuse my appearance. There has been a lot of trouble here. Yes, I had hoped you would let me serve you, but now that tragedy has so unexpectedly struck their Highnesses, of course I cannot leave for the present. I'm not a rat to desert a sinking ship," he added sententiously.

"A most loyal resolve," I remarked. "Have you any idea why the Prince was arrested?"

"No, sir, but even if I did it would not be for me to comment."

I found Marie Therese in her drawing-room draped haphazardly in a pink dressing-gown. When I had freed myself of my crutches she threw herself into my arms, considerably shaking my balance. I sat down.

"Oh, Eddie, I'm so glad you have come," she sobbed. "They took him away at dawn—and ever since, people in uniforms have been searching the house and taking away papers out of the secretariat and Heinrich's office and bedroom. And after that a rather nice man, not in uniform, called on me. He was quite polite and civilized, but he asked me the most absurd questions."

"Such as?"

"Oh, had my marriage been a happy one? Had I ever felt myself neglected? Me, neglected!" She started to laugh through her tears. "But he seemed to know quite a lot about my private life, how I really don't know."

"Was he Viennese?"

"Oh yes." Who in Vienna didn't know, I thought.

"But I simply couldn't understand what he wanted," she continued. "If he hoped to seduce me, or to jail me for adultery instead? Still, I told him how happily married Heinrich and I had been for over twenty years."

"But didn't he ask you questions about Heinrich's political opinions?"

"Not really. He knew all about the Falcons, of course. It didn't seem to interest him very much, nor when I told him of Heinrich's charitable activities, especially in the Sudeten, and how he was trying to unite the youth of the world. 'Don't worry unduly, your Highness,' he reassured me. 'Your husband has been merely taken into custody to answer some questions and probably won't be detained for long. But meanwhile, don't leave the house.' And then he kissed my hand quite politely and left. So you see, I am more or less imprisoned here too. What is it all about, Eddie?"

"I wish I knew, Marie Therese. Frankly I am as puzzled as you are. Has Heinrich ever actively opposed Hitler?"

"Oh no. Though he hated him, he was too careful to provoke him in any way. Heinrich has great self-control and patience. He can bide his time. Oh, Eddie," she then wailed, "I'm so worried about his heart. Being jailed suddenly like that must have been a dreadful shock to him, and I don't even know if he took his medicine with him. I'll have to consult Dr Koritschoner immediately as to what can be done about it."

"Dr Koritschoner left two days ago for Prague."

"Without telling me? How very inconsiderate."

"I scarcely think he could help it. He would have been arrested had he stayed."

She looked at me without comprehension.

"But why, Eddie?"

"Because he is a Jew. They have been imprisoned Baron Rothschild."

"Not Louis? Why, I dined with him only last week! Oh, Eddie, what is happening? I mean, if it was only against Jews one could perhaps understand, but Heinrich and some of my closest relations? What have the Germans done to my beloved country and its people. We have been *Vergewaltigt* overnight."

"If you mean raped," I said, which I was sure was what she meant since it was almost impossible for her not to think of everything in connection with sex, "I am not certain it was entirely against Austria's will."

"How can you know, not being a female or Austrian? Of course one flirts, but one doesn't want to be brutally taken, which Hitler has now done to my country."

Then she flung herself on the sofa.

"Eddie, I've decided you must help me free Heinrich," she surprisingly said. "I know I can trust you and I am not allowed to leave the palace and I am obviously under surveillance all the time. It's a miracle they let you in—no one else has been allowed to enter."

"But what can I possibly do, Marie Therese? I have no powers whatsoever."

"But I have—enormous powers—if you help me." From out of her bosom she drew some scented and crumpled pieces of paper and gave them to me.

"Read it!" she ordered. I unfolded the sheets. They were very thin and covered with tiny but quite legible handwritten script.

Every European country from north to south was listed and underneath each, hundreds of names and addresses.

"But what does it mean?"

"They are the leaders of the young Falcons Heinrich trained. Each of them has about a thousand youths under his command. All that is needed is that they are told to march and they will free Heinrich and my country."

"But by whose orders?"

"Mine. Heinrich never feared death, but he dreaded he might one day be imprisoned on some trumped-up charge and not be able to act. So he gave me this and told me if needs be I must rally his Falcons."

"Is this the only copy?" Fear gripped me and my hand in which I held the paper shook, knowing it was dynamite. Perhaps she saw my consternation.

"Yes. Thank God they didn't search my person. All you need do, Eddie, is call one or two of these leaders, inform them of what has happened—they will pass on the message to the others. You can easily do it from the Embassy and many thousands will come to our rescue."

"But are the Falcons armed? Don't you understand they will have to face fully-armed German troops? All there will be is the most awful bloodbath."

"Oh no," Marie Therese smiled. "You have always underrated my intelligence, Eddie. They will carry no weapons. They will demonstrate for peace and freedom and for Heinrich's release. And what can Hitler do? Not even he would dare order his troops to shoot children. There would be no stopping them. And they are not only Austrian boys, but from all over Europe, even from England. Imagine what would happen if there were any incidents. Why, there would be war! However little people care what one nation does to another, none would suffer the murder of their innocent children without rising in arms."

I had to grant that for once Marie Therese's logic seemed faultless. And I was tempted. I visualized the young blue-shirted Falcons sweeping the brown-shirts out of Vienna with no one daring to oppose them and the Viennese public probably acclaiming them with as much, or perhaps more, enthusiasm than they had the Nazis. And I only needed to give the word for them to march.

"Does anyone know of this list?"

"No, of course not. It is all secret. Some of the names mentioned are those of youth organizers or those who headed various sporting associations, some belonged to the Hitler Youth, some to the *Heimwehr,* some were Italian fascists, there were even some English fascists; Heinrich recruited his Falcons from all over the world. But they all have quite respectable covers. No one knows—they are sworn not to reveal who their leader is."

And then I realized in what danger both Heinrich and Marie Therese were. If even a vestige of the powers they could unleash were known to Hitler, they were doomed—as long as there was proof; and I held it in my hand.

I temporized. "Heinrich will probably be back in a couple of days. If all this is secret, there is nothing he can be accused of except of charitably supporting various youth and sports organizations. But if the Falcons were given marching orders now, his life and yours would be at risk. It is not a responsibility I dare take or want to."

"You think they might try to kill him?" I saw that I had frightened her. "Surely they would not dare make a martyr out of him?"

Perhaps not, I thought, knowing she was right. I doubted Hitler would take the risk in case all the youth of Europe rose. The balance was still even—as long as the paper I held in my hands was destroyed.

As always in Marie Therese's overheated rooms a fire burnt brightly under the mirrored mantelpiece. I threw in the incriminating list of countries and names and watched it flare, wondering if I had stopped a world conflagration or started one.

"But Eddie, why did you do that?" she asked reproachfully.

"Because I thought it best," I said firmly. "When Heinrich is back he can sort things out. I can't make myself responsible for risking so many lives."

"But not even in a good cause?"

"No."

She sighed. "And it was such a splendid plan. Oh well, don't look so worried, Eddie. Come, let me smooth those lines from your forehead."

Her chestnut-coloured hair spilt all around my face, its fragrance reminding me of the past as she bent to embrace me.

When I finally left her room I was startled to find the footman, whom I now knew as Fritz Lang, waiting for me in
front of the door. I had a sudden suspicion that he had been
listening, but since I was sure he did not know any English
what could he have hoped to hear?

"Sir, I have been waiting for you," he said. "I felt I must
warn you. Anyone who leaves the palace is searched. If you
have anything on your person that they might think suspicious, give it to me and I will keep it safe for you."

Thank God I had destroyed the paper, I thought.

"How very considerate of you, Fritz, but probably you
know better than I what they think suspicious." I pulled a
packet of cigarettes out of my pocket, my lighter, a shimmering piece of quartz I had collected on one of my walks and
forgotten, some cash, my credentials and a folded-up copy of
*The Times Literary Supplement.*

"That's all," I said. "Satisfied?"

"Sir, I was just trying to help. But perhaps it would be best
if you left that newspaper with me."

"But it's not worth keeping," I said, "throw it away—I've
read it."

At the gate, much to my relief, I was not searched after
all. The sergeant looked at me glumly as he helped me climb
into the Rolls.

"It has been over two hours. I didn't know what I was expected to do, call His Excellency, storm the palace or go to
sleep. I have been on duty since six o'clock."

I apologized as best I could. Once more we threaded our
way through streets crowded with flag-waving, screaming,
chanting people. Many were women.

At the Embassy I found my mother and Sir John drinking
coffee. Both looked at me with more questioning concern
than I felt was necessary.

"Well?" Sir John asked. "You look as if you need a cup,"
pushing one towards me.

"I think I'd rather have some gin for once, if you don't
mind, sir."

He shrugged. "Help yourself."

I went to the cabinet where he kept drinks for his guests
and poured myself a generous amount, hoping he had not noticed that I had added neither tonic nor water. I drank it and
felt better.

"Everything all right at the palace? Were you allowed to see the Princess?"

"Yes, though she is more or less under arrest and naturally very worried and anxious. She has been questioned—interrogated."

"About Heinrich?"

"As far as I could make out, not really. It seems all the detective wanted to know about was her marriage and her private life. Totally incomprehensible."

I saw Sir John and my mother exchange looks.

"Not to me, alas," Sir John said. "Have you seen today's papers?"

"No, there wasn't time."

"Here they are." He pushed a pile towards me.

I scanned the thickly printed headlines:

FÜHRER TO THE RESCUE REVOLUTION AVERTED THROUGH THE FÜHRER'S INTERVENTION     GERMAN TROOPS WELCOMED BY ALL     OUR POPULATION RESTORE ORDER     WE HAVE COME HOME AT LAST, HEIM INS REICH

and so on, one after the other.

"Do they report any of the arrests?" I asked, after having scanned the headlines with distaste.

"Only in small print and not mentioning any names. They only say that some undesirable trouble-makers have been taken into *Schutzhaft*, which presumably means protective custody. Hitler is here, you know."

"No, where?"

"In the Hofburg with his gang. It stands to reason that any opposition is feared and gives them a good excuse to lock up anyone they please. But you had better read this article. It is out of the main Sudeten German paper; though there are several somewhat less offensive ones, but on the same subject, in the Austrian press." He pushed it towards me.

I read with ever-mounting horror and indignation.

DRUNKEN HOMOSEXUAL ORGIES IN SCHLOSS AND PALACE! It has long been known that certain youth organizations sponsored and financially supported by Prince H. merely served to cover up perverse practices, here not necessary to be described or explained. The members of these groups were sworn to secrecy as to what went on in the turreted Schloss and in its private theatre, where even foreign actors performed. What sort of plays can be imagined, considering the Prince's tastes! And in his town palace as well, where his drunken masked and costumed guests, knowing they could not be recognized, indulged in the same obscene pleasures. An end has been made to all this! Just as our Führer will not permit subversive activities against the State, can we tolerate our children and even those of other nations being subjected to sodomy. The Prince is now cooling his ardour in prison.

"But this is the most ridiculous of lies!" I exclaimed, throwing down the paper.

"And about the cleverest and most ingenious I've ever encountered," Sir John replied. "One could almost admire the fiendish genius of Hitler and his propaganda machine, because that article and the others were probably cooked up weeks ago in preparation for the invasion.

"Had Prince Heinrich been accused of anything else, his Falcons would have rallied to his defence—which would have embarrassed Hitler. Now none of them will dare, or want to. The whole far-spread organization will collapse. Fearful of shame and disgrace and above all of being laughed at or persecuted, these—I am sure totally innocent—boys will never march for peace or freedom again. They will change their blue shirts to brown or black and many will no doubt have no alternative but to follow Hitler's orders in the future. As for Prince Heinrich, deprived of all power, totally discredited, they will probably release him in a day or two. Hitler need fear him no more."

"But can't Heinrich clear his name? Surely there is no proof?"

"As if that made the slightest difference to them. Besides, they can always get one of their adherents to testify to anything."

"But can't Heinrich at least sue the newspapers?"

"How? His name was never mentioned. This part of the world abounds in Schlosses and Princes. How can he risk coming forward and saying it was he who had been wrongly accused? It would only cause further scandal and defamation which is exactly what they want. They are damn clever, you know. Besides, so many of the facts fit most neatly: that he was devoted to the welfare of young people and spent a fortune on supporting them; that he was not a womanizer as are most men of his class. All this is well known. Also that his wife sought affection elsewhere."

At last I understood why Marie Therese had been questioned about her marriage.

A sudden fear assailed me. "But could there have been any truth in those accusations?"

"*Et tu, Brute?* Even you! And many of his friends will think the same."

My mother, who had quietly listened to all this without interrupting, as if she had chosen to withdraw from its horror, now broke out suddenly: "How can you, Eddie? Just because a man is good and charitable and fond of children, since he had none of his own, and more responsible and moral than most of his kind, how dare you doubt him?"

"But I don't."

I saw that she was not convinced.

"Better they had killed him," she said bitterly, "than this!"

"What! And made a martyr out of him?" Sir John asked. "They are much too intelligent for that. Prince Heinrich has a worldwide reputation as a benefactor of youth. There might well have been international repercussions had he died in prison. Now there won't be any. No doubt they will free him with apologies that it was all a mistake in a day or two. But the proud Falcon's wings," he added, "have not only been clipped but broken. He will never fly again."

As a matter of fact he did—once more. He had been allowed to return to the palace after a couple of days and he and Marie Therese immediately afterwards moved with their household to Prague. A week later he was reported dead. His plane, the "Falcon," which he piloted himself crashed in flames somewhere in the Sudeten mountains. The accident "believed to be due to a sudden heart attack".

Many obituaries followed, praising Prince Heinrich Hohenturn's achievements in the world of sport, his many charities were acclaimed; there was no more mention of anything else.

A memorial service was held in St Stephen's Cathedral. I did not go. I felt too guilty. I thought of Schwarzensee. Would fate always single me out to bear responsibilities I was unfit to carry?

Was I to blame for Heinrich's death—as I had been for Beck's? Had I not burnt that paper but called on the young Falcons to march, they might have come in time to save their leader.

No good telling myself it might have started a war and what was one life in comparison to that of so many. Because if even one innocent man was allowed to be hounded to death by such monstrous methods, what would thousands not have to face in the future?

# Chapter Twenty-four

My plaster cast had been removed in what used to be the Koritschoner clinic and was now renamed Hermann Schmidt Sanatorium. I was X-rayed by a young German doctor and my ankle pronounced healed.

There was no one I knew left except for the matron. Perhaps she noticed my surprise at still finding her there, knowing how devoted she had been to Dr Koritschoner.

In any case she apologized when we were momentarily alone together, but not before she had looked carefully behind her and then to right and left for fear of being overheard—a safety measure that was soon to be known in Austria, as well as later in Czechoslovakia and probably even in Germany, as *"Der deutsche Blick"*.

"What else could I do?" she asked. "I am an old woman and will not easily find another job having worked so long for a Jew. Here, at least for the time being, my knowledge of the clinic and my capacity to deal with staff makes me indispensable. And although I suppose I should loathe the new patients we get here, mainly prominent Nazis, sick is sick, whether they be Nazis or Chinamen or Hottentots." And then in a whisper: "Did they all reach Prague safely?"

"Yes."

"Thank God for that."

"I will be seeing them quite soon."

"Give the doctor my most respectful regards and tell him how it is with me. He will understand."

I had meanwhile bought a small second-hand car and maps of Czechoslovakia, and a week later left with my mother to take up my new appointment in Prague. Sir John was already there.

On arrival we booked rooms in the Ambassador Hotel which had been recommended to us because of its conveniently central position.

It was situated in the modern part of the town on the Va-

clavske Namiésti. The statue of St Wenceslaus guarded the
square in front of the large, imposing National History
Museum. But the rest of the long wide street that descended
from it was lined with modern unattractive apartment buildings and shops. Mid-way between them was our hotel. It
boasted a seemingly very popular bar and underneath it there
was a large, much-frequented night-club. Both were very
noisy.

There was certainly nothing ambassadorial about the hotel's guests. It seemed more the haunt of swarthy businessmen
from Balkan countries than diplomats.

Having established my mother in a room which looked
rather oriental too, with a curtained bed in a pillared alcove,
I went in search of the Koritschoners' house. I knew no
Czech, but everyone seemed able to speak German as did my
taxi-driver.

First another shop-lined street, then a wide square with
some fine buildings and a towering, medieval-looking church,
then the streets narrowed into dark arcaded tunnels under
ironwork or stone balconies and suddenly the river, spanned
by the Charles bridge—Carluv Most—or Karlsbrücke. Whatever it is called in any language, it remains one of the world's
architectural marvels.

"Held together only by white of eggs," the taxi-driver said
with pride. "Built in the year 1357 and still stands firm."

How many millions of eggs, I wondered, as I looked at the
great blocks of stone so accurately joined, at the stupendous
arches that supported the immense structure and the huge
bastions that protected it from the onslaught of the swiftly-
flowing turbulent river underneath.

Two watch-towers soaring in gothic splendour barred exit
and entrance to the bridge. But the safeguarding portcullises
had long been removed, allowing free passage to pedestrians
as well as cars.

The bridge's stone parapet was graced by the most varied
assortment of baroque saints carved in stone. Whatever their
agonies and their martyrdoms might have been in the past,
they displayed their suffering with such exuberant and elo-
quent elegance of gesture that one could feel neither piety
nor pity, only pleasure, on beholding them.

Looking down, the river flowed fast and wide. Looking up,
the old part of the town with its medieval buildings, patrician
houses and palaces climbed in terraced tiers among gardens,
higher and higher till it reached to underneath the great block

of the former Imperial Castle—now the seat of the Czech president—outlined against the sky as was the many-spired gothic lacework of the Cathedral of St Vitus that guarded it from above.

At the end of the bridge my taxi stopped.

"I could take you round, but since you have no luggage this is the quickest way. Just down those steps and you will be on the *Campa*. It's the tall walled house on the right—you can't miss it."

I thanked him, paid him and climbed down the steps to find myself almost under the bridge on a narrow strip of beach. Small boats were drawn up on it and it was fringed by a row of obviously old but nondescript and rather derelict-looking houses. Only one, its tall gabled roof showing above a high wall, seemed to fit the driver's description. I had to circumvent a considerable enclosure until I got to its front, to be stopped by an iron-barred gate. The house was almost like a small fortress, I thought—rather formidable. There was no bell as far as I could ascertain so I knocked, first gently, and since this brought no response, as loudly as I could.

From somewhere someone must have seen me, perhaps from above, because it was Dr Koritschoner who opened the door and led me into a paved courtyard that was not formidable at all. It was shaded by old apple trees in full blossom and there were borders of bright tulips and beds of pinks, lavender and herbs.

"Welcome, Mr. Livingstone," he said. "We were expecting you any day now. Sit down." There were deck-chairs and I did. "How is your ankle?"

"Perfectly healed, thanks to you."

I told him about the clinic and the matron.

"A sensible woman and she is absolutely right, you know. Anyone in or associated with the medical profession must maintain these principles. No matter how abhorrent the political or idealistic views of our patients, the power we are given over them—that of life or death—must never be abused. You know our oath, that of Hippocrates?"

"Of course."

His grizzled beard rose in a smile. "Nice to have you here, Mr Livingstone. Esther and Alexander are so much looking forward to seeing you."

"How is he?"

"Rather well, considering everything."

"And you, doctor?"

"This used to be my home. I still have many friends here. I took my degree at Prague University—I lecture there now. I share an office with colleagues—they are glad to have me. There is an operating theatre at my disposal in most of the hospitals whenever I need it. All in all I would say I was fortunate."

"But the clinic? Have you no regrets?"

"Nothing one has created is ever lost. The clinic was built to serve mankind and will continue to do so—creating it mattered more to me than owning it. As long as I keep my skill I will never be in financial need. I have more private patients here than I can manage, including our friend the Princess. She is here now, as you probably know. Poor lady! Prince Heinrich's death has upset her more than anything else that ever happened to her in her happy frivolous life. It has deprived her of all the secure protection and support on which she could always depend."

"What evil character assassination," I said, with all the indignation I felt. "I suppose Heinrich thought there was nothing left but to kill himself?"

"I rather doubt he did. He was a very religious man and his faith forbids self-destruction. Certainly the whole horrible business would have affected his heart, weak as it was, but as long as he took the medicines I prescribed for him he would have been safe. But someone who knew this might, if he wished him dead, have replaced the pills with others, or even tampered with his plane, knowing his heart condition would be blamed for his end."

"Murder?"

The doctor shrugged. "How can one be sure of anything except that we are up against people of the most infernal cruelty and guile. But here is Esther to welcome you."

She came running into the courtyard on sandalled feet, her long suntanned legs bare. She wore a short cotton frock and her warm smile told me that she was quite unreservedly glad to see me again. I knew I felt the same about her as she took my hand and led me into the house. After the bright sunlight outside it seemed very dark, as did the room into which she took me. It had only small gothic windows recessed in the stone wall, so thick that there was space for wide seats underneath. It was a sombrely rich and splendid room, oriental carpets covering most of its stone floors, medieval tapestries its walls, or shelves filled with very ancient-looking books bound in ivory-coloured vellum. Even the antique furniture, mostly oak, the chair backs and seats covered in gold-stamped leather, belonged to the same period.

"It amused my father," Esther said, seeing my amazement, "to keep the room much as it must have been when our family first settled here after having been cast out of Spain in the fifteenth century. We are Sephardic Jews—so was my mother—that's why I am as swarthy as a Moor." She smiled.

"The ceilings are rather fine." They were indeed—low, crossed by great beams and the beams painted with a strange scroll-work or ornamental designs in colours softened by time into mellow beauty. And everywhere, on tables and shelves, were bronze and silver ornaments and strangely-shaped and iridescently-coloured glass vessels and globes that I could recognize as many centuries old.

"But what lovely things," I exclaimed.

"Well, yes. My father's family have always been collectors and connoisseurs," she said, "and some of these objects are very rare and valuable. But come, Alexander is waiting most anxiously. Don't be too startled when you see him. It's a surprise for you. I promised not to tell you what it is. He lives in what used to be my nursery right at the top of the house.

"It is really the attic which my mother had converted," she said, as she led me up narrow polished stairs past several ban-istered landings and into a very large room that had windows on three sides, though these were partially curtained. There was a tapestried four-poster, a grand piano, some comfortable upholstered furniture, a large desk with a typewriter on it, and books all over the place, a radio and a gramophone. The inner roof structure was exposed, the enormous oak beams that supported it—black with age—arching above. The rest was plainly white-washed.

"But where is he?" I asked. A door at the far end of the room opened.

And there stood the Alexander I had known in all his radi-ant beauty, fair hair curling about his young face. He was wearing flannel trousers, just as he used to at Schwarzen-see—thinking them very English—a T-shirt and a bright scarf around his neck. His body seemed as slim and lithe as in his early youth and his face unchanged.

What can one do if one beholds a miracle, except drop on to one's knees and pray, or flee in terror? But Esther's steady-ing hand was on my shoulder.

"It's only a mask," she whispered.

And when he approached nearer, I saw this was true. The

mask was of a rubber-like material closely resembling the texture and colour of human skin, but feature for feature was an exact reproduction of Alexander's former face.

He embraced me, held me close for a moment, then led me to the desk and pulled a chair out for me beside it, sat down and started to type rapidly and efficiently.

"Fooled you, didn't I. Eddie? As I have so often before."

"Yes," was all I could answer.

"Quite an improvement, don't you think? Under this I will never grow old or ugly, like Dorian Gray. Do you remember?"

"Of course—and how you tore up my best drawing for fear of it."

He paused for a moment in his typing. Perhaps he felt my emotion or was trying to control his own; the hand that grasped mine once more trembled slightly—with the other he typed out: "Stiff upper lip, as my mother always said. The trouble is mine were burnt away. Tell me, is the mask like me?"

"Quite extraordinarily so," I managed to say.

"Esther and I made it. First moulding the face in wax, then having the rubber cast over it. It was really quite easy. I still had a lot of photographs of myself, but even without them I would have remembered my face, having painted it up for my various performances in front of a mirror for so many years. It's much more comfortable than the bandage. My hair is a wig, of course, attached to it. And I can take the whole thing on and off within seconds."

I stared at the type that emerged from the page almost as fast as anyone could have spoken, and at the agile long fingers, scarred no more, that performed so efficiently.

"Nice room, don't you think?"

"Perfect," I said.

"Ask Esther to show you my bathroom. She calls it the Devil's kitchen. I quite enjoy cooking for myself sometimes, though there is an old woman who usually feeds me. I also experiment in there."

Esther was looking over his shoulder at what he was writing.

"Come," she said, "the Devil's kitchen used to be my night-nursery. It has been put to all sorts of uses now."

It had indeed, as I saw. It was quite a large room. In one corner there was a bath and basin and WC screened off. All the rest of the considerable space was filled with a varied assortment of strange contraptions: ropes and pulleys hung from the ceiling, there was a small trampoline on which, to my surprise, lay a revolver. There were, too, a climbing ladder, dumb-bells, roller skates, shelves with jars and bottles and, indeed, an electric stove on which something pungently odorous was simmering in a pot.

Esther turned off a switch. "God knows what he is brewing here now. If it was only food it would be all right, but he's been reading books on chemistry and tries the most dangerous experiments. Well, what do you think of the mask? He is delighted with it, though he says he was even more beautiful than that."

She looked at me and saw, I suppose, how upset I was. "Sorry, Eddie," she said, "but he is ever so much happier since he has been wearing it."

"It's a very good likeness," was all I could say. And then: "Isn't there some danger he might be recognized?"

"No. He only wears it in the house which he never leaves in the daytime. I do take him for walks at night, but then he covers his head with a hat and we evade car and street lights. You see, he needs some exercise. That's why we got him all those contraptions. He takes great pride in keeping fit. He is stronger than you and I now and ten times as energetic and enterprising. Twice he has escaped out of the window at night only with the help of a rope—he is as agile as a cat. Still, I doubt anyone here would recognize him, even masked. He never acted in Prague, nor has he ever been here. And his young friends have probably never heard of Plevke the actor."

"Friends?"

"Quite a group," she said. "Some went to university with me, some are medical students who attend my uncle's lectures—some of them are Jewish. Twice a week they congregate in his room and we have concerts. They bring whatever instruments they have or sing Czech folk-songs. Or there are political discussions of the most inflammatory nature—most of them are impassioned Czech nationalists. And Alexander has learned the language perfectly. He is not like others, Eddie. Sometimes I wonder if he is real; such genius is abnormal."

"I know," I said. "I've always known. And these students—do they realize why he is masked and can't speak?"

"No, he doesn't want them to. I keep the room rather dark and if any do notice, I tell them that all Englishmen are eccentric. And since they have come to trust him with their conspiracies, they think his mask is merely there to conceal his identity and that he is a dangerous anarchist who lost his voice in an explosion in hiding here."

"But are they all anarchists?"

"No, just very patriotic young Czechs."

"But what do they conspire about?"

She looked at me rather strangely, her enormous dark eyes seeming to stare not at me, but into some far distance. And then, with quite unexpected violence, she said: "To fight the people that killed my parents, that deprived my uncle of his clinic, that persecute all of our kind in Germany and now in Austria. And who knows how soon they will start here? We must not let them, Eddie."

"I wouldn't worry about that," I reassured her, seeing how moved she was. "I very much doubt the Germans will ever venture to enter Czechoslovakia. The frontiers are well-fortified. The Czechs have a well-trained army. Hitler would never take that risk! It would mean war."

"But if?"

"But, dear Esther, if it came to such a situation, what could a few students do?"

"We could at least be prepared, organize an escape route for Jews before it is too late; and then go underground, sabotage, blow up trains and bridges, deter and harass the Germans in any way we can. The whole Czech nation will be with us. And this is my country after all, the only home I have left. Can you blame me for wanting to defend it to the last?"

I looked at her with amazement, at the small head so proudly poised above the long strong neck, at her stern face, at her tall slim body—more that of a boy than a girl.

"So you want to play a Czech Joan of Arc. I am sure Alexander inspired you to do so." I laughed, if rather uneasily.

"It's no joke, Eddie. We are dedicated. Each of us has his role to play. Alexander's is, perhaps, the most difficult. In any case, we hope for your help."

"But how?" I asked, feeling extremely nervous. "I can't speak any Czech and if it comes to shooting I am, I know, no good at that either." And I glanced at the revolver lying on the trampoline.

"He only uses it for practice in here," she said. "It has a silencer. No, Eddie, we don't want you to assassinate anyone.

Just to gather information in the diplomatic circles in which you can move freely and to tell us what you hear."

"You want me to spy?" I exclaimed, with some righteous indignation.

"Certainly not. I know how delicate your conscience is. It is not your Embassy's official secrets we want you to reveal, but simply gossip. You will no doubt hear a lot of it in the Hohenturn Palace here in which the Princess now entertains, in spite of her recent bereavement, much as she did in Vienna."

A bell clattered. "There—Alexander's become impatient," she exclaimed. "That's the way he summons me."

We found him sitting at his desk, swinging what looked like a brass cow-bell. He gestured for us to sit down.

"What have you been up to for so long?" he typed out. "Making love?"

I saw Esther's dusky cheeks flush. Then she did something rather odd—she kicked his leg, not very hard, but not gently either.

"Stop fooling, Alexander," she said, "I told Eddie something about our work and asked for his help."

"Will you, Eddie?" he typed out.

"Within decent limits."

"Thank you. I knew I could trust you to oblige. I need some more cash, another thousand will do changed into Korunas, I have certain expenses. You had better bank at the Naródni Banca from now on."

"I can show you where it is tomorrow," Esther said. "I also want to show you and your mother something else which I think you might like. Does she mind climbing stairs?"

"No, I don't think so. She is very agile for her age. But why?" I asked, puzzled.

"Because I want her to see a little house, but one must climb many steps to it. It has been left in my uncle's and my care by Jewish friends who have gone to Switzerland. The rent is extremely reasonable, but they would prefer it in foreign currency and they hoped we could find a western diplomat to take it, because then whatever might happen here it would be protected. It is completely furnished and you could move in tomorrow, if your mother likes it."

"She certainly doesn't like the hotel—Esther, it sounds perfect!"

"And it's quite near here, too, and close to your Embassy.

Also there is a maid who has been looking after it and would be most willing to work for you."

"It seems ideal, exactly what we hoped to find."

I looked at my watch and saw with consternation how late it was. I started up. "I will have to be off now, though. I haven't even been to our Embassy yet."

Alexander was typing. "Come back soon, Eddie!"

"Of course I will."

"To see me or Esther? She's so wonderfully capable, isn't she? Not as physically attractive, of course, as was Marie Therese, but not too bad. In fact I'm not certain I am not falling in love with her. I might even ask her to marry me."

"How dare you, Alexander," she exclaimed. She tore the page out of the typewriter, pushed it into the fireplace and to my surprise lit it with a match and watched it burn.

"We have to destroy all the nonsense he writes," she said over her shoulder, "some of it being highly dangerous if found, now that he writes as easily in Czech as in any other language. Not that our old housekeeper can read any of them, but she is careless with the rubbish."

She got up from her crouching position and bent over Alexander.

"Monster," she said, with great tenderness, and then led me downstairs.

"But is what he wrote true?"

"Of course not. He was just teasing."

"It sounded almost as if he was jealous. But what reason could he possibly have?"

"None. Except that he is fond of both of us. You see, we are all he has left in life."

"But surely you would never consider marrying him?" I asked, surprised at the distaste I suddenly felt.

"And why not? Because he is disfigured? I've known even worse cases in the clinic. I have seen what is left of his poor face behind the mask hundreds of times by now—I scarcely notice."

"But do you love him?"

"In a way, very much. But there is no point in discussing this because he quite simply will never ask me to marry him. Too proud, too vain to offer even me, his nurse, what he believes would only be accepted with compassion."

"And if you asked him yourself, if that is what you really want most?"

"I can't," she said simply. Then: "I'll come and fetch you

at your hotel tomorrow morning. Give my regards to your mother."

She opened the front door of the walled garden. "If you walk ahead instead of turning round on to the *Campa*, you will pass the Maltese Palace and the Buquoi Palace, which is now the French Embassy. It is a pretty square. But then, as you will soon find out, this—the old part of Prague—is very beautiful. Perhaps one day we can explore it together." She smiled and then vanished behind the heavy door. I heard her lock it.

I hailed a taxi and was driven to our Embassy.

It was not a very prepossessing building, at least not from the outside. Large and gaunt and rather austere, it had, although obviously built in the eighteenth century, none of the flamboyant baroque décor that ornamented most of Prague's old palaces. The chancelleries were unattractive—dark, very cold, even if it was summer weather outside. I found Sir John wrapped in a tartan plaid and on his head a knitted cap.

"Not quite my official dress," he said, "but I can't risk catching cold just now. There is more work than I expected to find. I'm glad you have come. How is your mother?"

I told him about the house Esther thought might suit us.

"Reasonably priced, you say?" From him an inevitable question.

I told him how much the rent was.

"Well, that's not exorbitant," he had to admit. "Must be something wrong with it. If the drains are as bad as ours here, all I can say is that I'm sorry for your mother. I don't mind peeling paint, shabby furniture, chipped china, frayed carpets—all of which I have found here—but I do dislike smells."

"And what have you been doing since I saw you last, sir?"

"Firstly presenting myself to President Benes. He speaks very fluent German and English. An intelligent man, if rather evasive, I would think; but so I have come to notice are most Czechs. But perhaps no wonder, considering their history. I had tea with his wife, quite good tea as a matter of fact, and I rather like her. No pretensions, a kindly, well-meaning woman and devoted to her husband and to her country. But both the president and she are, of course, very worried about the situation in the Sudetenland. Hitler's demands are ever more outrageous. If they were met, this country would not only be split apart but become defenceless. From the Czech point of view it cannot be permitted. And I don't put much trust in this investigating mission they are sending from London headed by a Lord Runciman—nor in their capacity to decide on the rights and wrongs of Sudeten Germans. Thank God it has nothing to do with me. His Lordship and his considerable staff of assistants will be staying in a hotel, but I suppose I will have to invite them for a meal."

"Do you know him?"

"Never met him. Poor man—I don't envy him his task. I am told he is fairly impartial and decent, but in the end he is as much under orders from our government as I am—to appease at all costs. We are simply not ready for war. We have to buy time as best we can, even if it is at the risk of destroying another nation," he said bitterly.

Then much to my surprise he asked: "Are you still on friendly terms with Princess Hohenturn?"

"I think so, though I haven't seen her since Heinrich's death. Why?"

"Well, only because the aristocracy here is equally divided, I would say, into those who are pro-Hitler and those who are patriotic Czechs. Both parties are competing to persuade Runciman to their views. And they do still have some power. The silver is being polished, the chandeliers washed, the furniture cleaned or refurbished in all the palaces of Prague and in many castles, in order to entertain the Runciman mission with impressive splendour. And so I believe will Princess Marie Therese. Even if recently a widow, she seems quite a merry one. It is in her house that most of the aristocracy congregates here now. Since nearly all of them are her or Prince Heinrich's relations, I doubt she would be on one side or the other—still it would be quite interesting to know. She is not only immensely wealthy but, so I'm told—" he eyed me wickedly—"still very persuasive."

"How old is Lord Runciman?" I could not help but ask.

"Well into his seventies, I think. Still, who knows? In any case, Eddie, I would be grateful if you informed me of what goes on there."

Thinking of Esther, I wondered if by now even Sir John expected me to spy.

Probably he read my mind. "I would not wish you to betray any confidences," he said. "Just to give me a general impression of what you think is brewing in the Hohenturn Palace."

Next morning Esther came to fetch us at our hotel. We drove over the great bridge and beyond it into a large square, fringed by ornate palaces and arcaded buildings. Overlooking it and dominating it all was a church of monumental dimensions, its domed roofs and cupolas sheathed in copper that had weathered into bright green. It was a very baroque church, quite unclassical as to architecture, irregular in shape, with its tall bell-tower set sideways; and yet there was such harmony in the whole and such fluid beauty as it rose skyward, that it made me think of music expressed in stone.

"St Nicholas," Esther said. The taxi stopped at a corner of the square. "Now we must climb," she warned.

We did indeed.

To the right, small connected gabled houses rose in tiers, one always slightly higher than the next as they followed the steps as we did. Above on its hill was the Presidential Palace. To the left, there was an ever-widening view over the tiled and slated roofs of the Old Town as we ascended.

Into the front door of one of the little houses about midway between those lowest and those highest up, Esther thrust a key.

There was a small hall, a dining-room and a very modern kitchen. On the floor above, a large drawing-room and a bathroom. On the second floor, another bathroom and three bedrooms with French windows opening on to the most entrancing of scenes. For each of the houses had a garden that had climbed with them in terraces up the hill, each in full spring blossom. Some were walled and on the stone balustrade stood urns and gods and goddesses; some gardens had tiny pavilions or arbours.

"But it is too lovely," my mother gasped—whether out of breath from the long climb or with enthusiasm, I did not know. The latter, I soon learnt. Because the house was perfect, beautifully furnished with valuable antiques and had every modern convenience imaginable. We moved in that night.

# Chapter Twenty-five

Next day I called on Marie Therese. The entrance to her palace was rather forbidding. Two muscular Negro slaves carved in stone stooped under its portals, seeming to carry the weight of the entire palace on their bowed heads.

There was a bell, which I rang, and the door was opened.

"Nice to see you again, sir," the footman said, smiling at me. "You remember me, Fritz Lang? There was a time I hoped that I might serve you as a valet. And now with my master so tragically dead I can make a change. If you yourself have no need of me, perhaps your Embassy does?"

"I've only just arrived here," I said, brusquely. What was it about this perfectly harmless, if rather obsequious and somewhat too familiar, servant that always made me feel uneasy?

I turned to look at him once more. Then I remembered. There was something about his build, the shape of his head and his thick neck, and above all in his manner, that from the day I first met him had recalled Beck.

"Will the Princess be able to see me?" I asked.

"Oh yes, she is receiving this morning."

He guided me up stairs, much like those of the Hohenturn Palace in Vienna, to a drawing-room obviously only recently redecorated in what Marie Therese called the English style—frilled chintz everywhere—and she herself in extraordinary contrast to the cheerful interior, dressed entirely in black, a veil, also black, suspended from a white crape-edged heart-shaped widow's cap such as I had only seen on pictures of Mary Stuart. A large diamond cross adorned her neck.

"Why do you look so distrubed, Eddie?" Marie Therese asked anxiously, "as if you had seen a ghost."

"Perhaps I have."

"It's not me, is it?"

"No, it's not you. Even in that absurd costume you seem very much alive. Is that what widows wear here? It has a certain nun-like charm."

"That is the impression I hoped to give," she said primly. "You see, I am a changed woman. I spend my time in prayer and try to seek God's guidance as to how best to continue Heinrich's work on earth. I did love him most!"

And as I knew her to be quite incapable of lying, I believed her.

"I couldn't come and tell you how sorry I was when I heard. You had already left for Prague," I apologized.

"Oh, those terrible tales," she exclaimed. "Never was Heinrich *de l'autre côté*—" I remembered the odd expression she had used before—" he had no *côté* at all, he disliked sex of any kind. He was too pure, saintly almost. They killed him. They broke his brave, proud heart. Oh, if only we had called his young Falcons to defend him. Now it's too late. The whole organization—which Heinrich spent his life in building—has fallen apart, all because of this monstrous accusation. But I will clear his name! That is why I don't hide and retire from the world as I would wish to, lest people might think I have anything to be ashamed about. I see as many as before, more perhaps.

"Some of my friends have moved here. But we all miss Vienna. None of us feel at home among Czechs, but by now we all prefer them to Germans. I have even started to learn their awful language so as not to have to speak German here. You see, I am the leader of the Czech faction in society. It is still small but it is growing."

"How most extraordinary," was all I could say.

"I can't do much about my friends and relations in the Sudeten—they are all for Hitler. But there are some important families here who, strange as it may seem, have for centuries always been devoted to this country and its people. Within the framework of the monarchy, of course. In the past loyal to the Emperor," she added, "nevertheless, preferring to live on their estates here and in shabby old Prague instead of elegant Vienna. These have rallied to my cause."

"But what is it?"

"Not to let Hitler in, not by the back door of the Sudeten or any front door either. We will fight to the last for our country's independence.

"When we heard that the president might have to give the order for mobilization of the Czech armed forces," she continued, looking solemn, "I called on Mrs Benes to assure her of the loyalty of the Bohemian nobles if it came to having to fight for Czechoslovakia. Mrs Benes seemed slightly surprised, but promised to tell the president. And do you know, Eddie, I actually managed to address her in Czech. I had learnt my little speech by heart. Fortunately for me she then spoke German and we became quite friendly.

"What are you laughing at, Eddie," she then exclaimed indignantly. "It is all very serious."

I was indeed doubled up with laughter.

"At you," I gasped, when I could speak. "And your friends. It was about the last thing I expected, that you become a Czech patriot. Have you read Tolstoy's *War and Peace*?"

"You know I never have time to read, especially not those long and tedious Russians. Why?"

"Because there was almost the same absurd situation in Russia when Napoleon threatened to invade the country. A wave of patriotism even in society. Everyone suddenly remembered they were Russians, but only a few spoke it. The aristocracy thought it inelegant to do so. They spoke French or German, or even English, among themselves and Russian only with their servants."

"Rather like us here with the Czechs," Marie Therese admitted.

"And what are your further plans, and those of your friends?"

"Mainly now to win Lord Runciman and his mission to opt for our side. Being a lord, surely he will understand the aristocratic point of view?"

"I rather doubt it. He is a Liberal and only became a lord last year."

"Strange customs you have in England, dispensing titles just like that!"

"For services rendered to King and Country, as yours presumably once were."

"I suppose so. The Hohenturns were given theirs by Frederick the Second."

"Of Prussia?"

"Oh, Eddie, really! By Frederick the Second, Holy Roman Emperor, and King of Sicily and Jerusalem, in the twelfth century. I thought everyone knew that!"

"Probably—in your snobbish society."

"Snobbish?" she repeated, amazed. "Snobs are people who aspire to be like us. What on earth could we be snobbish about, being what we are? But listen, I am giving a large dinner party for this lord and his mission the moment they ar-

rive. I will invite all the prettiest women and the most
handsome men of our way of thinking. Surely he can be persuaded to our point of view, before my pro-Hitler relations
get hold of him?"

She looked at me appealingly.

"I wish you all the luck in the world, Marie Therese, but I
do think he will have his orders from London to remain
uncommitted to either side."

"Darling," she said, "I know nothing of politics, but I do
know that women have certain powers in influencing men."

"As indeed you have," referring more to her feminine
charms than her prospects of succeeding in the cause she had
so astonishingly adopted. "The only trouble is Lord Runciman is a very old man. Besides, he has a wife."

"What are wives to me?" Marie Therese asked. "As for
age, surely I could still fan a flame even out of ashes. In spite
of bereavement and sorrow, I believe I have not quite lost my
touch."

"No," I had to admit. Even in her strange and sombre
clothes she managed to look irresistible.

"How many lovers now, Marie Therese?" I could not refrain from asking.

"What a cruel question, Eddie. Surely you can see that I
am in deep mourning. But there are, of course, certain things
that I need so as to preserve my health and good looks."

"I thought Dr Koritschoner saw to that."

"Well, not entirely—although it is a great help having him
living here now. Thank Hitler for something. Besides, my
physical well-being is none of your concern any more,
Eddie—or is it?"

"It certainly is not."

"Really?" She laughed enchantingly and I was only allowed to leave her an hour later.

A few days passed during which I settled into my work at
the Embassy and my mother installed herself most comfortably on the top floor of the little house. She transformed one
bedroom that led on to the terrace garden into her study by
covering the bed with my Chinese shawl and sofa cushions,
and setting out the things she cherished. The Tsarevna's gold
box glittered with undiminished splendour on her writing
table. Beside it stood the miniature of Tsar Alexander the
First and the icon that Alexander had given me; also a photograph of my father, faded but elaborately framed in silver,
and one of myself when I was seven, looking grim since I

was to be sent to prep school. Heavy parcels of books with which she always travelled had taken me all one morning to carry up to her study.

One day towards evening we called on the Koritschoners. We had telephoned the time of our arrival. The doctor himself received us and took us up to Alexander's room. Esther was there. She laid down some tapestry work and rose to greet us. So did Alexander, putting away a book. A fire was burning brightly. It seemed a very cosy domestic scene that we had interrupted.

If my mother was confused by Alexander's mask, she did not show it, except by starting to talk rather hurriedly and nervously. She is still of a generation that believes silence impolite and that embarrassment can be dispelled by even the most random efforts at conversation. After having praised our new house effusively and having thanked them for it, she started to talk about the book she was intending to write.

"Having come here will give me so much more opportunity to study Rudolph the Second, since in his later life he lived mainly in Prague. Such an extraordinary man! If not a great emperor, he had interests far beyond his time—artistic and scientific. And not a curiosity that he did not collect, human or otherwise, and summon to his court—astronomers and mathematicians, astrologers and alchemists."

"Yes, Tycho Brahe and Kepler, I remember," the doctor said. For some reason my mother's chatter seemed to interest him.

"And artists! One of the greatest picture collections in the world is all due to htim. And yet they say he was mad—and in some ways he must have been. All those gruesome relics. Surely he cannot have believed in their virtue? Nor in the genuineness of shrivelled carcasses of supposed mermaids, twisted roots of man-shaped mandragoras, stones, plants, presumed to have magical connotations, all of which he acquired?"

"We of the medical profession, in our studies through the ages," the doctor said, smiling at my mother, "have only advanced by taking anything or nothing for granted, even magical powers of objects, since—if believed in—they influence the human mind and health. You must go and see the Alchemists' street, its tiny buildings still almost unchanged," he added, "some with their original ovens and smelting pots. It is where the emperor put his alchemists to work. The secret passage by which he could visit them from the Hradschin is gone; so of course are they. The street is a tourist attraction now."

"I'd love to take you there, Mrs Livingstone," Esther said. "It's rather interesting."

"And they made gold?" my mother asked the doctor, after having thanked her.

"That experiment rarely proved successful and, if so, was usually a deception by some clever charlatan. Gold can only be made from gold, as they must have known by then. But they were in search of something infinitely more precious. The Stone of Wisdom which could transform all things and which, powdered and infused, would give those that partook of it eternal life."

"And did anyone ever discover it?" my mother asked, by now not nervous any more but fascinated.

"Who knows?" the doctor replied. "They say a rabbi did. Rabbi Loew lived in the time of Rudolph the Second. He was so famed as a miracle-worker and magician that even the emperor consulted him secretly."

"Oh, was it he who created the Golem? I read about it somewhere. Please tell me more! It's so important for my book."

Esther looked up from her embroidery.

"Nothing but a silly legend," she said, "fit only to frighten the superstitious. The Golem never existed and, if he did, what remained of him after he had fallen into dust and was immured in the roof of our synagogue hundreds of years ago and walled in so no one would believe he still walked."

She looked back at Alexander, almost as if she wanted to reassure him. He was sitting quietly and in silence, contemplating all of us alertly I could feel; even if his eyes were scarcely visible under the mask, I saw them move.

"All superstitions, however absurd some of them seem, are a warning of our subconscious. If they only reach our mind in symbolic form they are, nevertheless, significant and should not be ignored. The Golem is one of them. From time to time he reappears when there is danger to Prague and its people and is seen by Jews and Christians alike, showing—" the doctor said with faint irony—"no discrimination. But then he isn't human."

"A ghost?"

"As far as I can remember," the old doctor mused, "the legend says the rabbi formed a creature from clay and instilled into it the elixir of eternal life. And the thing, though roughly of human shape but without human soul or brain or face, came to life and served him. But since the rabbi had transgressed against Moses' fourth commandment in making an image, he tried to insure himself against God's anger by inscribing the sacred name in letters of light on to the creature he had made and, through those, he controlled it and it remained obedient to him and to God.

"Nevertheless, one day the Golem escaped his master and could not be recalled. The rabbi, who had not partaken of the elixir, eventually died a natural death and was buried in the old Jewish cemetery here, and even his tomb is still thought to have miraculous powers. Many pilgrimages are made to it by believers. Meanwhile, the Golem has been seen throughout the centuries whenever Prague was threatened by invasion. And now they say he walks once more. He does no harm to those that meet him, except for inspiring the most abject fear."

"But what does he look like?" my mother asked.

"Quite ordinary. Like any orthodox Jew, dressed in a black frock-coat and the wide-brimmed black hat we wear for the synagogue. Except for one thing, the shining letters on his brow."

"And have you ever seen this phantom?"

"Only once and quite recently. And not in the vicinity of the old ghetto or near the cemetery, where it is supposed to haunt, but on the *Campa* here underneath our house. I saw it from my window."

"Really, Uncle," Esther exclaimed. "You will frighten Mrs Livingstone with your ghost stories. Even if you invent them to divert her, I doubt she is enjoying them as much as you do."

But my mother, looking far from fearful, seemed enthralled.

"And you were not terrified?" she asked.

"No. I don't fear the supernatural or inhuman—I have learnt to fear mankind much more. And if God wished to warn me in this way of coming danger I accept it with gratitude, for it tells me the God of Israel is still with us, even if he uses the Golem as messenger."

Esther rose from her chair. "What about some music?" she asked. "My uncle gets rather carried away once he starts on these abstruse subjects and the ancient legends in which our country abounds. He will be telling you next how St

Wenceslaus will return out of the mountain into which he vanished with his knights, if Prague is threatened.

"Come along, Alexander, let's play." He put down a pad of paper on which he had been writing, but did not offer it to any of us to read and went to the piano. "We have been practising from Dvorak's 'New World Symphony' together," Esther said, sitting down beside him.

I am not very musical, but it seemed to me that they performed well and in perfect harmony and I listened with pleasure. So evidently did the doctor and my mother, both applauding when it was over.

"I knew that Alexander played, but not that you did, Esther."

"My mother taught me; she was an accomplished pianist. I am just an amateur but, like all Czechs, I love music. I have not wanted to play since my mother died; now for Alexander's sake I have started again."

It was almost dark when we left the house.

"How wonderfully dedicated to Alexander that girl is. It's almost saintly the way she sacrifices herself to make him happy."

"She loves him," I said. "She told me so."

Perhaps my mother heard a certain bitterness in my voice. "But aren't you glad?"

"Of course," I said. "It's only that I sometimes resent that even now he should have such power over anyone who comes under his spell."

My mother was silent, then suddenly said: "Let's go by way of the *Campa*."

"But that is in the wrong direction," I protested.

"It's still early. Besides, I hoped we might see the Golem."

"Mother, really. Surely you didn't believe that story?"

"And why not? There are, as you should know, more things in heaven and earth."

We went. Above the great bridge with its statues the sun had set, leaving traces of rose and orange from the evening sky reflected in the waters of the now placidly flowing river. On the *Campa* the light had faded except for the faint glow from some windows of the houses that overlooked it. The narrow strip of shore was already deep in shadow.

I gazed up at the window of what I knew as Alexander's room, then someone drew the curtains. Esther?

I felt my mother's hand touch mine. "Look behind you," she whispered. "I think it's the Golem."

In the shadows of some trees a black immobile figure was just discernible.

I confess I was startled. "It might be anyone," I whispered back, "but I will find out." And with more courage than I felt, I called out "Good evening," in Czech.

Whoever it was moved, turned as if to flee and then approached us instead. It was a man in a black overcoat and wearing a hat.

"Good evening," he said in German. "I thought I recognized your voice, sir. It's the young Englishman from the Embassy, isn't it?"

I could see his face by now. It was that of the footman I knew as Fritz Lang.

"What are you doing here?" I asked.

"Merely out for a stroll. The air is cool and fresh near the river in the evenings."

"Are you still employed by the Princess?"

"Oh yes, and hard work it is these days, what with all the preparations for the English mission. I haven't much time off and, if so, I seek some quiet place like this. And you, sir?"

My mother had been listening in silence.

"I am escorting my mother home. We have been visiting friends."

He glanced quickly up at the windows of the Koritschoners' house. Did he know where we had been, I wondered? But he said nothing, only bowed to my mother.

"I thought for a moment you were the Golem," she said. "He walks the *Campa* at night, I hear."

His friendly face changed. Dark as it was, I thought I discerned an expression on it of sudden terror.

"My lady, I don't know what you are referring to. I have never heard of anyone called Golem. Good night, sir." And he vanished with great speed into the darkness.

"He knew the legend, of course," my mother said, as we climbed the many steps to our house. "Did you see how frightened he looked?"

"Yes, but I don't understand why. He isn't Czech."

"And you know him quite well?"

"I have often seen him at Marie Therese's and at Hohenturn. He did me a good turn once, or tried to, possibly at some risk to himself. Do you remember when Prince Heinrich was locked up and Marie Therese under guard in Vienna and I went to her house?"

"Yes, of course."

"Well, Fritz warned me that I would be searched when I left the palace and offered to keep any incriminating papers I had on me. I had none. Marie Therese and I had burnt them all. Still, it was rather decent of him to try to help me. He has been looking for another job as a valet and offered to become mine. I had to tell him I could not take him, then he begged me if I couldn't find him one at our Embassy. He said he was very pro-British. Do you think Sir John might want him?"

"Not on my recommendation," my mother said firmly. "I liked neither the man's face nor his manner nor what you have told me about him. In fact I wouldn't trust him an inch."

"Your famous instinct, once more!" I teased.

"What you call my instinct is merely a small amount of deductive power. Ask yourself—why should the man, being Sudeten German and most probably a National Socialist, have been so anxious to relieve you of incriminating papers? I doubt very much they would have searched a British diplomat at the palace gate. So he had orders to do so for them. As for his wanting those jobs—isn't it evident that he wants to spy? Also, I thought it highly suspicious his lurking under the Koritschoners' house tonight. Don't forget they are Jews and so are many of those young students that assemble there."

"A perfectly harmless servant," I protested, nevertheless struck by what she had said. "I doubt he has any political ambitions but his own betterment."

"And doesn't that amount to the same? I think you ought to warn the Koritschoners."

# Chapter Twenty-six

Finally the Runciman mission came to Prague. Some of them had brought their wives. All of them stayed in the Hotel Alcron. Presumably Lord Runciman had called on the President soon after his arrival, but in any case he and his staff dined at Marie Therese's three days later. So did I.

The palace had been built like all palaces, more for representation than for comfort, but was impressive—so, that night, was the list of titled Czechs invited to meet Lord Runciman. Everyone was in evening dress. Candlelight shone on jewels and decorations, on bare shoulders and on white ties, on gleaming silver, fine porcelain, hothouse flowers and on Marie Therese; her copper-coloured hair piled high, her dress—though black—of some material so transparent that she might as well have had nothing on at all. She looked irresistible.

Lord Runciman was seated at her right. If he was entranced by her as he should have been, he certainly did not show it. He was a very small man and looked, I thought, with his round blank face, rather like an old clown who had omitted to paint his features into even a semblance of the engagingly comic. The days when he had been obliged to please the public were obviously over. His advisers, though somewhat more usual as to appearance, were equally solemn-looking. Though they did full justice to the excellent food, they were reserved in their speech and, if polite, not very forthcoming. No doubt they took their mission very seriously and also perhaps had been warned to be discreet and not to be influenced by the insidious charm of the Continental aristocracy. Their wives were obviously nice women, modestly attired, neither glamorous as to dress nor appearance, nor do I think did they aspire to be anything but what they were, serious intellectuals.

My neighbour at the table thawed somewhat when she discovered I was English and from the Embassy.

"Don't you find all this very strange?" she asked. "So much blatant display in this day and age and with this country going through a crisis."

"It is all in honour of your mission," I said.

She glanced briefly at Marie Therese, who was indeed displaying a lot of her ample self. But not only that—voicing her opinions without any restraint and, since she had never found it necessary to lower her voice or conceal what she thought or felt, the whole table heard.

"And have you been to see Benes?"

I only just caught Lord Runciman's quiet, affirmative answer.

"And did he tell you of those of us who have declared our loyalty to the Republic?"

I saw him shake his head.

"What, he never mentioned it? Understandable, perhaps, that he felt it should be kept secret. We still have great powers, you know, on which he can now call, thanks to me."

Never, I realized, would Marie Therese's naïveté fail to delight me.

"The Princess seems very outspoken," my neighbour remarked, if with admiration or disapproval I could not judge, nor did I care—I was too fascinated by Marie Therese's performance.

"No doubt you will be going to the Sudetenland from here," she sang out, "to meet Henlein. My husband, God rest his soul—" she crossed her almost naked bosom piously— "never trusted him and neither should you, Lord Runciman. He is a snake in the grass and all for Hitler."

There was a slight diversion from the attention focused on her when the roast appeared. A large and unfamiliar-looking bird on a silver dish garnished with peacock's feathers, presumably its own.

Serving it, his hair powdered and in livery, was Fritz Lang. I refused the dish and ignored the slight smile of recognition he gave me. I thought of my mother's warning. If he was a German spy, certainly Marie Therese was giving him all the information he might need.

"And do you mean to say they eat peacocks in this country? At home the RSPCA would never allow it. It seems disgraceful to me," my neighbour said.

"Oh, it's considered a delicacy here, like tongues of nightingales and hearts of larks."

With pleasure I saw the distaste of her humourless face as

she toyed with what was on her plate. I turned to listen to
Marie Therese's next sally.

"And so you are touring the country," she proclaimed
loudly. "And of course, since most of those castles in which
you are staying belong to my relations, I am fully informed."

"It seemed the only possible accommodation for us that
could be found," said an elderly scholarly-looking man seated
at her left, as if apologetically, "if we were to see the country
at all. The small villages and towns could not offer such facilities."

"Well, all I can do is warn you. Don't be swayed by my
Sudeten German relations."

Though Lord Runciman's round clown's face remained impassive, he did raise his voice somewhat irritably.

"Princess," he said. "Ours is a quite impartial mission and
in all fairness we have to consider and study everyone's hopes
and wishes."

"Impartial," Marie Therese repeated indignantly. "When
the future of my country is at stake? Remember that in your
hands, Lord Runciman, may be the fate of our beloved nation!"

I could not help recalling what she had said about
Czechoslovakia and its people only six months before; but all
the more admirable did I think her moving performance.

However, looking at the dour faces of my compatriots, all
slightly embarrassed—adverse and distrustful as I knew they
were towards exhibitions of emotion and their ingrained puri-
tanism possibly affronted by Marie Therese's frank display of
her feminine attributes—I feared her gallant effort to save
Czechoslovakia had failed.

"You were wonderful, darling," I nevertheless compliment-
ed her as I bade her good night after her guests had left the
palace.

"Yes, wasn't I, Eddie? I am quite sure I have won Lord
Runciman to my side. My traitorous relations in the Sudeten
won't have a chance after this!"

She was to be proved mistaken.

The mission toured the country staying mainly in the
castles of the Sudeten lords. They pleaded their case more
adroitly than Marie Therese had been able to do or any of
her Czech adherents. The evasive Henlein, when he finally
condescended to meet Lord Runciman at Schloss Rothenhaus,
was unexpectedly conciliatory. He even declared himself
willing to try to intercede with Herr Hitler himself and hinted

that, if autonomy was granted the Sudetenland, it could still remain part of the Republic.

Trusting the assurances they had been given by Henlein, the mission finally returned to London.

The rest is history.

"I will never be able to look a Czech in the face again. It was a monstrous betrayal," Sir John said bitterly, after Chamberlain had returned to London from Munich and declared he had brought back "Peace for our time".

"I feel much the same," I admitted.

"Had the Czechs been allowed to fight when Hitler's troops were known to be preparing to attack, they could have put up a formidable resistance. Certainly strong enough to give the Germans a very bloody nose and, in time, other nations might have come to their aid." He sighed. "Now it's too late. I doubt even Hitler believed we would hand over this country to him without a shot being fired."

He stared at me angrily. "President Benes has resigned. I called on him to offer my sympathy and to tell him how deeply I regretted what had happened. He was coldly polite, that's all, and no wonder. Though he did say he knew it was not my fault. Was it, in any way?" Sir John seemed to be questioning himself, not me. "I did warn against appeasement in all my reports. A voice crying in the wilderness would have been of as much avail. Oh, those fools in London!"

Never had I seen Sir John so emotionally disturbed.

"Can't they understand that if Hitler, every time he threatens, is given all he wants there will be no end to his demands?"

"But, sir, if the only alternative is war?"

"It would not have been, had he been stopped earlier. Now, though I am a pacifist, I can only hope it will come soon. Better war than such dishonour. Benes told me he was going abroad to try and rally help for his stricken country. What is the use now, when there is no country left? Meanwhile they are electing a new president. He is said to be a patriotic Czech. Poor man—a mere powerless figurehead—Hitler will make mincemeat of him.

"I suppose we must see out the end, but after that I will retire from the Diplomatic Service."

"You will be sorely missed, sir."

"No necessity to flatter. I have never been popular either with my superiors or inferiors."

"And where will you retire to? Torquay or Brighton or Southport?"

"Why?" he asked, looking at me balefully.

"Well, so many people do—sea air and all that."

"I do not wish to be near the sea and be reminded of how once our proud ships sailed out to conquer an empire. I have a spinster sister who lives in a semi-detached house in Birmingham. I will rent two of her rooms. I can still afford to have them padded against any noise and firm locks against all intruders installed. There I will write down my recollections."

"Like Proust."

"Well, not exactly, though an admirable writer." A faint look of amusement brightened his face at last. "He and I don't have quite the same tastes."

■

Winter came early that year. Snow covered the domes and spires and streets as if wrapping Prague in a protective mantle. A silence as of mourning had descended on the town and its people who, muffled in scarves and overcoats against the bitter cold, seemed to be hiding their sad and anxious faces even from each other. There was no laughter, no more jokes to which the Czechs are so prone, and very little speech.

What was there left to say? An atmosphere of hopelessness and impending doom, as grey as the skies above, pervaded Prague. Even the turbulent river lay still, frozen into icy silence. There was nothing left to hope for, not even spring, because no one doubted that with the first thaw Hitler would march.

Meanwhile, since one cannot feel despondent all the time or guilty, my mother and I enjoyed the comforts of our little house. Compared to the Embassy in which Sir John refused to install central heating, declaring it was no longer worthwhile, it was warm and cosy, heated by big porcelain stoves.

My mother seldom left it. The innumerable slippery steps that led to it, covered by ice or snow or both, intimidated even her. She was busy writing her book on Rudolph the Second. If concerned about the political situation, she could quote so many historical precedents that though they did not reassure me, they seemed to satisfy her.

"Do you know," she asked me, "that when in 1648 the Swedes invaded Prague unexpectedly and the bridge tower was unguarded, some students rushed out and let down the portcullis? Aided by the citizens and even the Jewish community, they held the post and saved the old part of the town and the castle above from invasion. And though the Swedes besieged and bombarded the gate for fourteen weeks, they finally had to retire, defeated by a handful of students!"

"Mother, there was only one bridge then, there must be dozens now. I doubt such brave action would be of any avail against Hitler's army these days."

Nevertheless, in the course of some conversation, I asked Esther if she knew of the story.

"I was practically born under the Charles bridge. I know its history," she said, rather sharply. "I know every saint on it, too. I must say I always like St John Nepomuk, who preferred death to revealing a secret confessed to him. A real Czech! He died in the river on the spot below the bridge where his statue now stands. And of course I know about the siege. In the Old Synagogue there is a flag presented to my people in gratitude for their courageous help in defending Prague then."

"Won't you take me there once, Esther? I would like to know more about your religion."

"Well, you need only read the Bible. What I could show you is not impressive. The old cemetery? Overcrowded for centuries, the tombstones sloping and falling, covered with moss and lichen, everything decaying. You see, we Jews don't believe in cherishing what is left after death. Some famous rabbis are buried there; they are still shown some respect by Jewish pilgrims or perhaps even petitioners hoping for miracles, placing stones or pebbles on their graves. As for the Synagogue, ancient as it is, it's so humble compared to a baroque church. And yet both were built to glorify the same God. Ours seems to apologize for its very existence, to crouch in fear like my people have learnt to do. I hate its musty, fusty atmosphere and the chants forever bewailing the loss of Israel, God knows how many thousands of years ago! Though uncle is an Elder and has to attend, I don't any more."

One day she gave me a typewritten page. "I translated it from the Czech paper in which it appeared this morning," she told me. "I thought it might amuse your mother since she is so interested in the subject."

I scanned it. THE GOLEM WALKS ONCE MORE said the headline. "In the last months the legendary spectre supposed to haunt Prague in times of danger has reappeared. Not only has he been sighted where he used to be seen in former centuries in the street of the Alchemists, but lingering around the Presidential Castle and near palaces and foreign embassies. We have been able to interview an eye-witness who gave us the following report. He was passing the German Embassy at about half past ten at night when he heard a woman scream out 'The Golem, the Golem', pointing upward. And indeed, on the balcony above, stood a spectral black figure. Our correspondent swears he distinctly saw an eerie light that seemed to come from under the creature's hatted head and that then the spectre leaped down as if it had wings and vanished. Other passers-by, arrested by the old woman's cry and the extraordinary thing they had witnessed, dispersed awed and fearful. What can one make of this tale? Except that now, when our country is threatened, the ghosts of the past have come to obsess people's minds." The article was signed— "Rehtse."

"Rather odd," I said, "but my mother will be fascinated since she loves anything mysterious, and I can show it to my ambassador. Although he is given the translation of the more important press reports every day, he might have missed this."

"Of course," she said, "if you think it would be of any interest to him. As for myself I think I have made it plain that I don't believe in ghosts." Her eyes sparkled as if with secret amusement.

How much I might have understood then, had I only been more perceptive.

I took the article to my mother.

"This poor nation," she said, "if all they have left to assist them now is the Golem!"

Sir John had different reasons for being interested when I showed the article to him. He seemed delighted. "I will call my German colleague to find out—obviously he must have been very cleverly burgled."

He had him on the telephone within minutes. A lengthy conversation followed, then he put down the receiver.

"Well, *Seine Excellenz* did admit this much. That though nothing was stolen, he had left some rather important papers on his desk when he went out to dine, instead of locking them in the safe as he usually does. On his return a frightened servant told him that, hearing a faint noise in the office, he had investigated and seen a dark and indistinct figure bending over the desk and a strange light emanating from its forehead. Certain that it was the Golem he had fled."

"The light might well have been the flash-light of a small camera," I suggested.

"Elementary, my dear Watson," Sir John said, managing to look very like Sherlock Holmes. "Exactly what I had deduced. If there is any more mention of this so-called spectre in the papers again, let me know."

There was—a few weeks later. This time it had been the turn of the Italian Embassy where much the same had happened, except that there had been no witnesses except for a youth who had called the alarm. After that, Sir John admonished us to put every one of his papers into the safe each evening and hand him the keys before he went home. Since this meant a lot of extra work for the staff, we cursed the Golem wholeheartedly.

So I suppose did the Czech police, obliged to guard the various embassies, having to stand in the cold outside them all through the night. No investigation of theirs brought any results and their work was made difficult by constant reports of the Golem having been seen here, there and everywhere throughout Prague. The news of his walking once more had spread. People were afraid to go out at night for fear of encountering him. Anyone dressed in black was suspect, any shadow mistaken for him. Descriptions varied—ten feet tall or dwarf-sized, horned like the Devil himself with flaming eyes, leaving a stench of sulphur, flying through the air like a bat or crawling over roof-tops on all fours like a beast.

We were kept fully informed of all this by the Czech maid that served us. Even in diplomatic circles the apparition was discussed. It was something to talk about, more diverting and less delicate a subject than politics, and acquired the delightfully spine-chilling charm of all ghostly tales. Yet it was clear that the profound unease and anxiety that beset the whole nation that winter had found a fit expression in the Golem's appearances.

I still frequently visited the Koritschoners and Alexander. But only on evenings when I knew their young student friends would not be there was I invited. Esther did not even need to apologize. How could a patriotic Czech trust an Englishman after Munich?

After Christmas, which we spent quietly except for exchanging presents with Alexander and the Koritschoners, I went to see Marie Therese.

A footman let me into the palace—but it was not Fritz Lang.

This one was much younger and, though he spoke German, by his accent obviously a Czech.

"What has happened to Fritz?" I asked.

"He has gone. Boasted he did not need to be a servant any more."

I found Marie Therese in her drawing-room. Sofas, chairs and tables were littered with dresses, hats and shoes, none of them black. Her maid was with her.

"Why, Eddie," she exclaimed, "you have neglected me of late. Still, I'm glad to see you. I am packing—as you might notice."

"But why?"

"Because I am leaving for Monte Carlo. I simply can't stand the cold and the gloom of Prague any more. Let's admit it—I failed with Lord Runciman. But then, he wasn't a real lord, was he? Had he been, he would not have sold us out like any shopkeeper. '*Glücklich ist—wer vergist was nicht mehr zu ändern ist,*' " she trilled melodiously from the *Fledermaus*, wrapped a boa of pink ostrich feathers round her neck and waltzed round the room.

"But have you friends in Monte Carlo?" I asked, surprised, finding it difficult to imagine her in any surroundings but those in which I had known her for so long. "Where will you live—in a hotel?"

"Certainly not. Heinrich once bought a villa there. We lent it to a cousin, a Russian grand duke. He has since died. So all I need do is move in. And I won't be lonely. I am taking my Rosenkavalier with me—he suffers as I do from the Czech climate of late. Some sun will do us both good!"

"You are incredible, Marie Therese!"

"Don't I know it," she chuckled.

It was the last time I was to see her.

More and more I knew I was becoming attached to Esther. Sometimes I even wondered if I was not falling in love with her; but if so, I did not dare admit it even to myself, so treacherous did it seem towards Alexander. Nor had she ever encouraged me to believe that she felt anything but friendship for me.

She is not even pretty, I told myself. And yet her narrow dark face with its enormous eyes, as mysterious and oriental as those of the Mother of God on the Tsarevna's Russian icon, haunted me.

Of the admirable integrity of her character I was by then convinced. She was not only intelligent, but good, capable and courageous. She combined qualities rarely found in so young a person, or in anyone. But did I desire her? I thought of Marie Therese—absurd, foolish, fat, incurably frivolous, and how much I had loved her, in spite of all her faults—or perhaps because of them.

How contrasting were the two women! Marie Therese seemed to express in her person all the rich, florid and exuberant spirit of the baroque; Esther all the austere, pure grace of the gothic.

I simply could not make out what I really felt about her. Affection certainly, and concern. Because it seemed to me that of late she had become even thinner than she usually was and that her face was pale.

"What's the matter, Esther?" I asked. "Why do you look so exhausted?"

Rather wearily she smiled. "Too many sleepless nights. Alexander never rests. He's not human."

"What you need is some fresh air and exercise."

"Exercise," she echoed. "As if I didn't have enough of that."

Uncertain as to what she might be referring, I ignored this.

"Come out with me to the Petřin," I pleaded. "It's not far. I have seen children and even grown-ups tobogganing and skiing on its slopes—we might try. I will buy a sledge."

"You don't have to," Esther said, "there is my old one in the cellar that I used as a child."

A day later we went. The Petřin is one of Prague's many hills, but almost in the centre of the old part of the town. Planted with fruit trees, it is delightful in the spring when they are in bloom, a pleasant recreation park in the summer with its many shady walks, even more enchanting under snow; the trees sparkling as if in crystal blossom, castle and cathedral above towering in ermine-mantled splendour and the slopes below criss-crossed by the bright flashes of children's colourful clothes as they descended rapidly on their sleighs down the hill.

They shrieked and laughed. So, I must confess, did we—I completely forgetting my age!—Esther clinging to me as I inefficiently steered the toboggan through the trees. Finally we plunged into a snowdrift and capsized. Esther was the first to extricate herself.

"Lovely," she said, looking down at me. But so, it struck

me forcibly all of a sudden, was she. Slim and tall in her tight-fitting ski suit, her face glowing pink from the cold and radiant with animation.

"You are nothing but a child," I exclaimed, "for all your solemn seriousness."

"If given the opportunity, who doesn't happily revert to childhood? Are you any better?"

And her usually so sombre eyes were bright with laughter. But only momentarily—then they grew sad again.

"Come," she said, "we have to get back or Alexander will fret. He so much hates to be left out of things."

"Always Alexander," I protested. "Don't you want any life of your own?"

She ignored this. "I have been thinking how much he would enjoy this sort of outing. Don't you think we could manage it somehow? If he wore a cap and a muffler over his mask?"

# Chapter Twenty-seven

The next time we went to the Petřin we took Alexander with us. He proved very much more efficient at guiding the sleigh down the slopes than I. Blinded as he almost must have been by mask and scarf, his performance excelled all of my and Esther's efforts, as usual! Later we bombarded each other with snowballs and it was only too pathetically evident how much he was enjoying himself.

As we trudged home with our sleigh through the deep snow towards evening, passing the Maltese Palace, we saw a solitary figure standing in front of the French Embassy. Though I could not see the man's face distinctly, there was something familiar, I thought, about his build.

"Alexander," Esther called, loudly and indignantly. "Stop it!" He had lifted her on to the sleigh and was pulling her at great speed towards the house. As if suddenly alerted by her call the man came towards us. I recognized him then; it was Marie Therese's footman, Fritz Lang.

"Good evening, Mr Livingstone," he said, grinning.

"But what are you doing here out in the cold and dark, Fritz?" I asked.

"I was thinking of applying for a job with the French. The Princess is closing the palace here and going to the south of France."

"Yes, I know," I said. "But isn't it rather late in the evening to apply here? The Embassy offices must be closed by now."

"As indeed I have discovered. My watch must have been at fault. No matter, I will have to try another time—since your Embassy would not take me. And you, I see, have been enjoying local winter sports, sir? With your friends?"

Esther had got off the toboggan. She looked at Fritz as if she, too, recognized him and I was surprised at the sudden fear I thought I read in her face.

"You are going to Dr Koritschoner's house, no doubt. Let

me help you with your sledge," Fritz said, taking hold of the rope and walking ahead of us with it. When we came to the gate Alexander bent to open it. His muffler slipped.

"Why, if it isn't Count Plevke after all," Fritz exclaimed. "Congratulations that you survived, sir!"

Alexander turned and then something so dreadful happened that to recall it is almost as terrible to me as remembering Beck's death so long ago.

Alexander took Fritz by the throat, held him with one hand and with the other brushed off both his mask and wig.

I cannot describe the horror revealed. I might have been prepared to see a hideously disfigured and scarred face—but not this. It did not resemble anything human.

There was a shriek of such terror from Lang as I hope I will never have to hear again. "The Golem," he yelled. Then he sank to the ground. Alexander replaced his mask and walked calmly into the house. I stood as if paralysed.

Esther bent over the prostrate Lang. He lay quite still. She unbuttoned his coat and shirt and felt his heart.

"I think the man's dead, Eddie," she said. "Call my uncle—hurry."

I forced myself to move, but my limbs felt as heavy as lead and when I reached the courtyard I vomited. I found Dr Koritschoner reading in the library. I gasped out what had happened as best I could. I suppose that I looked as sick as I felt. He took a small phial out of his desk drawer, extracted two pills and bade me swallow them.

"You will feel better in a few moments," he said, "but now come, I may need your help. If the man is still alive we will have to carry him inside."

"Where is Alexander?" I asked.

"Upstairs. Can't you hear his typewriter?"

How could he be calmly typing after what he had done? Coldblooded murder. Of his having strangled Fritz Lang as soon as he realized the man had recognized him, I had no doubt.

We went. The man was still lying there in the snow. He did not move.

"He is dead, Uncle," Esther said. "I made certain."

We stared at Fritz Lang's face, at the wide-open eyes and the contorted mouth. It was a frozen mask of terror. The doctor bent over him but did not touch him.

"Esther," he commanded, "put on your gloves. See if there are any marks on his neck."

I marvelled at her being able to bring herself, even if gloved, to closely examine the dead man's throat, then remembered she was a trained nurse.

"No, Uncle, nothing." I heard the relief in her voice. "Is it possible he died from shock when he saw Alexander's real face?"

"Died of fright? Rare, but it has been known to happen."

"But Uncle, what shall we do with him now? Call the police?"

"Better not. I would prefer us not getting involved in any way."

"But we can't just leave him here, lying in front of our house."

Whatever pill the doctor had given me, and the relief that Alexander had not killed after all, had restored some of my mental capacities.

"If we put him on the sleigh and I pulled him to the French Embassy and dropped him where we first met him? No one would connect him then with this house."

"But what if you were seen?"

"I would tell the truth; that I had been tobogganing on the Petřín and seen this man lying in the snow, that I recognized he was dead, loaded him on my sleigh and had taken him to the French Embassy as it was the closest place I knew where I might get help."

"And did you?"

"No, I rang and rang and no one came."

"Then why didn't you call the police?"

"Because I can't speak Czech and didn't know how to manage it."

"And so you left him there?"

"It might do, Uncle," Esther said, her face pale but determined. "In case Eddie should meet anyone. He might not at this hour. Tip the body out in front of the embassy," she ordered. "Take the toboggan on your back afterwards; eliminate as you return, as best you can with your feet, all marks it has left. Probably it will snow again tonight anyway. Now, Eddie, help me lift him."

I was once more amazed at how strong and capable and devoid of emotion this girl, in spite of her youth, had become. She showed no distaste or fear as she, almost without my assistance, heaved the heavy inanimate body on to the sleigh.

Remembering that this was not the first time I had dealt

with violent death for Alexander's sake, I pulled my gruesome burden through the soft snow. In front of the French Embassy I tipped out what was left of Fritz Lang. If one could really die of fear having seen Alexander's face, I wondered why I had survived.

Having followed Esther's instructions, I returned to the house.

She was at the door. "Everything all right?" she asked anxiously after she had let me in.

"Yes, I think so. I didn't meet anyone. The Embassy didn't even seem to be policed tonight. Perhaps they have caught the Golem."

She looked at me rather strangely and then did something very unexpected and sweet. She kissed me. Not on the mouth, but on the brow and eyes. She held my face in her two hands and then cradled my head against her shoulder as protectively and gently as a mother might a child, stroking my hair with such soothing tenderness that I felt restored to sanity.

"You have had a shock, Eddie, but you took it bravely," she said. "Thank you. Come now—Alexander and I have decided we owe you an explanation for what happened."

As we climbed the stairs, she added: "He has been busy the last hour writing it. He wanted my uncle to hear it too, and for me to read it out to you both. He is waiting."

She paused suddenly. "There is only one thing," she said. "He is desperately unhappy that you saw his face. He didn't want you to know—ever."

What could I say? "I didn't see it," I stammered. "Everything happened too quickly. You can tell him that."

My reward was a smile of such understanding, appreciation and gratitude for what she knew was a lie that I will never forget it.

In Alexander's room we found him at his desk sitting in front of his typewriter wearing his mask. The doctor was already seated. I too sat down. Alexander handed Esther several closely-typewritten pages.

"Is the audience ready?" she asked, trying very ineffectually I thought to sound cheerful. "The curtain's going up.

"It's a sort of confession," she then said. "Also of mine. You won't like it, Uncle. If we had to keep so much secret from you, please forgive us. But we feared you might guess and connect Alexander's night walks with the Golem."

The old doctor looked up at his niece, startled.

"Please then explain, Esther."

Alexander made an impatient gesture towards the paper in her hand and she started to read instead of answering.

"This is an apology of sorts to you, Doctor, who have been so good to me and equally to you, Eddie, and an explanation of why this Fritz Lang had to die. I did not deliberately kill him; I barely touched his throat. Knowledge of his own guilt and the fear of the supernatural that I had deliberately instilled in him did. He deserved death. But once a murderer, always a murderer, Eddie will think and perhaps it's true of me—for by whatever means possible I wanted to eliminate Lang."

The doctor moved uneasily in his chair.

"But what does all this mean, Esther?" he asked. "I don't understand."

"I'm afraid you soon will, Uncle—" and she read on, though her voice trembled slightly.

"Because it was Fritz Lang who murdered Esther's parents and made me what I am. It was he, too, who in the Nazis' pay defamed Prince Heinrich and his Falcons and probably even arranged his death. As his valet he had every opportunity to do so, either by tampering with his plane or his medicines."

"Then someone did? I always thought it possible," the doctor exclaimed.

Esther went on reading.

"On the night the Koritschoners' house was burnt, I had seen Fritz Lang—whom I had first noticed because of a certain resemblance to Beck—hand out the fuel to those boys. I don't doubt he told them it would be more fun to fire a Jewish home than to light a bonfire. I followed them and he followed me. When I got there the house was ablaze, but Esther's parents were alive calling from a window for help. 'We can still get in,' I said. 'Go in yourself *verdammter Engländer* and burn with your Jews,' and I heard him laugh as I tried to enter the house through the flames. Well, you know what happened."

Esther paused momentarily, then bravely continued.

"When Lang saw what was left of me after I had been found, he must have been certain I could not live. Nevertheless, it must have come as a relief to him when he heard later I had died, since I was the only witness against him. I also knew more—that he was a homosexual, since he had boasted to me of his successful seduction of some of Heinrich's young

Falcons. It was quite evident when the Heinrich scandal came who had made the accusation.

"After we had arrived here I was looking out of the window one evening. Lang was on the *Campa* staring up at this house. I was wearing my mask, but though it was rather dark I feared he might have recognized me because of it and know I had not died. I knew then that he would want to make sure I was Alexander Plevke. I did not want to frighten Esther or the doctor by telling them. I had to deal with this myself. Because I was certain that if he guessed my identity he would try to kill me. I knew too much. How would he do it, I wondered? If he found out about my nightly walks a quick knife-thrust in a dark street, or he might try and strangle me. From then on I took my revolver with me at night. But what I feared most, totally ruthless as I knew him to be, was that he might set fire to this house and burn us all in our beds. I had to eliminate him somehow. Yet I didn't want to kill once more, believe me, Eddie. All I wanted was to frighten him away. It was then that I became the Golem."

The doctor looked up startled and I wondered if Alexander had suddenly gone mad.

"Esther will prove it."

She laid down the paper, went into the next room and returned with a bundle of black clothes and a large black hat. She put them on a chair. The doctor and I stared at the black frockcoat, then at Esther. She was smiling faintly.

"Let me explain, Uncle."

"Indeed, I hope you will," he said severely. "What foolish nonsense is this?"

"It has proved the safest of all Alexander's disguises and I painted the sacred letters on his brow—may God forgive if I did wrong—with phosphorescent paint, so that in the dark no one could mistake him for anyone but the Golem. And since in the nights he walked without a mask, all those who saw his face fled."

I shuddered. I could well believe it.

"But why this extraordinary masquerade?"

She went and bent over Alexander who was still sitting quietly at his desk. Though I heard her whisper something to him—how did he communicate with her if he didn't write, I wondered? By touch. I saw his hand rested on hers briefly. Then he got up, made a sort of bow and went into the other room.

"It's all right," she said, turning to us. "He is tired and disturbed, but he wants you to know everything now. Let me explain.

"After Alexander had read all about the Golem—he found the tale in one of my uncle's old books—and that the creature had no human face, at first he only wanted to frighten Lang. Successfully too. The man ran like a hare when he caught sight of him on the *Campa* one night. It was almost funny."

Esther composed her features, seeing her uncle's stern look, then more seriously she continued.

"When Alexander saw how successful his costume was, he thought he might put it to other uses. Both he and I had become rather involved and interested in the patriotic activities of our friends from the university. What they needed most was information so they could be prepared to resist the Germans if they should come. In his disguise he was able to get into embassies—since anyone who saw him fled—photograph documents and bring back information which was then, through the students, passed on to the right quarters. There were lists of names the Germans had already made out of those to be arrested. Many Czechs and Jews could be warned what to expect and many have since been able to leave the country. I doubt even President Benes would have resigned and gone abroad had it not been for the information he was given that Hitler had ordered his troops to march in early spring, no matter what concessions had been made."

She paused a moment. Her uncle looked at her uneasily, but she gave him a reassuring smile.

"I often followed Alexander on those missions, either draped like an old woman in a shawl or dressed as a man, and gave the alarm. 'Golem, Golem,' I would scream and, terrified, everyone ran—which made it easier for Alexander to escape into one of the alleys and passages under Prague, the networks of which we had learned to know well.

"No wonder you thought I looked tired lately, Eddie, but it was all in a good cause and for Alexander it has meant a new life. He has found a way to use—" she paused momentarily—"his disfigurement to help others. Once more he has a part to act, greater than any he has played on the stage. Surely you understand how much it means to him?"

I did. Striving to conceal my emotion, I asked: "But what about the danger to you both?"

"As if he cared! It was I who wrote those articles about the Golem and sent them to the newspaper under a pseudonym. I feared you might have guessed that 'Rehtse' was only Esther spelt backwards. Some sort of vanity, I suppose, since those were my first journalistic efforts. And when you told Mrs Livingstone all about the Golem, Uncle, I was fearful you might discover our activities, because the Golem you saw on the *Campa* was Alexander himself."

The old doctor passed his hand wearily over his brow. "I should have known," he said. "But Esther, the risk!"

"The police might shoot you or Alexander," I seconded the doctor's protest.

"Nonsense. They do not shoot at ghosts or old women. Besides, they are Czech. They know what it means when the Golem walks."

"These activities must stop, Esther," the doctor pleaded. "I will forgive you all your deceptions if you promise they will."

"I can't do that, Uncle. I'm sorry. I can't promise anything except that I will be careful. We are committed to certain plans."

She stood up very straight and tall, her small dark head held high.

"The time is over, Uncle, when we Jews should bow down in submission. We, the young, want to fight those that persecute our kind. An eye for an eye and a tooth for a tooth! Please understand, Uncle! Why else did you name me Esther? Except that I should help my people as best I can? Have you forgotten *purim* and the Book of Esther?"

And though I only remembered it vaguely myself, as she stood there as proudly as the brave young Biblical queen must have done so long ago, pleading for her people, I knew at last that I loved her.

She went and bent over the old man with all the tender compassion which was so much a part of her strange fierce nature.

"We want your blessing, Uncle, for what we have to do." I saw his trembling hand touch her forehead and I heard him murmur some words in Hebrew.

Then she stood up and said briskly: "I will have to take Uncle to bed now and cover up Alexander who has fallen asleep on his trampoline. For once I don't think he is going to vault from it into the night. At last he is tired out. And so rather am I. Lang's death shocked him—he did not mean to

kill him. Please believe that. Good night, Eddie, and thanks
for all your help."

I went home, my mind in such turmoil that I scarcely noticed the blinding curtain of snow falling on Prague.

# Chapter Twenty-eight

Within the following week it was rumoured that President Hacha had been summoned to Hitler and with it the thaw came. Though it was still very cold, the river cracked open hurling great blocks of ice against the stone bastions that supported the Charles bridge. The roar of the surging waters could be heard from afar.

Always before its sound had been welcomed as a sign of approaching spring in Prague. It was not welcomed by its citizens that year.

Soon the news spread that Hacha had returned from his meeting with the Führer. All the old man had been able to save was Prague itself from the total destruction by air which Hitler had declared it would suffer, if what was left of Czechoslovakia did not instantly and without resistance accept becoming German.

*"Zlata Praha"* as the Czechscall it. *"Zlata"* not only meaning the golden one, but the treasured and beloved. This ancient and historic city, that had started as a small river settlement in the tenth century and gradually grown, prospered and flowered throughout a thousand years into the architectural marvel it had become, the pride and glory of the Czech nation, threatened with total destruction in a day by a madman!

Thanks only to Hacha's total capitulation was it spared.

However, Hitler could not resist confirming his victory by a triumphant occupation of the country and its capital.

In early March his troops entered Czechoslovakia.

■

As a matter of fact it was not to prove all that glorious a conquest. Though there was no resistance, the weather was inclement. It snowed heavily. Many of the splendid new tanks got stuck and had to be abandoned on the way. A lot of Hitler's brave soldiers suffered frost-bite and discomfort, if nothing else. The Czechs looked up at the grey sky—it was all they had left to look up to by then—and decided their patron saint, St Wenceslaus, had sent the snow from heaven to deter and harass the enemy.

Nevertheless, that morning the new part of the town was occupied by German troops and it was said that Hitler would pass over the Charles bridge, taking the historical route to the castle above as kings and emperors had in the past.

The bridge was lined with Sudeten Germans hastily assembled to greet their Führer. They waved German flags and chanted *"Sieg Heil."* There were few Czechs about and, if so, they averted their faces. I walked through almost empty streets down to the tower that once guarded the bridge.

To my surprise I was told I could not pass.

There was some commotion in front of it.

"What's happened?" I asked a bystander, in German since I knew no Czech.

He turned from me with such an expression of hatred on his face that I quailed. "Hitler!" he said.

Then I saw why I could not pass. What must have been the erstwhile portcullis, a heavy oak barrier, blocked the entrance to the bridge.

I climbed down the steps to the *Campa*, just in time to hear even louder than the roar of the river in spate the thunder of marching boots above. I looked up. Very smart in their black and silver SS uniforms—goose-stepping as if on parade— came what I supposed must be Hitler's favourite troops and bodyguards, presumably led by himself in this triumphant march across the historic Charles bridge. Then there was a sudden halt and a battering against the gate of the watch-tower that had formerly guarded the Old Town of Prague from all invasion.

I could hear exclamations. Then I saw something thrown from above. It looked like a parcel, but there was a loud explosion as it hit the bridge and a burst of flame. Screams were audible as the front lines of the SS troops fell and most of the rest retreated in confusion. I looked up to from where the bomb must have fallen. And then I saw a black-clad figure standing as still as one of the gothic statues that ornamented the parapet of the tower.

So obviously had others. "The Golem," a woman's voice screamed distinctly.

A volley of shots was fired. With one great leap the spectre vanished into the depths of the foaming, churning river.

I stared as if hypnotized into the swirling waters, knowing that no one could survive among the crushing, breaking ice without being pulverized within minutes. I knew Alexander must be dead.

A hand touched my shoulder. I turned to see what I took to be an old woman draped from head to foot in a black woollen shawl. It was Esther.

"It's no use staying here, Eddie," she said quietly. "It's over. Now no one will ever see his poor face again. Come into the house or they will shoot us too. We can watch what is happening just as well from the windows there."

Only when we had reached Alexander's room and I realized how I was trembling, and that I could scarcely speak, did I know that only Esther's icy calm could sustain me.

Together we stood at the window. Except for some field ambulances that had come to collect the dead and the dying, the bridge had been cleared of troops.

And the great river in its spring spate flowed on.

"It is what he wanted most of all, Eddie. Do not grieve for him. One stupendous last act! You cannot know how unhappy he was, how he hated his disfigurement, his speechlessness. He didn't want to risk the lives of others, only his own. It was of no value to him any more. True, the students helped in manning the gate, but that was all he would permit them to do except for assisting us in making the bomb. He left a letter for you, certain he would die. Here it is. He wouldn't let me read it." She gave it to me.

It was in an envelope addressed *"Gentilhomme Anglais."*

Before I opened it I asked: "How can you be so calm, Esther? I thought you loved him."

"I did. I still do. I always will. That's why I can accept his death with composure—and so must you. Read—then perhaps you will understand."

And I read: "My dearest Eddie. This is goodbye. If I have to kill once more it is to rid the world of a monster. By now I hope Hitler will be dead and so will I. Have no regrets about me. I have often wanted to end my life but a shabby little suicide didn't seem grand enough. You know my vanity. Look after Esther. She loves you—you must know that. Take her to England and to safety. Use my fortune to make yourselves and the Doctor comfortable there. And remember that I have always loved you and admired and trusted you more than anyone else in the world. Alexander."

Most unmanly tears were streaming down my face. Ashamed I tried to wipe them away.

Esther gently took the letter from my hand and read it.

"Is it true, Esther?"

"What?" she asked.

"That perhaps you are fond of me? After all, we have only each other now."

"And our memories," she said.

Then to my amazement she laughed. "Silly old Eddie. How little you know about women."

And somehow I felt everything would be all right between us after that.

■

The incident on the bridge was not mentioned in any of the by then German-controlled Prague newspapers. Hitler's life had not been endangered—he had crossed over on one of the other bridges, of which there were thirteen, safely concealed in an armoured car.

But no Czech was ever to forget that brave effort by a few students to stop the German army. Even if it had proved futile, national pride had been re-established.

Hitler did not forget either. When Herr von Neurath had been installed as *Reichprotektor*, he ordered the university founded by Charles IV in 1348 to be closed, and a dozen Czech students accused of having protested at this were shot.

I had to inform my mother and Sir John as to what had happened. Their reactions varied only slightly, except that my mother could not believe at first that Alexander was dead.

"But I saw it. He must have been riddled with bullets even before he leapt into the river," I had to tell her.

"But wasn't he a strong swimmer? Even if wounded, couldn't he have reached the shore somehow?"

"Mother, not even the most powerful swimmer could have remained alive in that river. He would have been pounded to death within minutes by the breaking ice. How can you doubt he is dead?"

"Well," she said, rather hesitantly, "only because of history and his extraordinary likeness to Alexander the First. Many witnessed the Tsar's death and funeral and yet, afterwards, he was seen all over Russia in different disguises and forms, as the Golem is still seen here. Certain legendary figures seem to reenact their roles from time to time on the world's stage. I've often thought how like the miracle-making Rabbi Loew the old doctor is—and those brave students who once more held the bridge, just as they did in the Thirty Years War. It is very strange how many historical events repeat."

She seemed to have forgotten me. She was looking at the gem-studded golden box which she always kept on her desk and at the miniature of Alexander the First.

"Mother," I exclaimed impatiently, my nerves strained to the utmost by what I had seen and had had to tell her. "All this historical business is beside the point. Read this." And I handed her Alexander's last words to me.

She bent over it and read, then looked up. Her eyes were moist.

"How he must have suffered," she murmured. "No wonder he faced death with such sublime courage!"

Then she suddenly smiled through her tears. "And do you want to marry Esther?"

"If she will have me."

And to my surprise, since she had always in the past been jealous of my few attachments to women, she said simply: "I am so glad."

Sir John was amazed when I told him of what I had seen on the bridge.

"Not a word of this has reached me," he said, "but I suppose both Germans and Czechs have reason to keep it quiet. Mind you, I don't like assassination, but in this case had it succeeded it might have changed the whole course of history and spared us a war. It must have given Hitler quite a shock. He is sulking in the Presidential Palace at present, too fearful to show himself, making proclamations only through the radio.

"How incredibly clever—the Golem impersonation by your young friend," he then said appreciatively. "One marvels at such ingenuity and courage; but then, he was half English. It always shows in the end. And you know, however regrettable and perhaps futile his death, the fact that he gave his life in defence of a nation which we so cruelly abandoned to its fate does, at least, do something to restore one's British self-respect."

He sat for a while in silence, toying with a pencil, then with sudden violence snapped it in two.

"Well, that's that," he said, discarding the two ends. "What's over is over, but some things remain to be attended to. Please tell your friends, the Koritschoners, to pack whatever they value and I will take it to England with my luggage. I dont' know if you realize what danger they will be in now, not only because they are Jews, but because that intrepid young woman's association with the students might become known and she will be arrested. They must leave immediately—I will order a special plane to fly them to England and hang the expense to His Majesty's Government for once. And you and your mother might just as well go with them. Our usefulness here is over—not that we were much help to the Czechs. I will be leaving shortly too."

I thanked him with all the gratitude I felt.

"I will let you know when we can expect the plane. In a couple of days, I hope. Meanwhile, I must prepare credentials for the Koritschoners that prove them to be members of my staff. Those in power can hardly object to them flying home—after all, we are not at war yet."

We reached London safely that week and by autumn there was war.

# Chapter Twenty-nine

At the time I write this, Esther and I have been married for seven years. Though we have no children of our own we have an adopted son.

When war started, I enlisted. But before that I had bought with Alexander's money a large country house set in extensive grounds. It is in Gloucestershire, not far from my home.

It was transformed into a modern clinic with all the most up-to-date medical equipment, an operating theatre, X-ray rooms and laboratories. The many bedrooms became wards and staff were soon engaged.

When war started in earnest a year later, the old Doctor could once more patch up burnt or shattered faces and heal broken bodies as well as minds. He seemed to gain a new lease of life. His valuable services amply proved his gratitude to a country that had accepted him without question, and to a people from whom he knew he need never fear persecution.

Esther assisted him as a nurse. My mother helped too, with all household matters such as catering, staff and book-keeping—when she was not busy doing the same for Sir John, whom she had persuaded to rent a pretty cottage in Burford instead of settling in Birmingham.

Meanwhile I had got my pilot's license and joined the RAF. I knew that I would never be much good at soldiering on the ground; neither did I prove to be so in the air. Though we did manage to shoot down some German planes, we were far outnumbered at the time and our losses were great. I had few regrets when, after having been forced to crash-land my plane, I was invalided out of the service. If I was to walk with a limp for the rest of my days—my ankle, already once broken, was beyond even Dr Koritschoner's skill to repair completely—I was relieved that my fighting days were over. I was no hero. To kill or be killed, even if for King and Country, had not appealed to me and to try and keep men alive seemed more satisfactory than destroying them. For this the clinic gave me every opportunity. I worked at Esther's side doing the many odd jobs of which I was capable and trying to restore hope and confidence in those of our patients who had lost it.

And perhaps some of the happiness Esther and I had found in each other spilled over and helped those who had not dared believe that life could still be good.

Throughout the war I had continued the payments to Alexander's school for aspiring young actors and the home for aged ones, but I had, of course, not been able to send any money to Frau Margarethe Reinecke in Germany.

Once the war was over I knew that I must find out if she was still alive. I telephoned the bank and after some difficulties they found the old address—it was still the village of Schwarzensee.

I wrote, but no answer came. Perhaps she had moved elsewhere, perhaps she had died. We had bombed Schleswig-Holstein quite thoroughly, destroying most of Hamburg and some of the smaller towns and villages too.

"I rather feel that Alexander would have wanted you to go and see what has happened to the woman," Esther said. "After all, he did love her once."

"As much as Faust did Gretchen—if at all."

"Besides, didn't you say there was a child?"

"Probably not his."

"Well, I think you had better find out. And anyway, my love—" and her large dark eyes, that used to be so sad, sparkled with laughter—"a few days' separation will give me a most welcome rest from you."

Schleswig-Holstein was then in the British Zone and occupied by our forces. I went in uniform; I thought it would make things easier and it did. My rank helped too and I was given every facility in my enquiries. A jeep and a driver took me to Schwarzensee.

The jungle had encroached once more, almost obscuring the drive. The great heraldic gates with their Russian emblems were gone. The two lodges were shuttered and so were the windows of the main house. Weeds grew in the courtyard. Everything looked neglected and deserted.

"Seems no one lives here any more," the corporal said. "Where to now, sir?"

I still remembered the way to the village. I directed him to it and told him to stop at an inn which looked unchanged. The landlord scanned my uniform, somewhat fearfully I thought. He was a portly, elderly man with a scarred cheek. He poured me a beer.

"I am looking for a family called Reinecke. Do they still live here?" I asked.

"Why should they be investigated?" he exclaimed indignantly. "For all his faults, Reinecke was never for Hitler—none of us here were."

"I have not come to investigate anyone."

"To requisition food then? You won't find much of that at the Reineckes'. The farm is run-down, creditors always at the door, six children to feed and the man always drinking away whatever little money there is. If it wasn't for the Bastard they would have starved in the war."

"The bastard?"

"It's their eldest—that's what Reinecke calls him. He is not a bad lad, rather wild, always in trouble with gamekeepers, but perhaps he has some right to fish in the Schwarzensee—since it might have been his."

"And his mother?"

"Well, she does the best she can, poor woman. For a while, before the war, the family was quite well off."

"Because certain payments were made?"

"How do you know?" He stared at me and I at him. Recognition dawned at the same moment to both of us.

"Why, Mr Livingstone!" he exclaimed. "After all this time, to see you again!"

"Yes, Ivan, I've come back. Do you remember when you insisted on giving me my bath at Schwarzensee?"

"Oh, sir!" He laughed. "What days those were with the Tsarevna still alive! And Count Plevke became, did he not, the famous actor he always wanted to be. Before the war we could read about him in the newspapers, even here. What a little devil he was, always up to some mischief." Unconsciously, I think, his hand went to his scarred cheek. "And the tales he invented. How is he now?"

"He is dead, Ivan."

"The war? My brother Fritz, too, on the eastern front. You remember him?"

"Of course. I'm sorry." We were both silent for some moments.

"More beer?" he asked, after a while.

"No, thank you."

"Well, I think I need one. Who would have thought to see

you again, Mr Livingstone. And those payments to the Reineckes before the war came from Graf Plevke?"

"Yes."

"Reinecke never confessed to that. Perhaps he was
ashamed. Do you remember Herr Beck, who was factor of
Schwarzensee?"

"Only too well."

"He went abroad to South America—they say, with most
of the Plevke fortune. We thought it was him who sent the
money, trying to repay at least to Alexander's son some of
what he had stolen. Guilt, you know."

Didn't I—thinking of Beck.

"Ivan, where can I find the boy?"

He looked at his watch. "Fishing in the Schwarzensee as he
does most evenings. Believe me, I've done everything I could
for the lad for his father's sake, but these have been hard
years."

"If it is at all possible, I'll help from now on. Tell me
where the Reineckes live." He gave me the address. It was
the same as the one I had.

"Strange. I wrote there, but got no answer."

"Not really," he said. "In their deplorable situation every
knock on the door means a threat, even what the postman
delivers. They probably never dared to open your letter."

"Ivan—you have been such a help. Is there anything I can
do for you?"

"No, thank you. Business is picking up now. But save the
boy from Reinecke, if you can. I assure you, he's well worth
saving."

And so we parted with the usual conventional Germanic
handshake, but this time it was a warm confirmation of understanding and friendship.

I found the derelict place that must once have been a pros-
perous farm. The surrounding fields were untilled, the cow-
sheds and pigsties empty, the thatched roofs partially gone. A
few hens scratched in the dusty yard, that was all.

The front door was locked.

I went around to the back and found my way through an
open door into an incredibly dirty and squalid kitchen. With
squeaks of terror, several small flaxen-haired children fled,
scuttling away like frightened mice.

Probably alerted by them their mother appeared. She was
heavily built and wore the blue-patterned cotton Holstein
peasant dress.

"What do you want?" she asked defensively, having scanned my uniform. "We have no food to spare."

"I am here on behalf of Count Alexander Plevke," I said "He and I were friends. He has since died."

She looked at me with eyes as pale and faded and worn as her blue dress. Comprehension seemed to come only slowly. Then with a gesture that was not without a certain dignity, she removed her soiled apron, straightened her heavy body and ushered me into what must once have been the parlour. There were still a few pieces of solid oak furniture, but whatever upholstery remained was dirty, frayed and torn. She drew a chair foward for me. As I lowered myself into it, I realized that not only its cover but its springs too were gone.

"It used to be a nice room," she apologized. "But what is the use of keeping it neat now? Soon they will take away the last good furniture I have left too. That is what it has come to." She sank on to a battered sofa.

"And so Alexander is dead?"

I could read neither surprise nor regret in her tired face.

"In the war?"

"Yes. He charged me to see to it that you would never be in want. I am here for that reason. Payments to you could not be continued in the war—now they can."

Only gradually did this seem to penetrate her mind.

"Who are you?" she asked.

"Once I used to be Alexander's tutor, long ago at Schloss Schwarzensee. I remember you, although we never met. I saw you in the church at the Tsarevna's—Countess Plevke's—funeral. How much I admired your pretty hat!"

A pathetic effort at coquetry changed her face momentarily into a semblance of youthfulness.

"*Ach, yes,*" she said. It was the finest hat I ever owned, feathers and velvet ribbons. Fancy you remembering!"

"Tell me about your son. How old is he now?"

"My eldest is sixteen."

"And his name?"

"Well, his real name is Alexander Reinecke, since my husband accepted him as his own, though he was born out of wedlock. But when the other children came, he turned against him. My husband is not a bad man, but when he is drunk he doesn't seem to know what he is doing and is cruel to the boy, beating him for no reason except that he is not his own flesh and blood."

"And Alexander goes to school?"

"No. We couldn't afford to let him. He is the only one who still does some work around here. And he is clever. He taught himself to read and write. In the war they wanted him to join the Hitler *Jugend*. But he hid in the forest or on some farm whenever they came recruiting. The farmers like him. He is good with animals—heals them when they are sick. In exchange for his curing them they give us a little food."

"And does he know who his real father was?"

"Oh yes. Everyone does around here. He is proud of it. He believed that as soon as the war was over his father would come and take him to England. Well, now it's too late!" She sighed heavily.

"But would you have let him go?"

"Of course," she said. "He's not a child any more—he will soon be a man. And once he is, he will either kill my husband or he him. But what can I do? If I had some money I would send him away myself, much as I would miss him. He deserved better than this, but how can I spare him? Except for him the little ones would starve.

"And yet he is such a bright lad, it's a shame the life he has to live and what he has to suffer. Yet he never complains. A real aristocrat, even if he is my son."

"And does he resemble Alexander?"

She considered this. "I don't think so," she said at last. "In looks perhaps, but I wouldn't really know, since I mostly met his father in the dark and by now I can't even remember his face. But the boy's different, more simple. He hasn't Alexander's winning ways, but he is not so selfish either. He is good and kind."

"So then, perhaps, he takes after you?"

She rewarded me with the first smile she had given me since we met.

"Where can I find him?"

"Do you know how to get to the lake? He will be fishing there now, if the gamekeepers haven't caught him."

"I will be back after I have seen him, Frau Reinecke," I said, "and then I would like to meet your husband so that we can discuss the future. I think that at least as far as money is concerned your worries are over."

She looked at me dumbly, unbelievingly, with eyes in which all hope seemed long ago to have faded.

I climbed back into the jeep.

"Sorry you had to wait so long," I said to the corporal.

"I'm accustomed to it, sir."

I directed him to the lake. But before we approached the water's edge I asked him to stop. "I can find my way," I said.

I knew it only too well and a sort of revulsion seized me. What had compelled me to return to the scene of a crime I had spent a lifetime trying to forget, in search of a boy whom I doubted Alexander had even been sure existed. Why did I need to see him? All that was necessary was to provide for the Reineckes and leave Schwarzensee.

I nearly turned back, but then—as if drawn against my will—I reached the picnic ground. The lake shimmered darkly through the foliage of the weeping willows.

On the small platform that overlooked it squatted a boy in tattered shorts, his bare back marked by welts and bruises. If I felt pity, I also felt the same distaste as I had at the squalor of Mrs Reinecke's story. He was bending over a fishing line. He must have heard me approach, because he jumped up and stood poised to dive into the lake.

"Don't swim away," I called. "I mean you no harm."

Then he turned. It was Alexander as I had seen him first. The golden hair and skin, the lovely face, the slim graceful body.

Time had stopped. So, I felt, had my heart.

"I thought you were a gamekeeper," he said. Then evidently recognizing my uniform, he gave me the dazzling smile I knew so well. "You are my father? I always hoped you would come for me after the war was over."

I had recovered enough to stammer: "No, Alexander, only a friend of his. He charged me to see if you were all right."

"But you will take me to him, and to England?"

"Your father is dead," I had to say, too brutally perhaps, but after all the boy had never known him.

"Dead," he echoed, and I saw all the radiance go out of his face.

But where the real Alexander would have burst into hysterical tears of disappointment and frustration, this one did not. I saw his throat move as if he stifled a sob, then he looked at me dry-eyed, in control of his emotions.

"In the war?" he asked quietly.

"Yes, he died a hero's death. He was a brave man."

"So then I will never see England or him or my grandmother?" He could not quite keep the despair out of his voice.

And then, on an incomprehensibly rash and sudden impulse, I have since never regretted, I said: "Look here—I was very fond of your father. We were great friends. Do you think you could accept me in his place and come to England with me?"

His eyes searched my face. They were as large and luminous as Alexander's had been, but their gaze was steadier. They did not dazzle, tantalize and flatter as his had. They simply seemed to question my integrity. It was as if they searched my soul.

"But why should you want me? I have no education. I'm a bastard and I'm not much use at anything but fishing and curing sick animals."

"For your father's sake and perhaps, now that I have met you, for yours. If I can settle things with your parents, will you come home with me?"

"It's no good even thinking about it," he said hopelessly. "Reinecke will never let me go."

"Your mother would."

"You talked to her?"

"Yes. Your father left a lot of money, most of it will be yours one day."

"I don't need much—not for myself anyway."

"But we could provide handsomely for your family if they let you go."

He seemed to ponder this. Was I trying to tempt him as I once had Alexander? Would everything repeat itself inevitably?

"Your father was a very famous actor. Do you want to become one too, when you are grown up?" I asked fearfully.

"Me?" He laughed. "No. I would be no good at play-acting, not that I have ever been to a theatre. All I want is to be a vet. I like animals more than people and I have always heard they take good care of them in England. Could I learn about it there?"

The relief I felt was somewhat tempered by disappointment; it seemed a very modest ambition.

"You would have to go to school at first, of course, and then study. But there is no reason why you shouldn't become a veterinary surgeon if that is what you really want."

"More than anything else in the world!"

It was what Alexander had said about becoming an actor, so long ago.

"You have had no schooling, your mother told me, but she said you have taught yourself to read and write?"

"Yes, even a little English. I can read it, if not pronounce it well."

"But how on earth did you learn that?"

"From the people that bought the Schloss after my father sold it. They lent me books from the library there. They were kind to me. They were my only friends, except for Ivan who keeps the pub."

"The house looked deserted—have they moved somewhere else?"

"They are dead. Hitler gassed them—they were Jews," he said, quite matter-of-factly.

"Is that why you did not join the Hitler *Jugend*?"

"Yes, even though I wanted to get away from Reinecke."

He sprang up. "Look, the sun is setting. If I don't lay my eel-lines now there will be nothing for us to eat for the next week."

I walked away for the last time from where the Tsarevna had nearly been pushed to her death because of me, where I had embraced and lain with this boy's grandmother and helped to dispose of his great-grandfather's murdered body. I looked back once more . . . There stood—young and beautiful—the last incarnation of them all, glorified by the setting sun's rays.

"Back to the farm," I told the weary corporal.

There I met Herr Reinecke. An unpleasant and indeed brutal-looking man, his powerful frame was gaunt and emaciated, probably due to lack of food and excess of drink.

When I made my offer, he blustered, protesting he loved his eldest son; yet made it quite clear that if I paid enough he would let him go.

I wrote out a cheque for a considerable sum in any currency.

He studied it.

"How much is it in Reichmarks?" he asked.

I told him—and saw I had won.

"If I give you this, you will have to sign an agreement of adoption," I warned.

"Well, if the boy is worth all that to you, take him. I certainly won't miss him." Having pocketed the cheque he slumped out of the house.

I looked at Mrs Reinecke. How dared I hope for approval when I had just bought her son?

"Better so," she said, with placid resignation. "I don't think you will be disappointed. He's a good lad, even if not as

bright as his father was. Do you have a wife and family?"
she then asked.

"A wife, yes, but no children. She will cherish the boy as if
he was her own. She loved his father."

"She too?"

"Yes, perhaps more than all of us."

The adoption arrangements were easily made in Kiel.
Those in authority were only too anxious to oblige anyone
connected with the occupation forces then.

I telegraphed Esther—"Returning with Alexander's son tomorrow."

It would, I hoped, at least spare her the shock she might
otherwise have had on seeing him.

When I brought him to her she nevertheless paled. "So
Alexander has come back to us," she said. "Is it to happen all
over again?"

It did not and never will. Except for his physical likeness
to his father the reborn Alexander, whom we have come to
love as if he were our own son, proves to be a perfectly ordinary, cheerful, good-natured boy of quite uncomplicated dis-
position—fond of sports, excelling in these at school more
than at his lessons. He has none of his father's brilliance of
mind, neither is he cursed by such devastating charm. If he
manages to pass his final exams it will be because he is conscientious, tenacious and painstaking—qualities probably inherited from his peasant mother. His resolve to become a
veterinary surgeon remains firm.

Meanwhile his two grandmothers spoil him. The fair
Elaine, now grey-haired, sees him frequently and always
shows him the plaque in the church commemorating his father's last resting place, behind which the ashes from Dr
Koritschoner's fireplace are walled in.

My mother loves the boy too, though slightly disconcerted
at having to realize that his likeness to both Alexanders, the
Tsar and his own father, are merely superficial. She has
started to ponder if he is not in character more like Tsar
Alexander the Second, a gentle, rather simple and humane
ruler.

Nevertheless, after having carefully removed the erotic
painting, she has given him the Tsarevna's golden box. He
treasures it, not because of its value or beauty, but because it
came from Schwarzensee.

"Pandora's Box," as she always called it—out of which all
evil spirits have, it would seem, finally escaped.

## More Bestsellers from SIGNET

- [ ] **EMPIRE by Etta Revesz.** (#E9564—$2.95)
- [ ] **BEYOND FOREVER by J. Bradford Olesker.** (#E9565—$1.95)*
- [ ] **HUNGRY AS THE SEA by Wilbur Smith.** (#E9599—$3.50)
- [ ] **TULSA GOLD by Elroy Schwartz.** (#E9566—$2.75)*
- [ ] **THE CHILD PLAYER by William Dobson.** (#J9604—$1.95)*
- [ ] **THE UNICORN AFFAIR by James Fritzhand with Frank Glicksman.** (#J9605—$2.50)*
- [ ] **EDDIE MACON'S RUN by James McLendon.** (#E9518—$2.95)
- [ ] **THE INTRUDER by Brooke Leimas.** (#E9524—$2.50)*
- [ ] **THE SUMMER VISITORS by Brooke Leimas.** (#J9247—$1.95)*
- [ ] **THE DEAD ZONE by Stephen King.** (#E9338—$3.50)
- [ ] **NIGHT SHIFT by Stephen King.** (#E9746—$2.95)
- [ ] **'SALEM'S LOT by Stephen King.** (#E9545—$2.95)
- [ ] **THE SHINING by Stephen King.** (#E9216—$2.95)
- [ ] **THE STAND by Stephen King.** (#E9708—$3.50)
- [ ] **THE SURROGATE by Nick Sharman.** (#E9293—$2.50)*
- [ ] **THE SCOURGE by Nick Sharman.** (#E9114—$2.25)*

*\* Price slightly higher in Canada*

## ABOUT THE AUTHOR

The striking atmosphere and narrative detail of MAS-QUERADE can be traced partly to Cecilia Sternberg's own life. Miss Sternberg made her debut in the twilight years of "old Vienna," and moved through the various levels of society in Europe, from the gilded lives of the aristocracy to the harsher realities of workers and peasants. She now lives in London.